On the Hunt for the Wizard King

An Age of Wizards Novel

MICHELLE MILES

This is a work of fiction. All characters, organizations and events portrayed in this novel are either products of the author's imagination or used fictitiously.

ON THE HUNT FOR THE WIZARD KING

Cover Design by Erin Dameron-Hill

Copyright © 2017 Michelle Miles
Dusty Tome Publishing

ISBN: 978-1-7333887-1-9

Praise for On the Hunt for the Wizard King

"We really got to watch all of the characters grow and change throughout the book. No one was what you expected. Miles did a great job of keeping you guess and wondering what was around the next corner." —5 stars, Amazon Reviewer

"Wow! This story is so full of magic with action and adventure I could not put it down. The land of fae is an exciting magical world where anything can happen, and I definitely was not expecting some of the twist and turns that transpired."
—5 stars, Amazon Reviewer

Dedication

For Janice.

Pronunciation Guide

PEOPLE:
Aoife (EE-fa) Burke
Sean O'Connell
Fiona (FEE-o-nuh) – Aoife's mother
Niall (NEE-ull) – the "Wizard King" and ruler of Illyia
Deaglan (deck-LAN) – Niall's father
Cian (KEE-an) – Ruler of Anatolia
Sunnie Burke – Aoife's half-sister
Liam Burke – Aoife's step-father
Caleb O'Brien – Sean's buddy and partner
Eimhear (M-hear) – a dark sorceress whose restless soul is looking
for a new host
Queen Siobhan (shiv-AWN) – Queen of Anatolia, mother to Niall
and Cian
Brigid (Bridge-ID) – a *sidhe* (SHE) who can break spells on others
King Ardan – King of Anatolia who is ill and dying
Bryant – Deputy Director of the Inter-dimensional Portal
Protection Agency
Isla (EYE-la) – Siobhan's midwife

PLACES:
Anatolia, Cian's kingdom
Illyria, Niall's kingdom
Kydonia, neutral kingdom
Cliffs of Mhothair (MO-air) – where the Towers of Illyria are
Lambridge Castle – home of Prince Cian
Brookdale – Human realm, where Aoife hails from
Ridgeclere Castle – Where Inter-dimensional Portal Protection
Agency is housed

Part One

Schisms

Prologue

In the Land of Faery before Time was altered

"Push, my queen!"

Even though Queen Siobhan knew the midwife meant well, Isla's adamant command she push over and over grated on her nerves. She'd been in labor since nightfall. Her newly crowned husband, Ardan, had not made an appearance in the bedchamber as yet.

Just as well. She wasn't ready to see him anyway.

"Ah, I can see the crown o' his head. One more push. There! There he is!"

Isla delivered the baby and the child squawked with the sudden realization he'd left his warm, safe place. She wrapped him in swaddling clothes and carried him to the queen, gently placing him in her arms.

"Yer son, Your Majesty," she said, a smile in her voice. "Healthy. Ten fingers and toes."

He was so small with his wrinkled newborn face and tiny hands flailing. Siobhan looked down at the small child in her arms. *Alive.* The child survived. At last, she'd given her husband an heir.

"He's hungry, Your Majesty. Ye should feed him."

"Oh, aye, of course." She held the baby to her breast and watched as he started to feed amazed she had managed to carry a second child to term.

Through her pregnancy, she worried she would not. And if she had, the baby would be stillborn. Relief had flooded her when Isla announced he was healthy. Aye, he was pink and round and perfect in every way. After her miscarriages, she thought for certain Deaglan had cursed her womb, preventing her from having any child expect his.

Deaglan. Now was not the time to think of him. She made a solemn vow she would never think of him again when their torrid love affair ended in disaster. It had left her with a young son to care

1

for and a wicked scandal in her wake. Her parents had been horrified to learn of her pregnancy. It threatened to ruin everything they had built. Every alliance they had made with the king of Anatolia. She had begged their forgiveness. When they insisted she abort the child, she refused.

Instead, she wrote a lengthy letter with her confession to her betrothed, Prince Ardan. She begged his forgiveness and told him she would understand should he not wish to continue with their betrothal.

To her surprise—and some dismay—the prince had forgiven her and agreed to marry her and raise the child as his own though as a bastard and not of royal blood he could not inherit the throne.

Siobhan's marriage had not turned out as she hoped but then she did what she had to do for her son. He would be allowed to live under the same castle roof. They'd still be together. Ardan spared them from a life of shame because she'd been selfless with the confession of her sins. She'd agreed to meet with the High Bishop weekly to cleanse her soul and prepare her for marriage. That weekly meeting continued even after they said their vows. Gods, but she hated that sanctimonious prig.

"I ken yer exhausted, Majesty. Mayhap I should find ye a wet nurse so ye can rest?"

Siobhan leaned back into the soft down pillows as she held the baby. It had been a long labor, so long she had lost track of time.

"I am tired," she said with a yawn, but she loved holding him, watching his sweet face as he slept, his tiny hands curled into fists. She wasn't ready to give him up yet.

"Send for Niall," she said. "I wish for him to meet his brother."

"The boy is waiting outside, Majesty. But we should tidy up a bit, aye?"

The queen gave her a nod and Isla went about cleaning the bedchamber to make it ready for her to receive visitors.

When finished, the midwife signaled a servant girl standing by the door to fetch Niall. The queen finished nursing and pulled the baby away, covering up and cuddling him close to her.

Niall's nanny held him by the hand as she walked him into the bedchamber. He was barely tall enough to see over the edge of the high four-poster bed.

"Do I have a brother, Mummy?" he asked.

She smiled down at him, nodding, and held the baby so he

could get a better look. "You do. And someday he will be big enough for you to play with."

Niall stood on tiptoe and gazed down at the babe swaddled so tight only his little face was visible. Siobhan watched as the boy scrunched his face in a scowl of disdain. Unease shifted through her. Her eldest boy didn't seem at all pleased with the arrival of a baby brother.

King Ardan entered then, no doubt hearing the news he had a son and heir to the throne. The arrogant High Bishop trailed her husband reeking of high morals and hypocrisy. She cradled the babe tight in one arm and reached for Niall with her free hand, pulling him closer to her, too. Her jaw tightened into a hard knot. Displeasure rippled through her. Why had the High Bishop come, too?

He'd never approved of her marriage to Ardan. He made that abundantly clear from their first meeting. He disliked that she had a bastard and thought it made her nothing more than a common whore, even though her son had been born out of a deep love.

Despite counsel from his high and mighty bishop, Ardan had married her anyway, accepting her flaws and all.

He may have accepted her but it was clear he didn't approve of her bastard son either, and her illicit love affair still hung in the air between them like a rotting carcass. He ignored her boy, no matter how she tried to appease her husband.

Both men halted at the foot of the bed gazing at them.

"Run along with your nanny, Niall," Siobhan said. "Come visit me after you break your fast."

Ardan waited until the nanny took Niall away to ask, "A boy?"

"Aye," Siobhan said.

He moved to the side of the bed and perched on the edge. The High Bishop crowded closer, peering down at the babe with a critical eye. "A great day for the kingdom, Your Majesty. The crown prince has been born."

"May I hold him?" Ardan held his arms out.

The queen handed him to her husband and the baby protested loudly, his wails echoing off the stone walls. The child's face turned a bright shade of red, but that did not dissuade the king from holding the baby and rising from the edge of the bed. "Good lungs," he said with a smile. "Welcome to the world, Prince Cian."

"Cian? That's what you've decided to call him?" Siobhan asked.

"Aye, a strong name. A family name." He bounced the baby against his shoulder to quiet him. "And one day he'll be a great leader."

"A fine name, to be sure, Your Majesty. We'll plan a proper naming ceremony as soon as Her Majesty is able." The High Bishop wedged himself between Siobhan and the king, his black robes completely obscuring her view from her husband and child. She swallowed the panic that tried to rise, reminding herself no one was there to do the baby harm.

Siobhan wanted to tell the man to take himself off, that he wasn't welcome there, that if anyone was planning a naming ceremony for her child, it would be her. He wasn't welcome in her bedchamber. It was a sacred place. *And it was a private moment between husband and wife.* But she couldn't tell him any of that for fear of retribution. He would force her to stay at confession and prayers longer. He would needle her and berate her for all her past mistakes. He would never let her forget them. She clamped her mouth closed so tight, her jaw ached.

Siobhan leaned up on her pillows and watched with rapt awe as Ardan kissed the baby, rocking him and walking with him until he quieted in his arms. In that moment, she forgot about the vile High Bishop and was simply content to see her husband happy he finally had the son he always wanted. *His son.*

Where would that leave her Niall? A bastard without royal blood unable to inherit anything? He would be treated less than a second son. For that she had only herself to blame. Ardan had never warmed up to the boy. He'd kept him at a distinct distance. Though, to be fair, he had never promised to love the boy only, to provide for him and allow Siobhan to raise him within the castle walls.

"Ye have a way with him, Your Majesty," Isla said. "No doubt ye'll make a fine father."

With one last kiss, he handed the baby to the midwife. "We must feast as soon as Her Majesty is well." He turned back to Siobhan and leaned down, kissing her forehead. "Thank you for my son. Rest now. I'll be back in the morn."

As Ardan and the High Bishop left the bedchamber, a calming sense of peace went over her. For that brief moment, she knew all would be right with the world.

"Isla, will you see to the baby, please?" she asked.

4

"Aye. Ye ken I will. Did ye decide to use a wet nurse or no, Majesty?"

"No, Isla. Let me rest for a bit and then bring him back in a few hours."

"Aye, Your Majesty."

The queen drifted off to sleep before the midwife made it out of the bedchamber.

Darkness pressed around the wizard, Deaglan, as he stood on the edge of the wilderness south of Lambridge Castle. Pale yellow light lit up the windows from top to bottom. He had attuned his magic to the queen and knew the time had come. Somewhere deep inside the castle walls, the queen gave birth to a child—a boy.

He gripped his walking staff so tight his hand cramped. He conjured an image in his mind's eye of the woman he once loved, now the queen of Anatolia. How he delighted in unraveling her long plaits, running his fingers through her wavy locks in their stolen moments. He had once caressed every inch of her creamy skin and kissed secret parts of her while she gazed at him with adoration in her black eyes. She was an exotic beauty—*his* exotic beauty—and he loved her as no one else would ever love her with an intense fire that still burned deep and hot. She had forsaken their love and for what? Marriage to the then-crown prince of Anatolia. Title. Money.

She had betrayed him when she left. It cut him to the bone. Only when she was gone did he learn of her pregnancy and her intent to divide him from his child forever. He knew when the boy was born. Just as he knew she'd named him Niall after his own wizard father. Mayhap to drive home her point she would raise him with royalty, with the rich, but not his wizard, pauper father.

The entire kingdom had turned out for their nuptials. Even Deaglan, though he remained in the shadows so she would not know he had been there.

It had been widely rumored the queen could no longer carry a baby to term or that she might die trying to give birth. That did not bode well for the king, as he was desperate to sire an heir. Those same rumors insisted the gods had cursed her because of her illegitimate son. They were wrong. The gods had nothing to do with it. So this night, when the queen went into labor, Deaglan knew he had to be near the castle.

His wizard magic attuned to the woman he once loved, watching over her from a distance. He could feel her presence; Siobhan had not changed in the years since their separation. She was still the most enchanting woman in the realm.

It did not escape his notice the boy exhibited magical abilities. He could sense the wizard magic in him even from this distance. They were connected, the two of them. Niall shared his wizard blood. He would one day be as powerful as Deaglan. And then Siobhan would have no choice but to seek him out. She would not know how to handle Niall.

But that would be in the distant future. A future Deaglan could foresee.

This night the queen birthed a son. He had hoped it would be a son. Precisely why he had lifted the curse on Siobhan so he could carry out his plans. Not long after the child was born, the old midwife headed his direction. He used his powers of sifting and moved to her so she wouldn't have to walk so far. She crested the ridge and halted. Even in the blue-white veil of moonlight, he could see the wariness in her aged face.

"Are ye the wizard?"

"I am. Do you have the child?"

She glanced down at the bundle in her arms. "He isna dead. I couldna tell her he was stillborn."

"Nay?" He motioned her toward him. "That does pose an interesting dilemma."

Her refusal to tell the queen the child was dead altered his plan. No matter. He would execute his contingency plan, which was less than ideal but would still work.

"I dinna like telling stories to Her Majesty. Nor dinna I like handing over the newborn to ye."

"The child will not be harmed," he assured her. "I merely wish to place a protection spell on him." He pulled the cloth from the baby's face. The newborn was wrinkled and pink. Such an ugly little thing.

"I did what ye asked. I brought ye the wee prince."

"You did well. For that I thank you and will allow you to live." He held out his arm. "Give me the child."

She hesitated as she clutched the baby against her bosom. "Do ye not even want to ken his name?"

"I do not," he said and sighed with his impatience. "Hand him to me."

"I dinna ken."

"If you refuse now, dearie, then all within the castle will suffer. And I know you do not wish to bring harm to anyone in Lambridge. Especially your own family. Isn't that right?"

Her eyes went wide and round in the moonlight. She shook her head.

"The child."

She handed over the baby. He was a small thing. Weak and insignificant.

"What do ye plan to do?"

"He will be well, I assure you. For the protection spell to work, I must return to the woods. Wait here until my return. I will be back before sunrise." He started for the edge of the trees.

"His name is Cian," she called.

Deaglan stiffened at the sound of the woman's voice, cringing with the knowledge of having the boy's name. He glanced down at the child, only a slight pang of remorse going through him. It quickly passed as he continued to the woods. He sifted and arrived at the edge of the trees. He was well aware of the lightning sprites flickering through the darkness as he made his way to the sacred *crann bethadh*. They flitted around his head, following him to the foot of the great tree.

The *crann bethadh* was more than a century old. There were particular knots, nooks and crannies on the trunk. Local folklore told of the tree "breathing" on nights much like this—a full moon brightened the sky and blotted out the stars. Moonbeams streamed down through the canopy of overhead leaves around the great tree leaving slashes of that ominous white light.

The baby squawked in his arms, reminding Deaglan of the true reason he was there. He placed the child in one of the nooks. The child cried out in distress, no doubt wanting to be fed. He leaned down and placed one kiss on the crown of the babe's head. The baby's visage turned from Fae to human. The powerful glamour spell would hide his true appearance from those in the human realm. He waved his hand over the child, chanting ancient words from an ancient spell to suppress and conceal all manner of magic within him as well as alter his mortality. The child would grow into a man who looked and acted human. There would be no trace of Fae within him. He would live—and die—as a human.

Deaglan held the staff out to his side and recited the spell he had long ago memorized. The sprites flittered away from him, disappearing into the darkness. All but one.

This one buzzed in front of him and a moment later transformed from two inches tall to the size of a human. Next to her he opened the portal to the human realm to the nursery he'd found when he first concocted his scheme. He had not intended to switch the babes, but the midwife failed him. She would have to return with a child and so he would give her one.

"You know what to do," he told the sprite.

She smiled and gave him a nod, making her shimmering blonde curls sparkle and bounce in the half-light. She picked up the Fae baby from the tree. He took one last look at him to make sure his spells worked. When he nodded approval, the tree sprite was gone and a moment later returned with a squirming howling infant—a human infant. Using his magic, he changed the appearance of the babe to that of a Fae. Another glamour spell though this one would not have to be as strong as the one he placed on the Fae child he sent into the human realm.

He took the baby from the sprite. With a wave of his magic, he turned her back to normal size. Holding the squirming child against him, he knew he had to get back to the midwife quickly. It would not be long before the infant cries would break the silence of the woods.

Pleased, he walked to the edge of the trees and then sifted back to the midwife. If he could not be with his son, then Queen Siobhan could not be with hers.

Chapter 1

Fiona, briefly Queen of Illyria, stood on the wooden porch of her human home in the late afternoon hours to watch the sunset. For the middle of a Texas summer, the evening had turned cool. Quite unusual for that time of year.

The day she had planned so long ago had finally arrived. It was the last day she would spend in the human realm.

She didn't want to acknowledge the nervous knots twisting her stomach. She had to ignore them. Standing rigid, she clutched her elbows and waited for the sun to dip below the horizon. It was her last sunset here in the place she'd never learned to call home. The last day she would masquerade as a human.

Would she miss it? She couldn't be sure about that. All she really knew was the driving need to get back to Faery. To get back her life. To get the revenge she so desperately wanted.

It had taken her years to plan and perfect the spells she would use. She had read everything she could get her hands on about time travel. Once she was at the Time Sphere in the Ivory Wood, she could finally stop looking back with regret and instead look back with hope.

As soon as the sun kissed the edge of the horizon and yellow-orange light faded in the summer sky, she turned back to the house and entered. Her steps were sure as she made her way up the stairs to the attic.

She reached for the attic stairs, remorse sweeping through her. She thought of Liam and how things had spun out of control with him. How they had once loved each other. How he had once cared for her with a heartfelt sweetness. Their life together had been good once, but the secrets and lies eventually came between them. The burden of her past kept her from forgetting it and moving on. It consumed her with a fiery anger she could no longer deny.

The day she realized Aoife was Niall's daughter, she knew what she had to do.

Her marriage to Liam had ended and she'd let it. The divorce was final. Even though Liam had tried to save what was left of it, she wasn't interested. All that mattered was getting back to Faery and changing history.

She climbed the attic stairs, stepping onto the creaky floor and flipped on the light, pausing to glance around at the stuffy room full of dust and cobwebs. She'd tried to be a proper human wife and mother. They'd decorated for the holidays as any normal couple with two young daughters. But things had shifted for her when she realized there was a chance she could right past wrongs.

How many years had it been since she'd been in the attic? She'd lost track. Ever since that meddling Sean O'Connell and Caleb O'Brien discovered her numerous trips back to Faery and put a stop to them. Once she had the tracking tattoo, she could not return without them knowing.

Fiona had no choice but to agree to the tattoo. For if she didn't, she would be captured and returned to Faery and imprisoned. The last thing she needed was to be thrown into a Fae prison.

Her gaze landed on the old steamer trunk, the one she'd picked up at a local antique store a few years ago. Despite the years of non-use in the attic, the trunk didn't have a speck of dust on it. It was the same when she found it in the antique store and she knew then she had to have it. She knew it was meant for her.

The Celtic knotwork with the sword through it was an addition she made later, when she realized the symbol was enchanted. A gift from Liam's grandmother. Fiona had never quite discovered where—or how—the woman managed to get her hands on an enchanted thing such as that. Fiona, though, needed it to complete her trunk. In some ways, it was as though the symbol had been made for it.

Fiona fell to her knees in front of it. She ran her hands over the lacquered wood before she allowed her fingertips to brush over the symbol.

She pulled the small vial of pink sparkling Tears of the Dryad from her pocket and held it up to the pale-yellow light from the one bulb overhead. Even after all these years, the Tears still shimmered.

She shoved open the lid. Inside were old clothes and newspaper clippings from the previous owner. She hadn't bothered to take them out because she hadn't cared if they remained or not. They were not her family heirlooms, but someone else's.

Pulling out the cork, she took a deep breath and then tipped the vial so one drop of the Tears slipped out and landed with a silent splash in the trunk. A moment later, the portal appeared in the middle of the trunk giving her a window into Faery. It had worked as she hoped.

Her heart skipped. It was there. Waiting for her. Ready for her to step inside and return to the place she belonged. Her home.

She couldn't deny her apprehension as she looked through the portal to her home. Her future. Her past. It had been so long since her life was there, how would it be to return? Was she making the right decision? Would she come to regret leaving Liam and the girls behind?

She pushed away the thoughts, firm in her resolve and convinced that, aye, this was the right decision.

On the last trip to Faery she was able to make, she took clothes for her final return trip. Her bow and arrows waited for her on the other side in a hidden copse of trees. But first, she had unfinished business in the human realm. She replaced the cork and stuck the vial back in her pocket.

Fiona gently closed the lid. Then she ran her finger over that Celtic knotwork again before pinching the tiny handle of the sword and pulling from the makeshift scabbard in the knotwork. She pricked her forefinger, squeezed, and watched as three drops—no more—of blood landed on the knotwork. She replaced the sword and then recited the enchantment. The symbol lit up for a brief moment before going dark. She reopened the lid to make sure the spell had worked.

It had. There was nothing inside save for the old clothes. But Fiona could see the shimmer of pink light in the trunk. The portal remained open yet she had "closed" it to others with her blood magic.

Fiona closed the trunk again and left the attic. It was time to say goodbye to her daughters. Likely Aoife would wonder why she was calling her. She would explain everything once she returned. But she couldn't leave this realm without hearing her daughter's voice one more time. Everything she was doing was for Aoife. She had to make sure she was safe.

As she turned from the trunk, the ripple of magic sizzled

through her with such force it knocked her to her hands and knees. She gulped in a deep breath, trying to keep from retching. The punch had been so powerful. It took her breath away.

Fiona focused her senses as she closed her eyes to see with her mind the magic swirling through the air. The sensation was familiar, a powerful punch not far from the house.

It had Niall's signature all over it. A prickly sensation spread through her. After all these years, had Niall found her? It had been long, long ago when she felt his magic wrap around her, through her. When they married and loved each other for one night. She would never forget the way his magic mingled with hers. That sharp metallic tang with a cloying sweetness blending with hers as though it was already meant to be a part of her. It was as well-known to her as her own magic.

"Niall."

Fiona whispered his name to the empty attic. A warm shudder went through her. Despite the years and realms separating them she could recall his handsome face with clarity, his catlike grace, his deep voice, his dominating presence.

She hurried down the stairs and out the front door. The only thing that mattered now was getting to the creek where she knew the magic originated.

If only she could sift. She'd lost the ability at some point. She had never figured out why but she could only assume some of her magic had been damaged as she came and went through that icy portal. Since she couldn't, she'd have to make her way to the creek on foot and broke into a run. Opening the portal in the trunk likely alerted Sean or Caleb. She dare not open another one.

As she neared the creek, she was certain she could sense the traces of Niall's magic piercing the air. She was right. A portal opened nearby but now seemed to be closed. She could see glittering light dancing in the air. Anyone else would ignore it and think it nothing but an anomaly but she knew better.

When she arrived at the edge of the embankment, she stopped short. Liam stood at the edge of the creek.

The shock of seeing him so soon after everything that had happened between them sent a pang of longing and sadness through her. She hadn't expected to see him. Liam sensed her presence. He turned to look at her. Their eyes met. Her knees weakened. The light breeze ruffled locks of his sandy blond hair.

His sharp blue gaze assessed her with mild interest before he turned back to the creek.

"What are you doing here?" she asked.

"I could ask the same of you."

She clenched her jaw, trying to decide how to answer. It was, by all accounts, his place. She knew why she was drawn there, but she did not know why he was. For whatever reason, the creek held certain magical properties that were stronger during certain times of year—Samhain and Beltane. She'd come close to escaping back to Faery one Samhain but Sean and Caleb stopped her.

Liam, though, came here seeking solace as she went to the attic seeking her own solace. He knew she was Fae but there were a great many other things he did not know. He did not know who Aoife's father truly was or that Niall still lived. Nor did he know how Fiona ended up in the human realm or even that she had magic. She doubted he would believe in portals or Tears of the Dryad. Humans tended to think of them as fanciful things and Liam was far from fanciful. If she told him a portal had been opened, he might think she'd gone mad.

"I...didn't know you were here," she said.

"Sorry to disappoint you with my presence."

His voice was flat and unfeeling, as though he had a bad taste in his mouth. His words struck a nerve. She clenched her fists as she tried to think of a nasty retort. She couldn't. Her hands relaxed. She wasn't going to let him get to her. She didn't want to part with final harsh words between them.

"You may think this is nuts but I felt something...some shift. It was powerful. Made me sick to my stomach." He glanced around the area, as though looking for something or someone before turning his gaze back to her.

A cold tingling sensation prickled her skin. He must have felt the sensation of the portal opening. Had he sensed Niall's magic? She didn't understand how he could have since he was human. She made her way down the embankment and paused next to him.

"Did you sense something as well? Is that why you're here?" he asked.

She bit her lip. The urge to tell him everything from the moment she stepped into this realm until now went through her. To be completely and utterly honest with him. Didn't he have a right to know about Sunnie anyway? She was a Halfling, yes, but

13

she also possessed magic and an allure most humans didn't understand.

"Liam, there's something I need to tell you."

"You're leaving again, aren't you? And this time you won't come back. Is that right?"

"I—"

He turned to her, grabbed her arms and held her, his fingers digging into her flesh. There was a fire in his blue eyes she hadn't seen in a long while. It startled her.

"Fiona, do you understand how much you mean to me? How much I love you?"

"B-but you and I...you said we had to separate. That you couldn't live like that anymore."

"Yes, that's true and I couldn't. So, I released you. I gave you the freedom you've always craved so you could come and go as you please. I never wanted to let you go."

Despite everything they had been through, she could hear the sincerity and determination in his words. He could not go with her. He wouldn't understand why she had to return, nor would he approve of what she had to do.

"Liam—"

"Take me with you," he said.

She cringed. She hoped he wouldn't ask that of her. "I cannot."

"Why? Because you have a lover to go back to in this mysterious place?" He gave her a little shake. "Did you not love me? Did I not love you enough?"

"Please don't make this more difficult." Tears clotted the back of her throat. "Where I'm going, you cannot follow."

He dropped his hands. "And how do you intend to get there? Magic?" He laughed at that as though it were a joke. "Magic. How foolish that sounds. I don't believe in magic."

There was a hard glint in his eyes, cutting her to the bone. Perhaps she deserved that. "Liam, I truly am sorry for everything I put you through. You didn't deserve any of it. You deserve someone who makes you happy."

"You made me happy once. You still could. If you stayed with me or let me go with you." He dropped his arms and stepped away, raking a hand through his hair. "I don't care where we go, where we live. Here. There. It doesn't matter."

She pressed her lips together, unsure how to respond. He made her happy once, too, when she'd arrived in the human realm, alone, scared, pregnant. They'd had a nice life together but that life was over now. If she hadn't discovered how she could change things, maybe she could have stayed and forsaken all she was. Been a proper wife. She could have stayed but wouldn't. She knew deep down she had to get back to Faery to keep Aoife safe.

And now he begged her to stay, making her decision all the more difficult.

"Liam—"

A high-pitched piercing sound cut through the air, making them both fall to their knees. Fiona gripped a handful of grass as she tried to lift her head that felt as though it was full of lead. The air around them rippled with magic she had sensed previously at the house.

When she finally lifted her head, she could see it waving in a circular motion in the air. It pulsed outward from the center forming a perfect circle. A bright light flashed making her blink against the sudden light and shield her eyes for she refused to look away.

A portal formed. She could see right through time and space to the realm on the other side. And for a brief moment, she caught a glimpse of Niall.

As two men stepped through, the rippling waves dissipated. They stood on the other side of the creek, the trickling water between them. One man tall and arrogant. The other shorter holding a silver staff with a sphere nestled in what looked like a silver dragon's claw. The sphere reminded her of a miniature version of the Time Sphere. They were dressed as Niall's guards. He'd sent them through to find her. He knew where she was which made getting back to Faery even more urgent.

Slowly, Fiona pushed to her feet. Fear knotted inside her. They had come for her.

Liam groaned and managed to stand up as well. Silence descended as they faced the men across from them.

"What the hell was that?" Liam asked.

Fiona moved closer to him, a shiver of panic sweeping through her. "Liam, I think you should leave."

"You should listen to the lady," the tall man said. "We don't want trouble. We just want her to come with us."

"I'm not going anywhere with you." Fiona lifted her chin,

meeting his icy gaze straight on.

Liam angled his body toward her, his hand gripping her elbow in a protective move. "Who are you people?"

"The queen is to come with us," the leader replied. "By force, if necessary, though His Majesty does not wish to harm her."

"Queen?" He glanced back at her with question in his eyes.

"Liam...I know you don't understand but you have to trust me."

"You're right. I don't understand," he said. "What's happening?"

"His Majesty waits," the man said. "May I suggest you not keep him waiting too long?"

She lowered her voice so only he could hear. "Liam, please go. It's not safe here."

Fiona dropped her hand by her side and cupped it. She could keep the panic at bay long enough to defend herself. He glanced down and saw the first flicker of light in her palm. He frowned as he looked back at her, his brows knit with question.

"What are you doing?"

"Saving your life. And mine."

As she flung out her hand, the ball of light had fully materialized. It hit the tall man square in the chest. He screamed and went down. The other one sprang into action. He used the silver staff as a pole vault and leapt over the narrow creek which would have been a feat for any human. He made it look easy. Fiona stumbled backward, reaching into her pocket for the Tears of the Dryad. She ran but he used the magic in the staff, punching her in the back. She tumbled to the ground, flinging her arms out to break her fall.

Liam was at her side, helping her to her feet. She implored him with her silent stare, wishing he would leave but knowing he wouldn't.

"If you continue to resist, you will return to Faery in pieces," the man said. Light swirled within the orb as he pointed it directly at her.

Panic and fear left her. Now there was only defiance, determination, self-preservation. She was going back to Faery but only on her terms.

"Do what you must," she said and lifted her chin.

"As you wish."

"No!" Liam shouted.

As light streamed from the staff, Liam did the unthinkable. He shoved her out of the way and dove in front of her, taking the hit square in the chest. Liam landed with a thud on his back in the grass, a sticky black substance on his chest.

It all happened so fast, she didn't have time to react. She stumbled to the ground with his violent shove and now picked herself up. Her gaze met Liam's confused one. He swiped his hand through the sticky black substance.

"Pitiful fragile human," the guard said.

Her anger flared, white-hot deep inside her. She turned her death stare on the man with the staff. Now he'd gone too far.

She balled her fists, her lips pressing together with her anger. "I'd send a message with you back to your king..."

A smirk played upon his lips. "But?"

"But you'll be dead."

She flung her arms out, opening her hands. White light spewed from her palms and smashed into him, shoving him backward until he stumbled on the edge of the embankment. The staff fell from his hand and landed in the water.

Dead. He was dead. She'd killed them both and she had no remorse for it.

"Fiona?"

"I'm here." She hurried back to Liam and fell to her knees next to him. She pulled his head into her lap, cradling him as she brushed her fingertips through his hair fighting back the tears. "Liam, why did you do a damn fool thing like that?"

"Couldn't let you die," he muttered.

His eyes closed, his body went limp and he was gone.

"Liam!"

The anguished scream ripped from Fiona's lungs before she could stop it. She didn't even get to say goodbye. She rocked back and forth, wishing she could do something to bring him back. Knowing she couldn't. Only someone with dark arts would be able to do that. She gently lowered his head to the ground and whisked away the tears.

She got to her feet and paused at the edge of the embankment. She couldn't leave two Fae guards there. She had to get rid of the bodies before some human happened along and found them. It would be hard to explain two dead men dressed strangely with pointed ears.

She dragged the guard out of the creek and put him next to the other dead man. With a calmness she didn't know she possessed, she took the Tears of the Dryad out of her pocket, removed the cork. Taking a deep breath, she thought of the place to send them and then let the drop release.

Once the portal was open, she shoved them both toward it with her feet, careful to keep out of the opening. Once they were inside the portal, it closed and was gone. Fiona expelled a breath and turned back to Liam. The slick black substance in the center of his chest smelled oddly of sulfur.

She dropped to one knee and placed a hand on the side of his face.

"I'm so sorry, Liam. I never wanted anything to happen to you."

A deep buzzing sounded around her. She lifted her head and peered through the inky darkness to see the first shimmer of a new portal opening. She'd been such an idiot. Niall could have been watching through the Time Sphere. He must have seen what had happened. He would send more men to get her.

She scrambled up the embankment as a flash of light punctured the shadows. She used another drop of the Tears to open a portal back to the house. She had to get back to the portal in the trunk. Hopefully her blood magic would keep it sealed even after she went through.

One drop, one thought, and she was back at the house.

And so was Sean O'Connell. He was getting out of his old red pickup moments after she arrived. She hoped he hadn't seen her open and close the portal or then he'd arrest her.

"Sean," she called and waved, trying her best to act as normal as possible. She stuck the vial in her pocket but it would only be a matter of time before Niall tracked her here. She had to make her escape quickly. "What are you doing here?"

"I think you know why I'm here."

"Do I?"

Her quickening heartbeat sped up even more, threatening to pound out of her chest. Sean worked for the Inter-dimensional Portal Protection Agency and had been tracking her almost the moment she entered the human realm all those years ago. He had been a constant thorn in her side. And when his boss thought he wasn't getting the job done, Caleb was assigned to keep a watchful eye on her, too. She liked Caleb less than Sean.

"I think you do. Did you open that portal?"

Fiona wasn't daft. She knew he likely referred to the one above their heads and the one she opened only moments ago. But to throw him off, she said, "No, but I felt it, too. Not far from here."

"Where?" His brows knit with question.

"Near the creek where Liam likes to fish." She had to get rid of him so she could make her escape. Even if that meant driving him to the scene of Liam's death. "Maybe you should check it out."

Suspicion was still written all over his face. "Maybe I should and maybe you should come with me."

Her mind shouted no. She couldn't go back there—Niall's men were still there. And so was Liam. "I shouldn't. After all, you wouldn't want me to be tempted by a portal, would you?"

He hmmed his response. "Fine, then I'll go alone but I want you to be here when I get back."

Sean started for his truck. She thought of the house, Niall, Aoife and the portal in the attic. She couldn't take a chance that Aoife would find her way to Faery. Knowing how fond Sean was of her, she knew he would be the only one she could trust to keep her out.

"Sean," she called. "Before you go, I have a request."

He paused, turned to look at her. "What's that?"

She closed the gap between them, pulling her keys out of her pocket. "Do something for me."

"If I can," he said with a nod.

"In case something happens to me…" She paused, choosing her words to make sure she didn't give anything away.

"You think something is going to happen to you?"

Her eyes drifted closed with impatience. "Just…I don't know. If something does, I need you to take care of the house for me, Sean. Make sure Aoife never comes here."

"Why?"

"It's not safe for her. Do you understand? She can never come here. Can you do that for me?"

"No, I'm not keeping Aoife out of her own house. She—"

"She can't come here. Ever. Tell her I sold you the house." She pressed the house key into his hand and then conjured a SOLD sign for the front yard. "Promise me."

He stared down at the key before closing his hand around it. "If you're that certain."

"I am."

He pocketed the key. "I'll be back."

With a nod, she said, "Be careful."

But she intended not to be there when he returned. As soon as his truck ambled down the street and out of sight, she ran into the house and up to the attic. She gulped air into her lungs to calm her labored breathing as she pulled the cell phone from her pocket. She had to call Aoife and Sunnie and tell them what had happened to Liam. It would be the last communication she would have with either of them.

It hurt her heart to leave them behind, to return to Faery without them. When her task was done and she could be sure Aoife was safe, she would come back for them both. She would figure out some way to make them both understand they were part Fae.

She called Sunnie first but it went straight to voicemail. She hadn't expected her to answer since she was on location. It was a blessing. She left a hasty message and then dialed Aoife. Her phone rang and then went to voicemail. She started to leave a message but hung up and redialed. Again, no answer. Determined to hear her daughter's voice once more, she called again and again until finally her oldest daughter answered, her voice thick with sleep on the other end.

"Mom?"

Relief flooded her.

"Aoife, there you are at last. I've called to let you know that your father passed away." It was an effort to keep her voice calm and devoid of emotion but she had to. She had to pretend if hadn't affected her.

"What do you mean he passed away? He's dead?"

"Yes, I'm sorry. He's gone." She couldn't hide the quiver then as she squeezed her eyes shut, reliving the horror. He had been killed because of her. "I'm sorry to have to break the news to you this way, but there's no time, really. Your sister is in Shanghai filming a movie but I called to let her know. I thought you needed to know, too."

"Mom, wait—"

"I have to go before it's too late."

She hung up before she told her daughter any more. She dialed the phone once more.

"9-1-1, what is your emergency?"

"There's a man by the creek. I...I think he's dead."

"What creek? Ma'am? Can you be more specific? Hello?"

Fiona hung up assailed by grief for all she was leaving behind.

She clutched the phone for a brief moment, her hand aching, before she flung it away with a tightness in her chest. It crashed against the far wall and shattered.

It was now or never. She had to get back to Faery before Niall found her in the human realm. Finding her would lead him to Aoife. Fiona hurried to the trunk and pushed open the lid. Light pulsed upward, flooding the dimly lit attic. Taking a deep breath, she stepped into the trunk.

To Faery.

To home.

Chapter 2

In the Human Realm before Time was altered

Waking up in the morgue had been the worst day of Liam Burke's life. Things could only go uphill from there. After all, he wasn't dead anymore. In fact, he was very much alive and very confused as to what had happened. Liam pried his eyes open and discovered he was lying on a cold metal slab in a colder freezer drawer. He was blinded by the garish fluorescent lighting in the room. He squinted and blinked several times to get his eyes used to the bright light. He could remember nothing except for his name before the stranger revived him.

"Welcome back from the dead."

A man stood next to him with a head of thick wavy copper brown hair and hazel eyes. Something seemed vaguely familiar about him but he couldn't place his face. He was young, with a three-day growth of stubble on his cheeks and chin.

"Where the hell am I?"

"Morgue in the sheriff's office. Let's get you out of here. We haven't much time." The man helped him to a sitting position.

When Liam swung his legs off the table, he spotted the second man standing at the door, a bow and arrow in his hands as he kept watch. There was something odd and out of place about the tall, slender man standing there with a medieval weapon. The strangest thing of all about the man was, perhaps, his pointed ears.

Something about those pointed ears seemed familiar to Liam. As though he had seen someone recently who had them. Someone he knew well yet he could not recall the face. But the familiar sensation niggled at him. He narrowed his eyes as he looked between the two strangers. He was certain he had never seen them before.

"Who are you people?"

"We've been ordered to bring you back with us."

He drew his brows together in confusion. "By who? Where are

you taking me?"

"He doesn't remember anything," the man at the door said. "You warned about that yourself."

"What's the last thing you remember?" the first man asked.

He tried to recall but all he got was a blank memory. He shook his head. "Nothing."

"The hit you took was severe."

"You said welcome back from the dead. Was I…dead?"

"In a manner of speaking, yes. You're alive now, though."

"Come on, Caleb. It won't be long before the sheriff returns," the second man urged.

"Right." Caleb clapped him on the shoulder. "Bryant will help you remember but we have to get you out of here first."

"I'm not going anywhere with you. I don't even know who you are. Who's Bryant? How did I die?"

Liam tried to keep the panic at bay as he attempted to remember how he died because he couldn't remember that either. He shoved him away as he hopped to the floor. He took a step backward, eyeing the man.

The man clenched his jaw, the muscles ticking there. "I'm Caleb and this is Owen." He thumbed toward the other guy. "We knew each other once. All your questions will be answered once we get out of here and get you to Bryant." Liam started to protest but he held up a hand to stop it. "Not now. Now you have to come with me."

Apprehension swept through him. Though he had no reason to trust Caleb, he was his ticket out of the morgue. He didn't want to hang around to see what was going to happen next. How would he explain to the sheriff he wasn't dead? Finally, he nodded.

"All right. I'll come with you."

Owen headed out the door first, followed by Caleb. Liam fell in step behind him. He realized he was in some sort of police office. There was a couple of jail cells off to one side and two desks butted up against each other. No one else was about.

"Just through here." Caleb pointed to the door.

They exited the building and stepped out into the gray morning light. Dawn pierced the night, the sky turning from indigo to pale blue to pink.

He expected to be led to a waiting car but instead they headed up the sidewalk to the street corner and turned left. Liam followed the men to the back of the sheriff's office as he glanced around the town. Though it seemed familiar, he couldn't quite recall where he was. As though he knew the place, but didn't.

Once they were away from the front of the building, Caleb made sure no one was watching. He pulled a small vial from his pocket, uncorked it and spilled one drop of the shimmering substance inside. Light sliced through the air revealing a yawning opening. Owen went through first.

"This way." Caleb waved him through.

"What is it?"

"A portal. We're leaving this realm." Caleb motioned for him to follow.

Liam stepped through and was immediately accosted by a blast of cold air slicing through him. He didn't have time to notice it much when he stepped out the other side. The portal closed behind him.

They were in a large room with stone walls lined with dusty bookshelves crammed full of books, scrolls and other odds and ends. An oversized wooden desk in the shape of a crescent was in the center. Behind that some sort of armoire. Clutter filled every nook and cranny. A giant window was on the opposite side of the desk with a clear bright view of the world outside. Two oversized wingback chairs flanked the window with a small table and chessboard in between.

"I'll get Bryant." Owen said it over his shoulder as he left the room, not waiting for a reply from either of them.

Liam stepped toward the window to gaze out. While the landscape did not seem odd, there was something otherworldly about it. Below he could see the rippling waters leading out to sea. Ships docked in the harbor. There was a bustle of activity of men, women, children as they made their way from ship to shore and over the stone bridge extending from what appeared to be a castle to the walled city. Beyond the city, craggy mountains and lush rolling hills underneath a brilliant pinkish blue sky dotted with a large pale moon surrounded by fluffy clouds. The room he was in appeared to be at the top of a tower.

"Beautiful, isn't it? No matter how many times I come back, the view always surprises me." Caleb joined him at the window.

"What is this place?"

"The kingdom of Kydonia in the realm of Faery. Welcome to

the Enchantment Enforcement Agency, Liam."

As a new voice spoke, Liam turned to face the speaker. He was a short, pudgy man with beady eyes and a hawk nose. He dressed in fine clothes and wore knee high boots. Liam had no idea what the Enchantment Enforcement Agency was or even where Kydonia was for that matter. The name of the kingdom gave him no frame of reference in this strange world.

"You hold me at a disadvantage, sir." It was an understatement as he looked around. His world had shifted off its axis, making him disoriented.

"Do I? You don't know who I am?"

Liam stared at him in uncomprehending silence trying to make sense of what Bryant asked him.

"He doesn't remember anything," Caleb said. "I tried to warn you."

"An unfortunate side effect. I see we have our work cut out for us, then. My name is Bryant. I'm the Deputy Director of the Inter-dimensional Portal Protection Agency which is a sub-bureau of the Enchantment Enforcement Agency. You already know Caleb and Owen, two of my operatives." Bryant gave him a thin-lipped smile that didn't quite reach his eyes. When Liam didn't respond, the man cleared his throat. "I'll have Mavis bring some tea. Perhaps something to help jog his memory. And we'll need lemon cakes and scones."

Lemon cakes and scones. It was as though Liam stepped into the past or an alternate universe. Perhaps going through that portal had done something to his brain and he was hallucinating. Perhaps he was still dead.

"I'll have her bring it up," Caleb said. "I'm returning to the human realm. I have unfinished business there."

"Aye, you do. The women are top priority. I don't want them getting back to Faery," Bryant said.

Caleb stole a glance at Liam before he gave his boss a nod and headed for the door. Bryant waved Liam to one of the chairs.

"Please sit. We have much to discuss and you have much to remember." Liam took a seat as Bryant reset the chessboard. "Would you like to play a game?"

"Not really."

"Pity. You used to be quite good."

Liam glanced from the chess pieces back to Bryant. "I don't

think I know how to play."

"Let's see, shall we?" Again, that smile. He spun the board to place the white pieces in front of Liam. "You move first."

Liam studied the board for a long time before he moved his first pawn.

"What do you remember?" Bryant followed suit and moved one of his pawns.

"Waking up in the morgue."

"Ah, not a fun way to wake, I'm sure."

"Not exactly."

"Then what do you remember?" Bryant asked.

"Caleb brought me here through a portal."

"And nothing before waking in the morgue?" He lifted a brow in question.

"No."

A woman entered carrying a tray with a silver teapot, cups and tea cakes and scones. She was tall and slender with long silken black hair and dark eyes. She had a silver circlet of some type of knotwork around her head and wore an ivory tunic under a dark green velvet vest. Her hair was plaited on either side of her head, revealing the delicate pointed tips of her ears. She poured Liam a steaming mug of the tawny liquid and handed it to him. He sipped it, the minty herbal flavor bursting in his mouth.

"Thank you, Mavis." Bryant grinned as he took a tea cake. She dipped a quick curtsy before leaving them alone once again.

"The portal was real?" Liam asked, getting back to the topic.

"It was real. Everything you're experiencing now is real, Liam. You are very much alive."

That answered one of his questions. He wasn't hallucinating and he wasn't dead. But who had killed him and why?

"Caleb had something to do with my resurrection, I presume?"

"He did along with some magical help."

Liam stared at Bryant a long moment before he got back to playing the game, mulling over Bryant's words. He didn't know if he believed in magic. Though perhaps he should since it saved his life. He had scoffed at the notion of magic when he... His thoughts trailed off. When he what? There was something—no, someone he told he didn't believe in magic but he couldn't remember who.

They lapsed into silence as they played the game. The

movement of the pieces on the board soothed Liam. Made him feel as though he were in complete control. He could anticipate Bryant's next move and envision his own move before he made it. The game was familiar to him, as though he had played it numerous times before.

"Checkmate."

Bryant chuckled. "I'd call that beginner's luck but I know better."

"We've played this before." Familiarity tingled through him as he looked at the board.

"Many times." Bryant nodded.

"And I usually win."

"Aye, though sometimes I think you let me win to make me feel better." He chuckled.

Liam looked up from the chessboard to Bryant and met his gaze. His face was familiar now and there was a sense of déjà vu that came over him. Was the vague memory of the two of them sitting across from each other with a chessboard between them real or imagined?

"The last time we played was...not in this room."

"Correct. But enough about that. Does the name Fiona mean anything to you?" He leaned back in the chair and laced his fingers over his round belly.

"No, should it?"

"Hmm. Another cup?" Bryant held up the tea pot and Liam nodded. He refilled his cup and waited, watching as Liam sipped it. He wiggled his fingers. "Think again, Liam. Fi-oh-na."

Liam thought about the name again but nothing came to mind. No conjured image or anything. He started to shake his head when the image of a woman burst through his mind. She had green eyes and a gorgeous mane of auburn hair that fell around her shoulders. A devastating smile and an infectious laugh. She had a regal look about her with her high cheekbones, thin straight nose, thick dark lashes.

"I...yes, I think I know her."

"She is your wife."

The cup clattered against the saucer as he bobbled it, tawny liquid spilling over the rim. "My wife?"

"You don't remember because something happened to you at that creek where you died."

Liam placed the cup on the silver tray. He rubbed his forehead as a headache formed. "I don't remember that either."

"Aye, I know. That's why you're going to remain here with me while I help you reconstruct your memories."

His brow wrinkled. "Who are you again?"

Bryant laughed. "We have plenty of time to get into all that. For now, I'd like to show you to your chamber where you'll be staying."

"How long do you plan to keep me here?"

"Oh, my friend, we have all the time in the world."

This time when he grinned it gave Liam an odd sensation, as though Bryant knew some secret he wasn't willing to part with yet.

Yet.

Liam had been granted free reign of the building. He discovered the Enchantment Enforcement Agency was housed inside the walls of a castle the inhabitants referred to as Ridgeclere. It ran more like a residence than a secret agency complete with servants who took care of the staff and agents. It seemed odd but then there were lots of odd things about being in Faery.

Liam settled into a daily routine. He did his best to bring normalcy to his days. Most of his memory had returned though some of it was still hazy. He was still trying to sort through the jumbled mess of his mind. He hadn't let on to Bryant. He wanted to see how long the man would go on with the charade before he realized Liam had recovered some of those memories.

He should have been furious at Fiona but he wasn't. He had a sort of calm as he thought of the woman with which he had spent so much of his life. She'd lied to him, deceived him into thinking she would stay with him forever in the human realm when all she was doing was using him to take care of her and the children while she made trips to and from Faery. He didn't know what she was doing there—here—but he suspected she was up to no good.

She'd never told him about her life before arriving in the human realm so long ago. He'd tried to prod her for information, to get her to talk about it but she was as silent as the grave.

Looking back, he didn't know why he allowed her to come and go as she pleased. He had been far too lenient and accepting of her strange ways. He knew that now. He should have reined her in a long time ago.

He'd remembered snippets of conversation she had with those two who had been assigned to watch her—Caleb and Sean. Something about going back to Faery to see a man named Niall. He didn't remember all of the details. It had become fuzzy in his mind.

Bryant had been the one to share with him how Sean and Caleb were assigned to keep Fiona out of Faery—and Aoife, too, though he didn't understand what threat the girl posed. Neither did he understand the threat Fiona posed, though he didn't ask questions.

He arrived in Bryant's office for their morning chess game, tea and scones. The cook had discovered orange currant was his favorite and made sure fresh ones were made daily. Their morning ritual was something they had been doing since he arrived. He'd lost track of time since time in Faery moved at a much different and strange pace than home. His watch had stopped working the moment he stepped through the portal. He could never quite tell how long a day actually lasted. Some days seemed shorter. Others longer but one thing remained consistent—life in Faery was much, much different than life in the human realm.

Liam took his seat across from Bryant as he set up the board. By now, Liam was so good at playing chess he didn't have to think about his next move. And Bryant still hadn't won a game.

"Good morning, Liam. I'm ready for my daily beating." He grinned good-naturedly.

Liam spun the white pieces toward Bryant. "You go first this time."

One bushy brow winged upward. "Changing things up a bit, are you?"

"I like to keep you guessing."

Liam waited as Bryant considered his first move. He leaned back in the chair, his hands resting on the arms. While he waited for the man to make the first move, he used the time to ask him questions to which he needed answers.

"Who is Niall?" He posed the question as casually as he could.

He watched Bryant's hand hover over his first pawn as he glanced up at him and then back down at the board. "Why do you ask?"

"Something I remembered."

"He's king of Illyria."

He did not elaborate on the connection he had with Fiona. Hearing the name Illyria sent a sense of familiarity through him. He'd seen that before on a map.

With his new-found freedom, Liam studied the map of Faery as well as other documents to familiarize himself with his new world. He spent many an afternoon in the confines of the library amidst dusty shelves.

Faery was split into quadrants. Illyria was a mountainous region to the east. The Towers of Illyria on the Cliffs of Mhothair was the home of King Niall. Anatolia was more of a forest region to the west with Lambridge Castle in the center as its ruling seat. That was home to Queen Siobhan and King Ardan. The aging king was ailing and thought not to live much longer. His son, Prince Cian, had yet to marry and had disappeared long ago. No one knew where the prince was or even if he was still alive.

Kydonia was to the north, sharing part of the mountain range with Illyria and the forest with Anatolia. On the northern border, the Sea of Celestial Fire bordered Ridgeclere Castle but the map ended there. If there were other places beyond the sea, it wasn't part of any map he could find. The southern region was simply marked as the Otherworld, also known as the Heartlands, and someone had scrawled in an untidy hand the words *wood elves, sky elves, fire elves, southern Fae.*

He recalled that map with detail, as though he had it right in front of him.

"Does that mean something to you?" Bryant asked.

"He lives in the Towers of Illyria," he replied as he moved his bishop.

A smile crossed his lips. "I see you've been studying. Good."

"There is still much I don't know."

Bryant nodded agreement and made another move. "Aye, there is. You will know everything in time."

"Why parcel it out to me? Why not tell me everything now?"

Another move and Liam realized his queen was in danger. He leaned back in his chair and gave Liam a thoughtful look over the chessboard. "If I told you everything right now it would be much too much and you wouldn't be able to comprehend."

Liam moved his queen out of danger. Something about the way Bryant talked put his senses on high alert. "What is it you're not telling me?"

Bryant didn't make another move as he steepled his fingers. He sighed. "You wish to know, truly?"

"I think it's time I do. I've been here weeks, Bryant, and so far, all I know is that Fiona was my wife, we had two children together and she's a Fae. You've told me nothing else or why I'm here in the first place."

"You think there's a reason why you're here?"

Liam clenched his jaw. "I think there is, yes. You wouldn't have gone to so much trouble to bring me here if it wasn't for a good reason."

He lifted one corner of his mouth in a half smile. "Very astute of you. What other observations have you made?"

Annoyance flickered through him. "Enough with the questions. Tell me what I want to know."

A beat of silence and then the man chuckled. "Very well. You are quite special, Liam, though you can't even remember it. It took a large team of my best agents and a lot of time to track you down but we finally did it. Caleb was one of those agents. That's why I assigned him to Fiona's case. That and Sean simply wasn't getting the job done."

"I don't understand."

"Sean was supposed to keep Fiona out of Faery but he failed time and time again. I sent in a second agent, Caleb, to assist and that's when we discovered who you are," Bryant continued.

"And who am I?"

"You, Liam, are what is known as a Changeling. You are a Fae."

Chapter 3

In the Human Realm before Time was altered

The black limo ambled up the street toward Sunnie Burke's childhood home. Her heart remained in her throat with sickly anticipation as she willed the driver to go faster. Fatigue had overridden her impatience to get home hours ago after flight delays and dragging suitcases through airports all the way from Shanghai. The last fifteen hours had been brutal but she'd finally made it back to Brookdale, Texas.

Back home.

When she got the call her father had passed away, all she could think of was getting home. She knew it would all but stop production on the movie but her priority was her family and she didn't care if she got fired or not.

That wasn't true. She cared. She worried about the consequences but she decided she'd ask for forgiveness later. The most important thing was getting home and finding out what her mother's cryptic voicemail meant.

Sunnie, I'm calling to let you know your father passed away. I'm sorry. I have to go before it's too late.

She'd listened to the message over and over until her phone battery died. Her mother's unemotional words haunted her. Her stomach was in a perpetual knot. By now, she had it memorized as well as every inflection of her mother's voice and she still couldn't make heads or tails of it. All she knew was her father was dead and she had to get home.

When the limo halted, the driver got out and opened her door. She paused on the sidewalk, shocked to see her older sister, Aoife, on the front porch. She slowly slid the sunglasses down her nose and looked over the rims at her mousy geeky sister standing there gaping at her with a dazed look.

Annoyance immediately pierced through her at the very idea Aoife, who had been absent for the last five years, arrived before her. But of course, she would have. She was closer to home and could drive here in a short amount of time. She couldn't remember the last time they'd spoken to or seen each other. All she could remember were all those negative emotions associated with her sister swirling through her.

Unwilling to let those emotions keep her from confronting her sister, Sunnie straightened her back and headed up the sidewalk, the click of her Christian Louboutins the only sound in the still day. She paused at the foot of the wood steps and pinpointed her with her gaze for a brief moment before glancing up at the house. It was as she remembered it when she left. The cracked sidewalk. The faded chipped paint. The shutters that needed replacing and a well-worn roof. The only difference now was that the grass needed cutting and the hedges trimmed.

She looked back at Aoife. She hadn't changed much in the last five years. She still had the stringy brown hair though she no longer wore the glasses. She was dressed in khaki shorts, red Keds and a white cardigan sweater set looking frumpy and the complete opposite of her.

Sometimes Sunnie was jealous of her sister's petite frame because she was far from it. She'd inherited her father's height and knew her only hope of wearing heels in a relationship was if the man was well over six feet tall.

"I'm surprised to see you here, Aoife." She could hear the slow Southern drawl in her words, even though she'd worked hours with her speech coach to get rid of it.

Growing up in a small town in Texas had forever given her that twang, though. The casting directors who thought it was endearing gave her work. More work than she could handle at times.

"What are you doing here?" Aoife clenched her fists as she stared her down, a coolness in her green eyes. That same coolness that had always been between them since they were teens.

Agitation flickered through her. What kind of question was that? She was here because she had to be here. She jerked her shades off to glare at her.

"Because my daddy is dead. I came on the first flight I could get. I've been traveling for over fifteen hours straight. I'm tired. I'm hungry. I want answers. Where's Mom?"

Aoife's eyes narrowed with her own irritation.

"Newsflash. Mom is missing and did you even bother to notice the sold sign in the yard?" She motioned toward the sign.

Shock pierced through Sunnie's annoyance as she looked at it, seeing it for the first time. How could this be? When she talked to Dad a few days ago, he hadn't mentioned putting the house up for sale. When had that happened? She swiveled back toward Aoife, this time narrowing her eyes.

"Where is Mother?"

Her tone was so cold Aoife sucked in a sharp breath. She quickly recovered, though, and fired back her own retort, her voice shaking a little.

"How should I know? I got here yesterday morning and she was gone. I haven't been able to find her."

If Aoife didn't know where Fiona was, then who would? Sunnie had expected to find her making funeral arrangements when she arrived. Not gone. She had hoped to get answers from Fiona, to find out what had happened to Liam. All she had was that one voicemail that told her nothing but the fact he was dead.

"What happened to Dad?" Her words were a rough whisper.

"Dad was murdered. That's all I know." Aoife said it matter-of-factly with only a hint of emotion.

The blood drained from Sunnie's face as her shoulders slumped and she pressed her hand against her roiling stomach. That was something she hadn't expected. "Murdered?"

"All I know is he was found dead by the creek."

"How did he die?" Her voice lifted an octave at the end of the sentence as she tried to control the roll of emotion through her.

"I don't know."

Aoife shrugged, genuinely perplexed. She was as much in the dark as she was which raked on Sunnie's nerves. Why hadn't Aoife done anything to find out who did it? Where was Fiona? Had she even tried to find her? And what of the police? Were they notified? She had more questions than answers and it frustrated her.

"Haven't you gone to the police to find out? What are they doing about it? Are they investigating? What are *you* doing about trying to find Mother?"

Aoife blinked owlish eyes and bit her lip as she remained silent.

Sunnie huffed. "As usual you're useless."

But she wasn't. Aoife was probably the smartest person Sunnie knew. And she had to be in as much shock.

"Did you know they were separated?" Aoife asked, sounding

hurt, as though discovering the truth was painful.

"Of course, I did. They split before Christmas. You would know that if you ever bothered to come home."

She hadn't meant to sound so angry, so spiteful. But it was true. Aoife hadn't stepped foot back in Brookdale since she took off for college. But could she blame her for not wanting to come back? Aoife left and never looked back. She admired that and wished she could be more like her. Even with her hectic schedule, she came home as much as she could.

She and her father had been close—at least she thought they had been. He'd talked to her about the split before it happened. Most likely to soften the blow when it came. If Aoife didn't know then it was likely she didn't know about the divorce either.

She hated the idea of her parents splitting but there was nothing to be done about it.

"Dad wanted a divorce but Mom wouldn't agree," Sunnie went on in a sour tone. "He left her anyway. The divorce was final two days ago."

Two days ago her father was alive. Now he was dead. Fiona was missing. Her sister stood on the porch looking as though she had no idea what to do next. Like her whole world had shattered. Well, *her* whole world had shattered, too. She'd lost her father, too. She'd lost her mother, too. All she had left of this house and this town were her happy childhood memories and even those she had started to question if they were truly happy memories.

Looking back, she recalled all the strife between her parents. How her mother would lock herself in the attic and refuse to let anyone inside. She would spend hours there alone. Sunnie and Aoife were never allowed. And sometimes there were days when Fiona was unable to get out of bed. And it frustrated Sunnie that Aoife remained silent.

"So, what? You don't have anything to say to that?" she demanded.

Aoife shook her head and her lower lip did a little quiver. She could see the tears filling her eyes. Sunnie huffed, wondering why Fiona had disappeared shortly after the mysterious death of Liam. And it occurred to her to ask Aoife the question that had been niggling at the back of her mind.

"Do you think Mother had anything to do with his death?" She sounded cold and distant.

Aoife composed herself and drew up straight, her glare like heated pinpoints of light. "No. And you shouldn't either."

Sunnie drew in a long slow breath then let it shudder out of her. "I don't think so, either. I'm glad you don't."

Even though she said it aloud, there was still a little doubt in the back of her mind. There was something about the strange situation with her parents that seemed off. Something she couldn't quite put her finger on.

Aoife, though, seemed convinced Fiona was innocent. Maybe Sunnie was being unreasonable. Her sister was three years her senior. She might not have been the prettiest girl in school, but she was the smartest. She made honor roll every semester and was able to get a scholarship into a great college. While Sunnie struggled with her school work, Aoife made it look easy. She always breezed through her homework.

Oh, sure, Sunnie had been popular in high school. She was the star in every school theater production. Her singing and dancing skills were moderate, but she could definitely act. There was a lot of self-imposed pressure to be the best, to dress better than anyone else, to make sure her appearance was perfect. Sometimes she envied the way Aoife could blend in with the crowd and not be seen.

That's why Sunnie knew college wasn't for her. She wanted to be an actress and moved to Los Angeles when she was eighteen. Those two years had been a complete whirlwind. She'd been in the right place at the right time and managed to land a couple of roles leading to bigger and better things, including her first starring role in a major movie.

The movie she left behind to rush home and find out about her father.

An overwhelming urge to hug Aoife came over her and she took a tentative step toward the wood steps but halted. She was unsure how her sudden affection would be received.

"I never hated you, you know. I wanted to be smart like you."

She didn't know what made her say it. Or why. But she had to tell Aoife. To let her know she wanted to be like her in that respect. That she looked up to her big sister. They hadn't had the best relationship as they got older. Sunnie was aware of how Fiona treated Aoife when she became a teenager. Sunnie hadn't felt that so much since Fiona tended to push her aside anyway.

She never understood why. What she did understand was Liam, her father, adored her. She was Daddy's Girl. The apple of his eye. And though she hadn't been able to return home as much as she liked because she was busy with her career, she called him often to keep in contact.

Aoife stared at her with wide eyes, the shock apparent. Warmth pushed into her cheeks and she was suddenly embarrassed by the unabashed admission.

"That's all I wanted to say." Sunnie turned on her heel and hurried to the limo.

"Where are you going?" Aoife called.

"To the cops. I'm going to find out what happened to Dad," she said without turning around.

If Aoife wasn't going to find out, then someone had to. She would find out the truth. Perhaps the sheriff could shed some light on the case.

The click of her ridiculous heels was the only sound as she made her way down the sidewalk. Hearing her shoes suddenly seemed so silly and vain after seeing Aoife in her sensible Keds. Her driver opened the back door for her and she slid inside. She didn't even know the guy until a few hours ago when he picked her up at the airport holding one of those ridiculous signs with her name on it.

Luckily the news media had not been alerted to her arrival back in the States. The paparazzi dogged her wherever she went and it was almost a relief to know she was without someone following her.

For now.

She knew it wouldn't be long before that changed.

"Where to now?" the driver asked.

"Take me to the sheriff's station."

Brookdale was a small town. There was only one sheriff and one deputy and no real police force. She hoped, though, she could find out more information about her father's death.

Her cell phone rang. It was her manager. An inward cringe assaulted her as she punched the answer button, not wanting to talk to her but knowing it was inevitable.

"Hey, Carla."

"What the hell do you think you're doing? You up and left the production without a word to anyone?"

"I left a note."

"A note isn't good enough, Sun. The director is pissed."

"My dad died." It took a lot to say it out loud. A lump formed in her throat and her eyes stung. "I had to come home."

There was a long silence on the other end of the phone. "God, Sunnie. I'm so sorry. What happened?"

"I don't know. My sister didn't know either and my mother is missing."

More silence and then a deep breath. "You take all the time you need, honey. I'll deal with the production company and the director."

"Thank you."

When she hung up, only a little relief went through her knowing that part of her life would be handled. She had no idea what would happen to the production in her absence. It was the starring role. Would they delay? She couldn't worry about it right now.

When the car pulled up outside the sheriff's station, she didn't wait for the driver to get her. She pushed open the door and hopped out, hurrying toward the door. Inside, she was greeted by the deputy on-duty. The woman had a thick mane of wavy blonde hair that rivaled Sunnie's and blue eyes fringed with dark lashes. Her name badge read E. Swanson.

"Can I help you?"

"My name is Sunnie Burke. I would like some information about my father's death, Liam Burke."

The woman regarded her as she slowly got to her feet. "There's not much to tell."

She huffed. "My sister said he was murdered."

"That he was," she said with a nod. "I'm sorry for your loss, Miss Burke."

"What can you tell me?"

"Not much. He was found on the outskirts of town by the creek. He'll be transported to the county morgue for an autopsy later today so we can determine the cause of death."

"I see...and what about my mother, Fiona?" she asked.

"What about her?"

"Did my sister file a missing person's report?"

"Fiona is missing, you say?" Sheriff McAllister stood in the doorway of his office with a questioning look on his aged face. A bushy eyebrow rose toward his thinning hairline. He hadn't made his presence known until then and Sunnie never heard him enter the room.

"Yes, and the house has a sold sign out front. Neither my father nor mother told me the house was up for sale. Why are you looking at me that way?"

"I find it suspicious Fiona Burke is missing shortly after the murder of her husband."

Sunnie stared at him as worry twisted in her gut. The sheriff didn't know her mother was missing and she likely had given them a giant piece of the puzzle. "You think my mother is responsible?"

"I didn't until now."

Sunnie pressed a hand against her cramping abdomen. This wasn't going the way she had intended at all. Aoife didn't think Fiona had anything to do with it, so, why should she? Aoife knew their mother better than she did. Aoife spent more time with Fiona. How could she have been so stupid? She should have kept her mouth shut until she could find out more.

"Where is your sister now?"

"Aoife is...staying with friends."

She didn't know why she lied but she didn't want the sheriff to take off for the house and question her. The last thing she needed was more strife with her sister when they had so much stress between them already. Wasn't it enough they had to deal with the death of her father and her mother's mysterious disappearance?

"Liam Burke is dead and Fiona is missing hours later. I'd like to question your sister to see what she knows."

"Are you implying my mother may have harmed my father?"

"No, I'm saying it outright." His steely gaze never left her face.

Her heart raced as dread pumped through her. She should not have come here. She should not have mentioned anything about her missing mother. Sunnie didn't truly believe she would have harmed her father, but the evidence was damning.

"My parents may have had their differences but my mother is *not* a killer."

"Then she needs to come in and tell us what happened."

"Sheriff, I know it seems strange she's gone, but my mother is...strange. She deals with grief in different ways than most people." More lies. Sunnie had never expected her acting to come in handy in real life. She should get an Oscar.

"How does she deal with her grief?" the sheriff asked.

"If I know my mother, then she would have gone somewhere to be alone. I can't see her harming him. It's not in her to do something so terrible." She clenched her jaw and held her breath, hoping he would buy it.

She believed her mother wasn't capable of killing her father. There was not a vengeful bone in her body. She rushed on to keep McAllister from asking more questions.

"What I came to find out was how my father died, sheriff. Not talk about my mother."

"Liam was found with a strange black substance on him. It smelled like sulfur."

Sulfur? A shortness of breath returned and pinpricks of light danced in her vision. "Could I...see him?"

"Absolutely not. The coroner will be here shortly to take him to the county for an autopsy."

"Yes, I realize that. Your deputy said as much. But I would like to see him. Please."

"Seems a little morbid to me," the sheriff said.

She clenched her fists. Why could he not understand? Knowing her father was dead and seeing it were two different things. She wanted to see him for herself, to know for sure he was gone. Otherwise, her mind would continue to hope it was all a hoax and he was alive somewhere.

"Please."

McAllister and Swanson exchanged a look. The deputy gave a little shrug and the sheriff huffed out a breath and waved her to follow him. He led her through the small sheriff station to the back where they kept the dead until they were ready to transport to the county morgue. It wasn't a big room. Just big enough to have a row of four drawers for the bodies.

A lump formed in her throat. She had to swallow hard to push it back down. Her nerves were on high alert as he pulled open the drawer.

There was nothing inside.

Her father wasn't there. A mixture of relief and terror clenched her.

"What the hell?"

McAllister shoved it closed and reached for the next one. Also empty. And the third one Empty. And the fourth. Also empty.

"Emma!" he shouted.

She came running. "What is it?"

"Did the coroner come to retrieve him?"

"No, sir."

"Are you absolutely sure?"

"Yes, sir. What happened?"

"Liam Burke's body is missing."

Upon hearing that, Sunnie's legs gave out from under her as she fainted straightaway.

Sunnie blinked her eyes open as someone helped her to a sitting position. The deputy pushed a cup of water into her hand.

"Here. Sip this."

Pain erupted from the back to the front of her head as she sat on the cold tile floor, numb, holding the glass of water. She craned her neck and looked up at the sheriff and the deputy who stood over her with concerned looks on their faces.

"You all right, Miss Burke?"

"Where is my father?" she demanded, ignoring the question.

The two exchanged a look. One that said neither of them had an answer for her.

"A dead man can't get up and walk away," Sunnie added.

"No, ma'am, he can't," McAllister said.

"Then where is he?"

Silence was her response. She pushed off the floor in an awkward move. It was hard to get to her feet in the heels and dress holding a cup of water. Some of it sloshed over the rim.

"I suggest you two find him and as soon as possible." She shoved the cup at Deputy Swanson. "Or I'll be calling my lawyer."

She stomped out of the police station, the click of her heels the only sound in the small space. It gave her some satisfaction to threaten with her lawyer even if it wouldn't do any good. Once outside, she stood a moment looking at the black limo parked at the curb. Something about it all struck her as ridiculous and inconsequential. Her father was dead—no, presumed dead. Her mother was missing. She barely knew her sister anymore and here she was parading around town in a limo wearing designer shoes and clothes as if she was somebody.

She was nobody in Brookdale. It was a far cry from Los

Angeles where people knew her and she was on the A list to all the best parties. She was a rising star. Admired. Envied.

But as she stood there watching the driver hop out and open the back door for her, it struck her how none of it mattered. The only thing that truly mattered was family and hers was broken.

Overwhelmed, tears formed in her eyes. She blinked them back, trying to remain strong. But she wasn't strong like Aoife. She wasn't able to carry the weight of the world on her shoulders. She was a weakling.

Sunnie hurried down the sidewalk and slipped into the backseat as the driver shoved the door closed. She kicked off her shoes and then tucked her legs underneath her. She dug around in her handbag for a tissue and finally found a crumpled one at the bottom.

"Where to now, miss?" the driver asked.

She didn't know. She couldn't go back to the house with Aoife there. All she could do was find a hotel. She should have rented a car instead of having a chauffeur but she hadn't expected to be in town very long.

"Miss?"

Aoife said their father was found by the creek on the outskirts of town. She knew that creek. He sometimes liked to fish there even though he never caught anything but perch. And when he did catch something, he always threw it back. She wanted to see the scene of the crime.

"Take me to the creek."

She gave him directions. They arrived a few minutes later. He pulled up alongside the curb.

"Wait here," she ordered.

"As you wish."

Barefoot, she stepped out of the car and paused, looking down the embankment at the crushed grass and what appeared to be footsteps next to it. A cold punch of air went right through her and she gasped as her skin prickled and gooseflesh rose on her exposed arms and legs. A sudden breeze went through her, tousling her hair and blowing it into her face. Her stomach cramped and she doubled over, feeling as though she might retch any moment.

Sunnie took several deep breaths trying to regain her composure but it didn't help. There was a strange sensation coursing through her, tingling her skin. Something seemed to urge her toward the crushed grass at the bottom of the embankment. Whatever it was, she was compelled to go down it.

When she made it down to the trampled grass, she knelt. An overwhelming urge to brush her fingers over the crushed grass swept through her. A black substance smudged across a few blades. Without thinking, she reached for it, her fingers sliding over the cool grass. The image pounded through her with a wicked force. She sucked in a sharp breath.

Aoife. Aoife had been there and done the exact same thing. She could see her as if she sat across from her. Her face was pinched with concern and confusion. Sunnie shuddered, the image still utterly clear. It even seemed as though Aoife looked right at Sunnie, which couldn't be true because she wasn't there.

The black sludge that came off on her fingers smelled of sulfur. Sunnie used a nearby carpet of grass to clean her fingers as she remained, staring down at the crushed place. As she did, an image formed of her father. He was lying on the ground with the same black sludge on his chest. He wiped his hand through it, held it up in front of his face. He called Fiona's name. She fell to her knees next to him, pulling his limp body into her lap. Fiona said something to him, but Sunnie couldn't make out the words. Then his eyes shuttered closed and he was gone.

As Fiona threw her head back and screamed, the image faded and was gone.

Sunnie bolted to her feet and stumbled back a step or two. How could this be? It was as though she had witnessed the past. She'd seen what had happened to her father. And she'd seen Aoife standing next to the place where he'd died.

It was almost as though she saw into the past.

"Not possible," she whispered.

Was it? If it was, how? How was it possible?

She could still smell the sulfur. On her hand and in the grass.

"Miss Burke? Are you all right?" the driver called.

The hairs on her body stood on end. Her heart did a funny pitter-patter as the memory lingered. But the memory morphed as she continued to stare at the vacant place. Her father was there, joined by two men. One seemed oddly familiar. He placed his hand on Liam's forehead and looked up at the second man. They exchanged dialogue she couldn't hear. The second man nodded and suddenly the two men disappeared in a flash. Police arrived and Sunnie understood how he ended up in the morgue.

"Do you need help, Miss Burke?"

"No. I'm coming up."

Getting back up the embankment was harder than getting down, especially in her tight dress. As she neared the top, the driver extended a hand to her. She grasped it and he pulled her up the rest of the way.

"Did you find what you were looking for?" he asked.

She had more questions than when she arrived. "Yes."

Something niggled at her—something that made her think there was a possibility her father wasn't dead. And if he wasn't, then where was he?

If he wasn't dead, could he have walked away from the morgue?

A cold shiver ran through her.

"Could you take me back to my house?"

"Of course, miss."

Taking a cue from her sister, Sunnie hoped she could find some answers there. She had a sudden urgent need to tell Aoife what she'd found at the morgue—nothing. Maybe by now Aoife had found something and together they could bond over the search for their missing parents.

It seemed to take the driver an inordinate amount of time to get back. Impatience crawled through her veins as they turned the corner and headed down the street. Parked at the curb outside the house was a red Ford pick-up truck and a bright yellow sports car.

"Stop back here, please. Out of sight of the house."

He pulled over and cut the engine. Sunnie peered through the tinted windows watching as a copper-haired man jumped out of the yellow sports car and walked with a purposeful stride to the front door. He entered without knocking.

Sunnie sat back in the leather seat and chewed her thumbnail. Another sense of familiarity went through her. She'd seen him before but couldn't place where or how she knew him. Who was he? Why was he there? And who did the truck belong to?

"Are you going up, miss?" the driver asked.

"Not yet."

She wasn't sure what to do. She glanced down at her bare feet and the ridiculous designer dress and had a sudden impulse to change.

"Pop the trunk," she ordered.

"Miss?"

"Just do it, all right? And stay in the car."

She didn't need questioning looks from him as she hopped out of the car and went to the back. She opened her suitcase and rummaged around until she found a pair of faded jeans, a cotton shirt and a pair of well-worn sneakers. Despite her love of couture, she appreciated a comfortable pair of jeans. She slammed the trunk and got back into the car.

"Put up the privacy window," she said.

He gave her a brief glance in the rearview mirror before complying. She quickly pulled on the jeans under her dress then shoved it off over her head, dropping it on the floorboard. She pulled the shirt on and then stuck her feet in the shoes.

Then went back to staring out the window, wide-eyed, waiting for something to happen. She didn't wait long. A few minutes later, two men emerged from the house. One was the man from the yellow sports car. The other she knew as Sean O'Connell. Why was he there?

They got in the truck. She knocked on the window in a panic.

"Follow that red truck," she said when he rolled it down. "And whatever you do, don't lose them."

The driver pulled away from the curb so slowly, she nearly yelled for him to go faster. He picked up the pace a little as they left town, got on the freeway and headed to the city.

It was mid-morning when the faded red truck made its way through the heart of downtown Dallas to what looked like an abandoned warehouse.

"Pull up over there and park."

Sunnie draped her body over the front seat, pointing and giving him directions on how to follow. He tried to hide his sigh of annoyance but she heard it all the same. She didn't care. If Sean and the mystery man knew something about her missing parents, then she wanted to know.

She watched intently as they got out of the truck and walked into the abandoned warehouse. And waited. And waited. And waited. Twenty minutes later, they still had not emerged.

"I'm going inside. Wait here."

"You aren't paying me enough for all this trouble," he grumbled.

"Then I'll pay you double," she snapped and slammed the door.

Sunnie hurried toward the warehouse. When she pushed the door open, it made a groan announcing her presence. It gave her renewed confidence and she shoved it open with purpose and stepped inside.

And stopped short.

In the center of the empty warehouse, with faint light slashing over it, was a stone dolman surrounded by greenery and flowering vines. There was nothing but empty space between the stones and yet a shimmer of light was visible around the inside edge of it.

"Miss? I think you're in the wrong place."

Sunnie blinked and focused on the man standing to the left of the dolman. She hadn't noticed him before he spoke. He was the tall man with copper brown hair she'd seen earlier. His piercing hazel eyes pinpointed her with a less than friendly stare. He walked toward her and for a moment she thought she saw a hint of recognition flicker over his features.

"Who are you and why were you in my house? And where's Sean? I saw him come in here with you. What did you do with him?" She hadn't meant for the questions to come out in a rush but she couldn't stop them from bubbling out.

It occurred to her as she stood there, looking at the brawny man, she might be in a bit of trouble. He could be a serial killer and she was handing herself over as his next victim. She took a tentative step backward toward the door.

"My name is Caleb O'Brien. I'm a friend of Sean's. You must be Sunnie Burke." He removed the scowl from his face and replaced it with a smile as he extended his hand.

She hesitated a moment before she finally reached for him and grasped his hand, giving it a one-two pump. "Yes, I am."

"Did you follow us here?"

"I think that's rather obvious. What is that?" She nodded toward the dolman behind him.

"Nothing you need worry about. Come on. We should go outside." He ushered her toward the door.

Sunnie craned her neck to look back at the strange stone archway in the center of the warehouse. It was definitely out of place. When they were outside, he shoved the door closed and punched a code on the keypad next to it. The green light turned red.

"You didn't answer my question. Why were you in my house? Does it have anything to do with my mother?" she demanded. "Did she have anything to do with trying to kill my father?"

"What do you know about that?" He tipped his head in question.

"She's missing is what I know. What do *you* know?"

"I know as much as you do."

"And my father? Where is he? He's missing, too."

He swallowed hard, his throat working. "I hate to tell you this, Miss Burke, but Liam is dead."

She shook her head before he finished. "No, he's not. I was at the sheriff's department before I came here. His body is missing."

He stared at her for a long moment, his eyes widening only slightly before he regained his composure. "Are you sure about that?"

She folded her arms across her chest. "Of course I'm sure. I saw it with my own eyes. He wasn't at the morgue. His body was gone. A dead man doesn't get up and walk away, Mr. O'Brien."

"I'd prefer if you'd call me Caleb." He reached for her to grip her by the arm. "Let's go somewhere where we can talk."

She jerked her arm away. "No. I want answers here. Now. I want to know where my parents are. My sister didn't know anything. That's why I went to the sheriff. He was useless and then I had to open my big mouth and tell him my mother is missing. Now he thinks she may have had something to do with it and I'm not sure I disagree. I don't understand any of this."

She was aware of the hysteria edging her voice but she couldn't stop it from happening. For the first time since stepping foot back in Brookdale, she was truly frightened and sick with worry for her parents. She wanted to believe her mother hadn't killed her father. But the sense something was off was still there in the back of her mind.

"Sunnie...we should talk somewhere else."

"So you can tell me you don't know anything either? I don't understand why you can't answer a simple question about why you were in my house."

He cleared his throat and glanced around as he shifted from one foot to the other. "I was helping Sean look for Fiona, too. We didn't know about Liam."

"Well, he's alive somewhere. And if you won't help me, then I'll find someone who will. And I know where to start."

She spun on her heel and headed back to the car.

"Where are you going?" he called.

"Back to the house to talk to my sister. Aoife will help me."

"No. You can't."

Before she knew what was happening, he grabbed her by the arm and spun her toward him. Both hands clamped on her upper arms as he held her in place.

"Let me go."

Sunnie didn't give him a chance to respond. She kicked him in the shin as hard as she could and then kneed him in the groin. When he doubled over in pain with a groan, she made a break for it and ran toward the car. When she was inside, she locked the doors.

"Take me back to the house and hurry."

She had no doubt he would follow her and that was fine with her. Aoife would know what to do. Aoife would help her. And if he did show up, she'd call the sheriff and report him for trespassing.

Chapter 4

In the Human Realm before Time was altered

Caleb watched Sunnie hurry toward the limo, knowing where she was headed. Indecision went through him as he heaved a sigh.

Bollocks. She'd discovered Liam was missing from the morgue. That bumbling idiot sheriff would know, too, and then they'd be out searching for Liam. Liam who was now safely ensconced behind the veil in Faery. He decided the best course of action was to play dumb but even that didn't seem to work in his favor.

He was reluctant to tell her any more in case she decided to go snooping around in the attic. Sean had been sure the trunk lured Aoife into Faery. It could potentially do the same to Sunnie. The last thing he needed was Sunnie disappearing into Faery. But since she had Fae blood like her mother and Aoife, the open portal would likely call to her, too. And then what sort of mess would they have on their hands?

Perhaps he could talk sense into her and keep her away from the attic. Out of danger. He glanced at Sean's old pickup wondering if he could drive it. Sean exchanged the tracking compass for his keys before he left for Faery. He had them in his pocket.

He wanted to find out what else she knew about Fiona and Liam. He didn't think she'd lie about Liam's missing body but he was also fearful she may have discovered some shred of truth he wasn't prepared to explain.

Caleb hurried to the truck and hopped in. He started the engine, the body of the truck rattling. He knew back roads out of downtown and a shortcut and could likely get there before she did. He put the gas pedal to the floor and sped like a fiend through town. It was all the old truck could do to keep up.

When he pulled up outside the house, he was relieved to see he beat her there. He parked and got out, walking with a hurried gait up to the front door to wait for her. He didn't have to wait long.

The limo ambled up the street and halted at the curb. When she got out, he could see the glare on her pretty face as she stared at him from across the yard.

"How did you get here before me?" she demanded.

"I know a shortcut." He took the steps in long strides and walked across the yard to her. "Sunnie, I want to help you but I can't do that if you won't talk to me."

She looked around him at the house. He could see the panic was ready to set in. "I want to see Aoife."

"She's not here."

She propped her hands on her hips. "How do you know that? Where is she?"

He clenched his jaw, unsure how to answer. He knew because Sean tried to stop her from entering the portal in the trunk and was unsuccessful. The call to their boss at the Inter-dimensional Portal Protection Agency hadn't gone so well. Bryant was less than happy that Fiona and Aoife made it back to Faery. Caleb didn't want to think how utterly annoyed he would be if Sunnie made it back there, too.

"She had to leave," he said.

"When is she coming back? I need to talk to her about Dad."

He certainly didn't know the answer to that. Aoife was in Faery, where time moved at a different pace than the human realm. A week or a month could have passed by in the hours she'd been gone.

"I don't have an answer for you, but—" When she started to reply, he held up a hand to stop her, "if you'll hear me out I think we can help each other."

She tipped her head to the side. "How?"

"I want to help you find answers to your questions. But you have to trust me."

Sunnie chewed her lower lip, a thoughtful look coming over her face. "I don't know you."

Oh, but he knew her. He'd known her since she was a little girl. Like Sean had known Aoife. Fiona was very familiar with the two of them. They'd been in Fiona's life since the first time she left to return to Faery. She'd found a way to travel through the realms and when she returned for the third time, he'd been ordered to put the tattoo on her. He remembered it like it was yesterday.

The Agency let you slide the first time, Fiona. Not this time, he'd said.
She had merely smiled. *Fine, then. What do you intend to do? Arrest me? If you do, then you'll be the one to explain it to Liam.*
Not arrest you, he said. *Mark you.*
She had lifted an eyebrow and nodded. *I understand, of course.* Then she merely turned, lifted her shirt and exposed her shoulder. *If you don't mind, I'd like to request the location be here.*

It didn't matter where she had the tattoo as long as she had it. The ink he used had been enchanted, linking it with a particular spell to the tracking compass. The very compass Caleb had given Sean before he departed for Faery.

"I know you don't know me. You probably don't remember me so it will be a leap of faith for you." He held his hands up as though he were surrendering. "But I promise you I want answers as much as you do."

She considered his words for a long moment before she finally gave a nod. "Where do you want to start?"

"Let's go somewhere quiet to talk. I know a place not far from here."

"Why can't we talk inside?" She nodded toward the house.

The last thing he needed was the magic of the portal calling her, drawing her to Faery. He had to get her as far from the house as possible. And he had to do it soon before she knew what was happening. Sunnie wasn't like Aoife. She didn't sense she was different than everyone else. Even though they'd been raised by the same parents, they were complete opposites. She had no idea she had Fae blood.

"I don't think it's safe here." He extended his hand. "Will you come with me?"

More indecision flashed across her face and then she finally gave a nod. "Yes. I need to dismiss my driver."

She walked to the driver's side window of the limo and leaned down. He could hear her talking, but couldn't make out the words. The man glanced from her to him and then back again, as though trying to decide if he should follow through with her instructions. Finally he nodded and pulled away from the curb. Sunnie walked back to him.

"I'm ready. Let's go."

"What did you tell him?"

"I told him to check into the hotel on the outskirts of town and wait for me there. He didn't want to do it. He doesn't think I should trust you," she said.

"What do you think?" He led her to his yellow sports car and opened the passenger door for her.

"I think I'm not sure about you yet." She glanced back at the car. "This is yours?"

"Yes. The truck belongs to Sean."

She slid in the leather bucket seat. Caleb got in behind the wheel and started the car. They didn't talk much as they drove to the small diner not far from the house. He knew it would be a quiet place to talk. But the real question was—how much should he tell Sunnie?

He gave her a cursory glance as he parked. Would she believe him when he told her who she was? Or would she think he'd lost his mind? They entered the diner and were seated right away at a table near the windows. As the waitress sauntered away after taking their drink order, he dropped his menu and turned to her.

"Are you going to tell me why you were in my house or not?" she asked.

She didn't waste time, did she? "I was there looking for answers to the whereabouts of your mother."

That much was true. They'd found a lot of clues in the attic. None of which boded well for Aoife or Sunnie. The Eradication Spell, the map to the Ivory Wood in Faery, and a few ripped pages out of books were the biggest indicators Fiona was planning something serious back in Faery. The Ivory Wood was known for the Time Sphere under a strong protection spell but probably one Fiona could break since she was so powerful. Neither Sean nor Caleb knew who Fiona wanted to eradicate. Caleb, though, had a suspicion it had something to do with Niall.

"And what did you find?"

"Not much of anything," he said and then abruptly changed the subject. "Sunnie, how much do you know about your mother?"

"I'm asking the questions here, bucko. What did you find?" She said it as though she were the one in control. He almost laughed. She was far from in control of this situation.

He sighed. She wasn't going to make things easy, was she? "Sean and I found clues leading to her possible location."

"And?" she asked when he paused, unwilling to continue.

He looked her over again. Her golden blonde hair hung over

both shoulders in cascading silken waves. She looked at him with suspicion in her blue eyes. There was no doubt she was beautiful with her classic features—her high cheekbones, her perfect nose and her full red lips. Unlike Aoife, her true appearance wasn't hidden behind a glamour. Well, except her ears. They were hidden behind the glamour so no one would see the delicate points indicating her true heritage.

But Caleb could see through it. He was Fae. He could see through glamour as Sean could. He also knew Aoife's true appearance wasn't anything with which her sister was familiar. While Aoife's glamour showed her to the world as frumpy, beneath that she was a beauty just like Sunnie.

He leaned back in the vinyl booth and laced his fingers on top of the table and repeated the question. "How much do you know about your mother, Sunnie?"

She blinked surprise. "What kind of question is that? She's my mother. I know her about as well as any daughter would know her mother."

He almost laughed at that because he knew differently. He knew Fiona kept her truth buried and hidden so deep, no one knew who she truly was. Not Liam and certainly not him or Sean.

Or Aoife.

"Would you say she keeps secrets from you?" he asked, prodding her.

"I suppose any parent has their secrets from their children. What is this about, Caleb? Where are you going with this? Are you going to tell me what you know about my mother's disappearance or not?"

He pressed his tongue to the roof of his mouth as he considered. Sunnie deserved the truth even if it would rock her world off its axis. Should he be the one to deliver that news? Probably not. It should be Fiona but since Fiona was missing in Faery…then it fell to Caleb and he would have to be the one to break the news to her.

"What if I told you she's not who she appears?" he asked, keeping his voice light and conversational.

She looked at him like he was insane. "Caleb, if this is some weird way to tell me I'm not my mother's daughter, then I prefer you just tell me instead of beating around the bush. Am I adopted or something?"

He started to reply when the waitress returned to take their order.

"Just coffee and apple pie for me," Caleb said.

"And you, miss?"

"A salad," she said. "With whatever light dressing you have."

"All we got is the house salad and Ranch dressing, miss."

She scowled. "Then put it on the side."

When the waitress sauntered away with the order in hand, Caleb leaned across the table and dropped his voice. "What I have to tell you, Sunnie, will make you think I'm lying. But I assure you what I say is the truth. The honest truth."

"The more you try to convince me it's the truth, the more I'm going to think you're lying."

It was a fair assessment. He could understand why she'd think that. So, he'd have to choose his words carefully to make sure she understood what he was about to tell her.

"Your mother comes from a different place than others."

Her pale brows knit with question. "What does *that* mean?"

"It means there is another realm beyond this one that exists."

After a long pause, she snorted in a most unladylike manner. "Right. That's a good one."

He didn't answer her right away. He held her gaze, as though by doing that he could will the information into her mind.

Color drained from her face. "My god. You're serious."

"I am."

The waitress returned with a large slice of apple pie, coffee and the saddest looking salad she had ever seen. She plopped it down in front of Sunnie who looked at it with disdain.

"Anything else?" the waitress asked.

Caleb flashed a winning smile and said, "No, thanks."

When she was out of earshot, Sunnie shoved the salad away.

"Something wrong with your salad?"

"I forgot this Podunk town thinks a salad is iceberg lettuce and over ripe tomatoes." She eyed his pie.

He pushed it to the center of the table in an offer to share. She took a large forkful and shoved it into her mouth. Her eyes closed in a look of sheer bliss as though it was the best pie she'd ever had.

"Good?"

She nodded. "Been a long time since I've had sweets," she said around the mouthful of pie. When she swallowed, she added,

"Caleb, whatever you're trying to tell me, say it and get it over with. I have to find my father since apparently he's either not dead or some sicko stole his body from the morgue."

An inward cringe went through him. She was right about that but he couldn't tell her Liam was in Faery having his memory restored by Bryant. Nor could he tell her Liam wasn't exactly in the running for Father of the Year. He'd done as much damage to the family as Fiona had, just in a different way. He'd made promises to Bryant to keep the women firmly planted in the human realm. The only problem with that plan was Fiona was sneakier and cleverer than they realized. They should have given her more credit.

"Your mother is from Faery." Sunnie was right. There was no use beating around the bush. He got right to the point.

Her fork froze halfway to her mouth with another bite of his apple pie as she stared at him from across the table. Her blue eyes widened ever so slightly before she managed to compose herself. She lowered the fork back to the plate.

"Faery?"

"Yes."

"Where the hell is Faery? I've never heard of that country."

He huffed out a breath and stabbed a rogue apple. "It's not a country, Sunnie, it's a…a…realm. A place beyond this world. Beyond the veil."

She gave him a look that said she thought he might be crazy. "You're not making sense."

By now she'd managed to demolish half his pie. He shoved it the rest of the way toward her thinking she needed the sugar rush more than he did.

"Sunnie, have you ever heard of All Saints' Eve?"

She cocked her head to the side. "I don't think so."

"Also known as All Hallows' Eve. You would know it as Halloween."

"What does Halloween have to do with my mother?" she demanded.

He took a deep breath. This was going to be more difficult than he thought.

"All Hallows' Eve or October 31, is the night before Samhain when the veil between the human realm and the Faery realm is at its weakest point. Some believe it's the day when the dead can come and go as they please into our world. That's where the idea of ghosts comes from.

"In Celtic folklore, it's the beginning of the season of dark when the harvest is done and when the *Fae* can come and go through the veil to the Otherworld. Or Faery," he explained. When she continued to give him a blank look, he rolled his eyes. "You were a child. Probably three or four when Fiona took you to the creek. All you wanted was candy but she had other plans."

"I don't remember that."

She wouldn't remember it. She had been so small, so young. And Fiona had been so determined. It was the night she had nearly disappeared back to Faery with both girls.

She sounded almost offended, as though she couldn't believe he knew something about their family she didn't. But he knew plenty. He, like Sean, had been watching the Burkes for a long time. He had also been the one to wipe the girls' memories after the fact.

He had to restore that memory now.

"It would be easier if I could show you," he said.

She lifted one shoulder and dropped it in a half shrug. "Then show me."

Taking a deep breath, he reached across the table and wrapped his fingers around her wrist. One of the things he could do with his Fae magic was project thoughts. Thoughts that included memories. He closed his eyes and recalled that day so long ago.

"Where are we going, Mommy?" Aoife asked. She was three years older than Sunnie and dressed in a princess Halloween costume.

There were a few human rituals Fiona allowed the girls to partake in—one of them was Trick or Treating. And so under the guise of that, she took the girls to the creek on the outskirts of town. She carried Sunnie on one hip and held Aoife by the hand as she led them to the edge of the creek bed.

"It's a grand adventure. Just wait and see, my little princess," Fiona said.

A bonfire had been placed, the wood standing at attention in a pyramid shape. Once they arrived, Fiona waved her hand and ignited the fire. Aoife clapped her hands and bounced up and down.

"Mommy, you made fire!"

"Aye, I did." Sunnie fussed in her arms and she dropped to her knees to Aoife's level. She looked the girl in the eyes and brushed locks of hair back from her pixie-like face. "Things are going to change for the better now, my princess. It won't be long now."

Sean and Caleb had hurried to the site once they got wind of her plan. They both had to stop her before she made it back to Faery with the children. Before things were forever altered. Liam was back at the house under a sleeping spell she'd cast so she could slip into the night unnoticed. But she hadn't gone unnoticed. Magic in the human realm was like a shining beacon to other Fae. He and Sean knew she'd cast a spell before leaving for the creek.

"Stop right there, Fiona." Sean stepped out of the shadows, the firelight flickering over his face.

They had tracked her to this place, both suspecting what she was about to do.

She got to her feet and turned to face him. "It's too late, Sean. It's Samhain. The veil is thin and any moment now the portal will open."

"I can stop you," he said. "And I will. Both of us will. You can't leave, Fiona. We can't allow it and you're not taking the children with you."

"We don't belong here and you know it. We belong in Faery."

"Where are you planning to go, Fiona? Back to Niall? To the Towers of Illyria?"

There was obvious discomfort in her face as she considered his questions. Before she could answer, Sean continued.

"And what about Liam?" he asked.

"What about him?" she challenged.

"You'd take his children and leave?" he pressed.

"Aoife doesn't belong to him. She belongs to only me."

"But Sunnie doesn't. Sunnie is just as much his as she is yours."

She glanced at the blonde girl. "She will understand in time why I did it. Why I had to leave. She's part Fae. Besides, it's too late. The spell has been cast. By the time Liam wakes, we will be long gone."

The white light crackled through the air, shimmering in the darkness. They all saw it and they all knew it was the portal opening to Faery. Fiona knew, as they did, Samhain was one of the four fire festivals. That's why she had come here to try to escape.

"The spell can be broken. Now, Caleb!"

Caleb lunged from the shadows and used his Fae magic to stop the portal from opening. Fiona scooped up Aoife in her other arm as she made a mad dash for it. But it was too late. With his hands palm out and the bluish light streaming from him, he managed to close it before she could get to it. She stopped short and shot them both a heated glare.

"You won this time," she said. "But you will not be so lucky the next time. And there will be a next time."

"We'll be ready for you on Beltane come spring," Sean said. "In the meantime, neither Sunnie nor Aoife will remember tonight." He looked at Caleb and gave him a nod. "Do it."

It was then Caleb had to remove the memory from both the young girls' minds. But Fiona, though…Fiona remembered and resented them both for their part in stopping her from returning to Faery.

Caleb opened his eyes and met Sunnie's. Tears pooled in those blue depths and her lip quivered.

"That's….that wasn't real," she whispered.

"It was real. Every bit of it. I removed those memories from you and your sister to protect you. To keep you safe."

"From who?"

He didn't know how much of a threat Niall was to either of the girls. Niall had been searching for Fiona for years and, Caleb suspected, finally found her. His guess was Liam had been a victim of Niall's magic. Liam played his own part in the whole sordid tale. In some ways, her own father was as dangerous to her as Niall was to Aoife. He didn't think Sunnie was ready for the rest of the story.

"From someone who could hurt you and Aoife," he said.

"So…" she began slowly, "are you telling me I'm from…Faery?"

"Fiona is. So is Aoife even though she was born in the human realm." Regret and guilt speared through him. He wasn't sure *why* he was about to lie to her. He only knew he had to. "But you…you were born to a human and a Fae. You're a Halfling."

A Halfing. A strange tingling sensation went through her as she stared at Caleb from across the table. Sunnie had never heard the terminology before in her life. And she didn't much like it. She didn't want to be a Halfling and she resented the very idea that she was anything other then what she was.

She also wasn't so sure Caleb was telling her the truth. If only she could talk to Aoife to find out if she had the same memory.

"You think I'm lying," he said as though he could read her thoughts.

She glared at him. "Are you still in my head?"

"No, I'm just good at reading expressions. How can I prove to you I'm telling the truth?"

"You can't." She folded her arms and looked outside the window at his flashy sports car.

If she were in any other place in any other situation, she might like Caleb. He seemed like her type—he had the car, the looks, the swagger. But as it was, he was her enemy and she refused to succumb to the charming way he tried to tell her she was something she knew she wasn't.

You're a Halfing.

"I think I can." Caleb slid from the booth and held his hand out to her. "Come with me."

She gave his offered hand a suspicious look. "Where?"

He huffed. "Just come. I told you trusting me would be a leap of faith. So…take the leap, Sunnie."

Taking a deep breath, she reached for his hand. His fingers enclosed hers and a flash of some memory went through her. Caleb standing at the front door with Sean asking Liam where they could find Fiona. Liam telling them to get off his front porch, that they weren't wanted there. And Liam's voice boomed inside her head so clear it was as though he stood right next to her.

I've had enough of you and that Agency you work for. Now get off my porch.

And Caleb's terse reply. *You work for them, too, Liam.*

She flinched and drew her hand back.

"Everything all right?" he asked.

She chewed her bottom lip. He may be telling her the truth but there was more to the story. He hadn't shared everything with her.

"Yes, I'm ready."

He tossed a few bills on the table to pay for their food and headed out the diner to the car. He opened the door for her before heading around the back of the car to get in behind the wheel. She tucked her hands in her lap and waited as he started the car and pulled out of the space.

"What is the Agency?"

"Where did you hear that term?" He sounded guarded and she could tell he knew the answer to her question and was reluctant to give it to her.

It was difficult for her to explain how she knew the term because she wasn't sure herself. The flash she saw when holding Caleb's hand was definitely a memory from her childhood.

"You asked me to take a leap of faith," she said, "but to do that I need answers."

He nodded as though in agreement. "The Inter-dimensional

Portal Protection Agency."

Sunnie almost laughed by the way he offered that up so easily. "Did you make that up?"

"No. It's where Sean and I work. Our job is to protect the portals between here and Faery. We were both assigned to keep watch over Fiona and make sure she stayed out."

You work for them, too, Liam.

A cold sensation went over her. "Is that where she is now? In Faery?"

"You believe me now?"

He cut her a glance as he parked the car by the creek where she'd been earlier that day. Where she had the other strange memory flash as though she had seen through the veil of time to the past when Aoife had been there, looking at the same crushed place in the grass looking for answers as Sunnie was looking for answers. She rubbed at the crease along her forehead.

"I don't know what I believe. What are we doing here?"

"There's something magical about this place, Sunnie. It's where your mother tried to escape when you were a child. And where Liam was killed."

"He's not dead," she said, her voice hard and sharp.

"If he's not then we have to figure out why and how. We'll start here."

"There's nothing here. I was here this morning and I found nothing." Nothing except something weird that happened to her. But she wasn't ready to acknowledge it.

"Then we look again. Magic is a strange thing. If you don't know what to look for, you can't see it. But if you do…" He broke off and smiled.

"You think there's something here?"

"It's worth a look, don't you think?"

Apprehension went through her as she looked over at the creek. She wasn't sure she wanted to go back down there. She would have to face what had happened to her before. Maybe even tell Caleb. He didn't leave her much choice when he pushed open the door and got out.

She followed him as he headed down the embankment. Sunnie was glad she had the forethought to change from her heels and dress to sneakers and jeans. It made navigating the slope much easier than it had earlier that morning.

As they made their way down, she saw the shimmering thing in the water. She hadn't noticed it earlier that day. Had it been there before and she missed it? She couldn't quite make it out but she knew it was something that didn't belong there.

"What is that?" She pointed to it.

Caleb beat her to the edge of the creek. She paused next to him and peered down at the long silver staff with the glowing orb nestled in what looked like a silver dragon's claw. The water sparkled around it, giving it an ethereal glow.

"Stay away from it." There was something urgent and commending in his voice.

Touch it. Take it. Pick up the staff, Sunnie.

The words whispered in her head, the voice a dark and forbidding presence urging her forward. As though something reached down into her inner psyche and compelled her to do as it commanded. She dropped to her knees at the edge of the creek.

"What are you doing, Sunnie?"

Though she knew Caleb was speaking, she ignored him because the pull from the staff overpowered her senses.

Embrace the magic. Take the staff.

She pinched the bridge of her nose between her thumb and forefinger. Was she hearing things? Or was the voice really there?

Become who you are meant to be, Sunnie.

That time she was certain she heard the words in her head. She glanced up at Caleb but he merely stood there, almost like he was frozen in time. Sunnie glanced back at the silver staff in the water and noticed something very strange about the ripples. It seemed almost as though they moved in slow motion.

She heard a commotion that caught her attention and she saw the men on the other side of the creek. Two of them. One of them had the staff. Somehow she knew this was not the present. She was seeing something that happened in the past. It was only a brief image before it faded. The next image that came into view was of one of them falling backward into the creek, releasing the staff into the water.

"I must take it."

She stretched out her hand but it was out of reach. Her knees dug into the soft ground as she reached toward it, her muscles straining. Her fingertips brushed the cool water.

"Don't touch it." Caleb's hand landed on her shoulder and

pulled her away from the water.

"I have to pick it up." Dark need pounded through her with such a violent fury, she shoved off his hand and reached for it again.

"Sunnie, no."

He practically tackled her like a defensive lineman pummeling the quarterback. He shoved her away from the edge of the creek, pushing her to the ground. His hands encircled her wrists like a vice as he held them in place over her head. His long, lean form pressed against her, covering her, as he looked down at her.

Her breath stilled in her throat as she met his steely hazel gaze. Shadow and light played upon his handsome features and she could see the hint of stubble on his cheeks and chin. She hadn't noticed it before when they were at the diner but she noticed it now. Caleb was the kind of man she could easily fall for if she wasn't a movie star and he wasn't…whatever he was. She wasn't quite sure who or what he was. Nor was she sure what made her want to pick up the staff.

He made no effort to move off her.

"I think it's safe to get off me now," she said.

"Not if you're going to try to pick that thing up again." His gaze searched her face for an answer.

"I won't. I don't know what came over me."

"I do. The magic spoke to you."

Should she tell him it called to her? Or would he think she was totally off her rocker then?

He released her wrists and moved off her. He helped her to her feet. She didn't want to admit how much she liked being held by him. With Caleb's body heat gone, a chilly shudder went through her and she clutched her elbows.

"Why would it do something like that?" she asked.

"I'm not sure. I need to contact my superior and find out what they want me to do with it. It can't stay here."

He pulled out his smartphone and started to dial a number and then stopped. He put the phone back in his pocket.

"No, I can't do that. He thinks I'm in Faery with Sean." He cursed under his breath.

"So?"

"I disobeyed a direct order. If I call him now, he'll know I didn't go and then he'll ask me why."

She lifted an eyebrow. "So why didn't you?"

"It's complicated." He ran a hand over his chin, the skin bristling against the stubble. "I can't leave that thing here, though."

Sunnie looked back at the staff and noticed the orb was no longer glowing. Nor did she feel anything from it. "It stopped glowing. I'm going to pick it up now."

"Sunnie, wait—"

She slipped away from him and dropped to her knees once more to reach the staff. Her hand dove in the cold water, the tips of her fingers brushing over the silver. She almost had it in her hand when she slipped and fell head first into the water with a squeal and a splash.

Though the water was shallow, Caleb was there in an instant wrapping his arms around her waist and pulling her out. Before she moved too far from the staff, though, she managed to grab it. He hauled her back to the bank of the creek, both of them soaking wet. She dropped the staff on the ground next to her.

"Got it." She gave him a triumphant grin.

He sucked in a sharp breath. "You shouldn't have. It's too dangerous."

"It's not glowing anymore."

No sooner had the words left her mouth than the orb flickered and came back to life. And when it did that, the dark oily voice started once again in her head. She was powerless to resist. She could not disobey.

Sunnie reached for the staff.

Chapter 5

In the Human Realm before Time was altered

As soon as the orb in the staff flickered back to life, Sunnie once again reached for it. Her eyes had turned an odd shade of silver and Caleb knew instantly she was under some sort of spell. He'd seen that staff before, knew it was dangerous though he couldn't place why or how. He couldn't let her touch it again. He dove for her before she could grasp it and shoved her to the ground, pinning her frame underneath him for the second time.

Her long slender form stretched beneath him, her breasts crushed against his chest, and she blinked, the blue returning to her eyes. A strange streak of white appeared in her golden blonde hair. It hadn't been there before she touched the staff but it was certainly there now.

Color stained her cheeks under his scrutiny.

"Get off me," she huffed. She gave him a half-hearted shove that indicated she *didn't* want him to get off her.

"Not until you promise you'll keep your hands off that staff."

She giggled. He realized what he said sounded like an innuendo. She knew, as he did, he didn't mean it that way.

"You know what I mean," he said with a grumble.

A breath fluttered between her parted lips. There was something alluring and sensual about that as he continued to hold her against the ground. Her body was warm and curved against him in all the right ways. Apparently he liked holding her *a lot* judging by the way his erection pressed into her thigh.

"Do I?" she asked, breathy as she lifted one pale brow as though she challenged him.

"You most certainly do."

"It seems there's more than one staff around here." And she giggled again.

"Cheeky girl, aren't you?"

"Do you think so?" She tilted her head back enough to jut out her chin, looking smug. Her lips parted as though in invitation.

"I know so."

He wanted to kiss her, damn it, even though he knew he shouldn't kiss her. It didn't help matters when her dainty pink tongue darted out and ran over her lower lip. She was teasing him now and she knew it. Her gaze went from his eyes, over his face, pausing briefly on his mouth and then back again.

"If you let me up, I promise to keep my hands to myself." She gave him a flirty grin.

"I'll release you but if you reach for it again, I'll have to stop you."

"Will it involve you tackling me again?"

He could see the pulse fluttering at the base of her throat. "It might."

"Pity I won't be reaching for it," she said with a wistful sigh.

"Aye, pity, indeed."

The last thing he needed was to get mixed up with Sunnie Burke. The movie starlet had had her share of trouble in the tabloids—he hated to admit those rags were a guilty pleasure. He'd read most of them about her and all her troubles with Hollywood's A List actors. She was clawing her way to the top and would stop at nothing to get where she wanted. She'd been spotted with big name actors, some single, some not. She'd also been rumored to be having an affair with the director of her current movie in progress.

But, Caleb wondered, how much of that was true?

She cleared her throat. "You're crushing me, you know."

There were a lot of ways he wanted to crush her. And they all involved her naked.

She was a dangerous thing to want.

Caleb released her and they sat up. Next to them, the orb had stopped glowing. They both glanced at the offending thing. He wondered what it had done to her to make her want to pick it up. What type of magic did it have for it to change her eyes silver and put a streak in her hair?

"It's as though I heard it call to me," she said, as though answering his unasked question.

His head jerked toward her as he narrowed his gaze, wondering if she had heard him think it. But she couldn't have. She was busy pulling her fingers through her damp locks to release the tangles, blissfully unaware of the change in her hair color. She wasn't even looking at him.

"It's strange. I've never experienced anything like it. Or what happened to me earlier when I was here at the creek." She said it so casually he might have ignored it if it hadn't been so significant.

"You were here before?"

"Yes. After I talked to my sister, I came looking for clues. Or answers or something." She paused, a faraway look on her pretty face.

"Did you find answers?"

She blinked and turned her head to meet his gaze. "I didn't."

"What happened to you here?"

"I knelt in the grass over there." She indicated the place where Liam had been found. "There was this black sludge on the grass. I touched it and then...I...well, it's as though I could see Aoife there doing the same thing. But I *knew* she wasn't there because I'd left her at the house standing on the porch."

The nape of his neck tingled. She had discovered one of her Fae abilities and didn't even know it.

"Then what do you think you saw?" he asked.

"I saw Aoife but in the past. That sounds ridiculous, doesn't it?"

"No."

"You believe me?" Her eyes were wide and imploring as though she hoped he believed her.

He nodded. "I believe you."

Because he knew the truth about Sunnie. He should have told her but he spit out the lie before he could stop the words. Telling her she was a Halfling was much easier than telling her she was full-blooded Fae.

"Does it mean something?" she asked.

It meant a lot. It meant the magic in the staff called to her though he couldn't understand why. Looking at the staff gave him a feeling of foreboding. As though it was something evil. Something not to be trifled with. Something eerily familiar. He couldn't shake the feeling he'd seen it somewhere before.

"You said the staff called to you, right?" he asked and she nodded. "And you think you saw your sister here, but in the past?" She nodded again. "Now do you believe you're a Halfling?"

Even now he could not tell her the truth. He was a coward. He should have confessed and told her who she truly was.

She blinked her owlish blue eyes as the color drained from her face and realization dawned on her. He could see the understanding there and knew she was, at least, starting to believe making him all the more guilty for his deception.

"I'm a Halfling."

"You are."

Sunnie dragged her lower lip through her teeth. "Then perhaps you should take me back to the house."

"Why?"

"Because I need to find my family." She climbed to her feet and brushed the dirt and grass off her damp clothes.

He cringed as he got to his feet. How was he going to tell her Fiona and Aoife were both in Faery? She'd want to follow immediately. She'd want to track them down because now that she knew she wasn't who she thought she was, she wanted answers.

And he couldn't blame her. He'd want answers, too. But he couldn't let her step into Faery.

At least not without him.

Not yet.

The only way he could think to control the situation was to take Sunnie with him through the portal in the warehouse. Then he could keep an eye on her while searching for Sean, Aoife and Fiona.

If Bryant found out he'd brought along the other sister, he'd be in for an ass-chewing of epic proportions. But the alternative of Sunnie disappearing into Faery alone was worse.

"I have a proposition for you," he said. "I'll help you find them on one condition."

She cocked her head to the side. "And what is that?"

"That you stick with me until tomorrow and then I'll take you to them."

"You said you didn't know where they were." Her tone was almost an accusation. She tipped her head to the side, one hand on her hip as she jutted out her breasts, reminding him once again of the starlet who wanted her own way and usually got it.

Also reminding him why he needed to keep her at arm's length.

"I don't exactly, but I have an idea where to look for them."

"Oh, Caleb, you're absolutely exasperating. Do you know where they are or not?"

"They're in Faery."

She laughed. "Yeah, right."

"It's the truth, Sunnie. Fiona opened a portal and Aoife accidentally followed her."

"Accidentally?" Disbelief was written all over her face.

"It's why Sean and I were supposed to go after her."

"Sean's there, too? Is everyone there but me? What about my father? Do you know where he is, too, and you're keeping it from me?" She folded her arms across her chest again, pushing her breasts together and up. It took all his strength not to look at them through the damp t-shirt.

He did know and the shame of it pressed through him like a darkness he could not rid. He knew the answers to most of her questions but he couldn't tell her. He couldn't tell her he used dark magic to resurrect her father. He couldn't tell her he had personally escorted Liam through the portal and delivered him to the man who had orchestrated everything from the moment Fiona arrived in the human realm years ago. How would Sunnie ever understand?

She barely had a grasp on the fact she thought she was half human, half Fae. Nor could she understand Faery was another place, another time beyond the human realm. Faery was a land unlike the human world to which she was accustomed.

"I couldn't say where Liam is." It wasn't quite a lie. While he knew Liam's exact location, he definitely couldn't tell her. "I was supposed to go with Sean but he asked me to stay behind and wait until tomorrow."

"Why?" Her gaze narrowed.

"He thought he could get to Fiona and Aoife quickly. He asked me to wait. I'm not sure why I'm telling you anything at all."

She scowled. "Then stop talking to me. I don't need your help. I'll find my dad on my own."

Sunnie started up the embankment and Caleb knew he'd made a mistake. He huffed as he went after her, the silver staff on the ground behind them once again forgotten. She knew he followed her and picked up the pace, climbing the embankment until she made it to the top.

"Sunnie, wait!"

She hurried down the sidewalk, putting as much distance between the two of them as she could. Her brisk pace changed into a dead run. Cursing under his breath, Caleb took off after her. But her legs were just as long as his and she was a quick runner. He knew from reading about her and by her fit form she kept in shape by jogging and she was putting that to good use now.

"Sunnie!" he called.

She refused to stop or turn to look at him. He'd scared her off and now she was like a feral cat running from animal control. Her damp blonde hair bounced behind her.

And then suddenly she was gone in a blink.

Caleb slowed to a halt, pressed his hands on his thighs as he tried to catch his breath. The girl had sifted and she probably didn't even know how she did it.

"Hell," he muttered.

He knew exactly where she was headed because he intended to follow her.

Caleb spun back toward the staff and snatched it up. He couldn't leave the dangerous relic here. The only safe place he could think to stash it for safekeeping was the attic in Fiona's house…right where he'd find Sunnie.

Sunnie stumbled and tripped over a crack on the sidewalk before she went flying. She spilled across the walkway leading up to the wood steps of her house. Unfortunately, her knees and elbows took the brunt of the blow when she landed and skidded. She cried out in pain as she came to a jarring halt.

What the hell happened? She was running, trying to get away from Caleb, thinking she had to get back to the house and then suddenly she was there.

She lifted her head and looked up at the dilapidated old house. It needed repairs but she was quite fond of it. She'd grown up there. And even though she and her sister didn't always get along, she had good memories of it.

It took some effort to shove off the sidewalk and stand. Her jeans were ripped, her knee skinned beneath it. Both her arms throbbed with pain. She lifted one arm and saw the bloody scrape and winced.

It wouldn't be long before Caleb showed up and tried to get her away from the house. She had to barricade herself inside.

The trunk, Sunnie.

Odd. She thought she heard someone calling her. She glanced

around and saw no one. The voice was distinctive in her head and very different from the one that commanded her to pick up the staff. This voice was bright and clear while the other was sinister, dark, dangerous.

She limped up the front steps to the door. When she tried the knob, it was locked. She knocked.

"Aoife?" she called through the door. "Are you in there? It's Sunnie. Let me in."

She knocked again and called through the door for her sister. There was still no answer. Holding her arm against her side, she trotted down the steps and glanced around the front yard. The FOR SALE-SOLD sign was still there. The hot summer breeze fluttered over her, her still damp clothes clinging to her.

She didn't have her keys. How was she going to get inside? She remembered the broken lock on the window in the back. That would be her way in. She hobbled around to the backyard and halted. Someone had the same idea about the window. The screen was off and the window open.

Aoife must have remembered the broken lock, too. That must be how she got inside. So why didn't she answer? Unless she was in Faery as Caleb had said.

It took some doing with her skinned-up elbow and knee, but she managed to climb through the window into the living room. She landed on the floor with a thud, cringing with the pain. When she got her bearings, she climbed to her feet and turned back toward the window, shoving it closed. She scanned the room, looking for signs someone had been there or anything out of place.

"Aoife? Are you here?"

No answer.

She listened for movement but heard nothing.

She'd been back at Christmas and everything appeared to be in its proper place. The same threadbare carpet and well-worn furniture. The strange thing was if the house had been sold, why was the furniture still there? And the pantry still stocked? Dishes still in the cabinets? It seemed more like her mother had left for vacation rather than forever.

That didn't make sense.

The trunk.

Again, that voice in her head but she knew she was alone. Gooseflesh broke out on her arms. She gripped her elbows and regretted it when the stinging pain shot up her arms, reminding her of her injuries. She recalled there was a first aid kit under the kitchen sink. She hobbled to the kitchen and patched up her skinned elbow and knee.

Go up into the attic, Sunnie.

Sunnie looked at the stairs, her heart palpitating at a sudden rapid beat. The attic was forbidden to her and Aoife. It had been all their life. She couldn't go up there.

"But I must."

She muttered the words aloud as she headed for the stairs, passing through the living room by the wall mirror. She caught a glimpse of her face in the reflection and it startled her. She sucked in a sharp breath. A streak of white swept from her right temple upward and to the back of her head. It hadn't been there that morning.

"What the…?"

How in the world did that happen? It was almost as though she had aged. Or, rather, her hair had aged. Her beautiful blonde tresses were marred.

The trunk. The trunk. The trunk.

Sunnie forgot her new appearance and headed for the stairs, taking them two at a time until she stood under the attic entrance. She didn't even hesitate to pull down the attic stairs and then bolt up them.

Once she was in the attic, a strange sensation went over her. She was on forbidden ground. Eyes wide, she glanced around at the dusty confines. A desk in the corner was littered with paper and books. Holiday decorations. An old steamer trunk off to one side.

She approached the desk. Hand and fingerprints had been left behind in the dust. Half-rolled paper scattered along the top of the desk along with two books. She picked up the first one and flipped it open, the aged cover crackling from use. The title page read *Hidden Dimensions and Fae Time Travel*. There was no author. A cold sensation prickled the back of her neck, making the fine hairs stand on end.

"Caleb was right. He was telling the truth."

She thumbed through the musty pages but found nothing she could understand because it was written in a strange language she had never seen before. She replaced it and picked up the second book titled *Hypothesis of Fae Magic in Other Realms*. This one, like the other, also written in a strange language.

You are a Halfing.

The words rang back in her head as an ominous feeling swept through her. A parchment partially open on the desk caught her attention. Discarding the book, she picked up the parchment. Someone had scrawled the words *Eradication Spell* along the top in a messy hand. As she glanced down the faded page of carefully written words, the strange language morphed into words she could read and understand.

It was a spell. A way to remove and take the magic from someone and absorb it. The cold tingling sensation at the base of her throat subsided and was replaced by shadows and darkness, a sort of gloom that spoke to the very depths of her soul. That reached into her and tugged a part of her she didn't know existed.

Until today.

The trunk. The trunk. The trunk.

"Yes, the trunk. I must go to it."

Dropping the parchment, Sunnie moved towards it. The symbol on the top came to life, lighting up the dark room. She sucked in a breath as she fell to her knees in front of it. A Celtic knotwork circle with a sword through it glowed, pulsed, beckoned.

She was powerless to resist. Her fingers brushed over the symbol but her finger caught on the tip of the small sword and pricked it. She gasped, pulled her finger away as a drop landed on the symbol. She stuck her finger in her mouth and sucked away the drop of blood as she heard that same voice in her head once again.

Open the trunk, Sunnie.

Something drove her to follow the command. She couldn't stop from opening the trunk even if she wanted to. As soon as the lid was open, sunlight burst upward into the room. She leaned forward to look over the edge.

It was no ordinary trunk. There was another world inside it.

Her heart started to beat faster and everything she learned from Caleb had to be true. He spoke the truth. She had to believe she was a Halfing, as he called her. Her mother was a Fae and so was her sister. And this…this place must be where they had gone. *Faery.*

There was only one way to find out. She rose to her full height, took a deep breath and stepped into the trunk. She expected to fall into space but instead her foot landed on solid ground.

She took another step and was inside the trunk and yet…she

wasn't. All around her were vibrant colors—the grass was lush and the greenest she'd ever seen. The sky above was a blend of pink and blue, the colors bleeding into each other. Beyond she could see what looked like a walled city. A pale moon surrounded by clouds hung low on the horizon, giving her enough of a view to know that wasn't part of her world. She was definitely in another place, another time. Another realm.

Beyond the veil.

A giant creature flapped through the sky, the large wings making a loud *whump-whump* sound as it went past. She squinted against the bright sunlight, shielding her eyes to make out the strange form. If she didn't know any better, she'd seen her first dragon. A black one. The sunlight illuminated the iridescent scales as it glided through the sky. The giant head turned and for a moment she was certain those red eyes pinpointed her.

She staggered backward, as though that would keep the beast from seeing her, and tripped over the edge of the trunk. She took a tumble backward, crashing against the ground and landed with a thud.

"Sunnie? Are you here?" That was Caleb's voice coming from somewhere inside the house, which was, oddly, behind her now.

She gasped as she looked through the rectangular opening of the trunk, the lid still open. Through the opening she could see the attic, the one bulb casting a dim shadow across the wood slatted floor and dust motes dancing a lazy dance in the half light. Her heart pounded a wicked tattoo.

"Sunnie?"

She couldn't let him find her. She dove forward and reached for the lid, snatched it and pulled it closed with a loud snap. Once the lid was closed, it disappeared. There was nothing there but air and it took several seconds for the realization of what she had done to sink into her addled mind. Horror spilled through her. She was stuck in whatever place this was with a blue-pink sky and a green landscape that rivaled spring in the Highlands.

Sunnie sat there, unsure what to do next, as tears welled in her eyes. She was irrevocably alone. She had no idea where she was or what to do next. She wasn't like Aoife. She didn't have the wherewithal to figure it out. She didn't know what to do. She drew her knees up to her chest, wrapped her arms around them and sniffed, letting all the negativity and fear seep into her bones.

No, she could not let it defeat her. For whatever reason, the trunk had called to her, beckoned her to open the lid and step through. Like the staff had beckoned her to pick it up. Her fingers still tingled from the sensation. Deep in her psyche, the memory of it burned through her as she flexed her fingers.

Sunnie straightened, got to her feet and smoothed her hands over her shirt. She was strong and smart and she would find a way back home. She wasn't a wimp. She would figure it out. She only wished she'd allowed Caleb to follow her through the trunk. He could help her. He would likely know where she'd ended up and what to do next.

Somehow, though, she knew what to do. Taking a deep breath, she started across the immaculate greens and headed for the walled city on the horizon.

Caleb entered the attic in time to see the lid to the trunk slam shut. He dropped the staff and ran to the trunk. He shoved it open only to find there was nothing unusual inside. Nothing but dusty clothes and old newspaper clippings.

Damn it!

Just like Aoife.

When he and Sean opened the trunk after Aoife's disappearance, there had been a shimmering pink edge around it indicating the portal was still active. He pulled out his smartphone and checked the app. The spike had been there moments before and if the portal was still active and open there would be a slight vibration in the air around him. Nothing. It appeared the portal had been closed.

He saw the drop of blood on the Celtic symbol. Sunnie must have pricked herself—an accident or on purpose? If Fiona used blood magic to open the portal, then blood magic would close it. Blood magic Sunnie didn't even know she possessed.

He pounded his fist against the lid of the trunk and swore a string of colorful expletives. He'd been such an idiot to let Sunnie out of his sight. But he couldn't sift even if he wanted to—he'd never possessed the ability. She'd sifted right before his eyes and she probably didn't even know what she did or how she did it.

Caleb glanced around the attic, his gaze landing on the

offending staff. He would have to alert Bryant to the presence of the Fae relic in the human realm, a task he didn't relish. He walked over, picked it up and leaned it against the wall near the trunk. Then he reached for his phone and called Bryant.

His boss had somehow figured out a way for the phone to work across realms. Caleb assumed it was some type of magic that made it possible. As Bryant answered, he braced himself for the backlash.

"There's something you need to know," Caleb said.

"Cal? Where are you? Are you still in the human realm?"

"I am. There's been a…problem." He chose his words with care.

"What is it?"

"I found a Fae relic by the creek. It's a silver staff."

There was a pause and silence, then, "What sort of silver staff?"

"It has an orb on the top clutched in a dragon claw. It's what Niall's men used to kill Liam," he said. "I can sense the power in it."

"A moment," Bryan said.

There was another long pause. In the background, Caleb could hear flipping pages and imagined Bryant was looking up something in one of his thick books that resided behind his desk in his office. Then he picked up the phone again.

"You said the orb is clutched in a dragon claw?"

"That's right."

"It's the lost Staff of Amsheer. It's a powerful Fae relic, to be sure, and is thought to choose who it wants to wield it. It's good you found it. Where is it?"

"In Fiona's attic. What do you want me to do with it?"

"Leave it. It will be safe there for the time being. I will retrieve it with my own portal. Now why aren't you and Sean in Faery like I ordered?"

"On my way." Caleb clicked off the phone before Bryant could ask any more questions.

He didn't want to explain Sean already entered and gone after Fiona and Aoife, nor did he want to explain how he chased Sunnie right through the portal in the trunk. With any luck, he would find them all before he had to confess any of it to Bryant.

With one last glance at the staff, Caleb descended the stairs to return to the warehouse in downtown.

Chapter 6

In the Land of Faery before Time was altered

"A Changeling?" Liam asked.

Before Bryant could answer, his phone rang. He pulled it out of his pocket and spoke low so Liam couldn't hear. He thought a cell phone in Faery was a strange oddity.

Liam had, of course, heard the term Changeling before. When his Irish granny came to visit, she would regale him with tales of Changelings and fairies and all sorts of magical creatures. He thought the stories were nothing more than the fanciful imaginings of an old woman. And when she didn't come to visit, she would mail him letters from across the pond. Sometimes she would include little trinkets.

Once she sent him a pendant that was a circlet of intricate Celtic knotwork with a mini sword through it. It was the most interesting thing she'd ever sent him. At some point over the years, though, he'd lost it. He'd turned the house upside down looking for it and had never found it. He even enlisted Fiona and the children into helping but to no avail. The loss of the trinket still pained him.

Bryant hung up and plastered a fake smile on his face. "Apologies. It was an important call. Now where were we?"

"I'm a Changeling."

"Ah, aye. Do you know what a Changeling is?" Bryant asked.

He nodded. "I know."

"Good then I won't have to go into great detail to explain that. You have questions no doubt."

"I do. Are you prepared to answer them now?"

Bryant gave him that oily smile that had become so familiar. And so hated. "I am."

"How did I die?"

"Ah, so we're starting there, are we? I thought for certain you'd want to know how you ended up in the human realm."

Liam sighed. "Is that the first question you wish to answer?" When Bryant responded merely with that smile, he sighed again. "All right then. How did I end up in the human realm?"

"I thought you'd never ask. You were obviously switched at birth for a human child. Who that human child was we don't know. Since we discovered your existence, we've been trying to find out who your counterpart is in this realm." Bryant looked more than pleased with his reply.

It wasn't much of an answer. He didn't give Liam any new details he couldn't deduce for himself. Obviously he had been switched at birth for a human child, but why?

"You intend to track him down?"

"Aye, so we can return him to his proper place. He's human and doesn't truly belong here. He'd likely want to return to his own realm, don't you think?"

"What if he doesn't want to return?" Liam asked. "He's been here his whole life."

"'Tis nothing for you to worry over. Next question." He waved it away as though it were nothing and only a trivial matter.

"If I'm Fae, then why do I look human?"

"Another brilliant question! To answer that, I will need some assistance."

Bryant walked to the door of his chamber and opened it. He spoke to someone in the drafty corridor and then stepped aside to allow a young woman to enter. She was a dark beauty, petite and slender with wide brown eyes under a veil of thick lashes and hair the color of a fiery sunset.

"This is Brigid. She is a *sidhe*. Brigid, meet Liam."

She dipped a curtsy by placing one foot behind her opposite ankle. When she rose to her full height, which wasn't very tall at all, she gave him a coquettish look through those thick lashes.

"Hello," he said.

She blushed and looked down.

"She's a bit shy." Bryant patted her shoulder. "Are you familiar with the *sidhe*, Liam?"

"I am not."

"A *sidhe* has very special magic. She can see through and break any spell including the one on you."

Liam's brows drew together in surprise. "There's a spell on me?"

"A glamour spell. One that hides your true appearance. Anyone who is a Fae can see right through it, but yours is particularly strong and difficult to see through. Even I have trouble seeing through the glamour to your true self. It's even more difficult to break the spell. It's beyond my capabilities. That's why I've called on Brigid." He waved her toward Liam. "My dear, if you will."

Brigid moved to stand in front of Liam, her upturned pixy face lined with concentration and her shyness forgotten. Though she looked at him, it seemed more like she looked through him or beyond him to a place only she could see. She lifted her hands, her fingers twitching, and her eyes fluttered closed. Her lips moved but only a whisper came out with words in a language he couldn't quite hear or understand. Her fingertips shimmered with a pale white light.

She stood on tiptoe to reach for him, placing her fingers on his cheeks. When the tips of her fingers met his skin, the tingling sensation shuddered through him. Her eyes opened and met his gaze and he couldn't help but think she was the most beautiful sight he'd ever seen before him. A slight smile pulled at the corners of her mouth.

But the smile quickly faded and turned into a silent scream of pain. Blue and red veins suddenly became visible under her pale skin. Bryant saw what was happening and tried to intervene but it was too late. A zap like an electrical current went through both of them and poor Brigid flew backward into a bookshelf while Liam crumpled to the ground, the smell of sulfur emanating off his body. He landed hard on the wood floor with a grunt, smacking his knee caps and slamming the heels of his hands. By the time he regained his composure and lifted his head, Bryant had the unconscious girl cradled in his arms.

"Is she…all right?" Liam tried to get to his feet but settled for dragging his limp body over to them.

"She's coming to now."

When her eyes opened, she looked up at Bryant and whispered. "Wizard magic."

But it was loud enough for Liam to hear. "Wizard magic? What does that mean?"

Bryant lifted his head. "It means, Liam, your glamour is a spell weaved by the most powerful magic in Faery. The magic of a wizard. I must get her to the healer." He rose and headed for the door.

"I'm coming with you," Liam said and followed.

The healer's quarters were on the other side of the castle. Liam's questions were put aside as he watched Bryant put the girl on one of the narrow beds. The healer, a wizened old man, hurried over.

"What happened?"

"The spell she tried to break was wizard magic."

The healer cursed under his breath as he put his hand on her forehead and closed his eyes. "It could have killed her. The damage is severe but not irreversible. Move away and allow me to heal her."

Bryant and Liam stepped back and watched the man go to work, using his own magic to envelop the girl.

"Will she be all right?" Liam asked.

"She's in excellent hands, so I have no doubt she will recover," Bryant said. "I'm sure you have more questions than ever now."

"I do. None you have the answer to, I assume," he replied.

"If you want to know who the wizard was that put the glamour spell on you, I cannot answer that. There are but a handful of wizards in this realm. It could be any of them. As for your next unasked question, I don't know your true lineage, though I sensed the magic within you from the day I met you. It flickers there with a dim light. You have great potential to become somewhat of a force, Liam. I want to help you learn the ways of magic and become who you were born to be."

"And who is that?" he asked.

"Why, a powerful Fae, of course. I've wasted enough time trying to coax the magic out of you. It's time to teach you." Bryant gave him a bright smile. "Shall we begin?"

"Begin?"

"Aye," he said and waved him toward the door. "Come to the library and I will give you your first and most important lesson. How to open a portal."

He didn't wait for a reply as he left the healer's room behind. Liam had no choice but to follow him through the corridors to the library. He had been in the room once or twice to browse the books and become familiar with this new realm. Bryant pushed open the doors and paused to let him pass, then closed them and stepped into the cavernous room.

Bookshelves lined the walls from the floor to the twenty-foot ceiling. The floor was a green marble with a Celtic knotwork circlet woven throughout the stonework. He had never noticed that before and was fascinated by it now as he watched Bryant follow the circlet as though he followed a pathway. As he took one careful step after another, the circlet glowed with a faint white light. Once he was in the center, he turned to Liam and motioned him toward the center.

"Now you."

Liam followed his steps as precisely as he could. It was made easier by the glowing circlet.

"Portals are dangerous things but are important to the Fae. It's our window to other realms. A way to travel unseen and unheard," Bryant said as he approached. "There are numerous ways to open them. One is with a magic potion which I believe is how Fiona was able to travel from the human realm to the Fae realm and back again."

"And the other way?"

"Why, with magic of course."

"You make it sound as though I know how to use it."

"You have a clever mind, Liam. It's why you were always able to beat me at chess." He chuckled and shook his head at the memory Bryant thought Liam no longer possessed. "So, aye, you do know how to use it. We were making such good progress before Niall's man tried to kill you."

"I thought he did kill me."

"I thought so, too, but now that I see the way Fae magic responded to the wizard spell surrounding you, I think I understand more."

Liam shifted from one foot to the other, tiring of the way Bryant was less than forthcoming with information. He huffed out a breath. "Enough with the cryptic messages, Bryant. Just tell me the truth, damn it."

"Niall's men used a silver staff to kill you. The smell of sulfur was on your clothes when Caleb revived you. That same smell was on you now when Brigid tried to remove the glamour spell. That tells me it's not merely a glamour spell but also a protection spell. Whoever the wizard was that was responsible wanted to make absolutely sure your true appearance was not revealed and you would be well protected from other magic. I never realized that before today." He ran his hand over his chin in contemplation.

"You believe the Fae magic and wizard magic reacted to each other?"

"Something like that." He waved away the notion. "I will research more on that later. Now it's time for you to open your first portal to a place you know well. Your attic."

"My attic? Why there?" Liam asked.

"Because that's where the silver staff remains. It cannot stay in the human realm and must be returned. And you're going to get it for me."

Liam looked at him as though he'd lost his ever-loving mind. "You're crazy. I don't know how to open a portal and I'm sure not going to pick up the weapon that nearly killed me."

"It won't hurt you," he said.

"And you know this how?"

"Well, it didn't kill you, did it? The Staff of Amsheer is meant for one person and one person only and it chooses who that is. It won't be you."

For a brief moment, Liam was offended Bryant sounded so certain the staff wouldn't choose him. He also was not wholly convinced it wouldn't hurt him, nor was he convinced he could even open the portal. Ever since he'd stepped foot into Faery nothing had seemed normal. While he could clearly remember Fiona and the life they had together, he could not understand why and how he had a wizard glamour spell over him. And if Fae could see through the glamour spell, why then had Fiona never seen through it? From what he understood about her she was a powerful Fae. Had she never cared to look hard enough to see him for who he truly was? All questions he needed answered.

"Let's get this over with. What do I need to do?"

"Close your eyes. Listen to your inner self. Find that magic thread that resides inside you."

Liam stared at him for a long moment before rolling his eyes and then closing them. He'd do what Bryant said and he'd prove the man wrong. He was no more a Changeling than Fiona was a human. He was certain everything Bryant had told him up to this point had been nothing but an elaborate story, though why he wanted to spin such a tale about him, he'd no clue. Why pick him? Because he'd spent the last twenty or so years with a woman he knew to be a Fae?

"The magic within you, Liam. It's bright. Look for it."

Bryant's voice sounded distant, as though he stood in a long tunnel and called back to him. He wanted to open his eyes to check.

"Keep your eyes closed," the man ordered, his voice taking on a hard edge.

Liam squeezed his eyes closed again and waited, wondering what this bright thread of magic looked like deep inside him. Again he shifted from one foot to the other, feeling ridiculous.

"It wants to come alive for you. All you have to do is look for it. Reach for it," Bryant said.

Warmth surrounded Liam, pulsing through him from the bottoms of his feet to the top of his head. He had never experienced anything quite like it before. It was calming, giving him a sense of peace he'd never felt.

And then suddenly he saw the bright pulse of light behind his eyes. Pushing through him and bursting in a brilliant flash of color. He sucked in a sharp breath as it went through him and made the tips of his fingers tingle.

It should have been strange but it wasn't. In fact, it seemed like the most natural thing in the world to pulse through him.

"Aye...that's it. Let the magic flow through you. Reach for that silvery thread. Pluck it. Use it."

Liam could see it as Bryant described it. His hand flailed for it, grasping it and then wrapped around the thread. He gave it a tug and pulled it to his chest. The intense warmth settled on his breastbone, seeping into his bones.

"You see it, don't you?" Bryant asked.

"I do."

"Good. Now, let's get that portal open."

"How?"

"Envision the attic. Do you see it in your mind's eye?"

"Yes," Liam said.

"Use the magic inside you, Liam, to break through the barrier of time and space. Imagine what that looks like, what that feels like."

Liam could clearly see the attic though he hadn't spent a lot of time there. That was Fiona's domain. He much preferred spending time by the creek. It was his solace. It was the place he went when he and Fiona fought or when he wanted to go somewhere quiet to think. But the attic was off limits to him.

He imagined it now with the cobwebs hanging from the corners, the dust covered furniture. A pulse of light centered in the middle of his chest and then flashed through him with a pop and a flash.

"Open your eyes, Liam."

He did and outside the circlet was a round opening hanging in the middle of the open space of the library. The edges shimmered bright white—much like the magic beating through him—and in the opening he could see the shadowy attic and the silver staff leaning against the wall.

"That's the portal?" Liam asked.

"Aye, it is. You did it. Good work."

"Now what?"

"Now you step through, grab the staff and return. You must be quick for the magic will not hold for a great length of time." Bryant clapped him on the back. "Good luck."

Liam looked back through the open portal, took a deep breath and then stepped through.

The frosty air hit him first in the face and then went through him, turning his bones to ice. But it only lasted a moment as he stepped through to the other side into the musty air. He glanced around to ensure the portal was still open before he moved toward the staff.

As soon as his fingers wrapped around it the memories came back in a rush.

He'd first met Bryant on a cold January morning by the creek when Sunnie was but a babe and Fiona was still plotting her way back to Faery. Bryant had come to him with an offer of employment—help him keep Fiona out of Faery. Watch her. Report everything she did back to him.

Liam recalled numerous times when Bryant would come to him, portable chessboard in hand, and he would tell the man everything he knew about Fiona, Aoife, even Sunnie.

Sunnie. His daughter. His only daughter.

He recalled Bryant telling him he was a Changeling and he would eventually return to Faery after he helped trap Fiona and Aoife with Caleb's help. When Liam refused, Bryant threatened him, blackmailed him into helping, leaving him no choice. He threatened to take Sunnie away from him back to Faery, never to see her again. Sean, though, knew nothing of the scheme. He was innocent in all of it.

All this pounded through him in a flash of memories colliding together.

Liam grabbed the Staff of Amsheer and turned back to the portal. As soon as he stepped through to the other side, it closed behind him.

"You did well today, Liam," Bryant said, eyeing the staff in his hands. "Tomorrow, I will help you remember more about your past."

But Liam didn't need help. He remembered everything. And he would make sure Bryant paid for what he did to him. The man held his hand out for the staff.

"Thank you for retrieving it."

Liam gripped it tighter in his hands, the memories still playing like an old movie flickering through his mind. He couldn't get the images to stop and he suspected it had something to do with the staff. The staff he still held tight in his hands. He didn't want to let it go. He wanted to remember the rage pulsing through him.

"Hand it over."

"No," Liam said.

Bryant lifted one brow. "No?"

"I know what you did to me, to my family. I know everything."

Bryant dropped his hand back to his side. "Ah, you remembered."

He glanced down at the staff. "The staff helped me remember."

The man's eyes widened only slightly before he regained his composure. "That's not possible. The staff could not have chosen you. It's meant for someone else."

"I see everything. Playing over and over and over in my mind. You were the one who destroyed my family. You were the one who poisoned my mind against Fiona and Aoife. Even Sunnie. You told me lies." Liam lifted the staff and pointed it at Bryant. "Now you'll answer to me."

Bryant held his hands up as if in surrender. "You can't do this, Liam. I'm the director of this agency. I'm the one who found you. Who changed your life."

"You changed my life all right. You *destroyed* it. Now I intend to repay the favor."

"Wait." There was an edge of panic in Bryant's voice. "You don't have to do this."

"Oh, I do."

A change shifted deep inside him. Maybe it was from the waking of his magic or that he held the staff in his hands. Or maybe it was because he had regained his memories and knew what a scumbag Bryant actually was. He didn't know what the cause was and it didn't matter. All that mattered now was getting what he wanted and what he wanted was to kill Bryant.

"Payback is a bitch, ain't it?"

Liam pointed the staff at the man.

But a sudden rap on the door interrupted him. They stared at each other a long, quiet moment. So long the person on the other side knocked again. Liam waved at Bryant with the staff to answer.

"Who is it?" Bryant called, not taking his gaze off him.

"Sir, we have an unauthorized entry into Faery through a portal," someone called through the door.

"I have to deal with that," Bryant said.

Liam lowered the staff. "Then deal with it."

He stepped to the door and pulled it open. The man on the other side of the door handed Bryant a rolled parchment.

"A messenger raven delivered this from one of our agents in Illyria, sir."

"Thank you. Wait for me outside. I'll have orders shortly."

As the man nodded understanding, Bryant closed the door. He unrolled the small parchment and read it over then looked up at Liam.

"It appears we have another visitor from the human realm. She used the same portal as Fiona and Aoife."

Liam's pulse throbbed a quick beat. The only person that could have followed was Sunnie. He snatched the parchment from Bryant's hand and read over the careful script.

Unauthorized entry from the portal under surveillance detected. Female visitor arrived in Illyria this morning dressed as a human. We await your orders.

He glanced up at Bryant. "It has to be Sunnie."

"Indeed it does." He took back the parchment.

"You've had the portal under surveillance? For how long?"

"Since Fiona created it. We've long known she would risk returning to Faery. The last time she tried it was on Samhain when the girls were small. She intended to bring them back with her," Bryant explained. "Without you."

A burning anger pulsed through him at the thought of Fiona leaving with his daughter. He didn't pretend to claim Aoife since she wasn't his by birthright. But Sunnie...Sunnie was his. He pressed the palm of his hand against the center of his chest and rubbed, trying to make the anger go away. In his other hand, he still gripped the silver staff.

"You knew about this?"

"I did. That's why Sean and Caleb were sent to watch her. I put too much faith in those two men to stop her. She was far more clever than I gave her credit and I should have known she would try to escape. I knew the moment she went through that portal. However, I didn't know she would try to make her way to the Ivory Wood. It was only after Sean and Caleb contacted me with that information I realized her ultimate plan."

"And what is that?"

"She intends to alter the past." He said it as though he were talking of nothing more than the weather.

Liam stared at the man in shocked silence. How could Fiona alter time? And what exactly was she going to alter? Did she regret their life together so much she had to change things? Did she intend to wipe out Sunnie's existence?

Bryant continued, unaware of Liam's inner turmoil. "My failsafe was to have a tracking tattoo placed on her. I have every confidence Sean and Caleb will find her."

"Are you certain about that?"

"I am." He sounded and looked smug. "I opened a portal for them earlier so they could track her down."

"And what happens if they don't find her in time?"

"Failure is not an option," Bryant said, still smiling. "As for Sunnie..." He glanced down at the parchment. "I have to find her and bring her in."

"*We* have to find her," Liam corrected. He pointed the staff once again at Bryant.

He lifted a bushy brow. "I will only allow your help if you hand over the staff."

"Not a chance." He tightened his grip on it.

"Liam, the Staff of Amsheer is powerful."

"So you said. That's why I intend to kill you with it when I learn the magic inside it." He said it so calm Bryant blinked surprise. "Killing you is what you deserve after what you did to me."

"You may try to kill me, but you will not succeed. Not with that."

"You don't know that."

"I *do* know it! The staff chooses who wields it and it has not chosen you."

"You keep saying that but do you not understand I *see* the memories? They continue to play in my head."

"That's because I gave you a tea blended with a special herb to jar your memory. You've been drinking it every day since your arrival here. The herb finally worked."

Liam glanced down at the staff in his hands and wondered if Bryant told him the truth. The man had become so adept at lying to him and Liam accepting those lies, he was no longer sure what was true.

What he did know to be true was the tea brought to him daily was something to which he looked forward. He drank the tea daily and knew his mind was getting stronger. He hadn't realized the connection to the tea until now.

"I swear to you that's the truth," Bryant said.

Liam slowly lowered the staff, his shoulders slumping. If he cooperated, maybe Bryant would allow him to come along to find Sunnie.

"If I hand it over, then I want to help find my daughter."

"Of course."

Reluctantly, he handed over the staff. He would have to trust Bryant, even though it was against his better judgment.

"Now, then. Let's find her before something dreadful happens." Bryant pulled the door open once again. The man was on the other side, waiting. "Find the girl and bring her in unharmed."

"As you say, sir."

Bryant closed the door. Nervous knots erupted in Liam's gut. The last time he talked to Sunnie, she was halfway around the world on a movie set. No doubt Fiona apprised her of his untimely death. It could be the only explanation for her arrival in Faery. He wondered how she would take the news of his resurrection.

He still intended to get his revenge on Bryant. For now, he'd let the man live.

For now.

Chapter 7

In the Human Realm before Time was altered

Caleb drove back to the downtown warehouse like a madman, hoping Sean's old truck would hold together long enough to get him there in one piece. He didn't want to leave his car parked outside the old warehouse since it was his only prized possession in this realm. The portal in the dolman would not be open much longer and he had to get to it before it closed.

He made it in record time and prepared for his trip through the portal. The only problem he faced now was how to track down Sunnie once he got to Faery. She didn't have a handy tracking tattoo like Fiona. He wondered, though, how both Aoife and Sunnie were able to enter the portal. It seemed rather careless of Fiona not to secure it when she'd been so careful before on her illegal trips to and from Faery.

He stood in front of the dolman, hesitating and wondering if he should take that first step through the portal. Once he was through, there would be no going back. He would not return to the human realm. And yet he worried about his car.

Caleb was not proud of the part he played in toying with the lives of Liam, Fiona, Aoife and Sunnie. But Bryant had given him no choice.

Whenever a Changeling was discovered in the human realm, that person was tracked and then put under surveillance in the hopes of returning the Fae. Caleb had discovered Liam's existence quite by accident by sensing the trace of magic in him. It was one of his Fae abilities. When Caleb reported it to Bryant, the man pounced like a wolf after his prey and ordered Caleb to keep a close eye on him. It was Caleb who alerted Bryant of Sunnie's lineage, knowing she was a product of Fiona and Liam.

He should have never lied to her, either. Telling her she was a Halfling seemed easier. Not telling her the truth about Liam's death and ultimate resurrection would, no doubt, come back to haunt him.

He had revived Liam at the behest of Bryant. The director was insistent on bringing the man back to life and returning him to the Fae realm. He didn't know why Bryant insisted on forcing Liam to keep Fiona and the girls in the human realm. Perhaps he was suspicious all along Fiona would return to Faery and then he could bring Liam through the veil as well.

The conversation he had with Bryant played over and over in his head.

You will revive him, Bryant said.

By the gods, I will not. It takes a certain form of black magic to do that—

And you will do it. Bryant's tone left no room for negotiation. When Caleb still refused he threatened him again. *Do you forget where you came from? I gave you a life. And I can take away that life. I want that man alive and brought to me at once.*

Why? Caleb asked.

He is a Changeling as you said. He belongs here in Faery. Now bring him to me.

It had been an added bonus Liam awoke without his memories but Caleb knew in time that would change. Sunnie didn't know anything about who she truly was and stepping into Faery could be dangerous for her. Dangerous because the magic inside her would finally be released.

Caleb took a deep breath and stepped through the portal.

It led him to the woods on the outskirts of a town near the Towers of Illyria. Before him the walled village was a bustle of activity with guards standing at the north and south gates, the only two ways in or out of the village.

It sprawled over four-square miles with a host of shops and residences. Most of the people who inhabited it were loyal to the wizard king. He knew what manner of king Niall had been—cruel when necessary and giving when it was warranted. The king often made sure the villagers had plenty of food to eat during the hard cold winters.

Caleb knelt at the base of a tree and found the clothes left behind by the Agency. He quickly changed out of his human clothes into the pants, tunic, vest and boots. He put a dagger at his waist and found a small purse of coins Sean left behind for him.

He moved from the woods and halted at the edge of the tree line to survey his surroundings. Where would Sunnie go? More importantly, where would she end up in Faery? Portals were fickle and depending on the user, it could have led anywhere. She wouldn't be hard to find, though, that much was certain since her manner of dress would be odd in the realm.

He wouldn't even know where to find Sean and Aoife or even if they'd found each other or Fiona yet.

Then he saw Sunnie's golden hair glistening in the late afternoon sunlight as she bounded down the hill toward the north gate. Even from this distance, he could see the guards stiffen as they prepared for her approach.

Swearing under his breath, he had to get to her as quickly as he could. He bolted toward her, pulling the blade from his waist as he ran. Before he could get there, Sunnie had arrived at the gate. The two guardsmen blocked her way inside the walled village. Though he couldn't hear what she was saying, her defensive body language said it all. The guard on the left reached for her, wrapping a hand around her upper arm. She struggled, trying to pull free.

Caleb knew his aim had to be true. He never slowed his pace as he aimed for the guard who had his hands on her and let the dagger fly. He guided it with a little bit of magic. The blade hit his intended mark—right between the guard's eyes.

Sunnie released an ear-splitting scream as the guard released her and crumpled to the ground. Meanwhile, the second guard unsheathed his sword and turned to face Caleb. Now unarmed, Caleb wasn't sure how he was going to fight him.

It also did not bode well for him that he'd killed one of the royal guards from the Towers of Illyria.

But he'd deal with that later.

Especially since the second guard charged him, sword drawn.

That gave Sunnie the opportunity she needed to slip through the gate and into the village.

Shit.

She couldn't go far as long as she was there, though.

In the meantime, he had to deal with the guy swinging a sword toward his head intending to decapitate him. His reaction time was better than the guardsman and he ducked, dropping to the ground and sliding toward the dead man. He retrieved his dagger in a quick fluid movement, spun, and released it. The blade embedded in the second guard's neck. The guard's eyes went wide when he realized he had been beaten. The sword dropped from his hand, landing on the ground with a thud.

Caleb waited until he was sure the man was dead before he recovered his dagger and took the guard's sword for good measure. He wiped the blade on his thigh and placed it back in the holder at his waist.

Now to find Sunnie.

Caleb killed a man right in front of her. It had been gruesome and horrible and wasn't pretend like making a movie. She ran through the gate and into the village only to stop short, unsure where to go and what to do next. She knew Caleb would be on her trail, though, and she had to find a way out of the village.

But then where would she go?

She moved through the village, aware of the looks the people dressed in bright colors gave her as she passed. The knees of her jeans were torn from the tumble she took on the sidewalk. Her bandaged arm still throbbed. She knew she wasn't looking her best. It would be nice if she had one of her old medieval costumes from the last movie she did. At least then she would somewhat blend in. As it was, though, she stuck out like a sore thumb.

In the center of the village, a large pole soared upward covered in ribbons and flowers. Young girls danced around it, their cheeks red. She could hear their giggles of happiness over the din of the crowd as they danced, also dressed in bright colors with wreaths of flowers in their hair.

Watching them, a memory struck her so hard and fast she stumbled backward. She and Aoife had done that very thing once when they were children. Fiona made wreaths of flowers much like the ones the village girls wore. They danced and danced around the pole going backward and forward, laughing and having the best time of their lives. Aoife's ribbon had been pale blue. Sunnie's had been yellow.

She could not recall where the pole was or even how old they had been. She only knew the memory was quite real. Had that been another memory Caleb took from her? Or did she actually remember it?

Sunnie could not deny the tingling of familiarity she had in the new realm. It was as though she belonged here even though she knew she did not—could not. She was a movie star, not a Halfing as Caleb said. Even though she suspected he told her the truth, a part of her wanted to disbelieve him.

Sunnie pressed a hand against her roiling stomach, the redolent smells around her making her queasy.

"Lassie, are ye a'right? Ye look a bit pale."

One of the shopkeepers had stepped out of his shop. She realized she leaned against the window and quickly pushed off it.

"I-I'm sorry. I didn't mean to lean on your window. I—"

"'Tis a'right." He waved away the notion as though it meant nothing.

Sunnie spotted Caleb entering the gate to the village then and her stomach flipped. She didn't want him to catch her. She couldn't let him catch her. Why couldn't he just leave her alone?

"Would ye like to come inside for a pint? Looks like ye could use it."

She glanced up at the sign over the door in the shape of a shield with a faded painting of a knight wielding a sword. *The Paladin's Tavern*. She had never been in a tavern before. She wasn't even sure if she'd ever had a pint before. It was a day for a lot of firsts.

Another first—not having her wallet or handbag or anything with her. She couldn't help but feel a little naked.

"I haven't any money," she said, still eyeing Caleb as he made his way through the throngs of people. His keen eyes searched the crowd looking for her. Her stomach knotted as her heart picked up the tempo.

"Don't ye worry yer pretty head about that. C'mon, 'tis on the house." He waved her inside.

Sunnie had no choice. She had to follow. A dimly lit tavern would be a great place to hide until Caleb was past the shop looking for her elsewhere.

Or so she hoped.

Inside, there were three burly men sitting at the bar. A few others sat at the wooden tables scattered around ignoring her presence. The place smelled like piss and ale and old man sweat. Her initial reaction was to scrunch up her nose in protest but she managed to keep her face neutral.

Especially when the three men at the bar turned to watch her enter before the tavern owner. The man scurried behind the bar and reached for a pewter mug.

"Eyes back in yer heads, lads. 'Aven't ye seen a lass before?"

Sunnie hurried through the tavern to the corner table with a half-melted taper stuck in an empty bottle and slid into the chair. She was acutely aware of the man in the middle watching her with his dark eyes set in a pudgy face, a stub of a cigar tucked in the corner of his mouth and stubble on the rolls of his cheeks and chin. She didn't like the looks of him at all.

"Aye, Pug, we seen one. Not one the likes of 'er, though," he said, still eyeing her.

Pug, the barkeeper and owner, slammed a glass down in front of him. The amber liquid sloshed over the rim. "Mind yer business," he said, his tone warning.

"Or what?"

"Or I'll call the Watch."

The man snorted. "That a threat?"

"Do as Pug says, man." The one to the left of Fatty spoke up. He nudged him to face forward and take his drink. "'Tis no' worth the trouble."

"As you say."

Pug rounded the end of the bar with the pewter mug in his hand. He placed it on the scarred wooden table in front of her. "There ye go, lassie."

"Thank you," she said.

She gripped the handle and lifted the mug. Inside was a thick dark brew she was certain she could chew. The yeasty smell accosted her nose and turned her sour stomach upside down. To be polite, she took a sip. Satisfied, Pug gave her a winning grin and headed back to the bar.

But the man in the middle wasn't done staring at her. He turned his head and looked over his shoulder. Even went so far as to give her a little wink. Aside from the fact she wanted to gag, the way he continued to ogle her unnerved her.

She knew there wasn't much she could do about it. She was a stranger in a strange land. She watched Pug behind the bar and tried to implore him with her eyes as she clutched the handle of the mug until her nail beds turned white and her hand cramped. Her senses were on high alert and she knew something bad was about to happen.

Fatty in the middle swung his leg over the stool and shoved his big body up and away from the bar. He turned toward her and she got her first good look at him. What she saw was a disgusting wretch of a man who had nothing but bad intentions.

"Ye leave her be, Talon," Pug called.

"Shut 'im up."

The man on his left spoke up again. "Pug is right. Leave her be."

But Talon gave a jerk of his head to the third man who brought out his dagger and stabbed her would-be rescuer with such a calm demeanor Sunnie knew she was in for real trouble then. Blood spurted through the man's fingers as he clutched his side and slid off the barstool. His legs gave out, folding under him in an unnatural way.

"By the gods, Talon! Was that necessary?" Pug asked.

Talon's henchman brought out another dagger and threatened him, telling him to shut up.

The rest of the patrons merely sat mute and watched events play out. No one made a move to get up and help her, Pug or the injured man on the floor.

Sunnie gripped the mug handle tighter in her hand.

"Yer a right pretty thing." His gaze raked over her.

Thankfully, he couldn't see much of anything since she was still seated. She was all too aware of the way his gaze lingered on her breasts underneath her T-shirt. That sick feeling returned and bile rose to the back of her throat. The other man joined him, standing a little behind him with a lascivious grin.

Sunnie knew what their intentions were. She'd run into men like these before but in her own world, in her own time. Most of the time she could brush them off with nothing more than a glare. But these men were different. They were armed with medieval weapons they wouldn't hesitate to use and a Neanderthal brain with one thought only.

She'd read enough history to know that women in these types of situations were considered property. They would do with her what they wished. That is, if they got their grubby hands on her.

She stumbled to her feet, still gripping the pewter mug. Her chair scrapped back violently along the wood floor before tipping over, landing with a clack.

"What do you want?"

Talon chuckled. "The lady wants to know what we want." He slapped his companion in the middle of his chest. "Do ye think she's that daft?"

"She don't look it," the man said and then licked his cracked lips.

They both smelled of sweat and booze. Her stomach cramped as she tried desperately to come up with a plan. She had only pretend-fought when she was acting—she certainly had never been in a real fight nor would she know how to fight.

"She'll fetch a nice price on the slave market, eh?" Talon added.

That was the last straw for her. She wasn't going to let any scumbag take her and try to sell her on the slave market. She could well imagine what type of slavery to which he referred. Her hand cramped around the handle and she reacted before she knew what she was doing. She flung the contents of the pewter mug into Talon's face.

The liquid splashed over him, dripping down his face and soaking into his soiled clothes. And it did nothing but anger him. He shoved the table out of the way as though it weighed nothing. Sunnie squealed and backed up into the corner as he advanced. His hand came up and clamped around her throat, giving her a little squeeze.

"Bloody wench. I should kill ye right here, right now." Again his gaze raked over her and this time he could see all of her. "But yer parts are worth a lot and I'd like to have a little fun with ye before I give ye up."

"Not on my watch. Release the lady."

The familiar voice floated out from behind Talon. He turned his head and angled his body so she could see Caleb standing on the other side of him, a sword in one hand and a dagger in the other.

"Who're you?"

"Someone you don't want to fuck with."

Talon cocked a grin. "That so?"

It was as though there was some silent communication between Talon and the other guy. While Talon still had a grip on Sunnie, his companion launched toward Caleb. He didn't even flinch when he brought up the sword gutting him, slicing him from neck to naval. He crumpled to the ground, a pool of crimson spreading beneath him.

"As I said, release the lady," Caleb said.

Slowly, Talon's fingers uncurled from her throat. He dropped his hand. Sunnie scurried around the knocked over table, careful not to brush against the brute of a man, and moved next to Caleb.

"We'll be going now," he said.

He replaced the dagger back in the holder at his hip and took Sunnie by the hand. They turned to go, moving past the dead man toward the door under Pug's watchful gaze. Caleb paused and reached into his pocket. He brought out two gold coins and left them on the bar in front of Pug.

"For the trouble," he said.

And then gave Sunnie an unceremonious rough shove toward the door. Once they were out in the street, he took her by the hand and charged through the crowd. He walked at a brisk pace, making her leg muscles burn from the sudden exertion.

"Slow down," she huffed at his back.

He spun to face her, shoving her against the wall of the nearest shop. His eyes blazed fury as he stared her down.

"What the hell were you thinking going in there?"

"I-I—"

"Don't you know how dangerous it is for you here? A beautiful woman traveling alone is nothing but an easy target for men like that." He chastised her as though she were a little girl.

She stopped short of preening at his compliment. She knew now was not the time. "I'm sorry," she said lamely.

"Why did you run from me?"

She bit her lip, unsure how to answer. "I don't know."

Because she didn't. She was afraid he would be angry with her for going through the portal. It hadn't occurred to her he had access to a portal, too. Of course he'd follow her here.

He definitely looked angry now but she suspected that had more to do with what happened in the tavern than her going through the portal. He was right. She shouldn't have run from him. She should have trusted him.

"I'm sorry," she said again.

"A tavern like that is no place for a lady." He clamped a hand around her upper arm and started down the street again. "Let's get you some proper clothes. And stop apologizing."

She almost apologized again for apologizing but bit her tongue. He led her through the throngs of people to a shop with a sign over the door reading Sybil's House of Cloth. A small brass bell on the door signaled their arrival. A woman behind the counter greeted them with a bright smile.

"Hello and welcome. How can I assist you today?"

"I need traveling clothes for my lady," Caleb said.

The woman looked Sunnie over with a critical eye. "Where are you from, lady?"

"She's visiting me from afar," Caleb answered before Sunnie could. He gave the woman a winning smile and patted his pocket making the coins inside jingle. "There's four gold pieces in it for you if you hurry."

"Four gold, you say? Let me see what I have in the back."

She disappeared behind a velvet curtain.

"Why didn't you let me answer her?" Sunnie asked.

"Because she wouldn't understand where you came from," he said. "It'd be best if you let me handle these types of situations."

"Oh, then you intend to travel with me from now on?"

"I do. Got a problem with that, sweetheart?"

She scowled at him, the woman's return cutting off any retort she might have had. She piled an armload of clothes including a pair of suede boots on the counter in front of them and surveyed Sunnie once again.

"'Tis all I've got. You know, your manner of dress is odd. I wouldn't normally notice but I had a lady this week dressed in similar odd clothing."

Hope rose in her. Was it possible this woman had seen her sister or her mother? "What did she look like?" she asked before Caleb could respond.

"A green-eyed girl with dark hair. She traveled with two children. Twins I think it were. He said she was his sister but I didn't think she looked a bit like them."

It sounded like Aoife to her. She must have found someone to help her locate their mother. Aoife was hot on their mother's trail and Sunnie was still trying to catch up. She and Caleb were wasting time in this clothing shop when they could be out looking for them.

"Do you know where they were headed?" Caleb asked.

"I'm afraid I don't."

"I'm sure that was Aoife," Sunnie said. "We have to hurry."

"How much for the clothes?" he asked.

"Five gold. Plus, the extra you promised me." A hard glint in the woman's eye said there was no room for negotiation.

Caleb reached into his pocket and pulled out the coins. He dropped them on the counter.

"I thank you," she said. Then to Sunnie, "You can change in there."

Sunnie grabbed the pile off the counter and went into the dressing room, closing the curtain behind her. She stripped out of her torn jeans and shirt and started to dress. When her hand bushed through her hair and over her ears, she halted. Something didn't feel right. The tips of her fingers grazed what should have been the rounded part of the top of her ear. But her ear wasn't round at all.

It was pointed.

Her heart rammed against her chest. What had happened to her? There wasn't a mirror in the little dressing room so she couldn't look. She quickly dressed, pulling on the suede boots and then stepped out of the room, her street clothes forgotten.

She glanced around the shop, but didn't find what she was looking for. "Do you have a mirror?"

"A what?"

"A looking glass," Caleb corrected. "I think that's what she means."

"Oh." The woman reached under the counter and brought out a small handheld mirror.

Sunnie took it in her shaking hand and held it up to her face. She tilted her head to get a good look at her ears and saw the delicate points. She also noticed her face was not the same face as she had before. There was some sort of ethereal glow about her, something that seemed to say she wasn't human. Her hair was still the same blonde but the white streak remained. Her face had accentuated high cheekbones, her eyes were large and round and the brightest blue she had ever seen.

She couldn't stop the strangled scream from wrenching from her lungs as she dropped the mirror on the counter. She pressed her hands against her cheeks.

"I...I look..."

"You look magnificent." He pulled her into his arms and hugged her hard. Then whispered in her ear, "Stay calm and I'll get you out of here." He turned back to the shopkeeper. "We appreciate your help."

Caleb wrapped an arm around Sunnie's shoulders and led her

from the shop into the busy street. Sunnie whimpered, trying to understand the strange thing she saw in the reflection of the mirror.

"What happened to me?" she asked.

"The glamour spell broke when you entered Faery," he said.

"Glamour spell?"

"Fiona put a glamour spell on you to hide your true appearance in the human realm."

"It's true then. You were telling me the truth. I think I need to sit." Pinpricks of light danced in her vision.

"No time for that. It won't be long before the dead guards are discovered. We have to get out of the village." He led them towards the south gate.

"Why would she do that? The glamour spell?"

"Because you lived in the human realm, Sunnie. Humans think Fae are a myth."

It made sense, she knew that. But she was having a hard time wrapping her mind around the idea that the face she knew so well was not the same face everyone saw in Faery. The white streak was a new addition. As soon as she got back home she intended to make an appointment with her stylist to get that fixed. She was much too young to have a streak of gray.

As they neared the south gate, Caleb picked up the pace. She wasn't accustomed to the quick stride and stumbled once or twice. They could hear shouts behind them.

"We have to hurry," Caleb said.

"What's happening?"

Before he could answer, several guards spilled in through the gate. She stole a glance behind her and saw more closing in on them.

"Caleb?"

He scanned the area looking for possible escape routes. There weren't any—even she knew that. Nor would the shopkeepers be generous enough to let two fugitives hide out in their place of business. Caleb halted.

"What are you doing?"

"Surrendering."

"But we have to find my mother. We can't surrender."

He shushed her with a hiss as he shook his head and lifted his hands in defeat. Four guards halted in front of him, swords drawn.

Behind them, four more guards. Sunnie glanced back and then forward, a lump of fear in her throat.

"You are under arrest," one of them said.

Before Caleb could say anything, a man stepped through the group of four and gave a subtle wave of his hand. Movie nerd that she was, it reminded Sunnie much of the way Obi-Wan waved his hand at the Stormtroopers in Mos Eisley when he and Luke were trying to get past them with the droids. It was an understated gesture that caused all the activity around them to halt. Everyone and everything froze as though time stopped.

Perplexed, Sunnie glanced around. The only three people that seemed to be moving and alert were her, Caleb and the newcomer standing in front of them.

He wasn't dressed in armor like the others. He was dressed like Caleb—cloth pants, tunic, padded vest, cloak, knee-high boots and a sword swinging at his side. He looked them over, first Caleb, then her. His gaze lingered on her for a long moment before he turned back to Caleb.

"Witnesses say you killed the guards at the north gate," the man said. "Lucky for you I happened along."

"Did you 'happen' along, Owen?" Caleb's voice was calm, cool, confident. He didn't seem flustered at all.

Sunnie's heart drummed against her chest. The man, Owen, gave a humorless chuckle.

"Who's the girl?" he asked, never taking his gaze from Caleb. But something about the way he said it told Sunnie he already knew.

"None of your concern."

"Unfortunately, it is my concern. She used a portal to get here—an unauthorized portal—and you're aiding her. Bryant won't be happy to know you're an accomplice to a prohibited visitor," he said.

A quirk of a smile lifted at the corner of Caleb's mouth. "Bryant sent you, did he?"

"You know he did. I can't let you and the girl go. You have to return with me to Ridgeclere. There's someone waiting to see her."

He glanced her way and goose flesh rose on her arms. She didn't like the sound of that at all.

"Then I suppose we should come quietly with you." Caleb reached for her hand and pulled her to him.

"Unless you want these guys arresting you for the murder of the guards?" Owen thumbed over his shoulder at the men standing behind him.

"I'd rather take my chances with Bryant," Caleb said.

"Very well then. Shall we go?"

Caleb gave a jerky nod of his head and squeezed her hand. With another wave of Owen's hand, they all disappeared in a flash from the village. For a moment, she felt as though she were falling through space. It reminded her of when she was running, trying to get away from Caleb and thinking about how she needed to get to the house when she tripped on the sidewalk and was suddenly there.

This trip seemed more violent. Her stomach clenched and threatened to heave as they arrived. She wrapped an arm around her middle, groaning. Dizziness swept through her as she tried to get her bearings. She leaned heavily on Caleb doing her best not to retch. When the feeling finally subsided, she opened her eyes and realized she was in what appeared to be the great hall of a castle.

"You all right?" Caleb asked, his voice low in her ear.

She nodded, though she wasn't entirely sure she was all right.

"What was *that?*"

"We sifted," Caleb said.

"She doesn't know how to sift?" Owen asked, sneering at her.

"She doesn't know a lot. Just get Bryant."

"Wait here."

Owen scowled before he turned on his booted foot. His receding footsteps were the only sounds. As they stood there, alone, she took in her surroundings. Off to one side was a curved staircase with a hand carved balustrade following it all the way up to the balcony overlooking the great hall. Opposite the staircase a giant fireplace lit with a blazing fire to warm the place. The stone floor was covered with a plush garnet rug. Before them two archways leading to other parts of the castle.

"Where are we?" she whispered.

"Ridgeclere Castle, Kydonia. It's where I work."

"I thought you said you worked for some agency."

"I do. The Inter-dimensional Portal Protection Agency. Bryant is the director."

Before she could ask any more questions, Owen returned and waved them forward. "The director will see you in the library."

Sunnie and Caleb followed him through one of the archways into a long hallway, then took a turn and went up another curved staircase. Two guards stood outside the large hand-carved double doors. Owen opened one of them and motioned them inside. The two guards followed.

As soon as she stepped across the threshold, a humming sensation went through Sunnie. Though the room was dimly lit, there was ample light from the nearby fireplace and several braziers to illuminate the green marble flooring, the floor to ceiling bookshelves soaring upward to the ceiling and…her father standing in the center of the room.

She sucked in a sharp breath and halted, her body threatening to go numb. She stood rooted in place, refusing to take another step as she looked at the man she thought was dead but wasn't.

"Daddy, is it you?" Her weak voice echoed through the cavernous room.

As he moved into the light, she got a good look at his face. He seemed older, more haggard, as though he'd been through an ordeal. Had he ever truly been dead? How did he end up in Faery, like her? Had he gone through a portal as well?

None of that mattered now, though, as she launched towards him and hugged him. Hard. As though she would never let go again.

"I knew you were alive. I just knew it!"

He pulled back from her, holding her by the shoulders and looking her over as though he couldn't believe she was actually there. "Sunnie, my angel, what are you doing here? I thought you were in Shanghai."

"Mother called me and told me you were dead. I rushed home to find out what happened. Instead I found Aoife."

"Aoife? You saw her?" A short pudgy man with a hawk nose spoke up then.

"Where is she?" Liam asked, ignoring him and cutting off any response Sunnie might give the man.

"The last time I saw her was at the house."

"Aye, the house with the portal," the pudgy one said, his words acid. "Fiona opened a portal there in the attic of your house. The only way Sunnie and Aoife could have followed her was if she used blood magic. It would have called to them, too. That's how she got here. Caleb, I thought you and Sean were tracking her and Fiona?

Why aren't you with Sean?"

Sunnie glanced at Caleb to see his jaw set in a hard line. His normally handsome face had an angry chiseled expression.

"Bryant, I'll explain everything when you debrief me."

"Aye, I'll debrief you both. She'll have to be put in an isolation chamber until we decide what to do with her."

Liam wrapped a protective arm around her, pulling her close. "She's not going anywhere with you, you lying scum."

Bryant had taken a step toward the two but halted. The two guards still in the room placed hands on the hilts of their swords, waiting for orders. The man's face drained of color.

He held up his hands as if in surrender. "All right. She can remain with you. I'll have a chamber made up for her next to yours."

That humming sensation hadn't left her. It continued to amplify, vibrating through her. Reminding her of the staff she saw in the human realm.

The staff. Yes, she needed to find it again.

Pick up the staff, Sunnie.

Behind Bryant, lying across a table as though it had been discarded and forgotten was the silver staff with the orb in the dragon claw. The orb was lit up, pulsing and matching the vibration she felt inside her. A quiet gasp escaped her as she stepped away from Liam.

"How did that get here? It was beside the creek the last time I saw it." She took another step toward it but Caleb clamped a hand around her upper arm.

"Sunnie, don't." His tone held a warning edge.

"By the gods, it's calling to her," Bryant said. "Guards, get her out of here."

"You stay away from my daughter." Liam positioned himself between Bryant and the guards. His steely gaze swung back to Caleb. "Take your hands off her at once."

Caleb slowly uncurled his fingers and then stepped away. "It's dangerous, Liam. You can't let her touch it."

Embrace the magic.

It was all she could hear in her head. The voices in the room around her had faded to nothing but a whisper. There was a clamor and some commotion behind her but all that mattered was getting her hands on that staff. She took another step and another and then reached down, grasping it and lifting it up.

As soon as she touched it, the sphere lit up in a continuous pulsating glow. The vibration exploded through her, pushing out through her limbs, her fingers, her toes. A shuddering gasp went through her as her head fell back.

You have embraced the magic. Now let it flow through you. Let it in.

The room came back into focus and she no longer felt like herself. She felt more than herself. Powerful. Magical. Invincible. A goddess. She had become part of the staff and it had become part of her. And it was glorious.

"Oh, gods," Bryant moaned.

"What is it?" Liam asked, panic in his voice. He reached for her, but Bryant held him back.

"Don't take it away. It could harm her."

"What's happening?"

"The Staff of Amsheer chose her. She's the only one who can wield it now."

Chapter 8

In the Land of Faery before Time was altered

Queen Siobhan stood alone in her private chamber gazing out the window over what was left of her kingdom, Anatolia. The forest in the distance still hosted nubs of burnt trees still trying to gasp for new life even years after the destruction. The destruction that came when the wizard king arrived and took everything from them. From her.

Moonlight draped the charred earth in a blue-white veil. High clouds drifted through the inky black sky and in the distance she could hear a wolf moan. It was commensurate to her own state of mind.

She knew who the wizard king was. Though he called himself king now, at one time he had been her son. He had been the boy wizard with too much power and too much mischief. The guilt of giving him up to his father continued to fester deep inside her psyche every day since the wizard took him away. It had taken a toll on her. Aged her. Yet she knew it was the right thing to do. It *had* to be the right thing to do.

The day Deaglan walked back into her life was forever emblazoned on her mind. She recalled it as though it were yesterday even though it had been uncountable decades since she had last seen him. She and King Ardan were at banquet celebrating Cian's sixth name day. She had tried to be the happy doting mother. She went to great lengths to convince their people and her husband she was indeed that woman. But inside she hated everything about her life. Her son, Niall, was neglected by his step-father, the king, while Prince Cian was given everything.

Ardan refused to even give Niall his own name day celebration. He said because the boy was a bastard, it should not be celebrated as the prince's.

Even Niall knew Ardan favored Cian and tortured his half-brother to no end with his magic. He could conjure any manner of thing. Spiders in his bed. Snakes slithering through his chamber. When Niall discovered Cian's fears or weaknesses, he exploited them. Siobhan had tried to rein him in but it was useless. The more powerful he became, the less control she had over him. The servants and commoners feared him as though he was nothing but a menace. When Deaglan arrived in Anatolia, Siobhan was faced with a horrible reality—one in which she would have to give up Niall.

Isn't it clear why I'm here? You cannot control him, dearie. How could you when he doesn't understand how to control his own magic? I can help him but to do that I will have to take him with me.

"You will take him over my dead body," she protested.

He was not moved. "So be it."

He'd given her no choice. She had to release Niall to Deaglan. It had shredded her heart.

"You're going with this man, Niall. He can help you control your magic." Her eyes had flooded with tears. *"He'll take good care of you and someday I will see you again."*

She'd hugged him so hard she thought he might break. Letting him go had shredded her heart.

She'd heard the stories of the powerful wizard king, the one who had conquered Illyria. She knew who he was. Just as she knew Niall was responsible for the attack on Anatolia after Cian returned without Lady Fiona.

A quiet knock on the door sounded before someone pushed it open and stepped inside. Her eyes fluttered closed. She inhaled a deep breath as she waited for the news her husband was dead.

"My queen, the end is nigh. The High Bishop asks for your presence at once," the maid said.

He wasn't dead yet but would be soon. Queen Siobhan exhaled her deep breath and turned toward the maid. "Then I shall come at once."

She picked up the skirts of her mourning dress and followed the maid down the corridor to the king's chamber where he'd been confined to his sick bed for the last several months. A mysterious illness had befallen him and he had yet to recover. The healer had tried everything to cure him but to no avail. The king began a slow descent into death. It was only a matter of time before he would succumb.

And then what? Since the attack on Anatolia by King Niall

years ago, Prince Cian had been missing. Siobhan had sent her best men searching to all the far reaches of the kingdom looking for him trying to find him. He had not surfaced.

That was another day emblazoned on her memory. Niall's attack on Anatolia nearly destroyed everything.

She arrived at her husband's chamber, her stomach roiling from the thought of seeing him near death. The last time she'd seen him his skin had been ghostly white and so thin it was nearly transparent. The High Bishop stood at the king's bedside with his pinched pompous face.

"Your Majesty," he said and bent his head in reverence.

Though he gave her the respect her title commanded she knew in truth the man had little of it for her.

"Your Grace, you sent for me?" She dipped a low curtsy in return to show her own begrudging respect for the man.

"His Majesty is not expected to survive the night. Has there been any news of the lost prince?"

A pang of sadness went through her as she stiffened. The gentry had taken to calling Cian the lost prince since his disappearance the night of the attack. His body had not been found among the dead. The High Bishop, though, presumed him dead since he hadn't been seen nor heard from since.

"None that I have received, Your Grace."

"Pity."

His face turned sour as he pressed his thin lips together. In that counterfeit strained expression, Siobhan was certain she saw a smirk buried there. The haughty High Bishop thought he would inherit the kingdom if Prince Cian did not make an appearance soon. She would be relegated to queen regent should the prince not turn up. When two moons passed if the prince still had not been found, the rule of the kingdom would be turned over to the High Bishop and then he could do whatever he wished with her.

Even banish her.

After the attack on Anatolia, her husband fell ill and never fully recovered. His health continued to decline slowly and eventually he wasn't able to leave his sickbed.

"Good of you to call on me so I can pay my last respects." Siobhan moved toward the bed.

The smell of death hung in the air and it was all she could do to keep her composure and not gag from the stench. The High

Bishop stepped out of the way to give her room at the king's bedside. She knew the man had been there for days, waiting and watching, circling like a vulture. She knew he was plotting against her, waiting for the death of the king so he could take whatever action he deemed necessary. She knew her life balanced on a precipice.

Siobhan put the reprehensible High Bishop out of her mind and focused on her husband. He looked frailer than he had a day ago. Facing the reality of his death sliced through her like a newly hammered sword. She could almost taste the metallic tang of death hanging in the stale air. She perched on the edge of his bed and took his bony hand in hers.

"Ardan, I'm here." With her free hand, she brushed a lock of hair from his forehead.

His eyes fluttered open and he focused on her, something he had not done in days. His dry cracked lips formed a faint smile. "Siobhan, my dearest. You've come."

"Of course I came. Why wouldn't I?" She placed a tender kiss on the back of his hand and then instantly regretted it. His skin was so pale, so thin, so cold it sent a tremor through her.

"I hoped you'd come," he said. "'Tis the last."

"No." She shook her head. "I refuse to believe that."

He coughed once. "Always the optimist. You know as I my time is near."

She couldn't stop the form of tears in her eyes. Their life may not have been perfect, but they had a life together. Over time she had grown to love him, as he had her even though it had not been apparent every day.

"I'm not ready for you to leave me," she whispered.

"Cian..." He coughed again. This time so violently blood seeped onto his lips. She reached for a nearby kerchief and dabbed it away.

"Shh. Don't talk. It's too much for you."

"Has Cian returned?"

The question was like a lance through her heart. She did what she could to give her dying husband hope. "Soon, my love. He will be here soon." A lie, she knew. But a necessary one to ease the mind of a dying man.

"Will you...send him to me?"

"I will. As soon as I see him, I will send him to you

straightaway."

"Good. That's good." He closed his eyes, as though satisfied with that answer.

She bowed her head over his hand, pressing the cold bony fingers against her forehead and trying hard to keep the tears at bay.

"There is something I wish you to know, my dearest."

She lifted her head and looked on his gaunt face. His cheeks and eyes were sunken giving him the appearance of a grotesque skeleton. It was difficult for her to see but she refused to look away. She refused to leave him until he breathed his last breath.

"What is that, my love?"

"The kingdom..."

"Aye?"

"Should Cian not return..." He sucked in a wheezing breath, trying hard to get the words out. "I have written my final wishes. The kingdom, dearest, will be yours to rule."

She blinked, surprise flickering through her as his words sank in. Ardan was giving her total rule over the kingdom. Warmth spread through her chest as she realized the truth of his words. The High Bishop would have no claim over Anatolia once Ardan was gone. Her kingdom, her title, would be safe.

"No!" the High Bishop said on a gasped breath. "I know of no such decree."

"That's because I wrote it in secret," Ardan said. His breathing had become labored as he pushed out the words. His eyes opened once again and focused on Siobhan. He dropped his voice to a low whisper. "The midwife. She knows. Find her."

Isla, the midwife, had been part of the family for generations. She had birthed all the princes and princesses for the last three hundred or so years. It made sense to Siobhan that Ardan would entrust the royal decree with her. She would be the only person that had been part of his life from his first breath.

Siobhan nodded. "I will. I swear it."

Ardan gave her a last smile and for a brief moment he looked like the young man she remembered, the man she married all those years ago. His eyes closed and he exhaled his last breath and was gone.

Siobhan held his frail hand against her cheek, letting the silent tears escape. He was gone.

Behind her she could hear the High Bishop huff with his frustration. "What did he say at the last? Where is this royal decree he claims to have written?"

"I cannot say." Nor would she. She would tell him nothing.

She had to find the midwife.

A rap sounded so loud in the silence it made her jump. Before the High Bishop could answer the door, it flew open in a rush. A messenger boy ran inside straight to the queen.

"Your Majesty, you must come at once!" He tugged at the sleeve of her gown, a wild look in his eyes and his face flushed. His chest heaved as he gulped in air.

"What is it?" While she recognized the boy, she did not know his name. She gently released her husband's hand and rose.

"Just come! Make haste!" He motioned for her to follow him and dashed away.

Her heart rose in her throat. Could there be news of her Cian? She gathered her skirts and started after him, her steps light and hurried. Even the High Bishop fell in step behind her as they hurried after the boy. They made their way down the curved stone staircase to the great hall.

A man sat at the long wood table, hunched over with his head cradled on his arms. He was dressed in rags. A small group gathered behind him. The midwife, the healer and a few of the servants stood about whispering with wide eyes. She could not see his face but her heart palpitated at an unnatural rate.

"Look! It's the lost prince, Your Majesty!"

She halted, her stomach plummeting to her toes as she looked him over. Hearing the boy's exclamation, the man lifted his head with such laborious effort it was as though it was full of lead. His face was dirty and he was so thin it looked as though he hadn't had a decent meal in weeks.

"Mother." His voice was weak as he spoke.

She rushed to him as he pushed upward to stand. He looked almost as frail as his father before he passed. She wrapped her arms around him in a gentle hug. Hugging her child gave her a semblance of joy amidst the grief.

"My boy. You're back. You're alive. I've missed you so. Where have you been?"

"Lost."

He shook his head and it seemed as though it took his

remaining strength to do even that much. He slipped one arm around her waist and dropped his head on her shoulder like he had when he was a little boy.

"Aye, where have you been? Tell us for we would all like to know." The High Bishop moved to stand behind Cian. His beady eyes bored into them as he looked on.

Burning anger burst through her chest. She glared at him over her son's shoulder. "Do not think to question my son as though he were nothing but a commoner." Every word was laced with acid.

"Your Majesty, I merely wish to know his whereabouts as you and the others do. Do you not wish to know?"

"In time, when he has more strength, he can tell us. For now, he needs a meal, a bath and rest."

She took his face in her hands looking into his eyes. Unsurpassed relief that her son was home flooded her. There was much she needed to tell him but now was not the time. Now he needed to recover from whatever ordeal he had endured. She, too, wondered where he had been. The last she saw him was when he rode out to fight Niall when he attacked Anatolia. That had been years ago.

But he was home now and that was all that truly mattered.

"My boy. You're safe now."

She motioned to the healer who sprang into action. He took the prince's arm and wrapped it around his neck.

"Help me get him upstairs, boy," he said to the young messenger.

Siobhan watched them take her son away, her heart a bit lighter than it had been only moments before. She could still feel the High Bishop's glare.

"It seems strange to me, Your Majesty, the lost prince would mysteriously turn up today of all days," he said. "And only moments after the king's death."

She turned her own fierce look on him. "Why is that, Your Grace?"

"I thought that obvious. The king is dead. And despite his royal decree you remain ruler, it has yet to be found and proven."

The midwife emitted a quiet gasp but Siobhan heard it. She remained unaffected, her defiant stare still fixed on the High Bishop. So, it was true. Her husband had given the midwife the royal decree turning over rule of the kingdom to her. She would address that soon enough. But now she clenched her fists at her side trying her best to maintain her composure. She would not let this man bully her any longer. She angled to face him.

"The prince has returned, Your Grace, and you have no rule here as long as he or I live. You will stay away from my son. You will not question him unless I am with him. Is that clear?"

He moved closer to her. He was taller than she and used his height to intimidate her. She was far from intimidated. He could tower over her all he liked but she would not cower.

"Tread lightly, Your Majesty. The prince is not well. You may rule as queen regent in his stead now but should something happen to him and the royal decree not be found, then by law the kingdom falls to me. Never forget that."

"Is that a threat?" She lifted her chin ever so slightly and looked down her nose at him, trying her best to match his intimidation tactics.

"Not at all." He gave her a thin-lipped smile. "Merely a reminder the law cannot be changed."

He sauntered away, his gold and ivory robes flapping behind him. Oh, she so hated that man and would give anything to have him removed from Lambridge Castle.

Anything.

When he was gone, the midwife moved to stand next to her. Her aged face gazed up at her with a mixture of question and fear.

"Your Majesty…the king is dead?" Isla's voice quivered.

Siobhan spun to face her, grasping her by the arm and leading her away from the great hall. "We must speak at once."

She led her back up the curved stairs to her private chamber. Once inside, she closed and barred the door then turned to the woman who had delivered the prince all those years ago.

"The royal decree my husband wrote. Do you have it?"

"Aye, Your Majesty." She reached into her pocket and pulled out the folded parchment. "I dinna trust the High Bishop so I kept the paper on me person at all times." She handed it over without hesitation.

Siobhan took it in her shaking hand and unfolded it. Judging by the age of the parchment and the many creases, it was obvious the midwife was a woman of her word. For that she was glad. The last person who needed to get his grimy hands on the final royal decree her husband wrote was the High Bishop.

I, King Ardan of Anatolia, hereby decree the following.

Upon my death, Prince Cian shall assume the throne and rule with his mother by his side as queen regent. I appoint her his most trusted adviser.

However, should the crown prince not return or is found dead, then all lands and title for the kingdom of Anatolia shall relegate to my wife and queen, Siobhan. The law of the land stating the High Bishop acts as steward when no ruler is present shall be abolished from this day forward. So it is written. So it shall be. Long may she reign.

He signed it in his careful script. His royal wax seal was affixed next to it making it official.

Siobhan read the decree through blurred eyes. She could not stop the tears from falling even if she tried.

"Thank you, my love," she whispered. She folded the parchment and slipped it into her pocket. "Thanks to you, too, Isla. With this decree, the kingdom will be safe."

But the midwife worried her hands together in front of her. Her brow creased in deep set lines and her mouth turned down. "Majesty, there is more I wish to tell ye."

"More? What more could there be? The kingdom is saved. Prince Cian is home and even if he does not recover—though I pray to the gods he does—then I can rest assured the kingdom will come to me no matter what."

"The prince…is nay the prince." She whispered it then pressed fingertips to her lips, her eyes wide and round and dancing with tears.

"What? What do you mean? Are you saying that man is an imposter?"

She shook her head quickly. "Nay! He is not."

"Then what is it?" the queen demanded. "Tell me now, woman, before I have it lashed out of you."

She pulled a kerchief from one of her pockets and wiped away the tears. "Is it true about the king?"

Siobhan stiffened and straightened her shoulders. "Aye, it is. He has passed. May the gods rest his soul."

Isla dabbed at her eyes again. "'Tis a sad yet joyful day, aye?"

Siobhan tipped her head to one side as she looked over the woman. There was something she wasn't telling her. "Aye, it is. What did you mean the prince wasn't the prince?"

"Och. N'er ye mind yer pretty head about it. 'Tis only the ramblings of an auld woman. I've a creak in me bones. I best see to it."

She hobbled to the door, accentuating that creak in her bones to make sure Siobhan knew she told the truth. But the queen could not shake the feeling the old woman had a secret she was harboring.

No matter. She would find out soon enough. For now, it was enough her son had returned home and he was alive.

After the old woman left, Siobhan slipped out of her chamber and hurried down the drafty corridor. After the attack on Anatolia, it had taken years to rebuild Lambridge Castle. There were some parts of the castle, though, that had not been rebuilt and there remained a draft through the hallways and corridors. During the hard winters, it was impossible to keep the castle warm even with a fire in every hearth.

When she arrived at her son's chamber, she pushed open the door. The healer stood on one side of the bed making a concoction in a wood bowl. He ground something with a pestle against the high sides, then reached for a small vial of some herb-like substance and sprinkled it in.

"How is he?" she asked.

He stopped what he was doing and met her gaze.

"Exhausted. I don't know where he's been, Your Majesty, but mayhap he will tell you in time. He's naught but skin and bones if you must know and it will be a small miracle if he lasts through the next few days. His recovery will be slow. I want you to understand that."

There was nothing apologetic about his tone of voice. He merely stated fact. He went back to finishing his concoction and then poured the herb mixture into a steaming mug.

"There. That should help ease his fatigue and allow him to sleep."

"What is that?"

"A sleeping potion to allow him to regain some strength. In the morn, he may be able to break his fast with real food. For now, this." He held up the mug. "Help me with him, aye?"

She nodded and hurried to the other side of the bed. She slipped her arms under him and lifted him up. The healer was right. He was skin and bones and seemed to weigh nothing. As she lifted him up, he grunted his disapproval but was too weak to protest much. The healer placed the mug at his lips and then tipped it.

"Drink it, lad."

Cian complied and then sputtered and coughed. "It's horrible."

"It may be horrible but it will save your life, mark me. Drink more."

The healer tipped the mug again and Cian took another long drink. He swallowed hard and then scowled as he waved him off. Siobhan released him and let him slide back into the cushioned pillows.

"That should do it. I'll check on him in a few hours."

"I'll be here."

"You've had a trying day, Your Majesty. Are you certain you—"

"I'll be *here*," she said again, her voice firm.

"Very well."

He left them alone, closing the chamber door with a quiet snap. Siobhan perched on the edge of the bed and watched her son fall into a long quiet sleep.

The sleeping potion kept Cian out for the next two days. Siobhan spent most of that time with him, keeping a constant bedside vigil. She'd taken to sleeping in the oversized chaise on the other side of the room. For the third night, she settled in with her thick fur blanket as she kept watch over her son. She refused to leave his bedside for fear the High Bishop would try to wake him and question him. She kept the fire poker at her side as a weapon on the off chance the man entered the chamber.

But her sleep was restless as she kept an ear open for the slightest sound. She was aware of every movement and stirring from Cian in the bed.

She was even aware of the creak of the door as someone pushed it open. Siobhan reached for the poker and gripped it in her hand, ready to do battle. Light from the outside corridor slashed inside as a form stood in the light. It was not the High Bishop. Rather the silhouette was shaped like a short, round woman.

The woman pushed the door closed and then tiptoed to the bed. Firelight from the nearby hearth flickered over her face and Siobhan could see it was Isla. She released her hold on the poker and held her breath as she watched and waited. The woman must have wanted to check on him since she had been there when he was born. Isla often felt a sort of connection to the babes after she'd delivered them.

The midwife tucked the bedclothes around Cian and brushed hair from his face. She was unaware of Siobhan's presence.

"Poor lad," she whispered. "I canna help but think this all my fault."

She eased down to the bed, the feather mattress sighing with her weight. Siobhan suspected Isla had a secret that had something to do with Cian. Mayhap now she would confess it all. Cian stirred, a quiet groan escaping his lips. From her vantage point, Siobhan could see his eyes flutter open. Her first instinct was to leap from the chaise and go to him, but something held her back.

"By the gods!"

"Isla? Where is my mother?" He sounded stronger than he had when he first arrived.

"I'll fetch her at once."

She started to rise but Cian stopped her with a hand on her arm. "No. There is no need. If she's resting, leave her."

"She'll want to know yer awake."

He yawned and closed his eyes again, his voice thick with sleep. "Tell her I awoke only a moment." He rolled to his side and settled in again.

Isla nodded but remained where she was, wringing her hands together. "There is something ye must ken. Something I've kept to meself all these long years."

This was it. The confession Siobhan had so longed to hear. She stiffened, her senses on high alert as she held her breath and waited. The woman must want to ease her mind now that the prince was home safe.

"I'm sure it can wait." He sounded groggy.

"Nay, it canna wait. I can no longer carry this burden of secrecy. I've carried it far too long. Far too many years."

Cian sighed. "If it will ease your troubled mind then tell me."

"Thank ye, Your Highness." She produced a kerchief from the depths of one of her pockets and held it between her shaking fingers. "I did something I canna change. I had no choice but to do as he said. If I didn't, he said he'd kill everyone at Lambridge."

Siobhan's stomach clenched. She didn't like where this was going.

"It was the day the queen delivered her son. A wee perfect

laddie with a fuzz of black hair. I canna forget the day."

No, she didn't like where this was going at all.

"I had no choice, ye ken. None. I had to take the babe from her and give the lad to the wizard."

Oh, gods, what had she done? Pinpricks of heat erupted all over Siobhan. She wanted to burst from her corner. She wanted to let her presence be known but she knew Isla wasn't yet finished with her story. Her body vibrated with all the rage and fear rolling through her.

"What does that mean? What wizard?" Cian rolled to his back and pushed up in the bed, alert and awake. His eyes were like black orbs in the shadowy room lit only by the flickering fire. She could see the lines of confusion on his face.

Siobhan could think of only one wizard who would threaten all those at Lambridge Castle. A tight knot formed in her stomach.

Isla sniffed. Tears glistened on her pudgy cheeks. "The wizard said he'd kill everyone. I gave the lad to him. He took him into the woods. He was only gone a moment, not long at all, and he returned with a babe. Another lad. But I ken. I ken it wasn't the same lad as I give him."

"I don't understand. What are you trying to tell me?" he asked.

She had a hard time getting the words out between sobs but it was clear what she had done. Slowly, Siobhan uncurled her body from the chaise. The fur landed in a soft whisper as she took a step out of the dark.

"It means the son I bore was taken away."

The sound of her voice made Isla jump to her feet. She stumbled a few steps backward as Siobhan rounded the end of the bed with all her fury and confronted the woman. The burning anger she had for the High Bishop returned tenfold now for the midwife.

"How could you? How could you do this to me? To my son? Where is he? *Where did he take him?*" The queen snatched the woman by the arms and jerked her with such a violent shake the woman cried out.

"Mother, stop!"

"I will not stop. She took my son. She...she..." A wracking sob escaped through her lips before she could stop it. Tears blurred her vision. She shoved the woman away. "You should be hanged. Or worse. I should have you cut into a thousand pieces and thrown into the nearest loch. You bloody traitor!"

Isla emitted a choking cry as she fell to her knees at the queen's feet. "Please, Majesty. I dinna have a choice. He told me he would kill you and the king and everyone. He said he would destroy Anatolia. I couldna let him do that."

"I don't understand," Cian said from the bed.

"Where did he take him in the woods?" Siobhan asked again, her words flinging down like acid.

"I dinna ken. I swear it!"

"Mother, who is this wizard? What the bloody hell is she talking about?"

Siobhan blinked away the tears and focused on Cian. He was not her son. Looking upon him now she realized. He was not hers. She'd raised someone else's child, though she didn't know it. And even though Cian looked Fae, she suspected he was not. Now that she knew the truth, she realized he had never once exhibited any Fae magic. He'd expressed a complete and utter hatred of all magic users. She thought that was because Niall had tortured him with his magic when they were children. While that was probably the root of the problem, she understood so much more about him.

He must be human.

"I will explain everything in time. For now the midwife must be dealt with."

"I beg for mercy, Majesty. Please!"

"You don't deserve it. However, you have served this family for generations. My husband trusted you. And you did keep the royal decree safe and out of the hands of the High Bishop. But that still does not excuse you for this heinous crime. For now, it's to the dungeons until I decide what to do with you. Guards!"

At her shouted order, they burst through the door.

"Arrest her and throw her in a cell at once. Make sure she's guarded night and day," the queen said.

Surprise crossed both their faces as they looked from Isla to her and back again.

"Your Majesty, are you certain you—"

"Do it. Or I'll have you hanged for disobedience. And post more guards at the door. I want no one but me and the healer getting in here."

They hurried to do her bidding, lifting the sobbing old woman off the floor and carrying her away. When the door shut behind them, Siobhan blew out a shaky breath. A sickness wavered through her as she tried to form the words to tell Cian the truth.

"Mother?" he asked, his voice quiet in the silence.

She perched on the edge of the bed and reached for his cold hand, placing it between hers. "I don't know where to begin, my son."

"At the beginning, Mother. Tell me everything."

She almost laughed. Would that she could. She could not tell him of her torrid affair with the wizard, Deaglan, though truly her troubles began with him. Their romance burned bright and hot like the flame of the nearby fire and died out quickly like the flash of a shooting star.

"The wizard she speaks of is Deaglan," she said at last. "He is Niall's father."

"Niall's father? My half-brother?"

"Aye."

"What does that have to do with the midwife?"

She sighed. She knew enough of the truth to realize Deaglan had never truly forgiven her for spurning him and sought revenge. Cian was that human child she had raised as future king of Anatolia.

"She said she took the baby—my baby—on the night he was born to the wizard in the woods."

"Why?" he demanded. "Why would she do that?"

Siobhan could only guess but she had no doubt it had something to do with keeping Niall from his father. That was before Niall's magic developed, before he became so unruly Deaglan came to take the child away.

"I cannot say. The wizard would have done only one thing with him," she said.

"And what is that?"

"He would have given him to the sprites in the forest to exchange for a human child."

Cian stared at her in silence for a long moment. He slipped his hand away from hers.

"Am I that child? Are you saying I'm human?" His voice was cold and hard.

"I believe so, aye."

It had to be the truth. He did not have magic like the rest of them. Even Siobhan had a few Fae abilities though they were not as powerful as other Fae.

"If I'm human, then why don't I look like one?" he demanded.

"Because you are under a powerful glamour spell." She peered at him intently, trying to see the shimmer of the glamour around him but she couldn't. And she knew who would have put that glamour spell on him.

"Who is the Fae child that took my place?"

She shook her head. "I know not. Only one person knows the answer to that."

"Deaglan," he guessed.

"Aye," she said with a nod. She reached for him, trying to take his hand again but he jerked it away. "This changes nothing, Cian. You are still crown prince. You can still—"

"No," he snapped. "I am nothing but a human. I'm not crown prince. I am nothing. I'm not even your son. I've no right to the crown. To this kingdom. Not anymore."

"But you do. You were raised by your father to rule. You *are* still my son. You may not be the son I gave birth to, but you are the son I raised and loved all these years. The only people that know about this are the three of us and I intend to deal with the midwife."

"You intend to kill her?" There was a hard glint in his eyes.

She stiffed. "Execute. I intend to *execute* her for treasonous crimes against the crown."

"And where does that leave me?"

"As ruler of Anatolia. By the gods, I swear I will find out the truth, Cian. I will find out why he did this to you and I will have my vengeance."

His laugh was humorless. "You think you can fight a wizard?"

Siobhan reached for him again. This time he didn't pull away as she wrapped her long fingers around his wrist. "I know I can."

He must have seen her determination in her face for a sort of calm washed over him and that hard glint flickered through his eyes as he looked at her. He slowly nodded.

"Aye, then. Find Deaglan. For your vengeance shall be mine as well."

Chapter 9

In the Land of Faery before Time was altered

"I am the Goddess of Light and Dark, the Keeper of War and Peace, the Maker of Life and Death."

When Sunnie spoke the words, an icy fingertip slid down Caleb's spine. He'd heard that somewhere before. A dark memory, one he intended never to resurrect surged to the surface with such a force it made his head pound. Sunnie no longer sounded like the girl he remembered or even the girl she was when she walked through the portal. She was different. Like before, her eyes turned a strange shade of silver similar to the orb in the dragon claw. Her blonde hair no longer had the one streak of white. Something about the magic had turned her hair white from root to tips.

He stole a glance at Bryant and Liam who stared at her in disbelief with wide eyes.

"The Staff of Amsheer took her," Bryant said.

A sinking sensation went through Caleb. *Not Amsheer…Eimhear.*

"Sunnie—" Liam said.

"I am not called Sunnie," she said. "I am called Eimhear."

The magic had completely taken her over. Magic she had no idea how to control or wield. Magic that was unlike any she had ever experienced. It wasn't called the Staff of Amsheer, it was the Staff of *Eimhear* and somehow through the ages, the name morphed into something else as the story was passed down from generation to generation.

Caleb, though, knew the truth. A truth he had not thought he would ever face again. A truth so dark and disturbing, he had buried it deep into the recesses of his mind.

"Bryant, stop this madness. Take the staff from her," Liam urged, the panic evident in his voice now. Worry lines creased his brow and around his eyes.

"The staff belongs to me. I am the only one who commands it and all those in this realm. All will bend the knee and pledge fealty to me."

She was focused solely on Liam and Bryant. Caleb took a tentative step toward her. Perhaps if he could take the staff away, she would come back to her true self.

Sunnie pointed the staff at first Bryant and then Liam. "You will bend the knee."

They exchanged a glance as Caleb inched closer to her with slow methodical steps so as not to garner her attention.

"Do it or die," she said.

The pulse in the orb grew brighter. Bryant gave in first as he sank to one knee and bent his head. But Liam refused. He remained standing, his hands balled into fists.

"Sunnie, listen to me. This isn't you. It's the magic talking. It's taken you over. But the real you must still be in there somewhere. I believe that."

Her silver unblinking eyes turned on Liam. When she looked at him there wasn't a shred of recognition in her face. She pointed the staff at him. A light burst from the orb punching him in the center of the chest. He cried out with the sudden pain and stumbled backward, crashing to the floor.

"A warning. Next time, death."

Caleb reached Sunnie and took that moment of distraction to grab the staff. When his hand wrapped around it a burning sensation went through him. But he wasn't to be dissuaded by a little pain. He gave the staff a jerk and yanked it free from Sunnie's grasp before she realized he had hold of it.

In the seconds it took to rip the staff away, she came back to herself. He saw the confusion in her eyes as she released it and then crumpled to the floor, unconscious.

"What did you do? You could have killed her, you damn fool." Bryant jumped to his feet. "Give me that thing before she wakes up."

"See to Liam," Caleb ordered.

Caleb shoved the staff into Bryant's hands and dropped to his knees, pulling her limp body into his lap. He pushed the curtain of hair from her face. Her powdery white skin shimmered more than before. It held an ethereal glow.

What the hell had the magic done to her?

"Sunnie, can you hear me?"

The only sign of life was the weak pulse in the long column of her neck. Across the room, Liam groaned as he made it to a sitting position. He raked a hand through his disheveled hair but it remained sticking up in spikes on top of his head.

"I'm all right." He shoved away Bryant's help. "She attacked me."

"She didn't know what she was doing," Caleb said. "She was under the spell of the staff."

"Aye, she was. And now she's tasted the magic inside her. She'll not rest until she has the staff in her hands again," Bryant said.

"Then take it out of here." Liam climbed to his feet, rubbing the singed place in the middle of his chest. "Lock it up. Do whatever it is you have to do with it."

"That won't be enough. It has to be destroyed."

"Then destroy it," Liam said.

"If I do that now it will kill her. She's tied to the staff."

Liam reached for Bryant's tunic, fisting it and pulling him toward him. "Then find a way to release her from it."

"That won't be so easy."

"I think Sunnie needs a healer," Caleb said before Liam could respond.

"Bring her to the healer. He can help."

Bryant shoved off Liam and headed for the door as Caleb scooped Sunnie into his arms. Liam fell in step behind them. Once they were in the infirmary, Caleb placed her on one of the narrow beds while Bryant fetched the healer. There was only one other patient there. A young woman with a pixie face slept in the next bed.

"Do you think she'll be all right?" Liam asked.

"I don't know." He hadn't seen a magical object take over someone before.

The healer accompanied Bryant to see his newest patient. "Step aside, men. Let me take care of the girl."

"She will live?" Liam asked.

"I won't know that until I examine her. Now be gone and let me do what I must for her."

Bryant, still holding the staff, said, "I'll lock the staff behind a ward and a protection spell. Maybe that will be enough to keep her from it."

Caleb doubted that but at least Bryant was willing to try. When he was gone, Liam turned his attention to the girl in the next bed.

He took her small hand in his, running his fingers over the back of her hand.

"Who is she?" Caleb asked.

"Her name is Brigid. She's a *sidhe*."

He was familiar with the *sidhe* and knew Bryant had them in his employ. He had never met one. Their magic was some of the most powerful of the Fae. They could remove any spell, light or dark.

"What happened to her?"

"She tried to remove my glamour spell but couldn't. She said it was wizard magic."

Caleb's head snapped to Liam and peered at him. Though he still looked human, Caleb could see the faint shimmer of the spell surrounding him. He had not seen that before—only sensed the magic surrounding him. Now that he looked closer, and that Liam was in Faery, he could see the shimmer was a different shade from a normal Fae glamour. Stepping through the portal into Faery must have done something to him—changed him. It was typical of crossing into the realm.

If Liam's glamour was wizard magic, then he suspected he knew who could be responsible. He knew of only one wizard that could have that much power to place over another. Hot pinpricks went through him as he realized their paths could indeed cross again unless the rumor was true and the man was dead, killed by the king of Illyria, his own son.

"Wizard magic?" He tried to sound as casual as possible.

"Aye, that's what she said before she lost consciousness." He met Caleb's gaze. "I thought wizards only existed in Harry Potter."

Caleb almost snorted laughter at his naiveté. "You know nothing of the realm you're in. You've crossed through the veil to the other side. You are in a place where anything is possible and every mythical creature exists."

"I don't believe in fairytales," Liam said.

"You should start believing them because they are real."

"I also don't believe Bryant told me the truth about who I am."

"And what is that?"

"That I'm a Changeling."

He knew the truth, but like his daughter refused to believe. He turned his gaze back to Sunnie, her eyes still closed as the healer worked his magic over her. Realization went through Caleb. Liam and Fiona were both Fae which meant the staff latched onto

Sunnie's Fae magic and took control of her. But why? Why had it picked her?

There had to be a way to break the connection between Sunnie and the staff. Maybe if he searched the archives for some shred of evidence about Eimhear and the staff he could find a way to release Sunnie from its dark spell. His memories were so faded from long ago, he could not recall much.

He could tell no one what he knew about Eimhear. It had happened long ago when he was but a child. The fuzzy memories were hard to grasp. He could only recall images and feelings— Eimhear with her stark white hair and haunting eyes striking fear into the hearts of all that crossed her path.

"I don't think Bryant lied to you," he said at last. He shoved away the awful memories.

"Why is that?"

"Because I can see the flicker of the glamour spell over you. If it was done with wizard magic, only a wizard can release you from it."

"Who is he?"

"The only wizard I know of besides the King of Illyria is Deaglan and the old man is dead."

Disappointment and frustration flickered over Liam's face before he managed to contain it. A muscle ticked along his clenched jaw.

"This King of Illyria is also a wizard?" he asked at last.

"He is but—"

"Then I wish to find him at once," Liam said.

"The girl is in a deep sleep," the healer announced before Caleb could answer. "There is nothing more that can be done for her now."

"Will she live?" Liam asked.

"For now, aye. Once she wakes, I will examine her further. Until then, we must allow her to rest."

As the healer left them, the silence between them stretched.

"You heard the man. There is nothing more that can be done for her," Caleb said.

"I'd like to stay with her awhile." Liam sat on the edge of Sunnie's bed. "In case she wakes."

Caleb nodded understanding as he left the infirmary. He was as concerned about Sunnie as Liam and he intended to find out what the Staff of Eimhear did to her, though he suspected. The library archives had to have a book or scroll that held the answer. Ridgeclere boasted having one of the more well-stocked libraries in the realm. When he arrived, he was relieved to see he would be alone to search through the dusty tomes.

He started with all the myths and legends he could think of, pulling book after book off the shelves and leafing through them. He found nothing of note. Only a mention here and there of the four sacred Fae relics but nothing about a magical staff.

Caleb made his way to the back of the library where shelves were stacked with dusty scrolls written in an aged hand. These would be the more ancient archives. Some of the ink had faded with time but perhaps he could find something buried there within the pages. He started with the first shelf. When he removed the scrolls, a puff of dust followed. He coughed as he inhaled some of it.

One scroll looked like a list of items one would find at a market. Another scroll was nothing but a love letter from a forlorn young man to his lady who had perished. He proclaimed he would take his own life so he would not have to live without her. A few drops of faded blood were on the bottom of the parchment indicating he had done as much.

There was a scroll recounting the heroics of a warrior who had rallied the villages and stopped the invasion of the Fir Bolg. From the description of the warrior, he was ten feet tall and could shoot lighting out of his eyes. Surely an embellishment by the author. It made Caleb snicker as he put it aside.

His fingers brushed over the top of another one. When he pulled away, it left a tingling sensation behind. He paused and looked back at the innocuous scroll parchment. His hand hovered over it as he hesitated. It left him with that tingling sensation once again.

Caleb picked up the scroll. As soon as he touched it the tingling zipped through him. He unrolled it with a careful hand. The parchment was so brittle it threatened to dissolve into dust. The writing on the scroll was precise and in a careful script as though the author took his or her time scribing the words.

I, Cadryn, write this by mine own hand in the dark of night with only the light of one taper to illuminate my parchment.

It is the story of Eimhear I must tell for no one should be allowed to wield the staff again. The magic inside it is dark and dangerous. I know, for I have seen it with my own eyes. I must write swiftly before the memory fades from my mind.

Caleb's eye paused on the name Eimhear, that cold icy fingertip returning to rake down the length of his spine.

"The Staff of Eimhear," he whispered, testing the words on his tongue.

He continued to read about Eimhear, a powerful Fae consumed by her own magic. Always searching for more power, more ways to use that power. She had created the orb clutched in the dragon claw that now resided on the top of the staff. She put her magic into the orb and enchanted the staff with a spell that bound her to it for she never wanted to be parted from it.

I believe Eimhear's intentions were true for she wanted nothing more than to protect her people. But the power consumed her, turned her away from the Light and into the Dark. She embraced all the magic and became one with it. As her power grew, she knew she was invincible and she knew no one would be able to defeat her. She called herself a sorceress and she had all the power to back up her claim.

Those in the realm feared her. She killed. She destroyed. But if she favored you, she bestowed many gifts upon you. Wealth and beauty. Status and lands.

She favored me most of all for I was her consort. She would not be parted from the staff, even when we were alone. She begged for a child, someone to pass the staff to when she was gone. If she had been in her right mind, I would have given that to her. But she had grown far too powerful, far too unstable.

When I refused her, she went into a rage. She destroyed all that she had given me. She had become consumed with the Dark.

"I will spare you, Cadryn, for I wish you to bear witness to all that once was and know it is because of you all will be destroyed."

As she spoke the words, my blood ran cold. I knew I could not stop her.

Her warpath lasted for days. She hunted my family to annihilation. All dead. All gone.

The memory was clear now in his mind's eye. How old had he been? Nothing but a child, he knew that. Eight? Nine? It had been so many years ago and he had lived far longer than he should have. After Eimhear destroyed Cadryn's family, her thirst for power grew. She destroyed his village. His mother had shoved him in a wardrobe, telling him to hide. She thought he might be spared.

His mother had been right about that. Eimhear spared him for whatever twisted reason. She found him in the wardrobe. She looked him over with those haunting silver eyes and decided she would take him with her on her next quest. She used her darkness to manifest his magic early and as she did, a piece of that darkness remained with him even to this day.

I will teach you, my little urchin, she had said. *You will become as powerful as me someday.*

The sordid tale of Eimhear's destructive warpath continued in graphic detail as Caleb read and remembered. The woman showed no mercy. Caleb skimmed over more of the writing toward the bottom where Cadryn described how he defeated her.

And that, too, Caleb recalled.

I knew it was wrong but I had to find a way to destroy her, though it pained me to do so.

I found the old wizard in the Sildara Mountains and begged for his help. His reluctance to help was apparent and yet he agreed.

This wizard's white magic battled against Eimhear's dark magic and her staff. Their magical war was fought on the field of Farn. So consumed with the magic was she, her hair had turned a stark white and her eyes silver. I knew what I must do. I knew I had to help defeat her for it was my fault she had turned into the Dark. I joined my power with the wizard's and together we spoke the enchantment and cast the spell that would forever erase Eimhear from corporal form. He put her essence inside the orb of the staff and gave it to me for safekeeping.

Even now the orb pulses with a faint glow. And somehow, even though she is gone, Eimhear's spirit still haunts me.

It was unclear what happened to the staff after that. He could find no more writings from Cadryn.

When Eimhear's spirit was put inside it, Caleb was once again alone in a world he was not prepared for or capable to navigate at his young age. The wizard delivered him to Bryant who taught him how to control the darkness inside him and how to wield it when it suited him…and Bryant.

Caleb carefully rolled up the parchment and carried it out of the library to find Liam and Bryant. But he had what he needed. From the writings, it was clear the only thing able to destroy her was a combination of wizard and Fae magic. Perhaps a combination of wizard and Fae magic again would remove her spirit from Sunnie without killing her.

He had to try.

Liam kept a bedside vigil between the young *sidhe* and his daughter in the infirmary. He'd lost track of time since Caleb, the healer and Bryant left. Not that he had anywhere to be. He refused to leave either of them, preferring to stay and watch over them in case one or both awoke.

Neither of them had.

Some time ago, Bryant returned and took to pacing the length of the room from one side to the other, his hands behind his back. He hadn't said a word when he returned, sans staff. Liam could only suppose he had done what he intended—locked it behind wards and protection spells to keep it from Sunnie's grasp. His nervousness was indicative of someone who had a stake in Sunnie's recovery, though why he cared was a mystery to Liam. Bryant didn't care about anyone but Bryant.

As far as Liam was concerned he didn't want that filthy liar near his daughter. He knew all too well the man's manipulation tactics. If he was allowed to get his hands on Sunnie, he'd twist her into something she—or Liam —wouldn't recognize.

Caleb returned to the infirmary carrying a scroll.

"I think I found something that might help," he announced.

"You found a way to reverse the effects of the staff?" Bryant halted mid-pace, a hopeful look on his face.

Caleb nodded. "From what I read here it's not called the Staff of *Amsheer*. It's the staff of Eimhear. She was—"

"She was consumed by dark magic in the Third Age and nearly destroyed all of Fae," Bryant interrupted. "I've heard that bedtime story before. She was nothing but a myth." He dismissed the story with a wave of his hand.

"She wasn't a myth." On an empty bed, Caleb unrolled the parchment. "Cadryn, her consort, recounts the story of her demise here. He says it took his magic as well as wizard magic to defeat her but she wasn't killed. Her essence, her spirit, was put *inside* the staff.

Inside the orb."

Liam rose and walked to stand behind Caleb, looking over his shoulder at the ancient parchment with the faded handwriting.

"This proves nothing." Bryant joined them, standing on Caleb's other side.

"It proves everything," Caleb countered. "It proves Eimhear was real. Not a myth."

Bryant laughed. "You don't actually believe that, do you?"

"I do." There was nothing humorous in Caleb's expression.

"What does this have to do with Sunnie?" Liam skimmed the writing, trying to piece together what was so significant about it.

"The legend says the staff chooses who wields it," Bryant said. "It chose Sunnie."

"Aye, it did."

"Why?" Liam asked.

Caleb shrugged. "I don't think it matters. What does matter is the spirit of Eimhear lives on. Sunnie called herself that when the staff took her over."

"This says she was destroyed." Liam pointed to the parchment. "She *died*."

"She didn't die." Caleb's patient tone held a hint of frustration.

"If her spirit was in the staff, then her spirit now resides inside Sunnie." Bryant ran a hand along his chin.

"There has to be a way we can extract Eimhear and save Sunnie," Caleb said with a nod. "But according to this we'll need a wizard to do it."

"Then let's find him," Liam said.

"I'm afraid it's not that easy." Bryant took to pacing again. "There is only one wizard I know of in this realm."

"The wizard king?"

"Not the wizard king. His father, Deaglan." Bryant said.

"But Deaglan is dead, isn't he?" Caleb asked.

Sunnie whimpered cutting off any response Liam might have had.

"She's coming around," Bryant said.

Liam pushed the man out of the way and moved to perch on the edge of the bed. "Sunnie, can you hear me?"

Her eyes were still closed as her head rolled from side to side.

"Pain…so much pain," she whispered. She sounded like his daughter once again.

"Sunnie?"

Her eyes popped open, still silver. "You will call me Eimhear."

"The magic still has her," Bryant said.

"Can't we do something?" Liam snapped.

"I am the Goddess of Light and Dark," she said again. "Keeper of War and Peace. Maker of Life and Death. *There is a wizard of both Fae and Wizard blood that will come into power and rule from a silver throne.*" She turned her head and looked at Caleb with her haunting silver eyes. "The prophecy must be destroyed. Take me to this wizard."

They all exchanged a curious glance. Bryant's brows drew together in question. Clearly he had no idea what prophecy she was talking about.

"I must destroy the wizard before the prophecy comes true."

"What is she talking about?" Liam asked.

"I have no idea," Caleb said with a shrug.

"The girl is delirious," Bryant said.

Liam opened his mouth to reply but his voice froze in his throat as the world seemed to tip on its axis. He gripped the edge of the bed to steady himself and watched as the floor and the others wavered in front of him. He couldn't focus on them long enough to see if they had been affected as well. His vision blurred and a sick sensation rippled through him, leaving him lightheaded and nauseated.

Just as quickly as it had happened, it was over. The only thing left behind was the lingering headache that felt like a hangover.

"What the hell was that?" Liam held his head in his hands, rubbing his temples, trying to make the headache go away.

"If it was what I think then we're all in a lot of trouble." Bryant picked himself up off the floor and brushed at the dust on his pants. "Someone used the Time Sphere. That was a ripple in time."

"The Time Sphere?" Liam asked.

"A magical orb that alters time." Caleb's voice was raspy, like he'd been up all night smoking non-filtered cigarettes. "Fiona was headed there."

Liam looked down at his now unconscious daughter, a plan forming in his mind. If he could get his hands on that Time Sphere, he could right all the wrongs that had been done to him. And with Sunnie's new magic...well, he would be invincible, wouldn't he?

"Then I should go to the Time Sphere, too."

"No, it's forbidden. There's a protection spell around it anyway. You'll never be able to break through that." There was a hint of panic in Bryant's voice.

"I won't have to, will I? Because if Fiona used it then the protection spell is already broken."

Bryant's face drained of color as the realization of his words struck him. He almost gave him a triumphant smile. All he needed was a map and he could find his way there.

"Hold everything. No one is going to the Time Sphere," Caleb said.

"Why not?"

"It's dangerous for one thing," Bryant replied. "If Fiona did go back in time then she's altered the past."

Liam pressed his lips together in annoyance. He would find a way to get past both Bryant and Caleb and get to that Time Sphere. He'd comb every map in the library if he had to. He glanced down at Sunnie and then at Brigid. His magic may not be at its full potential, but theirs were and he could use them to his advantage.

For now, he had to agree with the two men staring him down. Finally, he nodded.

"Perhaps you're right. It is dangerous and if Fiona has returned to the past, then there is nothing any of us can do to stop her." Liam rose. "I'm weary. I'll return for rest to my chamber. I'll ask the healer to contact me if Sunnie wakes again."

"A good idea. Let us all get some rest." Bryant ushered them all out of the infirmary.

But despite Liam's agreement to leave, it wasn't his agreement to leave the idea of the Time Sphere alone. He would find a way to find Fiona and get back his life.

Chapter 10

Sunnie was no longer the person she thought she was. No, she was someone different. She could distinctly hear the other voice in her head edging out her own subconscious. Pushing her true identity deeper and deeper into oblivion. It was hard for her to hold onto herself. She'd grown weak and lost the will to fight against whatever or whoever was in her head, invading her space and taking her over.

You hear me. Don't you, Sunnie?

The smooth voice dripped with sweetness. Once dark and oily, now it was warm and dark like molasses on a hot summer day. The words were soft and commanding yet gentle and firm.

"I hear you." She whispered the words to the darkness. Were her eyes open or closed? She couldn't tell. She couldn't see. "Go away."

I am more powerful than you. All I need is for you to take the magic inside you. Embrace it. Reach for it and awaken it. You've begun to feel it, haven't you?

Those words pushed through the dark recesses of her mind. Filling up all the empty spaces. Making her lightheaded. Making her drunk. Making her weak and subservient.

"Yes, and I don't like it. It scares me." A whimper escaped her, though she wasn't certain if she actually whimpered aloud or if it was merely in her head.

Do not let it scare you, dear child. Once you take it you will never be able to let it go. You will want it flowing through you, filling you. It is a feeling like no other, isn't it?

Yes. No! She didn't want to feel it. She didn't want to take the magic.

"Go away," Sunnie said again. Her face was damp even though she wasn't aware of the tears leaking out of her eyes.

I'm part of you now, Sunnie. You cannot vanquish me even if you try.

"Get out of my head. Get out! Get OUT!"

"Sunnie!"

The familiar voice was close to her. It took several minutes to realize to whom that voice belonged. Her father? No, he was dead. Or was he alive? She couldn't remember. She had a vague recollection of seeing him alive but then wondered if that had been a dream. Or a nightmare.

"Sunnie, wake up!"

Someone gave her a gentle shake. She peeled her eyes open and blinked, looking up into Caleb's handsome face. A hero's face. Yes, that's what he looked like. A hero. With his strong square chin and his eyes nothing but dark orbs in the shadows. There was a scruff of stubble along his cheeks and chin shimmering in the candlelight. His brow was furrowed. Her first impulse was to reach up and smooth away those lines with the pads of her fingers but she couldn't lift her arms. She was tired. So very tired.

"Caleb?"

Don't listen to him, dear child. He is nothing to you. He wants to harm you—me. He wants me gone. He wants to destroy what I've made.

"Caleb." She whimpered. Her eyes blurred with tears. "Help me. Please help me."

He wrapped her in his strong arms, pulling her to him and holding her close, rocking her gently to and fro. She could smell faint remnants of his cologne. Her hand flattened against his chest. Beneath her palm his heart pounded a strong sure beat.

"I want to, Sunnie, but I don't know how. Tell me how to help you."

Don't tell him anything! He's nothing to you. He's your enemy. He wants to hurt you.

Sunnie cried out at the searing pain through her head. Why was the voice there? How could she get her out?

"It...hurts. Burns."

He held her by her upper arms looking down at her. Candlelight and shadows flickered across his face. His handsome features morphed into something evil, something demonic, something terrifying. She screamed and shoved him away. Her legs wrapped in the bedding and it took several minutes—precious minutes—to free them. She tumbled out of the bed and crashed to the floor, banging her elbow. Sharp pain speared through her.

"Sunnie—"

His booted steps came around the end of the bed.

"Stay back! Stay away from me." She hovered on the floor on all fours. Her stomach cramped, threatening to heave.

She wasn't sure if she was telling him that for his own good or hers. The voice in her head continued to whisper.

Kill him, Sunnie. If you don't, he'll kill you.

She sat back on her heels and pressed her palms against the side of her head. "NO."

"No, what?" he asked.

He is your enemy. Kill him. Use the magic. Use it, Sunnie.

Her vision clouded as she sobbed. "I can't. Not him. Please."

Caleb knelt in front of her, reaching for her but she batted his hands away. She couldn't see his face in the darkness. She couldn't decide if he was the enemy or not. Didn't she know him? Hadn't she known him since she was a little girl? There was a memory...buried deep inside her she tried to find. But her mind had been altered. Her memories faded into a dreamlike fog and she couldn't find her way out.

Forget him. He is nothing to you.

"Who are you?" Sunnie whispered the words on a jagged breath.

"You know who I am. It's me, Caleb. I want to help you but I don't know how."

I am Eimhear. I am the only one you can trust. The only one who can release all the wild magic burning inside you. Aye, you feel it, don't you? You've always known it was there. You just didn't know how to wield it. Let it possess you. Let me possess you. Give in to it, Sunnie.

Sunnie sucked in a sharp breath. She whisked away the tears to clear her vision and focused as hard as she could on Caleb's face. He seemed familiar but she wasn't sure. She wasn't sure about anything anymore.

"I will...do no harm to him."

His brow furrowed with a mixture of concern and confusion. He didn't understand. He couldn't understand the war within her.

You pathetic little simpering fool. I had such high hopes for you. I thought you were the one. Don't you understand what I'm trying to do? I'm trying to save you from that woman you call sister.

Aoife. How did she know about Aoife? Instantly the image of her older sister burned through her mind. She was the girl who wore glasses with thick lenses. The most unpopular girl in school.

The one everyone made fun of. But smart. She was so smart. Sunnie was the popular one. The pretty one. The apple of Dad's eye. Aoife was…she didn't hate Aoife. She could never hate her. She wanted to be smart like Aoife. But she wasn't. She could never measure up. Even when their mother berated her for her failing grades.

Aye, I know about her. She thinks she's stronger than you, more beautiful, more everything. She's envied you her whole life and now she's come to take it away. She will take it away if you don't kill this man in front of you. Because he knows her, too. And he'll warn her. He'll find her. He'll tell her everything. You have to stop him. And her.

"A wizard of both Fae and Wizard blood will come into power and rule from a silver throne."

When she spoke, it was not her voice. It was Eimhear's.

"There's only one place that's written, Sunnie. Where did you read it?"

She didn't read it. It was in her head. In her mind. Pushing toward the forefront of her thoughts. Sunnie pressed the palms of her hands against her eye sockets and rubbed hard enough to see starbursts.

I know all your thoughts, your memories, your sister, Aoife. I know you want to destroy her.

Aoife. Eimhear did not understand their relationship. She misinterpreted it based on Sunnie's innermost feelings and memories. Yes, there had been some ill will between them but that was nothing more than teenage angst and sibling rivalry. It meant nothing. She looked up to her. Aoife wasn't evil. Aoife wasn't a wizard. She was her sister.

"Go away!"

The shout ripped from her lungs before she could stop it. A rustle of material indicated Caleb got to his feet. She dropped her hands, tried to focus on him as he retreated from her.

"Caleb, not you. Please, not you. I need you." Her voice wavered.

He halted, looked at her over his shoulder.

He is nothing to you. Kill him.

Her lip quivered as they looked at each other. His face was full of concern and indecision. She could see it written there as he tried to decide if she was worth helping. Maybe she wasn't. Maybe she was nothing. Maybe she would die here in this weird place she couldn't remember with the stranger in her head.

"Caleb…"

He moved toward her, dropped to a knee and reached for her. He caught her hands in his, holding them in his firm grasp. "Tell me what you need."

She didn't know. She couldn't know. She wasn't sure herself. How could she explain it to him?

Take the magic, Sunnie. It burns bright and deep inside you. All you have to do is wield it. Take it. Make it yours. Kill him and our journey will begin.

"I'm sorry," she whispered.

He gave her a small smile and brushed hair from her forehead. "Don't be."

She could no longer resist the voice inside her or the urge to use that burning bright light of magic. She reached for it and met Caleb's eyes. The light burst from her, punched through her.

He released her and flew backward across the room, landing with a thud on the wood floor and skidding several feet before coming to a halt. Only a little remorse went through her. His tunic was scorched, smoking in the center of his chest.

Good girl. Now…it truly begins.

Sunnie gave herself to the magic. The warmth cascaded through her, filling her, completing her. She could not deny how powerful it made her feel.

She unfolded her long lean form from the floor and stood, her heart pounding a wicked tattoo as she looked at Caleb's crumpled form on the floor. A sense of familiarity went over her as she looked at him. But it would for the girl knew him when she was young.

Was he dead? She couldn't tell. She didn't care. It didn't matter.

The door to the infirmary burst open. Liam stood on the other side, wild eyed. He glanced from Caleb's inert form to Sunnie and then back again.

"What happened?"

"I removed him." It was Eimhear's voice that replied not Sunnie's.

"Sunnie?"

"I am Eimhear. You will address me as such."

He stiffened and let the door close behind him. He peered at her from across the sea of empty beds, his eyes wide and curious. "My apologies, Eimhear."

"Aye, that is what I am called. What are you called?"

"Liam. I was…Sunnie's father."

"Were?"

"Did you kill her?"

She laughed a melodious deep laugh that went to her toes. "No, the simpering weakling still remains. Only remnants, though. Remnants I plan to eradicate."

His face drained of color. "She is—was—my daughter."

"She is weak. Like you."

He stiffened, anger flashing across his face. "I am not weak."

One eyebrow rose toward her hairline. "No? Then prove it to me."

His lips thinned into a straight line. "How?"

"Bring me my staff and then you will take me to Aoife."

His brows drew together in confusion. "Aoife? Why?"

"You will bring me my staff."

"I cannot. It's behind wards and a protection spell. I don't even know where it is."

But she did. That fool, Bryant, thought to hide it from her. But the magic inside it called to her. She knew exactly where it was.

"I do."

"Then tell me and I'll get it for you." He added in a stilted tone, "Eimhear."

"Oh, but you cannot get past the spells, can you?" She snapped her fingers.

The young *sidhe* in the bed next to her bolted upright. She sucked air deep into her lungs, her blue eyes wide as she blinked them open and glanced around.

"Take the girl," she said.

"Brigid?"

"The *sidhe* will be able to break through the spells."

Liam's gaze went from Sunnie to Brigid who looked as dazed and confused as the man. These two were clearly not worth having in her employ, but they were all she had and so she would make do and use them until they were no longer useful.

Liam moved toward the young *sidhe*, skirting the end of the bed and around to the other side giving Sunnie a wide berth.

"Did you kill Caleb?"

Sunnie looked at his unmoving body and shrugged. "I do not know nor do I care."

"Sunnie would care. She wouldn't hurt anyone. She—"

"I am not Sunnie!" Her voice thundered through the room, shaking the furniture and the rafters. She moved toward him and placed two fingers under his chin, tilting his face upward so their eyes met. "The sooner you accept that, the sooner I shall let you live."

Liam snapped his mouth closed as Eimhear stepped back from him, satisfied with his silence. Brigid jumped from the bed and launched her small form toward him. He caught her in his arms, held her close. Cowards. They were all cowards and didn't understand her power. She would have to restrain the magic boiling through her veins. She needed these two as much as they needed her, though they may not even realize that yet.

Across the room, Caleb groaned. The man was still alive. She turned toward him, lifted her hand, intending to finish the job when Liam and the little *sidhe* stepped in front of her.

"Don't. You don't have to kill him."

Again, her brow lifted. "He knows too much."

"He can help you. Us. Me. He knows where Aoife and the others went. He can help us find them. He can track them."

Interesting. She was not aware of such abilities the pitiful Fae man possessed. Mayhap there was some use for him yet.

"He knows where I can find Aoife?"

He nodded. "Aye, he does, my lady."

She lifted her head, her chin jutting out as she looked down her nose at Liam and his *sidhe*. "Very well. Then he will live for now. But when he is no longer useful, he dies. Now, let us retrieve my staff and then we will hunt down this woman."

As she passed by Liam, she caught a glimpse of her reflection in a nearby looking glass and halted. She was dressed in the strange clothes of the woman who called herself Sunnie. It would never do. At least, though, her hair was the proper shade—a striking white blonde. And her eyes, aye...her eyes were that glorious shade of silver. Her skin had turned from milky white to the pale shimmering shade she recalled so well when she was still in corporeal form.

But her clothes. No, they simply would not do.

With the snap of her fingers she changed her clothes from the odd ugly rags she'd worn before to the flowing, gorgeous gown she had been known for. Ivory trimmed in gold with a high-collared cloak embroidered in the same gold thread as her gown. Aye, that was better. With a satisfied smile, she headed for the door.

"Come along, Liam, if you wish to help me as you say you do."

"I do, my lady."

He trotted after her like the lap dog she knew he was dragging the little *sidhe* with him.

Fine. He could have his pet as Eimhear once had hers. Until Cadryn turned against her.

She didn't need directions in this place they called Ridgeclere. She knew every room, every corridor, every drafty hidden passageway. She'd lived here once. She ruled with an iron fist when it was still a castle, when Cadryn was her lover and all she ever wanted was an heir. An heir he couldn't give her.

Or wouldn't.

He had suffered for that decision.

Oh, aye, she knew Ridgeclere. And Bryant was nothing more than a puppet. Her puppet she could mold.

Her magic knew no bounds and at last her spirit had a host. She would once again rule this land, this castle. And this weakling who called herself Sunnie would soon disappear altogether as soon as she had control of that staff.

It had been put inside a locked wardrobe in the room Bryant was calling his workroom or office or some such nonsense. Once it had been a private bedchamber for guests. What had this man done to her home?

With a wave of her hand, she opened the door and stepped inside. Bryant was there and shot to his feet, eyes wide with shock and surprise. Again, with a wave of her hand she shoved him out of the way. He landed with a thud against the opposite wall, slid down to the floor and was out.

Good. Less to deal with. He was nothing but a nuisance anyway.

She pointed to the locked wardrobe, knowing she could not go near it for it was warded against all magic. *Her* magic.

"There," she said.

Brigid huddled against Liam. She looked up at him as though asking for his permission to approach the wardrobe. He gave her a little nod to encourage her.

"You can do it, Brigid."

Eimhear rolled her eyes.

Brigid approached the wardrobe, lifting her hands and placing them on the wood doors. She closed her eyes and went into a deep concentration. It took no more than a few minutes for the spells to be broken. Brigid pulled open one of the doors and inside was the staff.

The Staff of Eimhear.

It called to her. The light in the orb pulsed with a brightness. Smiling, she stepped toward it and lifted it from the wardrobe. A sigh of contentment escaped her lips.

"At last. We are one again."

"Are you?" Liam asked.

She turned toward him, lowering the staff so the dragon-clutched orb pointed directly at him. "Aye, we are. And you are no longer useful."

"Wait." He held his hands up. "Please."

"There is nothing you can say to change the outcome. You will meet your demise. You know all too well the girl who calls herself Sunnie and you will do nothing but get in my way."

"Sunnie is dead, isn't she?" he asked.

No, Dad! I'm not dead.

"She is." The girl tried to claw her way back to the top of her consciousness. Eimhear shoved the essence down deep again. "She is gone."

Pain flashed across his face. Such deep pain. How could he feel so much for the girl who was nothing? Barely a magic user. An amateur.

"We can help each other." He was grasping for something, anything, to keep himself alive. Useful.

A simpering smile spread on her lips. "Can we?"

"Aye, we can. I know this woman, Aoife. She trusts me."

Aoife is my sister. You stay away from her, you conniving—

She shoved Sunnie away again. "You said Caleb could track her."

"I did and he can. I can also help you get close to her. You want to destroy her, don't you?"

"I do."

Brigid glanced between the two of them with wide eyes. So annoyed was Eimhear she wanted to snuff her out with one swipe of her staff. But the man, Liam, seemed fond of her. And he seemed to think Eimhear needed him.

"We can help each other. Form an alliance, you and me. There's a Time Sphere somewhere in this realm. It can lead us to them."

She had never heard of such a thing. Her interest was piqued. "What is this Time Sphere?"

"A device for traveling forward or backward in time. It's here in this realm. Together we can find and use it. Alter your past, your present, your future. Whatever you wish."

A Time Sphere that can alter time? Oh, aye, she needed this. She *wanted* this. It would serve her well. She could return to her own time. With all the knowledge she had now, she could destroy that wizard and Cadryn. Or she could forget the past and build a better life for herself in the future.

This could serve her very well indeed.

"I wish to find this Time Sphere. And you, Liam..." She paused and looked at the young *sidhe*. "And you, too, dear child. You will both help me." Her gaze landed once again on Liam. "Won't you?"

"Aye, we will, my lady. We will help you any way we can," Liam said.

Brigid's head snapped toward him. Though Eimhear couldn't see her face, she knew the shock was evident there. It poured off her skin in sickly waves. If the man wasn't so fond of her, she'd snap her little neck. As it was, he liked her too much. Much too much for his own good. She'd let the little thing live for a while longer. Her skill at breaking spells may come in useful yet.

"Good, then. In the morn, you will take me to the Time Sphere."

She left the room with a flourish to seek her own chamber. Now that she was finally in human form once again she required rest. Something she had not needed for thousands of years and it irked her.

But it was a small price to pay for what was to come. She would at last have her revenge on the wizard who imprisoned her. Aye, he would finally meet the end he deserved.

Chapter 11

As Eimhear departed the room, a groan came from Bryant. Brigid hurried over and helped him up. Blood trickled down the side of his face.

"I'll get the healer," she said.

"No, I'm all right." He waved her off, wobbling toward his desk where he found a kerchief. He held it to the side of his head. His eyes widened when he saw the open wardrobe. "What the bloody hell happened here?"

"Eimhear is what happened. She made me give her the staff," Liam said.

"You damn fool. Do you have any idea what you've done?" Bryant glared at Liam, his face red with anger. "Now we'll never get it back from her."

"Aye, we will. I have a plan. I—"

The door burst open and Caleb barreled inside, sword drawn and eyes wild as he scanned the room. "Where is she? Where did she go?"

"Gone to rest," Liam said.

"Liam gave her the staff." Bryant's accusatory tone was laced with acid.

His gaze swung to the open wardrobe. He turned the sword on Liam. "Why the hell did you do that?"

Liam held up his hands in surrender. "I was buying our lives with that staff. She was going to kill you both but I stopped her."

Bryant looked at Brigid. "Is this true?"

She glanced at Liam. Fear was etched on her face as she looked back at Bryant and slowly nodded. "It is."

The man huffed out a breath as he fixed his gaze back on Liam. "What's your plan then?"

"I intend to take Eimhear to the Time Sphere."

"Have you lost your mind? You can't take her there," Caleb said.

"I can and I will," Liam said, his tone hard. "Once we get her there we take her back in time to this Cadryn person. We can destroy her before she becomes a powerful sorceress."

It was a plan he'd come up with on the fly. He hadn't thought it through beyond when he mentioned the Time Sphere to Eimhear. But she seemed intrigued by the idea and easily swayed with the temptation of altering time.

"We can't go back to Eimhear's time," Bryant said.

"Why not?"

"Two of Eimhear cannot exist in the same time."

"Eimhear is a spirit—"

"In Sunnie's body," Caleb said, interrupting Liam. "How are we supposed to separate Sunnie from Eimhear?"

"We can't. Not without killing her," Bryant said.

"Sunnie is *dead*. Don't you understand that? Eimhear killed her." Hysteria tinged his voice as he raked his hands through his hair, making a show of it.

If he was being honest with himself, Liam wasn't certain Sunnie was dead despite her changed outward appearance. And the way she talked and walked. If there was a small chance she was still in there somewhere, then he should *fight* to get her back.

But perhaps he shouldn't fight to get her back yet. He couldn't ignore the possibilities of having Eimhear on his side. She would be a great asset and ally. It was a way to get what he wanted as well as give the sorceress inside Sunnie what *she* wanted. He could use the girl for her magic and finally rid himself of Bryant.

And Fiona? She was another matter. His feelings for his ex-wife warred within him—a sort of love-hate relationship. He wanted her back and yet he wanted her to suffer for taking over his life the way she did. If he couldn't have her back, then perhaps he could make her suffer for all she'd put him through.

"No." Caleb shook his head. "I refuse to believe that. Sunnie is still in there. She has to be."

"We're going to the Time Sphere." Liam turned to Caleb. "And you're going to take us there."

"I don't know where the Time Sphere is," he said.

"I saw it on a map. We can find it." He saw a bit of recognition flash across Caleb's face. "You know where it is, don't you?"

He and Bryant exchanged a look before he replied. "No."

"I think you're lying."

"Liam, Fiona altered time. We cannot alter it further," Bryant said.

"That does not matter to me."

Fiona could do what she pleased but he was not going to be dissuaded from his new course of action.

"It should matter," Bryant said. "Things will begin to change if they haven't already and there won't be a damn thing we can do about it."

"Arguing will get us nowhere. The damage is done," Caleb interjected. He looked at Liam. "All right, fine. I'll take you to the Time Sphere if that's what you want but it has a protection spell around it."

"That doesn't matter. Brigid can break it," Liam said.

Brigid gasped. Defiance was written all over her face.

"I will not." She folded her arms over her chest and stepped toward Caleb and Bryant, as if they would shield her from him.

That's how it was going to be then. The line in the sand had been drawn. They were clearly on opposing sides now. So be it.

"You will do it," Liam said with certainty as he moved toward her.

"Or what? You'll kill an innocent *sidhe*?" Caleb stepped in front of her, blocking him. "I won't let you bully her."

He peered at the agent, annoyed. "You, your boss and this agency have caused me and my family enough trouble. We *are* going. She's breaking that spell and I'm getting what I want." He thumbed at his chest for emphasis. Determination crawled through him.

"And what is that?" Caleb asked.

"My life back."

Bryant let out a wicked bark of a laugh. "You think it's that simple? You think you can use the magic in the Time Sphere to get what you want? No one gets what they want with the Time Sphere. That type of magic and spellcasting never comes without a high price. Niall learned that the hard way when he killed his own father for his magic using an Eradication Spell."

"Nevertheless, we *are* going and if you won't cooperate then I will find a way to turn Eimhear against you all."

The reality of his statement was written on all of their faces. They knew as he did Eimhear was unstable and willing to do whatever it took to get to her end goal. She'd kill anyone who got in her way and it would mean nothing to her. She would do it without remorse.

"Go ahead," the director said through gritted teeth. "That's what you intend to do anyway."

"Enough." Caleb sliced his hand through the air with finality to end the dispute. "Bryant, we'll do as he says. I'll take him and Sunnie to the Time Sphere. Brigid will accompany us."

"I won't—"

"You will," Caleb said, cutting her off. "And we'll do everything Liam wants from now on." His sharp gaze met Liam's. "If that's what you want."

"It is." He couldn't stop the smug smile. "We leave in the morn. Come along, Brigid." He waved her toward him.

She remained in place and shook her head. "No. I'm not going anywhere with you."

A flash of anger went through him. He didn't like her resistance and likely had made an enemy of her. He'd work on her, though, and eventually she'd come around. He clenched his jaw so tight, his back teeth ached. Even so, he managed to grit out one last farewell. "I bid you all good night then. Until the morn."

Caleb watched Liam leave, the door banging closed behind him. Brigid reeled on him, fire flashing in her bright blue eyes.

"How could you force me to do that?"

"Calm down. I'm not going to force you to do anything." Caleb sheathed his sword.

"Just as I thought. You have a plan." Bryant tossed the bloodied rag on his nearby table. "Liam has lost his mind, Caleb. I had no idea he'd go off the deep end as he did. He's snapped. Tell me your plan."

Caleb couldn't agree more. Something had shifted inside Liam. He'd known the man for many years but something about his new behavior was different. He seemed unhinged, out of sorts. Not the kind, gentle man he recalled from the human realm. Liam loved Fiona with a fierce devotion, making it difficult for him and Sean to get close to her, to keep her out of Faery like they were supposed to do.

He knew, as Bryant did, Liam had been recruited to the agency to make sure Fiona and Aoife stayed firmly planted in the human realm. Sunnie wasn't considered as much of a threat, so they never thought she'd enter Faery. Even so, Bryant used Liam's love of Fiona and the girls as leverage to get his help. He had seemed to be fine with that arrangement until of late. Caleb knew using the resurrection spell would change Liam but he had no idea it would alter his personality so much. He was definitely not the same person he was before his death.

"I'll take them to the Time Sphere in the Ivory Wood but we're not going to let them use it. Brigid, you'll make a grand show of trying to break the protection spell even though the spell is likely already broken."

"Aye, it would be, wouldn't it?" Bryant said with a nod looking well pleased. "Fiona would have broken it to use the sphere."

"Right. We'll lure them there. You'll send a small garrison ahead to wait for us. When Brigid tries to break the spell, they'll take Eimhear and Liam into custody," he said.

"You think that will work?" the director asked, sounding doubtful.

"I know so. As long as you have iron shackles."

It had to work. Because even though he didn't much care for his superior, Bryant was right in that Liam *was* dangerous. Once they had Eimhear in iron shackles, her magic would be contained and she would be like a knight without armor—defenseless. Caleb didn't like Eimhear taking over Sunnie's body and mind. He had to search the archives to find a way to separate the two without hurting Sunnie because he believed deep down the girl was still in there somewhere.

"Very well then. I'll send my best men. The iron ought to hold them both when they're arrested. I'm coming with you."

Iron rendered magic useless and would keep Liam and Eimhear contained while they were transported back to Ridgeclere. As soon as they had Eimhear in custody, Caleb could start working on a way to rescue Sunnie.

"No, you stay here. You're the director. Besides, we need to make sure Liam thinks he's in control. We want him to be overconfident and let down his guard. That way we can take them both unaware in the Ivory Wood," Caleb said.

"Good idea. Then you two better rest for the mission ahead. It won't be an easy one."

Another ripple of time ripped through them, catching them all off guard. Caleb tried to stay on his feet, but the shudder was too powerful. He collided with the floor as a wave of sickness went through him. He heard a little shriek as Brigid landed next to him. This one lasted much longer than the first.

Bryant groaned. Caleb got to his hands and knees and lifted his head as pain pounded behind his eyes. It was all he could do to keep from heaving.

"Another time wave?" he asked on a gasp.

"Aye." Bryant held his arm against his thick middle, his face ashen. "I think I broke my arm."

"I'll get you to the infirmary." If he could get to his feet. The nausea hadn't subsided yet.

"Fiona must be on the move in the past. That can be the only explanation for the second rift," Bryant said. "Mayhap you should go back in time to find her."

"Don't be stupid. That will cause more problems and you know it." Caleb finally got to his feet and helped Bryant up.

"If it happens again we may be looking at irreparable damage."

"We'll worry about that when the time comes. For now, let's get you to the healer. Are you coming, Brigid?"

"No, someone needs to get provisions together for tomorrow. We'll need them."

"Good idea," he said with a nod.

She headed off to the kitchens as Caleb and Bryant made for the infirmary.

"You won't let anything happen to her, will you, Cal? She's young. This is her first mission…" Bryant's words trailed off.

"I'll protect her as best I can," he said.

Bryant seemed satisfied with that answer but Caleb wasn't so sure. There were too many unknowns going into the trek to the Time Sphere in the Ivory Wood. He hoped his plan worked.

It was late in the night when Caleb finally made his way to his chamber. He was restless and couldn't sleep and so ended up pacing the length of the room until the morn. His fatigue would eventually catch up to him but in the meantime he would focus on the upcoming battle with Eimhear and Liam.

Before he left Bryant in the infirmary, the director sent his best agents ahead to wait for them at the Time Sphere. That gave Caleb some comfort.

As dawn peeked over the edge of the world, a knock sounded on his door. He opened it to find Brigid on the other side.

"They're waiting for us in the courtyard," she said.

He knew who *they* were. "I'm ready."

"You look like you haven't slept all night."

"I haven't." He strapped his sword to his side, and then stuck the dagger in his boot.

"Are you sure you're up for this?" she asked.

"I have to be. I may be Sunnie's last hope. Let's go."

He couldn't read her expression as he waved her toward the open door. Maybe she thought he'd lost his mind wanting to help Sunnie and maybe she was right about that. But he had to help Sunnie. He had to find a way to get Eimhear out of her head. Even he wasn't sure why he was so determined to rescue her. The girl had done nothing special to garner his attention. He'd watched her grow up much like Sean had watched Aoife grow up but he had never had any sort of amorous feelings toward her.

Until recently.

He couldn't explain what had changed. Sunnie had never given him any reason to want her. She was a tabloid sensation with all sorts of things written about her and one producer or director or another. If he believed that sort of thing and he wasn't sure he did.

But Caleb had more to worry about than Sunnie. He had the psycho sorceress to contain and a young *sidhe* to protect.

Eimhear was still dressed in her flowing gowns of ivory with gilt edges holding the staff in one hand and letting its end rest on the ground. Liam had traded in his street clothes for black pants tucked neatly into knee-high boots polished to a high shine, a black tunic, black padded vest and black cloak to complete the ensemble. The only thing he lacked was a sword swinging at his side. He still had the faint shimmer of glamour around him.

Eimhear looked Brigid up and down, eyeing the knapsack she had slung over one shoulder. Then she gave Caleb a once over.

"I trust you have the map to this Time Sphere?" she asked.

Caleb tapped the side of his head. "It's right here."

She looked unconvinced as she lifted one brow. "Is it?"

"Aye, it is. I thought you said we were ready. Where are the horses?" Caleb asked.

"Horses?" She chuckled. "We need no horses."

With a wave of her hand, they sifted from the courtyard of Ridgeclere to outside the castle walls. It took a few minutes for Caleb's stomach to catch up with his body from the unexpected sift and for a moment it felt as though he'd been dropped off a twenty-foot story building. Liam wobbled a little on his feet as he pitched forward, hands on his knees as he sucked in deep breaths. Even Brigid looked a little green around the edges as she pressed a hand to her stomach.

They were outside the walls of Ridgeclere at the busy harbor where people bustled about. The air was redolent with fish, salt air and cooked meat. Merchants hawked their wares on the seawall boulevard as visitors came and went. And further down the harbor, cargo was offloaded several large ships and transferred to the nearby businesses either by cart or pack mule. In the distance, the craggy mountains loomed large as though overseeing the port below.

While the rest of them tried to recover, Eimhear looked around the port, inhaled a deep breath and exhaled with a smile.

"Ah, it has been so long since I have breathed the salt air of the port city. I have longed for it."

"You know this place?" Liam had his hands on his thighs as he bent over to regain his composure but as he spoke he looked up at her.

"Of course. I ruled here once. Ridgeclere was my home, my castle."

Shock pulsed through Caleb as he looked at her, suddenly understanding why she was so familiar with the layout of the castle. He noticed they garnered quite a few looks from passersby. The sorceress didn't exactly blend in with the normal townsfolk. And yet she seemed oblivious to it all as she turned to him.

"Now, then. Where is this Time Sphere of yours?" she asked in her glacial tone.

"We head south toward Illyria," Caleb said.

She said nothing as she looked south, as though she could see it in the distance. The only thing in the distance was the stone bridge leading from the harbor to the walled city.

"Where in Illyria?"

Caleb shifted from one foot to the other, not wanting to tell her. His nerves were on a sharp edge. He knew Bryant had only recently dispatched the men to the Ivory Wood the night before. It would take them several days to reach the Time Sphere on horseback. He hadn't accounted for Eimhear's magic or the ability to sift them all with the wave of her hand. He should have thought of that. Already his plan was failing.

When he didn't answer, she turned to him, pinning him with her ice cold gaze. "Well? Do you know or not?"

"He knows. He's not telling you," Liam said.

Her head lifted ever so slightly as she gazed down her nose at him. "I see. Then mayhap I should extract the location from his mind."

Cold dread swept over him as he stiffened. Altering the mind of others was a dark and powerful kind of magic. The kind he had been forced to do when he took Sunnie's and Aoife's memories. He couldn't help but wonder if Sunnie was in there somewhere driving that part of Eimhear.

"Shall I?" she asked again, a smile on her blood red lips.

Caleb still didn't answer.

"Very well."

She lifted her staff as the orb started to glow. She lowered it, angling the point to the top of his head. He took a step backward as soon as the heat penetrated through him. The probing magic poked into his mind, riffling through his memories searching for the one thing she sought—the map to the Ivory Wood.

The sharp pain of the intrusion burst through him, slicing into his core. He faltered, pitched forward and tried to push her out. But it was useless. Like pushing against a brick wall. He cried out as he squeezed his eyes shut.

"Stop!"

He heard Brigid shout and then movement. When he opened his eyes, she had stepped in front of him and put up her hand, shoving the magic from the orb back toward Eimhear. The sorceress lowered her staff, the spell broken.

"Well, well. Brave little thing, aren't you?"

Caleb realized Brigid stepped in front of him to break the spell with her own magic.

"I won't let you hurt him," she said.

"Be careful, little one, or it will be your undoing. I have what I need. The Time Sphere is located in the Ivory Wood in Illyria."

Brigid moved to his side. She wrapped an arm around his waist. "Can you stand?"

With her assistance, he straightened and glanced around the port. No one seemed to even notice them anymore. In fact, there was something hazy surrounding them. Eimhear must have put a concealment spell around them to keep others from noticing her magic.

"Shall we go?"

She started to wave her hand and sift them.

"Wait, my lady, please," Caleb said.

She halted, pinned him with her cold questioning stare.

"No more sifting," he said. "It may be easy for you, Eimhear, but it makes the rest of us ill."

Her gaze flickered from him to Brigid to Liam and then back again. "Does it? Pity."

She made a movement to sift but he stepped closer and grasped her hand. "I said no."

A pale brow lifted. "And who are you to tell me what to do?"

Caleb searched her gaze, looking for signs of Sunnie. He couldn't see anything in there other than the cold emptiness of Eimhear. He would have to find a way to reach her.

"If you sift us again it will damage Brigid's magic." It was a lie and a bold one. In truth, he had no idea if it would damage the *sidhe's* magic.

"Aye, he's right," she said, playing along. She moved to stand next to him. "Your magic is too strong, my lady. If you sift me again it will drain my power. I will not be able to break the protection spell at the Time Sphere."

Caleb couldn't help but like the girl standing next to him. She was a quick thinker behind her quiet exterior. Irritation flashed across Eimhear's face.

"Very well. How do you propose we get there then?"

He tried hard not to crack a smile. "The old fashioned way, my lady. On horseback."

Chapter 12

In the Land of Faery before Time was altered

Caleb acquired four horses from a local merchant. He offered him so much gold the man was hard pressed to turn down the offer even though he'd intended to take the horses on the voyage across the Sea of Celestial Fire.

Brigid rode next to him as he led them out of the port across the stone bridge and into the walled city that would take them to the main road out of town and south toward Illyria. The city, like the port, was a bustle of activity. The town reminded Caleb of the one at the foothills of the Towers of Illyria. Both sides of the street were lined with shops and open-air merchants hawking their wares.

Eimhear rode past him at a sudden gallop, her horse's hooves clopping on the cobblestone. He wanted to call out to her but she came to a halt in front of one of the taverns and dismounted, the staff clutched in her hand. She stood next to the horse as her keen eyes glanced around the city with a light he hadn't seen before.

Caleb pulled his horse to a stop. Brigid and Liam did the same.

"What's she doing?" Brigid whispered to him.

"No idea."

"Eimhear, why are we stopping?" Liam called.

She entered the tavern. The three of them quickly followed. As soon as they entered, they saw all eyes on Eimhear as she glanced around, her gaze pinpointing every patron until it settled on one man at the bar. Caleb recognized him—it was Talon from the previous encounter.

"You." She pointed the staff in his direction. The orb glowed. "You are called Talon, are you not?"

He slithered off the bar stool. "I am. What of it?"

Her eyes narrowed to slits. "You sell women and children as slaves. You will die."

A flicker of fear went over his face before he broke into a guffaw. He looked her up and down, clearly not threatened by her at all. "Who're you? Part of the Watch?"

"I am not. I am justice."

His response was to laugh again. Not the wisest of moves.

She attacked him. A stream of white magic pulsed from the orb and punched him in the chest. He flew backward and crumpled to the ground. Dead.

Caleb knew then Sunnie must still be in there somewhere. Eimhear must have used her memories when she saw the man. And now she had her revenge. No one moved or dared breathe.

"If any one of you sells women on the slave market, you will answer to me," she said. "That man is dead because he is a slaver. Are there more among you?"

Heads shook emphatically as they all turned back to their ale and mead, ignoring the dead man at the other end of the room.

"As it should be."

She swished past them and exited, moving with her fluid grace. They followed and watched as she halted in the center of town, her gown swirling around her. The orb in the staff had come to life again and storm clouds gathered overhead. Brigid moved closer to Caleb, looking up at him with question in her eyes but he had no answers as to what Eimhear, or Sunnie, was doing.

She paused in the center of town as the crowd largely ignored her, unaware she had murdered a man in the tavern. She placed the staff on the cobblestone next to her with a thump. The orb pulsed out a bright white light, illuminating the area around her. That got the attention of the townsfolk. Most of them halted to gape at her. Others grabbed their children and scurried away.

"I ruled this city long ago."

Her voice was a melodious song. Somewhere in her words Caleb could swear he heard Sunnie.

"This village was mine once. My lover had a shop there." She pointed with the staff to the baker. Her gaze took on a faraway look. "He was a jewel maker. The finest in the village. He did not fear me. He worshiped me until those villagers turned him against me and I conquered them. Now I see no fear behind their eyes. I wish to conquer it again." She sounded indifferent.

Caleb took a step toward her as she lifted the staff and slammed it against the cobblestones with a resounding clang. The vibration shuddered through everyone standing, including the three of them.

It set off an earthquake, creating chaos. Buildings crumbled around them, destroyed. People in the streets tried to run for cover but the violence of the quake was too much. Rocks and debris crashed around them.

Caleb lost his footing and stumbled sideways into Brigid who grabbed onto him. They clung to each other. He could no longer control his body as he melted to the ground taking her with him. He landed on one knee, rapping it against the cobblestone. Pain burst through him. But even so he never let go of Brigid as he cushioned her fall.

He met her wide-eyed gaze. He could clearly see the fear, the pain, the terror in her eyes. He gave her his best consoling smile, as if to say everything was going to be all right even though he didn't know if that was true.

Then all went quiet and everything stopped almost as suddenly as it began. Those who survived picked themselves up off the cobblestone. Some were injured from the falling debris but Caleb, Brigid and Liam had been spared because they'd made it toward the center of town near Eimhear.

There was a smile of satisfaction on her lips as she looked around at the destruction.

Caleb couldn't help but wonder if Sunnie was in there somewhere. How could she destroy an entire village and murder a man without so much as a thought? That was not the Sunnie he knew.

But then he didn't know if she was in control of her own body. Perhaps Eimhear's dark magic got to her somehow, tainted her, and she wanted nothing more to do with the Light. She had embraced the Dark.

He would not—could not—believe that of Sunnie. She was still in there somewhere. She was still the same good girl, if a little self-absorbed, as she was before.

Eimhear exhaled what sounded like a contented sigh. Caleb stumbled to his feet, helping Brigid. She bushed dirt off her clothes.

"Why did you do it?" Caleb asked.

"Because they should fear me."

"Fear does not conquer a village," Caleb said. "These people will never follow you."

"Power is taken, not earned. Fear of power keeps those who would rebel contained," she said.

"But—"

"Silence," she thundered as her glittering gaze turned on him. "I do not need them to follow me. I only need them to obey me. I did not ask for nor do I wish for your opinion. The only reason you still live is because you can lead us to this Time Sphere."

As soon as the words were out of her mouth, she faltered. Her body hunched forward and she put a hand to her head, squeezing her eyes closed with a groan of pain.

"No, he will *not* live. I *will* kill him," she said suddenly as though speaking to someone else.

Hope flickered through Caleb. Hope Sunnie was still in there fighting her way out. She must have done something to Eimhear to remind her of her presence and Eimhear, in turn, threatened Caleb.

Eimhear regained her composure and straightened. She took another deep breath and smoothed a hand down her skirt.

"Let us move onward." She headed for her horse.

Caleb glanced around at the fearful faces of the villagers, the injured, the dead, the destroyed buildings. "That's it then? You destroy the village and move on? What about these people? What about the dead?"

"They do not concern me."

"You destroyed their village for no reason?"

She halted, turned back to him with narrowed eyes. "I do not need to explain my actions to you."

"But these people—"

She flicked her staff toward him. A punch of magic went through him with a fury, making him double over and cough. Pain radiated through him. Brigid was at his side, reaching for him but he waved her off.

"That was a warning. Another word and you'll be dead." She mounted her horse.

"Are you all right?" Brigid whispered.

"I will be."

He stumbled toward his horse. Brigid wrapped her arm around his waist and helped him the rest of the way. He gave her a smile of thanks as he reached for this horse. She released him and headed to hers.

As he stuck his foot in the stirrup, a low vibration started but much different than the earthquake before. People scattered, heading back into what shops remained or running through the streets toward the gate of the walled city. He glanced at Eimhear to see if it was coming from her but she had halted in the center of the destruction and looked as perplexed as he. And then it happened. A ripple of time pulsed through them all with a wicked force. It was like before in Ridgeclere but this time stronger, more violent.

Caleb's horse whinnied and reared. He stumbled out of the way as it galloped off. Brigid collided with him. He wrapped his arms around her. She gripped his tunic in both her fists as they tried to steady their footing together. A bright flash exploded around them, knocking them both to the ground. He couldn't hang on to her. Everything went still.

His ears rang with a high-pitched squeal as he lay on the cobblestone. His head pounded with a fierce pain. He had lost sight of Eimhear and Liam but had no doubt they were still nearby. He groaned and rolled to his side.

Brigid lay next to him and whimpered. Blood trickled down the side of her face. It looked like she hit her head on some loose debris. He scooted next to her, pulled her into his arms and brushed away the dirt.

"Brigid, you're bleeding."

"I...hit my head."

"It doesn't look bad but I need something to stop the bleeding," he said.

A man's groan nearby caught his attention. The stranger who had appeared wasn't in the village before the time rift. He huddled on the ground wearing a dark brown cloak. He used the walking stick in one hand as leverage to push to his feet with a groan.

Caleb could see he was an old man. Wrinkles lined his aged face. He glanced around, unable to hide his confusion.

"Where is this place?"

"The village near Ridgeclere," Caleb replied. "Who are you?"

His lips thinned into a straight line as he looked around the destroyed village. "I don't remember this place." His gaze landed on Brigid then. "You're injured, dearie."

"She hit her head."

He moved toward them and lowered his aged body to the ground once again. He reached for her but Brigid jerked her head out of reach.

"No worries, dearie. I'm not going to hurt you. I'm going to help you."

She gave Caleb a questioning glance. He nodded as if to say it was all right. The man pressed two fingers against the wound on the side of her head. A moment later the wound was gone.

"Ha. I'd forgotten I could do things like that. How do you feel?"

"Better." She pushed out of Caleb's arms and managed to get to her feet. The men followed. "Thank you."

"Who are you?" Caleb asked.

"Deaglan," he said. "Can't say how I came to be here, though."

Caleb stared at him with wide-eyed surprise. Deaglan was supposed to be dead, killed by Niall for his magic. The time rift must have been a major one and altered much of the past, the present, the future. It was the only explanation for the man's sudden appearance.

"You're Deaglan," Caleb said, saying the words slowly. "The wizard king's father?"

He tilted his head toward the side and squinted at him in suspicion. "Aye, what of it?"

"I thought the old wizard was dead?" Brigid asked.

"Shh," Caleb said.

"I was dead, eh?" Deaglan chuckled. Then understanding flickered across his aged features. He scraped a hand over his chin, his skin bristling against the stubble. "I think I understand. There is only one magic powerful enough to alter time."

Caleb moved toward him. "Aye the Time Sphere."

"Who?" he asked. "Who used it?"

"Fiona."

"Fiona?" He blinked surprise. "She's here? In this realm?"

"She was but now she's gone to the past."

"By the gods, I thought I'd never hear that name again. Then Niall found her alive?"

"Niall used a spell to gain your power. It killed you," he explained. "You're supposed to be dead."

He gripped his walking staff so tight his knuckles turned white. Deep concentration lined his face. "I *was* dead and now I'm not. I'm alive and here and I need to get back to the Towers of Illyria."

"*You!*" Eimhear screeched the word so loud they all turned to see her hurrying through the destroyed village toward them. "I know you, wizard."

"I'm afraid you hold me at a disadvantage, my lady." He gave her a half-smile.

"You *do* know me. I am the Goddess of Light and Dark. Keeper of War and Peace. Maker of Life and Death."

His eyes widened. "Gods. Eimhear. But...how?"

"Ah, so you do remember me, old man. You should since you are the wizard who put me in the orb."

The words from the scroll came rushing back to Caleb as he looked on. *This* was the wizard? He searched those dark memories once again for that day so long ago when the wizard defeated her. He peered at Deaglan for a long, hard moment and realized with some horror he *was* that wizard...a much younger man at the time. He was the wizard who had delivered him to Bryant after Eimhear's banishment into the staff.

A lump of fear clotted his throat. Would Deaglan remember him? Would he know he had been that orphaned boy Eimhear had taken under her wing all those long years ago? Eimhear certainly didn't remember. At least, she hadn't acted like she remembered him. He was a boy then. Now, a man grown. And neither of them recognized him. He could live with that if only to keep the secret of his own darkness a little longer.

"I should have destroyed you when I had the chance but Cadryn wouldn't let me. How did you get out of the staff?" he asked.

She laughed. "Your magic weakened and I found a willing host. This girl." She waved her hands down Sunnie's body. "She has raw untapped magic. She has served me well." The orb lit up and she pointed it at Deaglan. "Now you will die, old man."

"Wait, Eimhear." Liam stepped in front of her and fixed his gaze on Deaglan. "You are a wizard?"

Deaglan looked him up and down. "Aye, I am."

"Then you can remove the glamour spell on me."

"He must die for what he did to me," Eimhear said, her voice cold, hard.

"Not until he removes this glamour spell." Liam turned toward her and pushed the staff upright away from Deaglan. "He can give me back my true identity."

"Who are you, laddie?" Deaglan asked, his eyes narrowing.

"My name is Liam," he said. "Eimhear, don't kill him. Let him break the spell."

A blonde brow lifted as she scrutinized Deaglan. "Very well. I will allow him to break the spell and then I will kill him."

Deaglan peered at the strange man with a critical eye. He could see the faint outline of the glamour around him as he stood next to the woman who claimed she was Eimhear. He would deal with her in time but for now he was curious about this glamour spell.

"How do you know I can break the spell?" Deaglan asked.

"It's wizard magic," Brigid said. "I tried but couldn't break it."

"You tried to break the spell, dearie?"

"Brigid is a *sidhe*," Caleb supplied. "She can break any spell except the one on Liam."

"It can only be broken by wizard magic," she said with a confirmation nod.

Deaglan turned his gaze back on Liam, squinting as though that would bring him more into focus. "Is that so? Come closer then. Let me have a look at you." He waved Liam toward him.

Liam halted directly in front of him. Indeed, Deaglan could see traces of magic shimmering around him, the faint outline of something familiar and ancient. The glamour over him gave the appearance of a human. But it wasn't only a glamour spell. There was also a magical suppression spell rendering his magic dormant for as long as it was in place as well as something to alter his mortality.

His stomach twisted into a tight knot. He recognized the magic as his own. There was only one individual Deaglan had ever cursed with such a powerful glamour spell.

He knew this man, though he had not laid eyes on him in decades. He was but a babe when Deaglan stole him from the queen and took him to the human realm to switch him for a human baby. This was the true Prince of Anatolia. The one who should have been called Cian.

"Where do you come from, human?"

"I am no human," he said. "I'm told I'm a Changeling."

Deaglan's stomach twisted tighter. Gods, it was true then. This was Cian, the crown prince of Anatolia. And the man called Cian was actually a human behind a glamour who never possessed magic. Deaglan never thought he would come face to face with either man ever again. This man was supposed to stay hidden in the human realm, away from Faery, forever. He had even altered his mortality so that he would age and eventually die.

As soon as the spells were broken, his true identity would be known.

"Can you do it or not?" Impatience edged Liam's voice.

"Aye, I can. But will I? That is the true question." He gave a half smile, wondering how he could keep from breaking the spell.

"You will do as he says," Eimhear snapped. She pointed the staff toward him once again as the orb lit up.

Deaglan had no choice. He had to do it. He glanced over at the other two who stood nearby with a mix of emotions on their faces.

"Aye, I will break the spell."

Liam took a deep breath as Deaglan reached for him and placed his fingertips on his forehead. He closed his eyes and chanted something under his breath. Words none of them would understand. Once Liam's true identity was discovered, what would it do to him and the realm? What would queen of Anatolia do when she learned the boy she raised was not her son at all?

As for the man who called himself Cian at Lambridge Castle, his true identity had never been discovered either. Deaglan took it to his grave once, he would take it there again.

First he removed the suppression spell. Liam convulsed once and Deaglan suspected the sudden surge of unfamiliar magic went through him like a lightning bolt. Even he could sense the magic pounding through his veins as it swept through his body. It was quite powerful but only because it had remained dormant for so long.

With that spell now gone, Deaglan started the removal of the glamour spell. A spark of fear went through him as he realized the calamity of the situation. All these years he had hoped to keep this man out of Faery and away from his mother as revenge for all she'd done to him so long ago. It made no matter now, certainly, and he should be glad he had the chance to right that wrong.

But he wasn't. He wished this man, this Liam, had stayed in the human realm like he belonged. Damn him.

With the chants complete, he opened his eyes and removed his hand. The man's visage changed. While most of his facial features remained the same, there were two distinct differences. The sandy blond hair was replaced with black much like his mother's,

Siobhan. The once sharp blue eyes were now haunting black orbs, dark as midnight and again like his mother. There was so much of her in him it pained Deaglan to look at him. No longer did Liam have the face of kindness. He now had the face of someone dark and menacing. Someone not to be trifled with.

"Is it done?" Liam asked.

Deaglan could only nod.

Liam ran his hands over his face as though he could feel a difference. He swept his hands through his hair, over his scalp and down the back of his neck as he sucked in a sharp breath and then expelled it.

"I feel different. Changed."

Brigid and Caleb exchanged a questioning look. Deaglan, though, knew what he meant. For the first time in his life, Liam was acutely aware of the magic flowing through him.

"I can't explain it," he continued. "There is warmth there. A…glow. As though I've come alive for the first time."

"What did you do to him? Did you harm him?" Eimhear demanded.

"I removed the spell as he asked," Deaglan said.

"I see a silvery thread deep inside me." Liam put his hands on either side of his head.

Gods. The man was describing the magic deep inside him and he didn't even realize it.

"Magic. He has *magic*," Brigid whispered. Only Deaglan and Caleb heard. Her wide eyes turned on Deaglan. "You gave him that?"

"No." Deaglan gave a hard shake of his head.

"It's been inside him the whole time." Understanding came over Caleb's face. "There was a suppression spell on him because he truly is a Fae."

Deaglan gave a weak nod as blood drained from his head in a whoosh that left him a little lightheaded.

"By the gods, man," Caleb breathed. "Who is he?"

Liam glanced around looking for something, anything, to use as a mirror.

"He is…a prince." Even though Deaglan whispered it, Caleb heard. He would find out the truth. And mayhap a little part of Deaglan wanted someone to know the truth so he would no longer carry the burden of the lie alone.

Liam hurried to a nearby shop window and stared at his reflection in the glass. He ran his hands over his face again as he inspected his new features.

"Now you die, old man."

Eimhear lowered her staff, the orb pulsing a bright white light.

"Go ahead and kill me, Eimhear. Even if you strike me down here, now, you will still not win. There is another who can and will break your hold on the girl."

Deaglan gripped his walking staff as he thought of the prophecy. The very one he'd written by his own hand so long ago. It had been foretold then of the half-Fae, half-wizard who would come into power. But there was more to that prophecy than even Eimhear did not know.

"*A wizard of both Fae and Wizard blood will come into power and rule from a silver throne.* Is that what you mean, old man?" She laughed. "I do not fear this Halfling."

Deaglan smirked. Fool. "Ah, but you do not know the rest of the prophecy, do you, Eimhear? *A wizard of both Fae and Wizard blood will come into power and rule from a silver throne. This half-Fae, half-wizard shall be Protector of the Realm, Ruler of the Kingdom, Guardian of the Staff of Eimhear and all the precious treasures of the Fae. And should the spirit of the sorceress be released, only the Guardian, Protector and Ruler can destroy her. So it is written. So it shall be.*"

"No!" she shrieked.

Her face had gone pale as she shoved her staff toward Deaglan, the orb a brilliant white light. Caleb lowered his body and charged, head-butting her in the midsection. She cried out and dropped the staff. It clattered to the ground. He spun to pick up the staff to keep it away from her. Her shriek caught Liam's attention who took offense to Caleb's attack. He threw out his hand and a bright pulse of magic released from his palm. It hit Caleb, making him fly backward, landing on the ground with a thud as he skidded to a halt at Deaglan's feet. So shocked by the sudden burst of magic from Liam, Eimhear froze in place, gaping at him.

"Get up. Get up!" Deaglan wrapped a hand around the man's upper arm and pulled him to his feet. "Brigid, get that staff."

On his order, Brigid was spurred into action. She dove for the staff, landed next to it and almost had her hand on it when Eimhear shrieked again and lunged for it at the same time. They both grabbed it and a tug-of-war ensued.

"He's going to use magic again," Deaglan said. "Stop him!"

Caleb pulled the knife from his belt as Liam charged toward the two women. He moved to intercept and slashed, flaying open Liam's cheek. Defenseless, he stepped backward as Brigid jerked the staff from Eimhear and rolled to her feet in one fluid impressive movement.

"Give it to me!" Eimhear held her hand out in desperation.

Deaglan snatched it away from Brigid. "Dangerous magic, that."

"Give it back!" Eimhear's hysteria was evident as she charged toward Deaglan.

The wizard lifted his hand and placed a protection spell around him, Brigid and Caleb. "Apologies, dearie, but I cannot allow you to have it again."

"Give it! Give it to me!" She sounded choked as she fell to her knees. The white in her pupils faded and turned back to a crystalline blue and something about the look on her face said she—Sunnie—was finally lucid.

"Sunnie. It's Sunnie. Let me out. I have to get to her," Caleb said. "Sunnie!"

"Caleb?" It was a moment of clarity as she met his gaze, her face a map of perplexity. "What…happened?"

Liam held his hand against his cheek, blood seeping through his fingers as he stared down Deaglan. "This isn't over yet."

She blinked up at him. "Daddy?"

"It's over," Deaglan said with an air of finality.

With a wave of his hand, he whisked the three of them from the destroyed village to the base of the Cliffs of Mhothair. Caleb released a strangled noise of frustration, clutching his midsection.

"Take me back, Deaglan. Now. I have to get back to Sunnie," Caleb said as soon as they came to a halt.

Brigid leaned down, her hands on her knees looking a little green around the edges. Sifting wasn't for everyone and it seemed to be particularly hard on her.

"Where are we?" she croaked.

"The Cliffs of Mhothair, home of the Towers of Illyria. You may wish to return, of course, but I cannot allow Eimhear to have the staff again."

"I can't sift, damn you. Take me back!" Caleb said.

"No," Deaglan said, his voice firm. "The staff will remain with me for safekeeping just as I have the Time Sphere for safekeeping. The magic inside it is too dangerous."

"Time Sphere?" Caleb asked. "You took it from the Ivory Wood?"

"No, laddie," he said with a chuckle. "I have it here in the towers."

Caleb started to object but Brigid interrupted.

"I can sift," Brigid said, her voice timid.

"You, dearie?" Deaglan clucked his tongue and shook his head. "She'll destroy you. She is far more powerful than you and so is the man called Liam."

"She won't," Caleb insisted. "Sunnie won't hurt her."

"You released the magic inside him, didn't you?" Brigid asked. "He didn't know he had magic until then."

Deaglan pressed his lips together. It would be impossible to keep the truth from the *sidhe*. Brigid understood all magic.

"Never mind Liam. He doesn't matter. Brigid, can you sift both of us?" Caleb turned to her, grasping her by the shoulders.

"I—"

"No." Deaglan cut off her response. "'Tis too dangerous. If you know what's good for you, you'll come with me to the towers."

Caleb paced as he raked a hand through his hair, the frustration emanating off him in waves. "But Sunnie…"

"She's a lost cause, laddie."

"But I *saw* her. She was there. Not Eimhear."

"Merely a moment of lucidity. The spirit of Eimhear will take over Sunnie again and she will be unable to control her or push her out."

"You don't know that." Caleb halted in front of him, his eyes wild and sparked with anger. "You *can't* know that. She doesn't have the staff."

"I can and I do. I'm the one who put her there. She doesn't need the staff any longer."

"Why in the staff?" Brigid asked.

"Because Cadryn, the fool, would not be parted from her. He would not allow me to destroy her as I should have. I tied her spirit to the staff and bade him and his future generations to guard it until the end of all time," Deaglan said.

That day was still vivid in Deaglan's mind. As though it had only happened yesterday. But no, it had happened long, long ago when he was a young and imprudent wizard.

"What happened to Cadryn?" she asked.

"He died. Childless."

"And the staff?" Caleb wanted to know.

"Stolen soon after his death. I searched for it but never found it. Until today." He glanced at the staff in his hand, the orb now unlit and quiet. "Are you coming with me or not?"

Caleb started to reply when Brigid placed a hand on his arm. "I think we should go with him. If the girl is truly lost, there is no way to help her anyway. Deaglan said so himself."

Caleb's jaw locked in a stubborn line.

"Aye, 'tis true. I can't help her. Only one person can."

"Who?" he demanded.

"Aoife."

When Deaglan had written the prophecy so long ago, he had intended Eimhear never be released from her imprisonment and if she had, by some strange incident, then there was only one person truly capable of destroying her. He had no idea that person would be Aoife, his own granddaughter. By a strange twist of fate, she had both wizard and Fae blood and would be the ultimate ruler of Illyria.

The long, cold silence stretched between them as Caleb stared at him. "If we go with you, will I be able to find Aoife?"

"Mayhap."

Caleb took Brigid by the hand. "Then take us with you."

"As you wish."

Before Caleb could change his mind, Deaglan sifted into the Towers of Illyria. He was home.

Liam watched Deaglan sift away, taking Caleb and Brigid with him. And the staff. A shriek of frustration came from Eimhear. He glanced at her as she fell to her knees and ripped her hands through her long hair. And then calm passed over her face as she regained her composure.

A moment ago, he thought he could see remnants of Sunnie but she was gone again and Eimhear was back in her place. Her eyes remained blue instead of silver like before. He wondered if the changing of her eye color was a side effect of the staff. He thought it must be.

"We will get it back." Liam held a hand down to her. He kept the other pressed against his bleeding cheek.

She grasped his hand and came to her feet. "Aye, we will. I will not be able to sustain the magic inside me for long without it."

"Why is that?"

"The magic from the staff is as much a part of this host body as my spirit, but it weakens without the staff."

"Sunnie—"

"No longer matters." Eimhear waved her hand as though waving away a gnat. "Only a vestige of her former self remains."

A pang of sorrow went through Liam regarding the loss of his only daughter. But it was quickly replaced by the dark coldness pressing into him and an urgency to follow where Deaglan had taken Caleb and Brigid.

"We must find the others," he said.

"Do you know how?" she asked. "Your magic is wild. Unstable. You know not how to use it."

Frustration flickered through Liam. "There has to be a way to follow them. You are a powerful sorceress, are you not?"

She stiffened. "I am."

"Then find a way to get us to the same place."

Annoyance flashed over her features before she got it under control. She closed her eyes and inhaled deeply.

"There is a metallic tang in the air. Remnants of wizard magic." Eimhear's eyes opened and focused on him. "He sifted. I could follow it."

"Then take us. There is still a chance they can lead us to the Time Sphere. And once we have that then we no longer need them. They are nothing to us."

Liam was certain something had changed deep inside him. Something besides his outward appearance. A surge went through him when the spell broke. But he could not control the wild magic boiling inside him even when he attacked Deaglan.

A glimmer of a smile played upon her lips. "And then we use the Time Sphere however we wish. We can both have what we want. We can go to any time. We can rule any realm as father and...daughter."

Was Eimhear starting to think of him as her father? A strange sensation went over him. Perhaps there was a small part of Sunnie still buried inside her. He regarded her and realized how advantageous a potential partnership could be between the two of them.

"If that is what you wish."

"It is." She held out her hand to him. "Come, Father, and let us find those who would do us harm and destroy them…and their realm."

She sifted them from the destroyed and deserted village in a flash of light. It was unlike anything he had ever experienced as they tumbled through space and landed at the base of the cliffs soaring upward into the sky. High above them two towers poked through the stratosphere, reaching for the stars. No one else was about.

"Where did they go?" he asked.

She closed her eyes and reached out again with her senses. When she looked at him, she pointed upward. "They went there."

Liam craned his neck to look up and see the towers. "Where is this place?"

"I know not. I am not familiar with it. But there is a source of eminent power there."

"Is it your staff?"

"Nay. This is something different."

"Then we must follow."

A sense of calm went over Liam as he realized how close they were to their ultimate destination. Before they could sift into the Towers, another time shift ripped through them. Liam stumbled to Eimhear and gripped her arm, trying to stay on his feet. It was useless, though. He went down, taking her with him.

Before they could recover, the time rift swept through them with a wicked violence. Everything went black as he was knocked unconscious at the foot of the cliffs.

Chapter 13

Caleb woke with a raging headache. At first disoriented, it took several moments for him to remember where he was and what had happened. He recalled sifting to the towers' library with Deaglan and Brigid before the time rift.

A female groan next to him alerted him to Brigid's presence. She was curled into a tight ball on the floor. Deaglan, too, was nearby and coming awake with a shake of his head.

"Another time rift?" Caleb asked.

"It would seem so," Deaglan said.

"Why does this keep happening?" Brigid asked with a groan.

"We must find the answer. For whatever is happening cannot be good for the realm," Deaglan said.

The wizard climbed to his feet, still holding the Staff of Eimhear in one hand and his walking staff in the other. He hobbled through the bookshelves of the library at as brisk a pace as he could. Caleb helped Brigid to her feet and they followed. The old wizard dragged a finger along the spines of the dusty books until he finally halted on one and pulled it from the shelf. The cover crackled when he opened it to pages yellowed with age.

"This should help answer some of those questions," he said.

"What is that book?"

"*Hidden Dimensions and Fae Time Travel.*" He licked his finger to turn page after page.

Caleb knew that book. It was the same one Fiona had in her attic. He and Sean had seen it on her dusty desk. Could this be another copy then? He could not understand how things happening in this realm and this time affected things that happened in the present in the human realm. Or even if things happening in Faery affected the human realm at all.

"Ah. Here it is. Come."

Deaglan waved them after him as he hurried deeper into the library past the shelves to the center of the expansive room where a crystal sphere rested atop a circular stone platform. It pulsed a pale golden glow.

"Is that it? The Time Sphere?" Caleb asked.

"Aye," Deaglan said with a nod. "A dangerous artifact, that. I should never have brought it here but I thought it would be safe. I could guard it closely with my own magic."

"This is what Fiona used to go back in time."

"It appears so." Deaglan pointed to a passage in the book. "*The mythical orb known as the Time Sphere has long been lost to the realm though some say it was hidden by a powerful Fae to keep it out of the hands of those who would abuse its power.*"

"But it's no longer hidden," Brigid pointed out. "You have it."

"Patience, dearie. And, aye, you are correct. I have it. I found it hidden deep within the caverns of the Azure Mountains. Shall I continue?" he asked, nodding toward the book.

"Please do," Caleb said.

"*It is known that anyone who uses the Time Sphere will not feel the effects of the alterations in time. However, those left behind in the realm will most certainly feel the effects of the changes by ripples or rifts. Much like dropping a pebble into still water, the size of the pebble determines the size of the ripples. So, too, do the changes in time. Any changes, even small ones, will cause these ripples. Some will be more violent than others.*" He paused and glanced up at both of them. "That is what we are feeling."

"So, whatever Aoife, Sean and Fiona are doing in the past is causing these…ripples," Caleb said.

"Aye. Saving my life, for instance, altered their future—our present—and that is why we felt such a large rift in time," he said.

"What about Niall? Will he think it strange you are suddenly alive?" Brigid asked.

Deaglan closed the book with a snap and grinned. "I cannot say, dearie. Shall we find out? We are in his castle after all."

He took off through the library, only pausing to replace the book on the shelf. Caleb and Brigid followed him past the shelves to the doors leading out of the library when they pounded open and there stood the king.

Everyone froze. Deaglan and Niall stared at each other a long silent moment. Niall's face drained of color, paling as though he'd seen a ghost and then he recovered almost as quickly. He brushed a hand over his face, his palm bristling against his beard. Caleb could see Deaglan's hand tighten on the staff, his knuckles turning white.

"Father, you gave me a fright. I didn't know you were in here. Where did you find that? I've been looking for it." Niall indicated the Staff of Eimhear.

"This?" Deaglan wiggled it. "I recovered it from the wrong hands."

"So strange. I lost it…" He paused and scrubbed a hand over his face. "No, that cannot be."

Deaglan straightened his shoulders. "*You* lost it?"

"Aye, in the human realm. Though I cannot say how I acquired it in the first place. It simply appeared one day." He peered at his father, his lips pressed together in a thin line. "I have an odd sense. I cannot say why."

"Mayhap you've been in the ale too much." Deaglan laughed it off but it was clear he was uneasy. "At any rate, I have it and will put it behind wards for safekeeping."

The king's gaze landed on the two of them then. "And who are they?" He nodded toward them.

Caleb stepped forward. "My name is Caleb O'Brien, Your Majesty. And this is Brigid. She is a *sidhe*."

"Father, did you bring them here?"

Before Deaglan could answer, Caleb said, "I came looking for Sean O'Connell. We both work for the Inter-dimensional Portal Protection Agency. He may be traveling with a woman named Aoife," Caleb said.

Niall stiffened. "What do you want with my daughter?"

"They were here then?" he asked.

Niall folded his arms over his chest. "Tell me what you want and mayhap I'll share that information with you."

"I want to find Sean, Aoife and her mother, Fiona. Our agency was assigned to keep them both out of Faery," Caleb said.

"And you did not succeed," Niall said and smirked.

"We didn't. We know Fiona wanted to go back in time to change the past," he said. "We know she used the Time Sphere."

Niall glanced from Caleb to Deaglan. His gaze paused on his father as he looked him over, contemplation creased on his face.

"I cannot shake the feeling as though you are not supposed to be here, Father. Like you were…dead."

"*Och*, I'm not dead," Deaglan said with a grin and a chuckle. But he gave Caleb a glance that said he knew otherwise. He cleared his throat and got the subject back on track. "They went back in time, did they?"

"Aye. I sent Sean and Aoife to find Fiona. She intends to kill me in the past."

"I don't think she'll accomplish that," Deaglan said.

"What makes you so sure?" His eyes narrowed at his father.

"You'll have to trust me on that one," he said. "You should remain here until their return."

"How will I know they'll make it back?"

"When the Time Sphere lights up again, you'll know."

"How long will I have to wait?"

Deaglan shrugged. "There is no rushing the Time Sphere, laddie. It will send them back when it's ready. You'll just have to be ready to make sure they make it all the way through."

"I'm staying, too," Caleb said. "I've got nothing to go back to."

Niall clenched his jaw, his face showing signs he was unhappy with their arrival. "Very well then. I will have guest chambers prepared for the two of you. When ready, I'll have one of my servants escort you there. Father, a word?" He waved toward the door.

Deaglan followed him out of the library, the doors closing with a snap behind them. Brigid exhaled a deep breath.

"I somehow think he's not happy we're here," she said.

"I think you're right. But I'm staying. You can return to Ridgeclere if you like."

She shook her head. "No. I've come this far, I may as well stay."

Surprise flickered through him as he looked her over, wondering why she'd want to stay. Surely not because of him. She was short and petite with still that shyness about her and yet there was something endearing about the way she looked at him. He gave a nod.

"If you wish. I need to send a letter to Bryant to tell him what's happening here."

He wandered through the library, past dusty books and the dormant Time Sphere. On the other side of the room, he found a stack of parchment, an inkwell and quill on a table. Brigid followed and took the seat opposite him.

"What do you suppose will happen to the timeline now that Deaglan is alive?" she asked.

Caleb pulled a sheet of parchment in front of him and scratched a note explaining to Bryant that Aoife, Sean and Fiona had all returned to the past. He told him the source of the time rifts and how Deaglan, who was once dead, was now very much alive.

"I don't know," he said. "It's been altered. I am sure there are other alterations we have yet to uncover."

"What about Eimhear and Liam? Shouldn't we alert King Niall to their presence?"

He halted writing, his hand hovering over the paper. He should mention that in his letter to Bryant as well. He dipped the quill in the ink. "I'm not sure. We should ask Deaglan."

They are a dangerous pair; however, Eimhear no longer possesses the staff. Deaglan took it and intends to hide it from her, he wrote.

He finished his note, rolled the parchment and sealed it with wax. "I need to find a messenger to send this to Bryant."

"There's no need for that." She held out her hand. "I can send it."

His brow drew together in question. "You can? How?"

"I am a *sidhe*." She smiled. "My magic is not limited to breaking spells. I can cast them, too."

She held the rolled parchment in the palm of her hand while she waved her other hand over it. It disappeared in a puff of purple smoke.

"There. I sent it to Bryant."

"And he'll get it?"

"Of course he will. He will find another *sidhe* to send a message back, I'm sure."

"How will the message find me?"

"It will find me," she said and got to her feet. "Come on. I'm famished. Let's see if we can find something to eat in this place."

Niall closed the door to the library and motioned for his father to walk with him. He was certain there was something out of sorts about the presence of Deaglan, but he could not discern what that was. When he entered the library and saw him standing there with the two strangers, an odd sensation went over him. He was almost certain he had buried his father on the cliffs long ago. He knew the risks of using the Time Sphere and he suspected sending Sean and Aoife back in time had altered something and his father was now alive.

"Do you trust this Caleb?" Niall asked.

"I cannot say. I know as much as you do," he said. "Do you think he is untrustworthy?"

"There's something about that fellow I don't like though I don't know why. Just a sense. A feeling."

"You have always been good at reading people, my son," Deaglan said.

"Mayhap I'm being overly sensitive. Fiona kept my daughter from me all these long years and I had to send her back to save her own life. I can only hope she, Fiona and Sean return to me unharmed."

"You must trust them to do the right thing, Niall," Deaglan said. "Fiona is powerful but she wouldn't do anything to destroy the life of her own child. Nor would she destroy you. Despite you kidnapping her, she fell in love with you. I watched her feelings develop, so I know of what I speak."

Niall wasn't so sure. He saw the look of determination in her eyes when she held the bow and arrow on him, when she told him they had a daughter. She said it to hurt him, to make sure he would suffer when she ripped it all away. Those words still rang in his head.

We conceived her the night we were married. She looks like you. She has your nose and your chin.

He prayed to the gods they would all come back to him. The silver staff was another enigma. He found it years ago in an ancient wardrobe in the castle. It had appeared—as though conjured—one day shortly after...again that thought his father should be dead. He shook it off and turned back to the staff. Mayhap he shouldn't have used it. Mayhap he shouldn't have tapped into the magic inside it. But he thought it would be an effective weapon when he sent it with his henchmen to recapture Fiona in the human realm. She had defeated them and the silver staff had been left behind for someone else to claim. Like a fool, he had not made haste to retrieve it. A regret he had now.

"I hope you're right, Father."

"I am. You should stay close to the Time Sphere and be present for their return. They'll likely need some magical help to cross the barrier of time. The pain will pass in time."

"They'll be in pain?"

"Travel through the Time Sphere is no easy task and it will be quite hard on them."

Niall was silent for a moment as he considered his father's words. "You believe they will return?" It was difficult to hide the tinge of doubt in his voice.

"I'm certain they will." He granted him a smile. "Now then I best get this put away. Oh, and by the way, I like the beard."

Niall's heart quickened with surprise as he watched his father walk away. He knew he must see to his guests but first, he had one thing to do. He took off through the corridor, his stride sure and purposeful as he left the castle walls behind and headed for the small cemetery on the cliffs. Strangers were buried there—the previous rulers of Illyria including the king and queen he murdered for their crown so long ago when he was a different man. Before he was king. As he made his way past gravestones, he looked at each name engraved there. The final headstone he came to looked new compared to the other weather-worn ones. And there, engraved in stone, was his father's name.

A coldness crept over him as he stared down at it. He knew the man he spoke to only moments ago was his father. He had no doubt since he knew so much of him and Fiona. And since that man *was* his father that meant only one thing.

Fiona had been successful in altering the timeline.

Chapter 14

Caleb and Brigid made their way to the kitchens where they were greeted with a less than friendly stare from the cook, a short stout woman.

"We're guests of the king and his father, Deaglan," Caleb explained when she demanded to know who they were.

"Humph. I was told of no guests arriving today," She folded her meaty arms over her chest and continued to stare them down. "Where is the king?"

"Our arrival was unannounced." Caleb flashed his best winning smile, hoping his charms would work on her but she was having none of it.

"Humph," she said again. "I will find the king and ask him myself."

"There's no need for that." Niall entered the kitchen on silent steps, his catlike grace apparent as he made his way to the cook's side. "They are guests here and welcome to anything in the kitchen."

"As you wish, Your Majesty. But I've nothing prepared at the moment. I'm busy with tonight's feast." She shot them another heated glare, her arms still folded. "They'll have to wait like the rest of you."

"Fair enough. I apologize if they've upset your kitchen order." Niall gave her a smile.

Her response was a snort of derision as she headed back to work. Niall gave them an apologetic glance.

"I'm afraid she's fiercely protective of her kitchen. I keep her here because she makes the best lemon cakes in the realm," he said after she'd gone. "Your chambers are prepared. If you'll follow me." He waved them toward the exit.

Brigid fell in step next to Caleb as they followed the king through the castle to one of the towers that held guest chambers. He halted in the middle of the corridor and pointed to first one, then the other.

"You are here, Caleb. And Brigid is directly across the hall. I hope you find them satisfactory."

"Thank you for allowing us to stay," Caleb said.

"We will feast in the great hall this evening shortly after dusk." He bid them farewell.

As he walked away, a puff of purple smoke appeared in front of Brigid. She gasped and held out her hand. A message scroll dropped into her palm.

"A response from Bryant, no doubt," she said.

"Let's read it in here." He thumbed over his shoulder to the door of his chamber.

She followed him inside and shut the door behind her. She unrolled the scroll, skimming the handwriting. "He's not happy."

Caleb took it from her.

It is all too imperative now that you find those women and return them. Even if that means you have to go back in time to do that. Once you have them in custody, they will be banished for all time to a hidden realm with no chance of escape back to Faery or the human realm. This must be done. They are far too dangerous to remain in Faery.

Caleb wondered why. Bryant had never explained why he believed the women to be dangerous to him or anyone else. His letter continued.

Eimhear may not possess the staff any longer but that doesn't mean she is not a threat. She must be stopped and soon and before any more damage to the realm is sustained. I trust you can handle that.

As far as Deaglan is concerned, I cannot help you with him. I have done what I could for you. Do not make that a wasted effort on my part.

"What does he mean about Deaglan?" She kept her intense gaze on him.

He crumpled the scroll in his fist and tossed it aside. "Nothing."

He didn't want to talk about it to her or anyone. It was his burden to bear and so far Deaglan hadn't realized who he was. But it was only a matter of time, wasn't it? Sooner or later Deaglan would recover his memories as Liam had after his own revival. He would be forced to face his past with the old wizard.

Bryant's words came back to him, haunting him still. *Do you forget where you came from? I made you. And I can unmake you as easily.*

Aye, it was true. Bryant had taken him in when he was but a child. He had given him shelter and food and raised him to be a good soldier. He supposed he could thank Deaglan for that but the old man seemed not to recall him at all.

Seeing the crumpled parchment on the floor unnerved him. He kicked it under the bed in a fit of frustration. "It doesn't matter."

"It does matter," she said. "Mayhap there's something I can do—"

"There is nothing you can do to help me. Nothing." He spun to face her as he bit out the words.

Annoyance pinched her face. She took a step back. "I'm sorry. I merely wanted to help."

He huffed out a breath and raked a hand through his hair as he sank to the edge of the bed.

"I didn't mean to snap at you."

As far as Caleb was concerned, he was nothing but a liar. He'd lied to Sunnie about her true heritage. He'd lied to Sean, too, by never telling him about his past. Bryant forced him to use his dark magic time and time again, turning him into something he didn't want to be. When he was assigned to the human realm, he used it as a second chance to change that side of him. Until Bryant forced him to use dark magic once again to revive Liam.

She perched on the edge of the mattress next to him, her hands curled in her lap. "You want to save Sunnie, don't you?"

Sunnie. Aye he wanted to help her though he couldn't say why. There was something about her that drew him to her. If he hadn't taken her to that creek, then maybe Eimhear would not have possessed her. If only he'd realized what that staff was before she'd touched it, but he'd forsaken that memory.

"Aye, but I don't know how," he said.

A long pause as she chewed on her lower lip. "Mayhap we can find the answer together."

He was all too aware of what she was trying to do. While he appreciated that, he didn't want to see her get hurt. Now that Deaglan was alive and back in the realm, it would only be a matter of time before the old wizard would remember who Caleb was. Then what would happen to him? To Brigid?

"You should return to Ridgeclere. There's nothing left for you to do here," he said.

She scooted closer to him on the bed. "There is something left for me to do here."

When he turned to look at her, their eyes met and he suddenly knew what she wanted. The heat of desire flashed through him. She was young and beautiful and it had been far too long since he'd enjoyed the pleasures of a woman. Back in the human realm, he had the reputation as a playboy. The kind of man that never settled for one woman because he knew his situation was temporary and he could never fall for a human woman.

But Brigid was different. She was Fae. Magic flowed through her veins. She understood how things worked in the Faery realm. She likely thought she understood him. She didn't. She couldn't. He was a man of secrets and lies and he would always despise that part of him.

Beyond that, he had a sort of allegiance to Sunnie. He'd made a solemn vow he would find her and free her from the dark sorceress. He would save her from her hell. He and Sunnie had no understanding between them since their relationship hadn't gone that far, but deep down he knew he didn't want anyone else.

Thinking of that now made him realize why he was such a playboy before. He had been waiting for her.

"Brigid, I—"

"I know. You want Sunnie. I can see that. I'm not her and could never measure up. But she may never come back to who she truly is." She looked away, staring at something across the room though not seeing it. "Magic is a dangerous thing. Especially dark magic like what has possessed Sunnie. It will snuff out any light magic and Sunnie will be all but dead."

He knew. He didn't want to think about that but he knew. Just as he knew the dark magic he'd used to bring Liam back to life still lingered inside him, mingling with his light magic. Turning a bit more of his heart black. They were alike in that, he and Sunnie, though Brigid couldn't see it. He hated Bryant had made him use it but there was nothing to be done about it now. No spell or enchantment could ever erase that.

Caleb reached for Brigid's hand, grasped it in his. She trembled against him. He didn't deserve her. He could never deserve her. He was a coward and weakling even though he gave a stronger outward appearance.

"I know, the gods help me. I know. I blame myself for what's happened to Sunnie. If I had taken her away from that house, I could have protected her. Maybe I could have saved her from touching the staff." Or even kept her from the creek.

"You cannot second guess your actions, Caleb. What happened, happened and there is nothing to change it."

Except the Time Sphere. More dangerous magic.

"It's possible this has been her destiny all along," she added.

Caleb didn't know if he believed in destinies. He once thought he had been destined for something far greater and yet his life had not turned out the way he had hoped.

Brigid turned to him, placing her free hand on his chest. "My life has not turned out as I had hoped, either. Mayhap, then, we can give each other comfort knowing we share that."

It was almost as though she had sensed his thoughts. He had been attracted to Sunnie when they were in the human realm. But maybe Brigid was right. He may never be able to save Sunnie.

Brigid was a *sidhe* with a youthful beautiful face. She understood him. She knew what she was asking. He brushed the back of his hand across her soft cheek, his eyes focused on her thick full lips. He couldn't stop himself from dipping his head and kissing her.

She sighed against his mouth, as though she had waited for that kiss all her life. She pressed against him, pulling closer. He could feel her quiver and the erratic beat of her heart. He had promised Bryant he would protect her. That didn't mean he had to bed her to do it.

He pulled away and stood, putting distance between them. "We can't do this."

She blinked her big eyes at him and swallowed hard, her throat working. Her lips, still damp from his kiss, turned down as disappointment etched her face. When she spoke, her words were thick with emotion. "It's because of Sunnie, isn't it?"

He didn't want to answer because he was afraid of the answer. Stalling, he went to the window, shoved aside the tapestries and gazed at the landscape unable to look at her.

"I know the truth even if you don't. You have feelings for her," she continued.

He did. He knew he did. And yet his only defensive mechanism was to lie. "I'm not so sure about that."

"I am." He heard movement and then footsteps toward the door. "Stop lying to yourself, Caleb, and face the truth. You may not love her yet but you will. My apologies for throwing myself at you."

"You don't—"

He turned to face her, but she had opened the door and disappeared, leaving him alone.

Outside the sun dipped toward the horizon and another day in Faery came to an end. How much time had passed in the human realm since he'd been in the Fae realm? It seemed as though only hours ago when Caleb stepped foot through the portal and arrived at the village in the shadow of the Towers of Illyria chasing Sunnie.

He had come full circle. Back to the towers awaiting the arrival of Sean, Aoife and Fiona. What had they done in the past? What had they changed? How would he explain to Sean about Sunnie's presence? He would leave it to Sean to break the news to Fiona and Aoife.

Caleb tried to sleep but couldn't. All he could think about was Brigid and the way he'd refused her. He'd hurt her, embarrassed her, and he hadn't meant to. He knew she was right in that he had feelings for Sunnie he couldn't acknowledge.

He'd mucked up everything now. She would likely never talk to him again.

By the time Caleb made his way downstairs to the great hall, the feast had ended. All but scraps were left by the previous diners. Brigid was nowhere to be found. Deaglan was not present. The only one sitting in the dark holding a mug of ale was Niall. Caleb couldn't tell if his bleary-eyed expression was because he was drunk or exhausted.

"Nice of you to join us." Niall lifted his mug in a half-hearted salute. "I'm afraid you're too late. Everyone has deserted us."

"I'm not that hungry." He picked up a plate and shoved several slices of roasted meat onto it.

"Have some ale." Niall shoved the wooden pitcher down the table to him. "Gods know I've had enough." He sat back in his chair and thumped his mug against the table, the contents sloshing.

Caleb poured a mug of ale as he sat at the table, spearing a bit of meat. "You have my thanks for allowing us to stay."

Niall peered at him from across the table with hooded eyes full of contempt and suspicion. It caught Caleb off guard and he tried hard not to notice as he forked the meat into his mouth.

"Aye, about that. Where did you come from?"

Ah, so that's the way of it. He understood Niall's suspicion then. He would have to tread carefully with this answer so he would not raise even more suspicions. It would be difficult to tell the king his father had appeared in the middle of the town, alive and well, after one of the time rifts.

"We arrived with Deaglan."

"Bollocks." He leaned forward, his elbows on the table, a hard glint in his eyes. "My father should be dead. I have the grave marker in the cemetery to prove it."

Caleb's hand froze halfway to his mouth. Slowly he lowered the fork as his stomach clenched into a hard, tight knot.

"I know something has changed," Niall continued. "I know there have been strange time rifts. I also know there is a woman in my employ whom I've never seen until a few days ago. Her name is Winnie. She claims to be my beloved's handmaid though I find it difficult to believe." He dipped his forefinger in the ale, pulled it out of the cup and watched the amber liquid slide off back into it. "But he's not dead. I know that now. What I don't know is how and why."

Caleb placed the fork against the table, his appetite gone. "I can't tell you because I don't know. All I know is he appeared and brought us here."

He did not tell him the why or the how of it. Niall could use his powers of deduction to figure that out. Nor did he find it necessary to mention Sunnie and Liam's presence. He had no idea where the father-daughter duo was now, though he supposed he should consult Deaglan about their whereabouts since they were a powerful force.

"When I saw him in the library, it was as though I'd seen a ghost."

So he *had* been shocked to see Deaglan.

Niall ran his finger around the rim of his cup. "It gives me hope, though. Hope they will return alive and well."

"They have to return," Caleb agreed with a nod. "I believe that."

"Good. Then you can break the news to them when they return."

"What news?"

"That they've been gone six human years."

"Six?" Caleb's brows drew together. How could that be? He had only left the human realm days ago, it seemed. He could not say how much time had passed within the realm of Faery since his arrival. Nor could he truly say how much time had passed in the human realm since his departure. It didn't seem possible that six human years had gone by, though.

"Aye, I've been keeping an eye on the human realm. I know it to be true. I believe these time rifts have done something to us here. It's altered our time in a way I cannot explain. And meanwhile time in the human realm sped up. Odd that." Niall pushed up from the table with a fluid grace. "Enjoy your meal."

"That's it? That's all you're going to ask me?" Caleb demanded.

"You have no answers or at least no answers you wish to share with me. But know this, Caleb. I will find the truth before too long. Let us hope I do not find you have lied to me."

Silence descended as he left the great hall. Caleb leaned back in the chair and blew out a breath. He had no doubt King Niall would make good on his threat. He was not someone to be crossed. He hadn't exactly lied to the king, but also had not told him the whole truth. He had not told him Fiona's human realm husband and the daughter they made together had also entered Faery and both possessed a magical ability that rivaled even that of Deaglan's.

Caleb pushed away from the table, his chair scraping against the floor. He made his way out of the great hall. It took him a moment to remember, but he finally found his way to Deaglan's workroom and knocked.

"Come."

Caleb entered. The wizard was at his workbench, his hands busy with a mortar and pestle.

"What troubles you, laddie?"

"What happens when Fiona and the others return?"

His hands stilled for a moment before going back to work. "I cannot say."

"Shouldn't we tell Niall about Liam and Sunnie? And, for that matter, shouldn't we be concerned where they are?"

"They cannot breach the towers. I've warded it against all magic." He straightened then with a grunt, his back stiff. "Why did the *sidhe* leave?"

Caleb's brows drew together. "What do you mean? Brigid left?"

He nodded. "She said she couldn't stay."

Fear trickled through him. It was his fault she'd left. "Did she say where she was going?"

"Sorry, laddie, I didn't question her. She only bid me farewell and thanked me and Niall for our hospitality before she sifted away."

All the breath went out of Caleb. He'd driven her away because he was nothing but a shallow bastard. He hoped she had returned to Ridgeclere where she'd be safe.

"I should go after her."

"She said you'd say that. She wanted me to tell you she would be fine and could find her way home on her own." Deaglan pinpointed him with a sharp look. "What happened between you two?"

He shook his head. "Nothing."

At least, nothing he wanted to tell Deaglan. He'd promised Bryant he would look out for her and he hadn't. If anything happened to her, he had no one to blame but himself.

Chapter 15

Niall made his way back to the library to wait and to watch. It had become something of a habit for him over the last several weeks. He'd been distraught when he sent Aoife and Sean back in time and spent most of his waking hours at the Time Sphere.

He hadn't bothered to shave, either. It had become less and less important over the weeks as he waited for their return. Hoped for their return. The knot of worry deep in his gut grew with each passing day.

As he waited, he'd taken to opening and closing portals to see how time passed in the human realm. A dangerous occupation, to be sure, since he never knew who or what he'd see on the other side. Mostly, though, he would open a portal back at the creek where he found Fiona and the mortal she'd married. And sometimes he would look in on the house they shared.

It was not much more than a ramshackle building with chipped and faded paint on the shutters, missing shingles, neglected hedges. It was clear years had passed there while in Faery it had seemed only weeks.

The Time Sphere was dark and quiet. He pulled up the chaise and lowered onto it, keeping one booted foot on the floor as he leaned back. Niall knew he should not have had so much ale, but it had been one those nights he could not resist the drink. Desperation for the return of his family had turned him to the ale in the hopes it would numb the pain. His eyes drooped and before long he'd dropped into a fitful sleep.

His dreams were erratic. He was at the base of the cliffs with his father. There were four travelers, three women and one man. Fiona was one of them but she was different. Older, it seemed. Not the same woman who had shared his bed. Her face was bruised, as though she'd been beaten.

Who did this to your face? If it was Cian, I'll kill him. And why are you dressed this way?

Deaglan nudged him aside and spoke, his voice calm. *Let her go, son. She's not who you think.*

Are you telling me this Fiona is an imposter?

No, she said. *Not an imposter. I'm not the Fiona of this time you know.*

The Time Sphere. She'd used it. She had gone back to a time when they were happy. When he loved her desperately before she'd left his bed. The others...one was his daughter, one a woman named Winnie and the man called Sean. He did not know these people and yet...he did know them.

I should have stayed. I wish I had stayed, Fiona said. Desperation laced her voice, her hands on his chest as she looked up at him, imploring. *Forgive me.*

When he demanded proof, Sean pulled the coin from his pocket. The one he'd given him from the old empire. The one that was from the future. Before he came and conquered the realm. Before he was king.

But king he was.

You can send us home with the second Time Sphere. Fiona insisted there was one in the Ivory Wood.

But there wasn't a second Time Sphere. If there was, he or his father would know about it. Even so, the group of travelers insisted it was there. He took them only to prove a second Time Sphere did not exist.

He had been right—it didn't exist. But it would because he and his father would create it. And they would send the travelers home.

I do hope you remember all I taught you, my son. The spells we are about to cast are powerful, Deaglan said. He uncorked a vial and jerked the shimmering blue substance with a violent shake. Niall caught it in his white magic.

A pop and then a blinding flash. Magic pulsed through them. Power crackled and sizzled. The ground shook and a second later the spherical object formed on the pedestal in front of them.

Winnie...I'll take her back to the towers with me and we'll find her mum, Niall said, making a promise to the lost, fragile girl. And then to Fiona, *Come back to me.*

Aye, I will. I promise.

And a kiss to seal that promise.

The three travelers grasped hands as he and Deaglan began the spell. The Time Sphere lit with a fierce pulsing. White light poured from it and a fog arose all around them.

Don't let go of each other, his last command.

Deaglan opened the time portal and the two of them pounded the magic through Fiona, Aoife and Sean and then there was a flash of light and they were gone.

A flash of light that pulsed against his closed eyes. Niall woke with a start, bolting to an upright position to light flooding the entire library. His head objected to the sudden movement but the pulsing light had not been a dream. It was real. And the dream had not been a dream. It had been a memory. A memory he did not know he possessed until that moment.

With a gasp, he rushed toward the Time Sphere and collapsed to his knees, watching the whirlwind of magic inside it, pulsing, throbbing, shattering the space-time barrier. And then it did something he had never witnessed before—it hummed. A vibrating sound that vibrated through him. Suddenly he saw the two timelines, as clear as if he were watching two alternate realities. The first, he'd killed his father for his power. The second, he had allowed him to live. And there in the middle of it all were three unconscious bodies—Fiona, Aoife and Sean.

Gods! It had been real. He had been remembering the final moments before sending them back through time.

Come back to me.

He heard the words as clear as if he had spoken them aloud.

"Aye, Fiona. Come back to me. I need you, dearest."

He cupped his hands, magic forming in the palms. He reached for them, stretching his hands toward the Time Sphere to pull them through the time portal when suddenly a zap and a crackle and the smell of burned flesh accosted his nose. The Time Sphere burned the tips of his fingers.

Fiona landed first, smacking her head hard on the floor with a sickening crack. Her head lolled to the side. Her face looked as though someone had bashed it with a battering ram. His stomach twisted into a tight knot. Before he could do anything about that, Aoife arrived, then Sean. All three of them collapsed in a heap on the floor in front of him.

"By the gods!"

He checked Fiona first. She seemed fine, but there was a large lump on her head. He didn't dare move her yet. Next to her, Aoife groaned.

"Aoife? Aoife, can you hear me?"

When her eyes blinked open, he breathed a sigh of relief.

"Thank the gods. Are you all right?"

"Niall?" she rasped. "Where's Sean?"

He knelt next to her and grasped her arm, helping her up. She winced, pressing her fingers to her forehead. Color drained from her face and he could tell she was in pain.

"He's here. He's all right. He hasn't come to yet. Neither has your mother."

Aoife tried to look for them but the pain seemed unbearable. She put her head in her hands with a groan.

"My father assures me the pain will pass."

Her head snapped up. "Deaglan? He's here?"

"Why wouldn't he be?"

Aye, of course. It seemed only natural his father would be there in the towers with him. He understood that now. He understood so much more now than he had when Caleb arrived with the *sidhe*. Before she could respond, Sean came to with a groan. Niall moved to help him.

"Easy, there."

"What happened?"

"You all returned via the Time Sphere. It was quite a thing to witness, to be sure," Niall said.

"Aoife? Fiona?"

"I'm here." Aoife dragged her body toward Sean as though she were an infant learning to crawl. He reached for her, wrapped her in his arms and hugged her tight.

Niall knew, then, what Sean meant to Aoife. Because Fiona meant that to him. They exchanged a quiet communication before Sean looked up and asked, "Fiona?"

"She's still out cold," Niall said. "I'm afraid to move her. She hit her head fairly hard when she landed. Who beat her?"

"It's a long story but it was Cian's men," Sean said. "What happened to us exactly?"

Niall explained to them how the Time Sphere came alive, describing it in detail and showing them his burned fingers. He did not tell them about the split in the timelines, nor did he bother to tell them of the odd memory-dream.

"You need to see a healer." Sean eyed his injured hands.

"I'll be fine," he said, waving it away as though it were nothing. "Staying here with all of you was more important."

"I'm so tired. I feel as though I've run a marathon and been hit by a Mack truck," Aoife said.

But Niall had no idea what a marathon or a Mack truck was.

"Me, too," Sean agreed.

"Let me get you to a room. You'll want to rest." He helped his daughter to her feet.

Before they could even take a step, the doors to the library banged open. Footsteps hurried through the room, past shelves and then there was Caleb. He stood there with his eyes wide and his hair mussed. The last time Niall had seen him was in the great hall. He couldn't decipher how long he'd been out though it seemed anywhere from a few moments to an eternity had passed.

"I didn't think I'd ever see the likes of you again," Caleb said. His face broke into a wide grin.

"How did you get here? Through the portal in the warehouse?" Sean asked.

"Yes." He glanced at Aoife, then Fiona. Something about that look made Niall want to step in front of him, hide her from his scrutiny. "You found them I see. About time."

"Aoife, this is Caleb. We worked together at the agency."

She shook his hand. "You seem somewhat familiar to me. Do I know you?"

Caleb smiled, shifting from one foot to the other. The movement would have been imperceptible if he hadn't been looking. "I was assigned to your mother, too, so I know all about her and you." He focused his attention back on Sean. "We have much to discuss. You've been gone a long time."

"How long is a long time?" Sean asked, sounding wary.

Niall peered at Caleb who met his gaze with question in his eyes. They'd had the conversation about time passing in the great hall not long ago. He gave a nod to Caleb.

He took a deep breath before he responded. "Six human years."

"Six years? How is that possible?" Aoife's voice was breathy with surprise.

"Mayhap you should sit down and explain it to them, Caleb." Niall waved toward the nearby chairs on the other side of the room. "I will stay with Fiona."

Because he couldn't bear to leave her side. And he didn't want her to be alone when she finally awoke. The three of them moved away, out of earshot, and Niall sat on the floor next to his wife, his queen, his beloved, and waited.

Caleb took a seat near the fire and waited as Sean and Aoife got comfortable, sitting together. They made a pretty couple, the two of them. It was clear to him their relationship had progressed to the next level. Sean had waited with a quiet patience while Aoife grew into a young beautiful woman. He couldn't help but wonder about Sunnie and what might have happened between them if she had not been possessed by Eimhear. He could not deny his own stirrings of feelings when he was with her.

"What happened?" Sean gave him a pointed look, his tone hard and serious.

Caleb decided to start with the truth. "I told you I'd give you forty-eight hours and then I'd follow. You never showed up and I had a feeling something had gone wrong. By the time I made it to Faery and to Niall's towers, it was too late. You had gone back in time to get Fiona. Why did you do something so insane?"

"Because I had to."

He glanced at Aoife as she looked up at him, met his gaze. And he knew, then, without a doubt they were romantically involved even though neither of them would come right out and say it. He didn't need to hear it. He knew by looking at the two of them.

Something about that struck a nerve deep down. All of a sudden all he wanted to do was divide them. If he couldn't be with Sunnie, then why should Sean be with Aoife?

"Bryant still wants the women returned to the human realm," Caleb said. The jealousy that raged through him was uncontrollable and he couldn't stop from saying it.

The girl stiffened as she looked at him, her eyes cold and hard and unforgiving. Unwilling. Unrelenting. Sean gave a quick shake of his head.

"No."

But Caleb was determined, his tone less friendly. "Bryant will want an answer soon and he'll want them back in the human realm."

"I'm not going back." Aoife lifted one thin brow as she looked at him, holding her head up and jutting out her chin in a stubborn move. When Sean and Caleb turned to her, she relented only a little. "It's just that…I don't belong there. Not anymore."

"She's right. She doesn't. She's Fae and a wizard. She belongs in

Faery." He smiled at her, laying a hand over hers, the adoration apparent as he gave her his rapt attention.

"Bryant won't be happy," Caleb said, still trying to drive that wedge. And unsure why he was so bent on doing it.

Anger flashed in her eyes. "I don't give a crap what this Bryant person thinks or wants. He's not in charge of me. I'm the daughter of the king of Illyria. I'm staying."

Caleb lifted his hands in surrender. He wasn't going to win this battle. "We'll talk more later, then. There is more I need to catch you up on, Sean."

"Later. Right now, I have a raging headache." Sean put a hand to his forehead and rubbed.

"Me, too," Aoife said.

"I'll take you to your rooms." Niall rejoined the conversation.

And that was that as they rose and Niall led them out of the library. But Caleb knew the conversation with Sean was far from over. He watched them leave, a sort of desperate jealousy clawing through him. Sean glanced over his shoulder at him as they exited the room, giving him a silent communication to let him know they would talk again.

She startled awake with a jolt, her head pounding at the base of her skull. A cool wind swept across her face, tickling her eyelashes as she blinked her eyes open. Something hard and jagged pressed into her back and that's when she realized she was on the ground. High above her, the soaring towers reached into the sky, the spires piercing through the wispy clouds giving it an ominous look.

Disoriented, it took her several moments to remember where she was, even who she was and for a moment the presence lingering inside her was silent.

My name is Sunnie Burke. I am the daughter of Liam and Fiona Burke. I am not a Halfling.

She recalled then her trip through Faery, grabbing the staff. Holding it and...no, she must not think of that. For the first time since touching that staff there was silence in her head. There wasn't someone or some*thing* trying to snuff her out.

Where was Caleb? The last she'd seen him he was inside the protective bubble the strange old man placed around them. He'd called out to her. He was desperate to get to her. He wanted to help her but something kept him from it. No, some*one* kept him from her. The old man.

For the first time since this whole nightmare began, she was lucid. Eimhear was silent in her head. Sunnie didn't want to poke around too much in the dark recesses of her mind to find her, either. She was merely grateful the sorceress was quiet.

For now.

Sunnie had no doubt she would be back but she had no idea how to keep her out or keep her from taking over again. While she had her own magic, she didn't know how to use it nor did she know how to protect herself from Eimhear's power.

A groan next to her and she turned her head. Her father was crumpled on his side.

But no, that couldn't be right either. He was dead. He was *supposed* to be dead.

She dragged her body toward him. "Daddy?"

He groaned again and moved to sit up, clutching his head in his hands with a moan. "What happened?"

She reached for him and placed her hand on his shoulder. In that one small motion, something inside her broke free. Eimhear surged upward, pushing and clawing her way to the surface. A cry ripped from her lungs as she reared back, rolling away from Liam and pushing the heel of her hand to the side of her head.

NO! I will not let you do this to me again, Sunnie said.

Foolish girl. You cannot think to stop me. I am here to stay.

The girl, Sunnie, tried to keep her out but had no idea how to do that. Eimhear thrust her away and came back to full consciousness again. The pain in her head subsided. She unfolded her long body from the ground. Then she held a hand down to Liam, her father.

Aye, the man was her father. She knew that now. She accepted it. Together they could rule the realm—all realms—as father and daughter. It would be a glorious empire.

"Eimhear?" he queried.

"I am here." She tilted her head back and looked up at the towers. "The others traveled there."

"Can you get us inside?" Liam asked.

Her eyes fluttered closed as she tested the magic. "It is warded. It is wizard magic and too strong for me to break."

"What about the *sidhe*? Could Brigid break it?"

"Mayhap, though she could not break the glamour spell on you."

"No, but if we helped her with our combined magic…maybe we could break the wards and get inside the towers."

True, it *was* wizard magic. Liam's suggestion was a good one. A deep memory surfaced of some lore she read once in a book. Something about combining Fae magic to break through spells and wards from other magic users. Other magic users such as a wizard.

"Clever. Aye, mayhap we could. We must find her."

She used her magic senses to find the little *sidhe*. The girl was not in the towers. She was trekking down the cliffs. "She is here."

"Here?"

"On the cliffs. We can take her. I will sift us to her."

In a flash, they moved across the cliffs and halted a few feet from Brigid. She was startled by their sudden appearance and stumbled before she regained her footing. Her eyes widened as she took a step backward, looking as though she was about to bolt. Liam threw out his hand, halting her with a binding spell.

"You cannot run from us," Eimhear said.

"Let me go," she said.

"You will help break the wards on the tower to get us inside," Eimhear continued as though she hadn't spoken.

"You know I can't do that. It's wizard magic," she said.

"We will combine our powers to break through," Eimhear said. "You will do it or die."

The girl glared at her. "You're going to kill me anyway. Why not go ahead and get it over with?"

Liam's head swiveled in Eimhear's direction. "We can't kill her. She may be useful once we have the Time Sphere."

Eimhear considered as she glanced between the two of them. When they had the Time Sphere, they could do whatever they wanted, go wherever and whenever they wished. But the past no longer interested her. Why go back when she had the world of time at her fingertips? She now looked toward the future. A future she could see in her mind's eye. One she could make with the magic of the Time Sphere and the orb in her staff. Liam was correct in that having a *sidhe* with them would be helpful.

"She *is* useful, Eimhear."

"Very well. You will live if you provide us the help we seek breaking the wards."

Liam released her as Eimhear moved to stand beside her. She glanced up at the towers, lifted her arms toward the sky. If only she had her staff, she would be much more powerful. For now, she would make do with what magic she had within the body she possessed.

Brigid lifted her arms, too, and together they sent a powerful spell breaker toward the towers. The area around the towers lit with a fantastic green-blue light. The magic sizzled, snapped and the protection spell cracked and fizzled and was gone.

A satisfied smile crossed Eimhear's lips. "Now we can sift inside and seek our revenge."

Chapter 16

In the Land of Faery before Time was altered

Things fell into an easy rhythm in the towers. Preparations for a celebratory feast and ball were underway to welcome home the travelers. Niall and Fiona had been reunited. Sean and Aoife were inseparable. Deaglan spent long days and long nights in his workroom keeping to himself. And Caleb? Where did that leave him? Alone, mostly. He'd driven away Brigid like an idiot.

He didn't know where Sunnie was or if she was all right. Where had she and Liam gone? Would they be back? He used the library resources in the towers to find a way to save her. He'd spent a couple of days searching the archives to no avail.

The third morning after the arrival of the time travelers, Caleb broke his fast alone in the great hall. Sean wondered in and took a seat at the long table opposite him, reaching for an oat cake.

"Are you ready to talk?" Caleb asked.

Sean dropped the oat cake on his plate. He reached for a couple slices of bacon. His steely gaze pierced Caleb.

"You want to tell me what crawled up your ass and died?"

So that's how it was to be then. Caleb clutched his cup until his finger muscles ached. He'd give his left nut for a cup of coffee in this world. Alas, no one had perfected roasting coffee beans in this realm. "I don't know what you mean."

"Yes, you do. It's clear you want to send Fiona and Aoife back to the human realm. I want to know why."

"Orders."

"Fuck orders. What's wrong with you, man? You were a dick the other day. I don't appreciate dick. What happened to you?"

Caleb wasn't sure where to begin as he shoved the cup away and leaned forward. "Bryant wants you back in the agency, that's all. And he wants Fiona and Aoife back in the human realm."

"That's not going to happen." Sean broke the oat cake in half, shoved it in his mouth. "And I'm not going back to the agency."

"You're leaving?" Caleb sat a little straighter as he looked at his friend across the table. Sean had a serious glint in his eyes, leaving no room for negotiation.

"Yes," he said.

"Bryant won't let you leave so easily."

"I don't give a shit," he said. "He can get over it. You both can."

"But we have unfinished business," Caleb said.

"Like what? My work as a portal agent is done."

"Like Sunnie being here in Faery." Caleb hadn't intended to blurt it out, nor had he intended to even tell Sean. If anything could keep Sean from leaving the agency that would. He needed Sean's help to find her, get her back. He'd explain the evil sorceress possession thing once they found her.

That stopped Sean cold as he peered at Caleb across the table. "She came through the portal?"

He nodded. "She started asking a lot of questions about Liam's death. She thought Fiona had something to do with it. I tried to keep her from the house but she wouldn't listen. She found the portal in the attic like Aoife did and like Aoife, she went through to Faery."

"How did she activate the portal in the trunk?"

"I don't know. I suspect Fiona tried to seal it with blood magic but the two of them were able to go through because they all share the same blood. I tracked Sunnie through Illyria but I eventually lost her trail. I don't know where she went."

More lies. They were becoming easier and easier to roll off the tongue. There was only a glimmer of a truth there—he truly didn't know where Sunnie was. He didn't bother to tell Sean that Liam was still alive or that he was the one responsible for bringing him back to life or even bringing him through the portal to Bryant. Sean had no knowledge of his other undercover work with Bryant, nor did he realize Liam was actually a Changeling.

"We should tell Fiona," Sean said.

Caleb's breath hitched as panic trickled through him. "No, we shouldn't. We should tell no one."

"Why?"

Caleb was unsure how to tell Sean Sunnie had been possessed by a dark sorceress. "No one knows she's here."

"Then we have to find her and get her back."

"That's why I need your help. Why you can't leave the agency. Once we have Sunnie back in custody, I'm sure Bryant will grant you a leave of absence."

Sean did not look pleased with that suggestion but he merely nodded. He shoved back from the table, his chair scraping along the floor. "We'll talk more, I'm sure."

As he started to walk away, Caleb called out to him. Sean halted, waited for him to speak.

Caleb made a snap decision. He didn't want to stick around for the celebration. He had to leave, to find Brigid and make sure she was all right, and he'd get her back to Ridgeclere. He'd make amends with her and maybe she'd let him escort her home. With her safe, he could concentrate on Sunnie and getting her back.

"I should return to the human realm. Seal that portal in the house to make sure no one else wanders through it."

"You do that." The razor words slashed through Caleb.

Caleb made no other gesture or comment to try to stop him from leaving. Sean simply turned and walked away.

He didn't know how long he sat there listening to the silence. The last thing Caleb wanted to do was make Sean an enemy but it appeared he had done just that. He should have never pressed to have Aoife and Fiona returned to the human realm, but he thought getting them back there was the safest thing to do since Liam and a rogue Sunnie were in Faery.

The bustle of activity started shortly after Sean left and Caleb knew he was no longer welcome in the great hall. They were preparing for the feast and ball later that night and it was clear he was in the way.

He left the great hall and halted, giving the castle one last look. He didn't know if he would ever return to this place again or see his friend again. He should have told Sean the truth. All of it. But it was too late now. And likely Sean would discover soon enough Liam was alive.

Unable to sift, he headed toward the stables to take one of the horses to make his way down the cliffs and away from Illyria. Halfway there, pain split the back of his head and he sprawled on the floor. For a moment, he was certain he saw stars. He blinked, trying to refocus and make the pain go away.

"Bring him. He may be of some use."

He recognized Eimhear's voice. He tried to turn his head, but it hurt too much. Someone grabbed him from behind and hauled him to his feet. He knew it had to be Liam.

"Bind his hands," she ordered.

"Is that necessary?" Caleb asked.

"It is." She moved to stand in front of him, looking him up and down. "I sense something of great power here. Is it the Time Sphere?"

"What Time Sphere?"

She gave a nod to Liam who still stood behind him. He smacked Caleb once again in the back of the head. Caleb's head exploded in second shower of pain.

"Do not lie to me. Is it here?"

"Yes," he groaned. "In the library."

"Someone's coming," Liam warned.

Liam shoved Caleb and they hurried out of the corridor. It was then Caleb realized Brigid was with them, bound and gagged. He could not help but take responsibility for her capture. It was his fault she left in the first place. She gave him a heated look before it softened and she realized he may be her only ally.

They ducked into a nearby chamber. Liam cracked the door to peer out and watched as Sean and Aoife walked past.

"There's a ball tonight welcoming the return of the princess and the queen," Caleb said. "You'll never get out of here unnoticed."

Liam's head swiveled in his direction. "The princess and the queen? Do you mean Aoife and Fiona?"

Immediately Caleb regretted his words. He pressed his lips together in a thin line and looked away, refusing to answer. Liam backhanded him, the slap jarring Caleb's pounding head. Brigid winced.

"Tell me. Is Fiona here?"

Liam raised his hand again.

"Stop. If I tell you, do you promise not to hurt her?" Caleb asked.

"I make no promises."

"We will destroy them," Eimhear said. "But mayhap we can make them suffer a bit first. Let us find this…Time Sphere. Once we have it in our possession we can alter time as we deem necessary."

"How do you mean?" Liam asked.

"I mean to destroy their realm first. Take away all they know. I mean to conquer it. And them."

The sudden realization of the cruelty Eimhear intended to inflict pounded through Caleb in concert with the pounding of his head. He understood what she meant and it terrified him.

"You mean to destroy Illyria?" he asked.

"Aye..." She lifted a thin pale brow along with the corner of her mouth in an evil half smile. "Their future looks bleaks in my mind's eye."

"You can't—"

Liam hit him again. "We can and we will. Fiona is here, yes?"

Caleb tasted the metallic tang of blood on the tip of his tongue. He glanced at Brigid who had tears pooling in her eyes. He nodded. "Yes, she is."

"Then we take the Time Sphere," Eimhear said.

"But first," Liam said, "I want them to know who has beaten them."

They waited in the shadows until the party was well underway. Caleb, like Brigid, had been bound and gagged. Liam waited until the princess and queen had been announced before he headed toward the great hall. He looked forward to seeing Fiona's face when he confronted her.

"Good luck, Father." She granted him a smile.

Somewhere along the way, Eimhear started calling him Father, though he knew she was not his daughter. She could never be. Could something of Sunnie still be buried there, deep down inside?

Liam gave her cheek a gentle pat. "To our victory."

She nodded agreement.

He glanced at Caleb. "Whatever happens, you two will come with us. We may need you yet." And then he pinpointed Brigid. "And you, of course, will be quite helpful."

Her eyes narrowed, shooting daggers at him but he ignored her.

Liam pushed open the doors to the great hall and sauntered inside with a confident gait. Sitting at the high table was Fiona, Niall, Aoife, Sean and Deaglan. There was no mistaking the look of shock on their faces as he strolled toward them. Fiona rose from her chair with a slow fluid grace, unfolding her body to her full height.

She hadn't changed since he'd last seen her. It seemed so long ago, that day by the creek when he begged her to take him with her wherever she was going. He'd been weak and tormented by the loss of her. He wanted her with him. He couldn't bear to be parted from her.

He had changed so much since that day when he died. He was stronger. He had Fae blood coursing through his veins. He was one of them. He belonged here in this realm.

And he would prove it to them all.

"Well, well. What a surprise to find you all here in Faery." His tone dripped disdain.

"You were dead. I saw the men kill you." Fiona's face drained of color as she stood peering at him from across the room.

Liam was aware of the spectators lining the room, their wide round eyes staring at them all waiting to see what would happen next. He faced two wizards, a powerful Fae female and a woman who was half-Fae, half-wizard. They could quite easily fry him, leaving him for dead right there.

But he suspected they would not dare do that to him in front of their people.

"And I identified the body," Sean added. "When I last saw you, Liam, you were lying on a metal slab in the morgue."

"It's true. I was dead on that slab but something happened to me there. Something brought me back." He wasn't willing to give up the truth of his resurrection yet. He would deal with Bryant and Caleb in his own time.

Aoife, the girl he'd raised from birth, sucked in a sharp breath. She looked older, wiser, and something about her skin emitted a golden radiance that had not been there before. "The Time Sph—"

"No," Niall snapped, the word slicing through the air.

It was true. The Time Sphere *was* here and they had used it to alter the past, to alter their future, perhaps even to alter their present. Niall and Deaglan exchanged a silent communication. Before Liam could reply, Deaglan waved his hand and they were sifted from the party to the library.

Caleb said the Time Sphere was in the library. Now that he was in the same room with it, he could sense the immense power humming through it, from it.

"How did you survive?" Fiona demanded. "There must have been something—"

"I am Fae." Liam straightened, his back stiff as he met her gaze dead on. He was finally proud to acknowledge the truth about his identity. He accepted it and made peace with the idea at last. He had power and he wasn't afraid to use it.

"I don't understand." Fiona sank to a nearby chair, her face pale.

"When I awoke in the morgue, I was surrounded by others who were determined to help me. Eventually I learned the truth. That as a babe I was taken from my Fae home and switched for a human child," Liam said.

"A Changeling," Aoife said on a gasp.

He did not miss the look of horror that passed over Deaglan's face before he managed to mask it. He ignored it and granted Aoife a smile.

"Once I learned the truth, there were so many things I understood that I had not before. Things about you, Fiona, my dear." He took a step toward Fiona but Niall moved in front of him, blocking him. "And things about Aoife."

"Me?" she squeaked.

"There was a distinct difference between you and Sunnie, though I never understood why. Fiona put you both under a glamour spell to hide your true appearance. I know that now though at the time I didn't quite grasp why you both seemed to shimmer," Liam said. "And Sunnie. She's Fae, too, isn't she?"

Fiona swallowed hard. "She is."

"Which means she, too, has magic," Niall said. "We should find her."

"*We* will do no such thing," Liam said. "You'll all stay away from her. She's *my* daughter."

Fiona started to protest when Niall waved her off. "We won't harm her."

"You'll stay away," Liam warned.

He could not tell them the Sunnie they all knew was no longer. She was someone far more powerful and far more dangerous. They may recognize her physical form, but Sunnie's spirit, her very essence, had been shoved down deep and overtaken by Eimhear. They would not understand that.

"How did you get here?" Sean asked, returning to the subject at hand.

Liam granted him a smile as he looked him over. "I followed your old friend Caleb. He showed me how to get into the realm through a portal."

It was a partial truth and one Liam wanted to dangle in front of Sean to make him rethink his friendship with the man.

"Caleb would never do that," Sean said.

"He would because he's one of my best operatives." A lie, he knew. Caleb was, in truth, one of Bryant's best operatives. He decided he could bend the truth to drive a wedge even further between the two men.

"He doesn't work for you. He works for Bryant at the Inter-dimensional Portal Protection Agency," Sean said.

"Everyone works for someone, Sean, and Bryant works for me." At least, he would from that day onward. He would do as Liam said…or he'd die.

"It was you." Fiona's voice wavered when she spoke. "You wanted to keep me out of Faery."

He wanted her kept out of Faery, yes. But not the way she thought. Bryant forced him to work with him to make sure Fiona and Aoife stayed planted in the human realm. He knew Fiona was married to the wizard king.

But it was Bryant who wanted her away from Faery because she was dangerous with her magic. Because she was married to the wizard king. Because she wanted to alter the past. For his response, he borrowed a bit of Bryant's logic.

"I tried my hardest, yes. That is true. I knew you were dangerous and with your wizard husband's help you had the ability to change things. To alter the past. I'd been following you for some time, watching you. I knew you were planning something. I knew you had some way to time travel and I intended to keep you in the human realm for as long as possible."

She pressed her fingertips against her lips. "But you were dead. I don't understand how this is happening."

"Altering the timeline changed more than we thought," Niall muttered.

It was a good guess. Liam resisted the urge to laugh. Liam's life had nothing to do with the alteration of the timeline. But no matter. As long as they thought that, they would not suspect there were other forces at work with him. Forces such as the dark sorceress, Eimhear.

"Yes, and I intend to alter it further."

Liam sifted away to the Time Sphere, drawn to the power. It sat on the pedestal, a pale glow lighting up the orb. He could not resist the power even if he wanted to. He reached for it, expecting it to be heavy when it fact, it was not. It weighed nothing. He wrapped it in his arms and sifted back to Eimhear waiting outside the great hall.

Impatience lined her youthful face. She held the staff. She must have retrieved it while he was dealing with Fiona and the others.

"What kept you?" she demanded.

"There were things that had to be said, Eimhear. You retrieved your staff?"

"The wards the old wizard put on his hiding place were not so strong. Were they, Brigid?" The girl didn't answer as Eimhear glanced at the staff, clearly happy to have it back in her possession. "You have the Time Sphere?"

"Yes." He held it up.

"Now we can have all we ever dreamed, Father…" she whispered.

"How do we use it?"

"Not we. I." Her eyes turned silver as they had once before when the staff first possessed her. "I will use it."

"Do you know how?"

She cut him a heated glance in answer.

"Do you wish revenge on this wizard king?" she asked.

"Aye, I do."

And the others but all that would come in time.

With a faint grin, she gave him a nod. She whispered a chant in a language he did not understand. The orb on the end of the staff lit up. She tipped it toward the Time Sphere, making it pulse with a bright white light like the orb in the dragon claw. A flash exploded around them and suddenly they were no longer inside the towers. They stood in a meadow dusted white. A faint wind blew. The air smelled of evergreen, winterberries and damp snow. The sun broke the horizon, illuminating the gray wintery sky with the first rays of dawn as snowflakes drifted down.

In the distance were the ruins of the Towers of Illyria.

Part Two

Metamorphosis

Chapter 17

In the Land of Faery present after Time was altered

A oife stood with Sean in the ruins of the library. The flash of light had come suddenly, crumbling everything around them in seconds. One moment it was there. The next everything was gone. The roof was partially missing exposing a stormy winter sky overhead. Snowflakes drifted to the cracked floor littered with books, their pages flapping in the bone-chilling wind. She fell against him as he wrapped his arms around her.

"Sean, what happened?" Her breath plumed white.

"Liam must have used the Time Sphere. He altered time."

"How could he alter time and destroy the towers?" She glanced around, clutching her elbows and shivered.

"I don't know. Let's find the others."

He took her hand and led her through the doors that now groaned with a strange squeak as he pushed them open. On the other side, things looked as bleak. Cracked floors and walls. The missing ceiling looked as though something had taken a chunk out of the towers.

Furniture was missing or destroyed. Tapestries were tattered and frayed as though they had been exposed to the elements for ages. There was no sign of anyone. Snow fluttered down from the darkening sky and dotted her shoulders and hair.

"Where did everyone go?" Her teeth chattered from the cold as she huddled closer to him. Her voice echoed in the silence.

He shook his head as he glanced around. "It's as though the place has been deserted for years."

"It's so dark and creepy in here. I never thought I would feel that way about this place."

They continued down the corridor leading into the great hall. Sean released her hand. He fumbled in the darkness until he found a torch. He pulled it from the bracket with a yank. It was covered in cobwebs.

"Do you have matches?" she asked.

"No, but you have magic. You can light it." He held it out to her.

She shook her head. "I don't know how."

"Yes, you do. Like your mother taught you. Reach for the magic."

Aoife concentrated on everything her mother taught her about reaching down for the silvery thread of magic deep inside her. She grasped it as she closed her eyes, the warmth cascading through her. She imagined a ball of fire in the palm of her hand.

"That's it," Sean encouraged.

She opened her eyes and saw the glow of a small flame in her palm. She lifted her hand and lit the torch. It blazed bright for a moment and then settled into a flickering flame.

"Good work."

Inside the great hall there was no sign of anyone, not even the feast they'd only had moments ago. The table in which they sat was tipped over on its side and broken chairs were scattered about giving it the look and feel as though it'd been long deserted.

"Did we go into the future or the past?" she asked.

"It's hard to tell. It seems as though we've leapt forward in time, though I don't know how that's possible."

"We don't know how he used the Time Sphere," she said.

A whimper in the darkness caught their attention. They exchanged a glance.

"There's someone here," Aoife whispered.

Sean crept closer to a form huddled on the ground. The flame from the torch flickered over a body. Aoife's stomach cramped with fear. She gasped when recognition hit her. She pressed a shaking hand against her abdomen.

"It's my mother."

Aoife knelt by Fiona's side and gently rolled her over. There was a large gash on her mother's head. Fiona groaned as she wrapped a hand around her upper arm to help her up.

"Mother, it's me."

"Aoife?" Fiona blinked, focus coming back into her face as she gazed up at Aoife. She squinted and then glanced over at Sean. "Sean. Thank the gods the two of you are all right. Where's Niall?"

"I don't know."

Sean handed Aoife the torch and then helped Fiona to her feet.

Her gown was covered in dust and debris. Aoife brushed it away.

"What happened?" she asked.

"I need to sit," Fiona said.

Aoife hurried to one of the tipped-over chairs and righted it as Sean led her to it. Fiona lowered to the chair and exhaled, her heated breath pluming white as she shivered.

"It's so cold."

"She needs water and something to stop the bleeding," he said.

Aoife reached under her skirt and ripped a portion of her petticoat into a long strip. She held it to her mother's head against the oozing blood. "We'll have to find some cloaks or something. We can't survive much longer in this cold."

"Are we still in the towers? It seems as though it's a different place," Fiona said.

"It's been destroyed," Aoife said.

"Tell us what happened, Fiona," he prompted.

"I'm not sure. Deaglan, Niall and I left the library and suddenly there was a flash of light and the towers crumbled around us." She blinked again and looked up at him. "It was almost as though we could feel time bending around us. I've never experienced anything like it before, even when we traveled through the Time Sphere."

"You three were separated?" he asked.

She nodded. "Are either of you hurt?"

"We're fine," Aoife said. "But I'm worried about you. Your head..."

"I'll be all right. It's just a scratch." She pushed Aoife's hand away and pressed the makeshift bandage against her wound. "I lost Deaglan and Niall. I'm not even sure how I ended up in the great hall. How did you manage to stay together?"

"I don't know," Sean said. "We haven't found anyone else."

Fiona's face paled a little. "No one?"

He shook his head. "No, but we haven't been through the towers. There could be others."

Aoife's teeth rattled in a violent chatter. "We need warmer clothes."

"You two stay here. I'll see what I can find in one of the private chambers," he said.

"Under the circumstances, Sean, I think we should stick together," Fiona said. "I'm well enough to walk. It's just my head that took a nasty bump."

"All right, then. Let's see what we can find."

Sean led them back into the corridor to head to the tower housing the private chambers when they heard it. A distinctive *whump whump*. They all halted and glanced upward at the gray sky as a dark shadow passed over it. Fiona's hand flew to her throat and her eyes widened.

"What is it?" Aoife peered at the creature winging its way across the sky. Whatever it was, it was large with a wide wingspan but it was far too high for her to make out anything other than that.

Her mother reached for her and gripped her hand hard. "It's a dragon. Where in the gods are we?"

Chapter 18

It had been nearly a fortnight since Siobhan and Cian rode out from Lambridge Castle in the pre-dawn hours. He had not quite recovered from his ordeal but he was insistent upon finding this wizard who had robbed him of his true identity.

And so was Siobhan. They headed toward the Towers of Illyria, crossing the border from one kingdom to the next. Cian knew his way, of course, because he had gone after Lady Fiona when she was kidnapped by the man he thought was his half-brother. He rode in brooding silence next to her. He hadn't spoken to her much since she executed the midwife for her deceit. Even the High Bishop had been appalled at her harsh punishment, though she didn't tell him what the true reason was for her death.

"Your Majesty, I do not understand why she has to die. She is an old woman and she has served this family for generations. What wrong could she have possibly done?" he asked.

"I know you do not understand, Your Grace, but she destroyed me and my family."

He paused, looking at her with his beady eyes peering out of his pasty white face. "I cannot let you do this to her."

"You will not stand in my way or I will have you arrested."

His face drained of even more color if that were possible. "You go too far, Your Majesty."

"I do not. I am the only one who understands the full calamity of the situation. The midwife will be executed and that is final."

"I can have you removed from power," he threatened.

Siobhan had been prepared for his defiance. She signaled her guards, the only ones she trusted. "You cannot. Not with the return of the prince. He is the rightful ruler now and I'm queen regent until he has recovered. I'm tired of your controlling ways." She paused then added in her most condescending tone and a stiff bow, "Your Grace."

With a wave of her hand, the guards took him away. He did not go quietly though.

"You will regret this, Your Majesty."

Mayhap she would but for the moment, she was glad to know the man was in the dungeon rotting away. She didn't care if he ever got out. She terminated the sobbing midwife the following day.

She and Cian departed for Illyria shortly after that. He had yet to speak a full sentence to her. She sighed.

They crested a ridge. In the distance, they could see the Towers of Illyria stretching into the late evening sky. A damp wind picked up and blew through them, tangling her long hair in front of her face.

"Mayhap we should camp here for the night before the sun sets," she suggested.

"As you wish." He pulled the horse to a stop and dismounted.

He had also not addressed her as anything since they discovered the truth about him. He refused to call her mother. Again, she sighed as she halted and dismounted. He set about gathering wood for the fire while she got out their provisions. They had enough to make it at least another week. Hopefully they'd be at the towers by then.

Cian returned, dumping the firewood on the ground. As he arranged it, she got out the bread and cheese and a flask of wine. There were oat cakes still, but that was for morning.

Siobhan settled on the ground slicing the cheese and bread as he made a small pyramid with the wood. He used the flint and lit the dry kindling. It took several moments for the fire to catch, but at last it was a nice warm blaze.

"You have to speak to me sometime." She handed him the cheese and bread.

"When there is something to say to you, I'll say it."

"Cian—"

"No, don't. What you did was unforgiveable."

"She betrayed me and your father."

"You are not my mother and he was not my father."

Her hand stilled, still holding the knife over the bread. "There you are mistaken. We raised you as our son, as the heir. We raised you to rule the kingdom of Anatolia."

"A lie." His voice was flat.

"It is not a lie," she said. "It is the truth. It is what the whole kingdom knows as the truth."

"I am not royal blood," he said. "And you know that. I will never rule Anatolia."

"You will," she insisted. "I plan to see to it."

He refused to say anymore as he reached for his own flask of wine and took a deep drink. His thoughtful gaze never left her. "Do you think things would have been different had I married Fiona?"

Siobhan stared at him, stunned by the question. "I don't doubt it. But you didn't want her."

"She didn't want me, either. She wanted Niall. She stayed with him when she had the chance to return with me."

Her brow furrowed. Siobhan had never been privy to this information. Cian had refused to tell her anything when he returned. "What do you mean by that?"

"When I went to fetch her and bring her back to Anatolia, my men and I camped at the foot of the cliffs. It was snowing then." His eyes took on a faraway look as he remembered. "We were planning our attack. I intended to invade but the cliffs were too treacherous to climb in the snow. The ground was too slick with ice. But then she came to me." He paused, took another drink.

"When did she come to you?"

"In our encampment. She said she managed to escape the towers but she didn't tell me how. I didn't ask. She told me Niall intended to kill me and take over Anatolia."

Siobhan remembered the attack on their kingdom but that was after Cian had returned from his trek to Illyria without Lady Fiona.

"Fiona…she told me she didn't want to marry me. She wanted to break the betrothal. She told me…" He paused again, swallowed hard. "She knew about the other women."

Siobhan stared at him across the fire, the orange-yellow light flickering over his face. She had known about the other women in his life, too. She had done nothing to stop him from his dalliances. She insisted he be discrete. Looking back, she should have squelched his carnal desires and insisted he be true to Lady Fiona.

She knew, too, about his certain perversions. The way he treated women and yet she looked away. She allowed it to continue. He was a cruel prince and probably not fit to rule Anatolia but he was still the boy she raised and despite knowing the truth, she still considered him her son. He was all she had left. Aye, discovering the truth he was truly not her son gave her some semblance of comfort to know she had not been solely responsible for the monster he had become. His return after losing him all those long years gave her hope at a second chance. Mayhap if they found the wizard king, they would find Deaglan.

He took a long drink and glanced back at her. "It enraged me. I wasn't going to let her go. I...I did things I'm not proud of, Mother."

Regret tinged his voice as a pained expression crossed his face. His disappearance and ordeal made him a different man. If he had regret for those horrible things he did, then he changed. Hope bloomed in her breast. Hope they would truly have a second chance to right the wrongs and rule Anatolia in peace.

And he had called her mother. She blinked the sudden burn of tears in her eyes.

"We have all done things we aren't proud of." She thought of Deaglan, their torrid affair and her illegitimate child, Niall. She couldn't share her jaded past with Cian. "Do you think I'm proud of executing the midwife or arresting the High Bishop? Nay, but they were both things that had to be done."

"You don't understand. I am...I wasn't a nice person to her. That's why she hated me. Why she didn't want to marry me. She had to get as far from me as possible."

"It matters not, Cian. All that matters is finding the truth about who you are and why Deaglan took my true born son from me. And I do intend to find the truth."

She had an inkling what the truth could be. Deaglan resented her for marrying Prince Ardan and taking Niall from him, allowing him to be raised by the king. That hadn't been a permanent situation. When Niall's powers surfaced, she hadn't a clue how to teach him to control it. When Deaglan returned to her for Niall, a part of her hoped he would take them both away. She would give up all she had if he'd asked. He hadn't. He'd taken Niall, spoiled him, and turned him into the feared wizard king.

She had many failings as a wife and a mother. Now that she was faced with the loss of yet another son, she could not bear it. She would not bear it.

"Don't you see? When we find your son where does that leave me? Returning to the human realm? To a place I don't even know or belong?" Cian asked. "Nor do I belong here or on a throne to which I have no right. I belong nowhere. I have nothing."

She understood then why he had brooded so much over the last few weeks. She had not considered how it would affect him other than she wanted the truth and she wanted vengeance. She had let her own selfish thinking get in her way, even though Cian had agreed to come with her to seek out the wizard king.

Things were more complicated than she wanted to admit. Things with Cian and Niall and Deaglan. She didn't know how she would feel if she saw the old wizard again. Would those same feelings be there? Those deep-seated feelings of love and lust and desire? Would she still want him as much as she had when she was but a girl and seduced by his charms into his bed?

She didn't know. And while she was determined to find him and to demand the truth of him, a small part of her wanted to know if she still harbored those feelings.

"You belong here, Cian," she said at last, her voice strong and sure. "No matter what happens. I will not let anyone send you back to the human realm. You are now the ruler of Anatolia, the king and ruler. No one, not even a wizard, can take that away from you."

Despite her certainty, the son she bore was the true prince and heir to the throne whoever he was. Not Cian. Even so, she wasn't going to allow that to change anything. Cian had been raised as a prince and prepared all his life to rule the kingdom. The king was dead. His time had come. He would rule and she would stand by his side as queen regent.

Cian took another swig of wine from the flask and gazed at the fire, his face taking on a faraway look. She couldn't read his expression and feared he was lapsing into another long brooding session.

"When I was gone…" he began and paused. He took another swig, shook his head. "Forget it."

"Tell me, Cian, please," she urged. "I'd like to know."

They had yet to talk about his disappearance. Whenever she tried to broach the subject, he would shake his head and refuse to discuss it. Now he seemed ready to talk.

"I should have been prepared for Niall's attack. I should have known he would retaliate somehow for my own botched attempt to take his towers and for vengeance for what I did to Fiona. But I was caught totally unawares."

Siobhan remembered that morning quite well. She had been removed from her bed by one of the servant girls and ushered through the secret passages to the chapel where she and the other women of the castle were barricaded inside. Despite her pleas for word about Cian, no one could tell her anything. She had feared the worst.

"Do you recall?" he asked.

She nodded. "I do."

"I rode out to battle that morning on my war horse full of arrogance and ego thinking I could beat him. The sky was ablaze with wizard fire. He'd brought his army and they breached the outer defenses with ease while Niall sat astride his own stallion at the back of the field, far enough away from the battle I knew he was a coward." He huffed with a humorless snicker. "I *thought* he was a coward. I was wrong."

A lump rose in Siobhan's throat as her mouth went desert dry. Her hands shook. She clasped them together, placing them in her lap so he wouldn't see, willing him to continue.

"I rode through the death and destruction to meet him. The ground was muddy with blood from horses and men. *My* men. The air had that stench of death and metallic tang of blood mixed with charred skin and the sulfuric pungency of wizard magic. I knew that smell. I'd smelled it most of my childhood when Niall tortured me with his magic."

Oh, gods. She had never expected to hear so much. A pang of sorrow pierced through her. But she remained silent and allowed him to continue. She wanted to hear the truth. She *needed* to hear the truth.

"Yet I rode out to him. His men did not attack me. He must have given them orders not to for he knew I would confront him. He *wanted* me to confront him." He took another quaff of wine. "He said, 'I knew you'd come to me.' I laughed at him. *Laughed.* As though he would not harm me. I even said as much. That I didn't believe he would hurt me. 'Oh, how wrong you are, my brother,' he said. And he did some bit of magic I didn't understand.

"The world crumbled around me. The landscape changed to a place I had never seen before and I knew then, still sitting astride my horse in all my armor, he had banished me to a realm from which I could never return. I was stranded. Trapped for all eternity.

"I wandered there trying to stay alive. To avoid the nightmare beasts that walked the land. There was nothing to eat there. Nothing to sustain me. I found water eventually but by then it was too late for my horse. He died and he didn't leave behind much meat. But I had no choice, did I?"

Bile rose to her throat. "Oh, Cian."

"I know he cursed me. Somehow that curse was broken," he continued as though she hadn't spoken. "I found myself roaming the woods beyond Lambridge and I knew I was home. So you see, you are not the only one who wants vengeance. I want my own. I intend to kill Niall for all the wrongs he did to me. He stole my bride. He cursed me. He forever altered my existence."

She didn't know what to say as she sat there, mute. In truth, it wasn't at all Niall who was responsible for altering his existence. That blame fell to Deaglan when he switched her son for him, this human who did not belong in Faery.

The sky brightened with the first rays of morning. They had talked all night.

"Cian—"

She was interrupted by a sudden bright flash in the distance and the rumble of the earth beneath them. They both sprang to their feet. Cian unsheathed his sword, though there didn't seem to be a nearby threat. In the distance, they could see the towers. Large black tendrils of smoke curled upward into the pale morning light from the ruins. The sky had turned a wintery gray as the cold wind whipped through them.

"By the gods." His breath turned white in the sudden cold. "What happened to the towers?"

She shook her head. She could not stop the shiver that went through her. "I've no idea. It's been destroyed but I don't understand how."

"Wizard magic?" he asked.

Again, she shook her head to indicate she didn't know.

Nearby, a groan sounded from the trees. They exchanged a look of surprise and question and then both headed in the direction of the sound. As they pushed through underbrush, they saw a man lying face down on the ground. She hurried over to him, leaving Cian in her wake.

"Mother, don't. It could be dangerous. It could be a trap."

She didn't heed his warning as she called out. "Sir? Are you hurt?"

He groaned in response as he rolled to his back. The grey morning light washed over his face. Siobhan sucked in a sharp breath.

There, on the ground, was her former lover. The man who took away her first born and her second. The man who was a wizard.

Deaglan.

Chapter 19

"What have you done, Eimhear?" Liam asked. The wind turned bitterly cold, sending icy pinpricks through his clothes to his skin. He clutched the Time Sphere in his hands so tight his nail beds turned blue. Next to him Brigid could not control her shivering and lowered her head, huddling closer to Caleb. Both were still bound and gagged.

"Is this not what you wanted?"

His teeth clacked together. "I-I wanted them to suffer, yes, but…"

"But what?" She turned on him, her eyes a stormy blue edged in white. Using the magic of the sphere and the staff had altered her appearance once again. "Are you not satisfied with this outcome?"

He glanced back at the ruins. His thirst for revenge did this, but he didn't want Fiona dead. He wanted her to suffer. He wanted Niall to suffer. He'd stolen their Time Sphere to get back at both of them. Now that it was done, he wasn't so sure he'd made the right decision.

"Do they live?"

"Is that what worries you? That I've killed your precious Fae folk?" She sneered at him. "Have you lost your nerve?"

"I have lost nothing." He glanced at her, seeing her not for the girl he raised but the dark sorceress within.

"I thought you wanted to rule together, to control the realm. Have I not given you that with the altering of time?"

"I never wanted to rule. You did. I wanted them to know I had beaten them at their own game."

"And you have. *We* have."

His jaw clenched, his eyes fixed on the ruins of the towers in the distance. "Where is Fiona and the others?"

She scowled, her brows drawing together as she glared at him. She waved her hand over the Time Sphere still in his arms. An image appeared in the orb showing Aoife, Sean and Fiona gazing up at the sky. He heard the faint squawk before he saw the beast. There, in the distance, the great creature winged its way across the overcast heavens.

"They are unharmed," she said.

But Fiona did not look unharmed. She looked as though she had a gash on her forehead. Aoife wrapped an arm around her mother's shoulders as Sean held a torch and waved them onward through the towers.

"Where did you send us?" Liam asked.

"The future to build our new kingdom. As it should be. There is no need to return to the past," she said. "The past is gone and all those I loved are dead. The future holds more power."

"I thought you wanted to return to the past. To alter your life."

"I did at first," she said with a nod. "Why should I go back and conquer the old world when I can conquer the new? Why not take control of the future while we can?" She reached for the orb, placed a hand on it. Her eyes lit up, turning that haunting shade of white. "The power is immense. Can you not feel it?"

He could feel it humming in his arms and warmth cascading from it.

"With this we have all the time in the realm. Illyria has been destroyed. We can shape the realm however we want. Don't you see that, Father?" She paused, blinking up at him. "You can now claim the throne and call yourself king."

But he never wanted a throne.

"What throne? You destroyed the Towers of Illyria."

And what else did she destroy with that one stroke of magic? Kydonia? Anatolia? How had the time rift affected those in the rest of the realm of Faery?

"Aye, I did. There will be no Protector of the Realm. You will be the Ruler of the Kingdom and only I will be Guardian of the Staff." She clutched it tighter in her grasp, closer to her body and then motioned for him to follow her. "Come. I will show you."

She headed away from the towers through the meadow that dipped into a soft rolling hill. Snow fell in earnest now. Even Eimhear was not immune to the frigid temperatures. She conjured a fur-lined cloak for herself then did the same for him.

"What about Brigid and Caleb?" he asked.

"What about them?"

His cheeks and nose had turned to ice as snow dotted his shoulders so he knew they had to be freezing. "Eimhear, stop. You cannot expect them to survive in this cold without a cloak at least."

She sighed. "Very well." And conjured one for each of them with a wave of the staff.

As they walked down the slope of the hill he could see the castle in the distance. It was smaller than Ridgeclere or Lambridge and made entirely of white stone with two towers on either side of the entrance.

"Your kingdom, Your Majesty," she said with a bow and a flourish.

He stared at the castle.

"The borders of Illyria, Anatolia and Kydonia are no more. This is your land now, Father. All of it."

With a wave of her hand and the magic of the staff, she sifted them inside to the throne room. Liam's stomach clenched as he looked at the silver throne sitting in the middle of the raised platform at the top of several stone steps. Next to the throne, a platform ready-made for the Time Sphere. He placed it gently on it. Giant pillars rose upward to the domed ceiling decorated with frescos in faded, chipped paint. The words of the prophecy Deaglan spoke came rushing back to him.

A wizard of both Fae and Wizard blood will come into power and rule from a silver throne.

He was not of wizard and Fae blood.

Aoife was as the daughter of Niall and Fiona.

Was Aoife the one to rule from the silver throne?

"It is yours for the taking." She waved to the throne.

He moved toward it, his booted feet echoing in the empty throne room. He paused in front of it, reaching for one of the arms and placed his hand against the cool silver. There was a symbol carved in the back of the chair. It looked like Celtic knotwork reminding him of his grandmother whom he had not thought of in years.

Liam ran his fingers over the carvings, tracing the curved lines. Why had he thought of his grandmother now? She wasn't truly his grandmother, was she? All those years she had told him tales of the Fae folk, of magic and a realm unlike any other. She sent him special things from Ireland. She'd sent him the broach of Celtic knotwork with the sword through it that had disappeared. She must have suspected he was not human. She must have suspected he *was* Fae.

He did not belong on a throne. He knew that. He turned to

look at the girl who had once been his daughter but was now someone else.

"I cannot take this throne," he said.

"Why not?"

"Because I am not royalty."

She huffed at that. "One does not need to be royalty to sit a throne. One only needs to be powerful, ruthless, cunning. With me at your side you are all those things. I will help you rule the realm. We will take what we wish, when we wish."

"Then perhaps you should sit on the throne."

She gave a ghost of a smile. "That sort of power does not interest me."

He understood. She was the conqueror while he, the ruler. "And the others? What of them?"

"They matter not. Their lives are expendable."

It didn't seem right. He shook his head. "No, Sun—" He caught himself before he said her name. "Eimhear."

Her gaze darkened. "Mayhap something else will sway you. Follow me. You, too." She nodded to Caleb and Brigid.

She led them through the castle to the dungeons, down a long winding stone staircase also made with alabaster stone. Her cloak billowed out behind her and the orb lit up, casting a blue-white ominous glow as they made their way down the length of cells. She halted at the last cell and stepped back, waiting for the others to catch up.

Liam moved to stand in front of the bars and peered inside. Shackled to the wall was an unconscious Niall. His arms were stretched upward against the wall. His head hung limp between his shoulders.

"What did you do?" he demanded.

"It is a gift," she said, sounding well pleased. "He is shackled with iron so he cannot hurt you. His magic is rendered useless."

Brigid made a choking sound behind her gag as she looked into the cell and saw the king. "He is here for you to do with as you wish, Father."

Liam stepped closer to the bars staring at the king. Eimhear managed to separate him from Fiona and the others. And what of Deaglan? The old wizard had not been a part of the vision in the Time Sphere.

Eimhear brushed past him and waved her hand, opening the

cell next to the king. She shoved Caleb and Brigid inside.

"Welcome to your new home." She slammed the cell door closed and waved her hand again. She sealed them inside with magic. "And don't think to be breaking out. These cells are made of iron."

"You could at least remove the gags and rope." Liam peered inside their cell at the two pitiful captives.

"Why?"

"It is the…humane thing to do."

Disdain creased her features as she heaved a sigh. "You've spent too long among humans, I think. But no matter. I will do as you wish."

She removed their bindings and gags with a spell. Caleb wrapped an arm around her shoulders, pulling her close.

"You plan to leave us here?" Caleb's voice was weak.

"I do." Eimhear nodded. She flicked her cloak behind her and started for the exit.

Liam fell in step behind her. "You can't leave them with no heat, no water, no nothing."

"They have cloaks," she said, unconcerned.

"Eimhear…it's freezing down here."

"Then mayhap we will not have to worry about them much longer."

He snatched her by the arm and spun her to face him. Her face registered surprise, then anger at the way he grabbed her.

"I forbid you to leave them here in these conditions."

"They are no concern of mine nor should they be a concern of *yours*."

"They'll die."

"So be it."

She started for the exit once more but Liam grabbed her arm again and jerked her to a halt. "You will not leave them here to die."

A beat of silence passed between them as her thin brow lifted. "Or what?"

"Or nothing. Give them heat, for pity's sake. And water."

Her jaw clenched and he could see the muscles ticking with her annoyance. She said nothing as the orb on her staff pulsed to a bright white light. Several torches along the wall between the cells lit with a bright golden flame. Across from the prisoners, a large fireplace blazed to life, emitting enough warmth to keep them warm.

"I assume that is sufficient?" she asked.

He glanced back to see Caleb and Brigid standing at the bars looking back at them. Firelight flickered over their ashen faces.

"The flames are magical. They will not go out," she added.

"Very well," Liam said.

"Good. Shall we dine?"

Before he could answer, she headed up the winding staircase. Liam gave the prisoners one more backward glance before falling into step behind her.

Eimhear may have taken over Sunnie's body but she hadn't completely destroyed her essence. At least not yet. The sorceress managed to shove her back into the darkest recesses of her mind, shutting her off from movement and her own magic. She no longer had full control of her own body, for god's sake. But she was still alive. She was still *there*. She could still feel what Eimhear felt, knew what Eimhear knew. Her spirit was not dead.

She could hear her father's footsteps behind her, his footfalls slow and deliberate. Sunnie had looked out of Eimhear's eyes and saw the anxiety on Liam's face when she imprisoned Caleb and Brigid. Sunnie knew she had to put them behind the iron bars to keep their magic in check. She knew the sorceress could not risk having them free inside the castle.

That was when she decided she would find a way to break them out of their prison. Caleb was the only one willing to help her. If she could free him then maybe he could help free her from this hell.

She also knew Eimhear decided Liam was *her* father and that greatly disturbed Sunnie. Her father didn't seem like the same man he was before. Something had changed in him. He was once kind and thoughtful with a slow Texas drawl. Now he was different with sharper edges. Not at all the man who had raised her. She knew he wasn't truly human, that his visage had been hidden behind a powerful glamour. It mourned her to think he would never be her daddy again nor would she be his little girl. Their relationship had been forever altered by that damn staff and Faery.

Eimhear, it seemed, had decided Liam would be the monarch in the new kingdom she wanted to build. She had decided he would sit quietly on the throne and do as she told him while she conquered the lands one by one. Even now she formulated her battle plans as she walked to the great hall and took a seat. She conjured all sorts of roasted meats, cheeses, fruits, bread, wine, ale. Everything imaginable for a grand feast.

When Liam hesitated to sit she glanced up at him. "Does the feast not please you?"

"What is your plan, Eimhear?" He stood opposite her, the long wooden table between them.

"My plan?" She plucked a bunch of red grapes off a nearby platter and placed them in front of her.

"For Niall and the others," he clarified.

"Niall is for you to contend with. The others will serve me when it suits me."

"You can't keep them here."

Annoyance flickered through Eimhear. "They are my prisoners. I can."

"Eimhear..." He paused, raked a hand over his face. Sunnie peeked out through Eimhear's eyes and saw the frustration lining his face. He reached for a chair and pulled it away from the table with a yank. When he sat, he heaved a sigh. "They have done nothing wrong."

Tread lightly, Dad.

Eimhear hissed at her. Sunnie shrank back a little. "You wanted your revenge on the wizard king. I have given you that."

His jaw clenched. When he remained silent, she continued.

"I have also given you a throne and your own kingdom in which to rule."

But you haven't, Sunnie thought. *You've given him nothing but the illusion of that.*

Eimhear gripped the edge of the table, her nails digging into the soft wood. Good. She'd heard Sunnie, then. The sorceress emitted another hiss.

"I didn't ask for that," he said, unaware of her inner battle.

"You are Fae. Embrace it."

She reached for the pitcher and poured a cup of wine. She sipped it, letting the sharp tang of it slide down her throat as she regarded him. Sunnie sensed her questioning her chosen path. Had she made a mistake selecting Liam as the one who would sit the throne while she conquered? Mayhap he was stronger in mind and spirit than she thought. And if he was, then that would pose a problem for her. She needed someone pliable and willing to do her bidding. She did not need someone to question her every move.

Liam would have to die.

Sunnie heard the thought from Eimhear loud and clear. No way would she let this dark sorceress kill her father. She jarred free from her internal prison and banged against her skull. Eimhear faltered, putting a hand to her head and sucking in a sharp breath. She lowered her head as a moan escaped her lips. She stood quickly, her chair scraping against the floor.

"I seem to have developed a headache. I shall retire."

Before Liam could respond, she sifted away from the great hall into one of the bedchambers. It was a large room with an oversized four-poster bed, a wardrobe, and a small sitting area with two chairs and a table beside the large double windows looking onto the meadow. She clutched her staff and hurried to the full-length mirror where she peered at her reflection. Anger lined her face. Her eyes were a haunting shade of ice blue.

"You listen to me, you simpering little fool," she said and Sunnie knew she was talking to her. "One more outburst like that and I will snuff you out of existence forever. Do you understand?"

Go ahead and try. I'm stronger than you think, Eimhear. And I won't let you harm him or the others. I WON'T.

She broke free once. She could do it again.

"As if you have any choice in the matter." The orb in the staff lit up. "My magic is far more powerful than you could ever be."

And Sunnie realized something. Though her essence may have been completely transferred from the staff to Sunnie's body, Eimhear still needed the staff to keep her magic charged. The magic inside Sunnie. Without it, she would be nothing.

If Sunnie could find a way to separate her from that staff, then maybe she could take over her own body once again. She could shove Eimhear out and get back to who she actually was.

Is it, Eimhear? We shall see.

Her expression faltered, changing from rage and hate as surprise flickered across her features. She quickly composed herself. Her brows knit together and her face darkened once again.

"I will kill you."

But you can't, can you? Because you need me alive to continue to draw upon my magic. I know that now.

Her breathing increased as her hands started to shake with her rage. "You don't know anything."

Don't I? As I said…we shall see.

Eimhear let out a shriek of frustration as she spun looking for something to throw, anything. She found a vase, grabbed it and flung it at the mirror. It shattered into a thousand shards, scattering on the floor at her feet.

The mirror may be shattered but I am still in your mind. That's something you cannot break.

For the first time since the ordeal began, Sunnie had hope.

Chapter 20

Caleb paced the length of the cell looking for a weakness. He found nothing. When he tried to touch one of the bars, the iron burned his skin with searing heat. He jerked his hand back, cradling it against his chest.

"It's no use, you know," Brigid said. "She doesn't plan to let us out of here."

He knew the iron rendered magic useless. Still he had to test it by touching the bars. Brigid leaned against the wall huddled within the confines of her cloak.

"What are we going to do?" Her voice was small in the shadowy darkness.

Caleb halted his pacing and glanced down at his burned hand. It didn't hurt but he knew without treatment it would become infected.

"I don't know but we'll think of something," he said.

"She wants us dead, you know."

"She doesn't care if I'm dead." He met her gaze. "You're too valuable to kill."

Her face paled and her shoulders slumped as she hunched forward. "Aye, I suppose you're right. She'll keep me around for as long as she can."

Caleb started to pace again, his boots scuffing along the stone floor as he went from one side of the cell to the other. It was clear Eimhear hadn't remembered him. Maybe she couldn't remember or she simply didn't want to. It seemed she had put the past behind her and was only looking forward to the future. He was unclear of her direction now that she had destroyed Illyria and wondered what happened to Anatolia and Kydonia. Had they suffered the same fate as well? What of Bryant and the agency? Were they gone, too?

Since their forced reunion, Brigid was distant and cold. He couldn't blame her after the way he treated her. He'd been mulling over how to apologize but couldn't think of anything that sounded sincere.

"Would you please stop pacing? You're making me tired watching you go back and forth," she said.

He halted. "What would you have me do?"

She was silent as she looked him over. "I don't know. Talk?"

"What's to talk about?" He started pacing again.

"You could tell me why you were such an asshole."

He paused and this time huffed out a breath. How could he answer? He couldn't tell her that was how he operated in the human realm—refusing to get close to a woman because he knew his situation was not permanent and because he was Fae. He had become a master of one-night stands. When things got too hot with a girl, he'd drop her and move on to the next.

But Brigid didn't deserve to be treated that way. She was a Fae. She understood who he was and where he came from.

"I'm sorry, Brigid. It was wrong of me."

Her eyes widened slightly as she stared at him from across the cell, quiet for a moment as she considered his words. "I accept your apology."

"You do?"

She nodded. "I don't know why but it seems like the right thing to do. I guess because we're stuck here together and I don't want you to hate me."

"I don't hate you. I could never hate you. It's just that…I don't have a good track record with women."

"That sounds like an excuse." Annoyance flashed in her eyes as she slid down the wall to the floor. She drew up her knees and circled her arms around her legs.

How could one so young be so wise? It was almost as though she knew him. He couldn't disagree with her. "You may be right. I have a lot of flaws, Brigid. I'm not perfect."

"No one is, Caleb." She lifted her head and looked up at him again. "Sit here with me. Tell me a story."

"What kind of story?"

"I don't know. Something of your childhood or mayhap even how you ended up at the agency."

"Long story, that." He dropped to the floor next to her.

She leaned her head on his shoulder. "We appear to have plenty of time." There was a smile in her voice.

"Right." He thought back to how he ended up in Bryant's care and then employ. "Are you certain you want to hear it?"

"I am."

"Once upon a time—"

She punched him in the shoulder. "No. Not like that. Tell me the truth."

If she could read his thoughts as he suspected, then she would know he wasn't so keen on telling her the truth. Mayhap the iron, though, suppressed that Fae ability and she couldn't read him now. If that were the case, he had a chance—a real chance—at winning her forgiveness for the way he treated her back in the towers. He took a deep breath, expelled it.

"You first. How did you end up at the agency?"

"All right, fine. If that's how you want to work it, I'll play by your rules. I'm afraid my story is nothing of interest. I joined voluntarily. My parents were against it, of course, but I thought I could make a difference. I could become something more than a farmer's daughter."

"You're from Kydonia?"

"Of course. My parents are still there." She paused as sadness came across her face. "Or were. I've no clue if they still live. I have a sister, too. Her name is Sybill. Her Fae magic far exceeds mine, though."

"They may still be alive. You can't give up hope. Why didn't she join if her magic was more powerful?"

"Bryant wanted her. He came to recruit her but she wasn't interested. She wanted nothing to do with the agency or him and refused. That's when I volunteered. I thought I could make a difference. That I could make something of my life."

Caleb couldn't help but feel responsible for their current predicament. "You will because we are going to get out of here."

"I hope so. All right your turn. How did you end up there?"

He took a deep breath and recalled every detail of that day long ago when he was a boy. The details he had long tried to forget. The ones he shoved back in a box and locked away thinking he would never have to face again. And yet, here he was. He'd never told anyone his story. Not even Sean.

"When I was a child, I lived in a small village in the heart of Kydonia." As he began, his heart sped up and his hands turned to ice. No lies, now. This was nothing but the truth. "Our village was raided and destroyed by an evil sorceress. Everyone was killed. Everyone but me."

She emitted a small gasp as she met his gaze. "That evil sorceress was Eimhear, wasn't it?"

He nodded. "I think she picked Sunnie because she looks much like Eimhear did back then. The resemblance is quite strong."

It was uncanny, actually, how much Sunnie looked like her. It took him awhile to make that connection.

"Does Bryant know this?"

"No one knows this." He paused then added, "Except Deaglan."

"He knows? How?"

"I'm getting to that. When my village was destroyed I was the lone survivor. Eimhear could not kill me. Instead she took me in and decided to train me. The story she was desperate for children is true. She saw me as a way to get what she wanted—a child. That's how I learned dark magic." He cut her a glance. "Bryant does know about that."

"You have...dark magic?"

"Some," he said with a nod. He knew how taboo it was to admit it. Most Fae would never reveal their knowledge of the dark power for fear they would be persecuted. Not all with dark power used it for evil. "You don't have to worry. I don't use it."

"I'm not worried." But there was the hint of an edge to her voice. "Go on."

"Cadryn tracked down Eimhear. He'd found a wizard to help him destroy her. It was Deaglan. Cadryn was still soft for her even after all the evil she'd done. She killed his family, one by one. She destroyed villages. She waged war against other kingdoms wanting more power and more rule. She was almost unstoppable."

"Until Deaglan put her in the staff."

"He put her in the orb," he corrected. "And enchanted the staff. It took Fae and wizard magic to contain her. I was orphaned once again. That's when he took me to Bryant at the agency and left me there, but said nothing to him of Eimhear or the staff. Bryant took me in and made me what I am today."

"I had no idea Bryant was so altruistic."

At that, he snorted. "Hardly. When Bryant discovered my dark power, he saw an opportunity and seized it. I had to become an agent as payment for him taking me in when I was a child."

Anger flickered over her youthful face. It was clear she did not approve. Caleb hadn't either but he didn't have much choice. He had been a child with no one to help guide him, no one to champion him. All he had was Bryant. Despite the things Bryant forced him to do, Caleb had a sense of loyalty to the man. He had saved him from a far worse fate of being a peasant orphan.

"You should tell Liam this story," she said.

He gave a shrug of one shoulder. "What can he do?"

"He's not a mindless follower. I've sensed resistance in him."

"He can't help me or you," Caleb said.

"The *sidhe* is right." The voice from the darkness startled them both.

Caleb got to his feet and squinted in the shadows to see Niall in the adjoining cell. His arms were still shackled, his wrists raw and red and bleeding. His skin held a sickly pallor.

"Your Majesty," Caleb said. "How long have you been listening?"

"Long enough. There *is* resistance in him. He fears her, too."

"How do you know? You've been unconscious," Brigid said.

"Was I?" He mustered a quirk of a smile. "It only appeared so. This man, Liam, is not a leader. Mayhap we can persuade him to help us defeat this sorceress. She took me away from my family and for that she deserves to die."

"How do we defeat her?" Caleb asked.

He held up his hands as if in surrender. "If I had my magic..."

"We don't either," Brigid said. "It's the iron."

"Then we must find another way and we will."

He sounded so sure, Caleb was inclined to believe him. "Then let's think of a plan."

Niall gave a slight nod. "Aye, let's."

Chapter 21

"Who is that?" Cian leaned forward to see around Siobhan to the man on the ground.

"I know him." Her whispered voice came out a rasp.

She dropped to her knees next to Deaglan, her heart in her throat as she placed a shaking hand on his shoulder. The last time she had been this close to him had been so long ago. Even so the memory burned through her mind, so vivid and clear it could have happened yesterday. It had been the last time they were intimate the last time she would see him as her lover. And all the while she knew she would leave him for Arden.

The only other time she'd seen him since was when he'd come to take Niall. She still regretted letting him go. She thought the boy would be better off with his wizard father. Instead he had turned into a tyrant who terrorized and destroyed the rulers of Illyria for his own gain. She had often wondered what would have happened to Niall had she continued to raise him. Would he turn out the same or worse?

He rolled to his back with a groan. His eyes blinked open and focused on her. Her heart skipped a beat. A lump formed in her throat as heat washed over her.

He looked like the same man she fell in love with all those years ago albeit a little older. His brows knit with question as he looked at her, as though he couldn't believe who he saw.

"Siobhan...is it you?" His words came out on a whisper in a plume of breath.

"Who is he?" Cian moved to stand behind her.

"Hello, Deaglan."

"Deaglan? The wizard?" There was an edge of incredulity to his voice.

"Cian, please," she chastised but never took her eyes off Deaglan. "Are you hurt?"

"I don't appear to be." He got to his feet without assistance and brushed debris from his robes. He glanced between her and the prince. "How did I get here?"

"I don't know. There was an odd flash and then you appeared. The towers are…" She paused, cutting a glance at the ruins in the distance.

He spun toward the towers. His face drained of color as he stared across the realm. "Gods, what did you do?" he whispered.

"What did who do?" she asked. "Deaglan, what happened?"

"I'm not sure but I believe time has been altered in some manner."

"What do you mean, time has altered?" Cian stepped next to her, standing close.

"I cannot say." He turned away from the towers, a sadness lining his face. "What are you two doing out here so far from home?"

Cian moved with such lightning speed, he was but a flash of movement. He pressed a dagger against Deaglan's throat. "We came to find you, old man. How fortunate we found you with such ease."

"Cian, don't!"

"What do you want with me? I'm nothing but an old man." The wizard's tone was wary and there was a glint of humor in his eyes, as though he were not afraid. And perhaps he wasn't. He was never afraid of much.

Snow fell harder now, dotting their hair and shoulders and gathering along the ground. The air had turned considerably colder, too. It seemed as though winter arrived quickly and in full force.

"I want you to remove this glamour spell on me."

He pressed his lips into a thin line as he narrowed his eyes. "I don't know what you mean."

Cian pressed the dagger deeper into his skin, drawing a droplet of blood. Siobhan sucked in a sharp breath. "Aye, you do. You are the one who put it on me."

Deaglan's eyes cut to Siobhan, the surprise evident.

"We know," she said. "The midwife you coerced into giving you the child confessed."

A brow lifted as if in defeat. "I see, then." He glanced back at Cian. "Remove the dagger and step away."

"I don't trust you," Cian said.

He chuckled. "I am an old man, laddie. I am far from dangerous. I will use it to do as you wish but cannot as long as you hold a blade to my throat."

"But you have magic."

"Aye, that I do. I won't use it to harm you or your mother."

Cian's hand wavered and then pressed against his throat. "She's not my mother and I don't believe you."

"Believe what you wish, laddie, but that is the truth. Remove the dagger so I can break the spell."

"Do as he says, Cian," Siobhan urged.

He hesitated before he finally removed the dagger and stuck it back in his belt. He took a step back as Deaglan swiped a hand over the small cut on his throat. It was instantly healed. He moved to stand in front of Cian.

"Is it the truth you want?" he asked then.

"We know the truth—"

"Silence, dearie," he said cutting her off. "I want to hear it from his own lips. Tell me, then, prince. Do you wish to know the truth?"

Cian didn't answer for several heartbeats. Finally, he nodded. "I wish to know. Did the midwife tell the truth?"

A small smile that did not reach his eyes broke out on Deaglan's impassive face. "She did."

Siobhan emitted a choking sound and pressed a hand against her mouth to stifle the cry she wanted to release. Though she knew it to be true, the confirmation still sliced pain through her. Somewhere in the human realm was her son.

"The glamour spell is one of my own. I put it on you many years ago when I brought you from the human realm to this one. You were but a babe then." Deaglan placed his hands on either side of Cian's face. "This won't hurt."

A light glowed from beneath his hands as Deaglan closed his eyes to concentrate. A flash of light blotted out the two of them and then dissipated leaving behind Cian's true appearance. Deaglan dropped his hands and stepped back.

While Cian had a similar facial structure as before, he no longer had the pointed Fae ears. They were rounded like a human's. His aura was not as vibrant as that of a Fae. And his eyes were no longer as sharp and assessing as they had once been.

Siobhan's knees weakened as she looked upon the boy she raised into manhood. The one who was supposed to be destined to be the crown prince of Anatolia. The one who would rule the kingdom now that her husband was dead and buried.

He ran his hands over his face, through his hair. "I don't feel any different."

"You won't. You don't have magic. Never have. But your appearance is human now." Deaglan turned to her and moved closer, his gaze traveling over her before meeting hers. "It has been many years, dearie."

She swallowed her tears and regained her composure enough to lift her head and look down her nose at him. "Why? Why did you do it?"

"I thought that would be clear. I never thought to see you again after you left, pregnant with our child. You took him from him."

Anger flashed through her bright and hot. "You took Cian away from me to get back at me for taking Niall away from you."

His response was a nod.

She balled her fists. "How could you?"

"I could ask the same of you, dearie. How could *you* take my boy from me? I never saw him until that day when I came to get him from you because you could not control him."

"His magic was unwieldy. Wild. Out of control. You knew it would come to that and you said *nothing*." She spit the hot words at him. Words she had longed to say to him when he took Niall from her and could not. They had met in secret and only for a brief moment.

"Would you have believed me had I warned you? All I got was a letter from you telling me you left to marry that prince. You didn't have the courage to tell me to my face." He held his hands up palm out as though in surrender. "You were determined to keep Niall at your side no matter what. I did what I did and I'm not proud of that. But it's over now. I should have realized our paths would cross again someday. We are forever entwined."

Burning emotion went through in a rush like a tidal wave. Her decision to spurn Deaglan for the sake of her family name came at a higher price than she knew. He was right in that they were forever entwined. He was the father of her eldest child, after all, and he took away the only child that was completely hers. How she mourned the loss of him and she didn't even know him.

He wrapped his finger around a tendril of her hair. She slapped his hand away as Cian reached for his dagger once again. She waved him off.

"You have no claim on me any longer, Deaglan. I am free of

you." A truth she wanted to believe.

"I don't think so, dearie."

"What does that mean?" Cian's brows drew together in confusion as he looked on, watching the two of them banter.

"Did she not tell you?" the old wizard asked. "She loved me once."

Cian took a step away from them. "Siobhan, you and the wizard …?"

"Niall is my son," Deaglan said. "And hers. Are you just now understanding that?"

She bit her lip to keep the threat of tears away. She couldn't look at Cian as the truth surfaced. She should have known it would have, though. She had been a dimwit to believe she could hide the truth forever. As she looked at him and thought back over all that had happened between them, she knew he was right about their intertwined lives. They had a son together though she had not seen Niall in many years.

"That's why you took him away all those years ago, isn't it?" Cian gave a bark of a laugh. "What a foolish child I was to think my mother…you…were the victim. I never put it together until today."

Deaglan scoffed. "You were glad he was gone. I know. I saw. I watched. Only a coward would deny that truth."

Cian's face turned dark red with anger. "I'm not a coward and I don't deny. I was glad you took him away. You said you weren't dangerous but you destroyed my life. You destroyed my *family's* life in the human realm. And the queen's."

"I destroyed a lot of people's lives when I was a young pompous wizard. I admit that now. But I cannot change the past, not even with magic spells or potions. It is what it is and it is my burden to bear for the rest of my days." He glanced from Cian back to Siobhan. "I regret I hurt you, dearie. Truly. I never wanted that. I only wanted to love you."

"You stole my son." Accusation laced her whispered tone.

"I wanted you to suffer as I suffered without my son. When you married the king and took Niall from me, it nearly destroyed me. That's why I gave the boy everything and why he turned out to be the feared wizard king. I helped him conquer Illyria."

"You made him into that. I've hated him all my life," Cian said. "I hated what he did to me, how he treated me. I hated him for stealing my bride."

Deaglan nodded. "Aye, I know Fiona was meant for you."

It occurred to Siobhan mayhap Deaglan had a hand in Fiona's kidnapping. She wondered if he had planned and helped execute the whole thing.

Cian's face washed of color. He knew, as Siobhan did, what manner of man he was. His jaw clenched, the muscles ticking along his jaw.

"But you are no prize. Prince or not, you don't deserve the throne."

"You will not speak to him like that," Siobhan snapped. "Anatolia knows no other prince."

"Do you intend to put him on the throne anyway? A human? A mistake, that." Deaglan shook his head.

"You have Illyria to rule," she said in her best haughty tone.

"I'm afraid I have nothing to rule." He waved toward the ruins. "I don't know what's happened to my son or Fiona or any of the people of Illyria. For all I know they could be dead and I must find them. Furthermore, how do we know Anatolia is even still standing?"

"Seems rather fitting you've lost everything as we have," Cian said, his words bitter.

Deaglan's eyes narrowed into slits. He lifted his hands. Siobhan sensed he was about to sift away and lunged toward him. She wrapped a hand around his upper arm, digging her fingers into him. Her rage returned. "Where is my true born son?"

He smirked. Snowflakes gathered on his hair in a fine blanket giving him a striking appearance that seemed to age him. "Your son, dearie, is here in Faery."

Chapter 22

A squawk overhead made Aoife glance up into the overcast sky. She shivered but this time not from the cold.

"I swear that thing is getting closer," she said.

"We have to keep searching," Fiona insisted.

"Fiona, there is no one else here," Sean said. "I think that's fairly obvious now."

"No." Lines of determination creased her face. Her lips pressed together in a thin stubborn line. "I have to find Niall."

"He's not here." Sean handed the torch to Aoife. He reached for Fiona, snatched her arm and spun her to face him. He gripped both upper arms and held her still. "He's gone, Fiona. The towers are nothing but ruins and he's not here."

Her chin quivered before she managed to get her emotions under control. "Then…where is he?" Her breath hitched, pluming in front of her.

"I don't know but we'll find him. I promise."

"We have to," she said. "I just got him back. I can't lose him again."

"We'll find him, Mother." Aoife laid a reassuring hand on her arm.

Another squawk followed this time by a response. They all looked skyward and saw not one but two dragons winging their way across the darkening sky. Night was coming—the day shorter than the last.

"I don't like the looks of this," Fiona said. "We should go deeper inside the towers. Mayhap we can find some food and keep warm until daybreak."

Sean nodded, taking the torch back from Aoife. "All right. We'll stop at the kitchens then head to the other tower. Hopefully it's still intact."

"Guys…" Aoife hadn't taken her eyes off the heavens. She counted a third dragon flapping its way across the sky. "I think there are three of them now."

They circled, moving closer to the ruins reminding Aoife of

buzzards circling a fresh kill waiting for the moment to strike. A cry of fear bubbled up into her throat but she bit her bottom lip to keep it contained. Fiona's gaze fixed skyward as well.

"Then we best get out of sight," she said.

They hurried away from the great hall to the kitchens. They found nothing but a deserted room covered in dust. The firebrick ovens had long since turned cold. Not even ash remained. Even the larder was empty. They all looked around in stunned silence. Aoife glanced between her mother and Sean. They had the same expression of disbelief.

"There's no food here," Sean said. "We should keep moving."

"I want to see Niall's chamber." When Sean started to object, Fiona gave a sharp shake of her head. "Do not argue with me, Sean. I want to see for myself if he's there or not."

He took Aoife's hand, squeezed it as he took in a slow breath. She sensed his frustration.

"All right. Then lead the way."

The king's chamber was in the east tower. It seemed to have fared better than the area with the great hall. Most of it was still intact. They made their way up the winding staircase. The only light was that of the torch Sean carried. The ones lining the wall were unlit and covered in cobwebs. Her mother halted at the oversized door and gave it a push with some effort.

Nothing could have prepared them for the ruin inside the chamber. Gossamer curtains at the windows lining the wall had seen better days—they were moth-eaten and tattered. A thick layer of dust covered every piece of furniture. The feather mattress sank in the center. The marble pedestal still hosted the bronze bust except it was now covered in a patina when once it was like a shiny copper penny. The luxurious rugs were frayed and threadbare. The large fireplace looked as though it had not hosted a fire in years.

Fiona stood rigid and still in the semi-darkness. Her muscles bunched into a tight knot along her back. The once warm and inviting room turned cold and dismal. Aoife gave Sean a questioning glance, but his gaze fixed on her mother. She glanced at Fiona, whose shoulders gave an imperceptible shudder so slight Aoife would have missed it had she not been looking.

"He's not here." Fiona pressed fingertips to her lips and shook her head. "Where is he, Sean?"

"I don't know."

"It looks like no one has been here in years," Aoife said.

"We were together one minute and then he was gone. And so was Deaglan." Fiona moved to the windows and pushed aside one of the shabby curtains. Beyond, Aoife could see the hint of the wintery sky and hear the squawk of the dragons. "This was once a glorious place and now it's as though it has been destroyed by time and neglect."

"Mother, I think we should go now." She shifted from one foot to the other.

But Fiona seemed not to hear her as she turned away from the window and stalked across the room to the old wardrobe. As she pulled the door handle, it snapped off in her hand. She flung it to the ground in a fit of anger, then pried open the door. The hinges crumbled and the door clattered to the stone floor.

"Fiona, I think Aoife's right. We should go."

"These are nothing but rags. How can this be?"

"Fiona?" Sean urged.

She spun toward them, her gaze raking over them in what was once their finery. "We cannot go traipsing through the muck in these clothes."

"There aren't any other clothes here," Aoife pointed out and shivered. A cold north wind blew in through the open windows.

Fiona put her hands on her hips and chewed her lower lip, her mind working. "How dimwitted of me. There is no need to look for clothes."

With a wave of her hands and a puff of purple smoke, she altered her clothes from her ball gown to boots, padded pants, a tunic, a padded vest, gloves and a fur-lined hooded cloak. She turned her gaze on Sean.

"Remain still."

She then performed the same spell on him and then Aoife, giving them all traveling clothes, gloves and a warm cloak.

"That will keep us warm enough I should think," Fiona said. "Let's go to Deaglan's workroom. He might have some potions we can use to find Niall and the others."

They headed toward the west tower where Deaglan's workroom was housed. They found it still intact and empty. Sean shoved open the door, the hinges groaning under the pressure. He held the torch up inside the room, lighting it as best he could with the one small blaze.

The desk still stood to one side under the window but it was coated in a fine layer of dust. Cobwebs hung in the corners from the ceiling. The workbench and shelves were also coated in dust and cobwebs.

"Deaglan's workroom, too?" Aoife whispered.

"I don't understand," Fiona said.

"Do you suppose Liam sent us forward in time?" Sean asked.

Fiona shook her head before he finished. "It doesn't make sense. Why would he do that? Why would he alter our future so much? To what end?"

"There has to be some other reason," Sean said. "Something that made him want to go forward in time. But why destroy the towers?"

While they conjectured, Aoife made her way to the large shelves over the workbench. Beneath the dust and dirt, vials filled with an array of colorful liquids and powders lined the shelf. One was of particular interest to her. She blew away the dust and reached for the pink substance.

"Look, Mother. Is it Tears of the Dryad?" she asked.

Fiona took the vial from her, turning it over in her hand and watching as the sparkly substance winked back at her in the half light. From what Aoife recalled, the Tears had a thicker consistency. This looked more like pink sparkles.

"No, though I think it almost is. We need actual Tears to make the potion complete. If we had that, we could use a portal to get to Niall."

"Where do we get Tears?" Sean asked.

"Deaglan told me once. He said he got them from the queen of the dryads in the Woodlands Forest. The home of the Elves."

Aoife could see her mother's mind working as she tried to figure out a way to get to the Woodlands Forest. She looked at her and Aoife knew then she was about to ask her to do some bit of magic.

"You can take us there," Fiona said.

"Mother, no. I don't know how."

"You can sift us."

"Fiona—"

"Quiet, Sean," Fiona snapped. "We need to make a portal to get to Niall and the only way we can do that is if we have tears from the queen of the dryads which means we have to make an official visit to the Elves. My magic has returned but I still cannot sift."

"What about Deaglan?" Aoife asked. "Shouldn't we find him, too?"

She was silent a moment as her gaze turned thoughtful. She gave a quick nod. "We should, aye."

Aoife examined the remaining contents of the shelf. "Maybe there are tears here and we can complete the potion," Aoife suggested. The last thing she wanted to do was attempt a trip to see the Elves. "Let's look around."

"We're not going anywhere tonight." Sean lit several candles with the torch. It gave the room a warmer glow but no less inviting with all the decay.

"Time is of the essence, Sean—"

"No, Fiona. We aren't going to risk our lives with those dragons still out there."

"He's right, Mother. Let's rest here tonight. We will go at first light."

Sean accepted they were staying the night but it was clear Fiona wasn't keen on the idea. He stood at Deaglan's desk leafing through the parchments. She pocketed the vial, a look of consternation on her face. Aoife busied herself with looking through the shelves to see if there was another vial of tears they could mix with pink substance.

"Fine. In the morn, then," Fiona conceded.

"I think I found something." He lifted one of the pages to the light, tilting it to and fro and peering at it with a squint. His head snapped up. "*A wizard of both Fae and Wizard blood will come into power and rule from a silver throne.*"

Fiona's eyes widened as she took a step back until she bumped against the workbench. She sagged against it. "No."

"That's what was written on the paper in the attic." Hot pinpricks broke out along Aoife's skin. Those words burned into her mind from the day she read them. "I read it before I stepped into the trunk. It's haunted me ever since."

"It's a prophecy." Sean's serious gaze met hers and something in that look told her he believed in the prophecy as much as Fiona.

Color siphoned out of Fiona's face. "Read it, Sean. I wish to hear it."

The paper wavered in the light as his hand trembled. "*A wizard of both Fae and Wizard blood will come into power and rule from a silver throne. This half-Fae, half-wizard shall be Protector of the Realm, Ruler of the Kingdom, Guardian of the Staff of Eimhear and all the precious treasures of the Fae.*" He paused and tilted the paper to get it closer to the candlelight. "There is more wording here but it's smudged. I can't read it but I can see the next line."

"What is it?" her mother urged.

"*And should the spirit of the sorceress be released, only the Guardian, Protector and Ruler can destroy her. So it is written. So it shall be.*"

He met Fiona's then Aoife's gaze. She glanced between the two of them, perplexed. "What does it mean? What sorceress?"

Fiona reached for her, taking her hands. "Aoife, don't you see? You are the one."

"The one what?" She resisted the urge to pull away as her mother held fast.

"You are the future, Aoife," Sean said. "You're the half-Fae, half-wizard. You will sit the silver throne. You will be Protector of the Realm, Ruler of the Kingdom. You will defeat this…sorceress whoever she is."

Her gut clenched. She jerked her hand away and pressed it against her stomach as she looked from Sean to Fiona and back again. "That doesn't make sense. For me to rule, my father would have to be——" She halted and clamped her mouth shut with a snap.

"Dead," Fiona finished. "Niall would have to be dead. I refuse to believe he's dead." She pressed her fist against her mouth.

"There is no silver throne here in the towers," Sean pointed out. "It only says 'Ruler of the Kingdom' but not what kingdom. It could reference some other land or some other ruler. It could mean any number of things."

"Aoife *is* the one. She has to be. The towers are in ruins now, aren't they?" Fiona said. "That means there has to be another ruling kingdom to take its place. How could Liam know that?"

"He couldn't have known without help," Sean said.

"Mayhap this sorceress?" Fiona asked. "What is the Staff of Eimhear? I've never heard of it."

"I don't want to rule anything," Aoife protested before Sean could answer. She spun the bracelet around her wrist in a fit of nerves, biting her lip trying not to let her emotions get the best of her.

"It is prophecy——" Fiona began.

"It is *not* my destiny," she snapped. "I don't believe in silly prophesies any more than I believe in destinies. My path has not been predetermined."

Sean tilted the paper under the candlelight. "This was written with a mystical quill."

"Oh, gods," Fiona breathed.

"What does *that* mean?" Aoife demanded.

"A mystical quill has magic," Sean explained, his tone patient. "It means whoever wrote this—I assume Deaglan—foresaw the future and scribed it on the parchment. It *is* a prophecy. It *will* come true. It *is* your destiny."

Aoife shook her head. Tears blurred her vision and clotted her throat. "No, I refuse to believe it. I don't want to sit any throne. I am not a ruler."

"But you will be," Fiona said.

Sean put an arm around her shoulders, pulled her close. He smelled of warmth and comfort and everything she loved. "Don't, Aoife. Don't think of it now. We'll find some way to break it if that's what you want."

But Aoife wasn't so sure the prophecy could be broken.

A dragon cry sounded outside. Another answered. She shuddered and turned into Sean, burying her face in his chest. He clutched her to him, his hand cupping the back of her head. She wanted only to hide in his warmth. She wanted things to go back to the way they were before Liam stole the Time Sphere. Or even before she stepped into that bloody trunk.

"They're getting closer," Fiona said. "They must sense us here."

"We should leave this place." Aoife's words were muffled against Sean's chest. She pushed him away and went back to searching the shelves.

"What are you looking for?" her mother asked.

"The Tears. There has to be some here. Deaglan was thorough. He wouldn't have left something like that potion undone without a way to finish it, would he?" Aoife turned back to the two of them.

"I'll help you look." Perhaps Sean read the determination on her face as he joined her.

"This is a waste of time when all you have to do is sift us, Aoife."

The tower shuddered around them as one of the dragons rammed into it. Fiona moved closer to the two of them, her shuddering breath hard and labored.

"I don't like the sound of that."

"Nor I," Sean agreed.

Aoife ignored them both as she continued to look through the small vials. There were different shapes and sizes. Her fingers landed on one squatty bottle with a cork in it and a faded label. It looked like the word "tears" was written in the squiggly handwriting.

The building shuddered again. The glass vials rattled on the shelf. Aoife snatched the one she found.

"Forget it. We'll take them all with us." Fiona grabbed a small knapsack and started filling it with as many vials as she could hold in both hands.

"This has to be it." Aoife spun to face Sean and her mother. "It's labeled *tears*."

"Let me see that." Aoife held it out to her. Fiona squinted at the label. "It says 'tears' but I'm not sure if it's what we need."

Nearby, a dragon squawked loud and furious. It sounded as though it was right outside the wood door. The tower rumbled again. Something—a dragon?—slammed into the door like a battering ram.

"Oh, god," Aoife whispered.

"Should we try it?" Sean asked.

"I think we have to." Fiona pulled the pink substance out of her pocket and popped the cork. She held out her hand for the vial. Aoife removed the cork placed it in her palm. Her mother took a deep breath. "Here goes nothing."

Outside the door, a dragon squawked and pounded it. The wood splintered with a resounding crack.

Aoife held her breath as Fiona poured the tears into the pink substance. It shimmered. A tinkling sound erupted from it.

"You did it," Sean said.

"I hope so. Let's see if this is going to work."

Before Fiona could test it, the wood door shattered. Fiona shrieked and stumbled away from the door, clutching the vial in her hand to keep it from spilling. Sean shoved Aoife behind him as a dragon small enough to fit inside charged toward them, opened its mouth and screeched.

Aoife's heart pumped wild and quick. Sean waved the torch at the dragon. The firelight reflected off the pale green scales and in its amber eyes but the flame did nothing to deter it from gaining entrance into the workroom. He stumbled as he stepped backward to avoid its snap. Aoife sidestepped out of his way as he tumbled to the ground, holding the torch like a weapon.

Fiona flung a bit of white magic at the thing but it was nothing more than a glancing blow across its iridescent scales. The dragon swiped her mother with its powerful head, knocking her into the desk. Papers went flying and the quill clattered to the ground. Candles toppled out of their holder to the wood floor and suddenly the place began to smolder. The dragon turned its attention to Aoife as Sean still struggled to get to his feet.

Aoife fisted her right hand and shoved it outward at the dragon as though she were going to punch it. The fiery red stone in the silver band of her ring lit up and emitted a stream of hot, bright red magic. It struck the dragon right between the eyes and drove it back, back, back out the door and into the corridor. She heard it shriek as it tumbled down the stone stairs.

And then everything went dead silent. Even the dragons outside the tower went quiet. Sean got to his feet and helped Fiona to hers. She flung magic down at the fire and snuffed it out before it managed to spread. They both looked at Aoife with eyes wide with surprise.

"What did you do?" Sean asked.

"I...I have no idea." Aoife looked down at the ring her father gave her. The stone had gone cold and dark but for a moment it blazed so bright, it lit up the room.

Guardian, come.

The voice boomed inside her head with such an intensity she winced. She pressed the heel of her hand against her head as she squeezed her eyes shut.

"Ow."

"What is it? What happened?" Fiona was at her side in an instant.

"Did you not hear that voice?" Aoife asked.

"What voice?"

Guardian, you have the ring of power, aye? Come to the window.

The voice sounded again in her head. Aoife shrugged off Sean and Fiona and went to the window, but the desk still blocked it.

"Help me move this thing," she said.

"Why?" Sean asked.

Come to the window, Guardian.

"Just do it!"

Together, they moved the desk out of the way. Aoife yanked on the lock until it finally gave way. She shoved open the window. Cold air burst inside, hitting Aoife in the face. She could see nothing but shadows outside the tower.

"What are you doing? Have you gone mad?" Fiona practically shrieked the words.

Aoife heard the flapping before she saw it. The large beast made its way to the open window.

"Aoife! Close that window at once."

"No, Mother. I think it wanted me to open it." She leaned out, the icy breeze pricking her face. She could see the dragon as it hovered closer. Overhead the clouds broke and moonlight peeked through, illuminating the shimmering black scales as two red eyes met hers.

You are called Guardian.

"I am called Aoife," she corrected. "Who are you?"

I am called Nero.

"Gods, she's talking to it. Sean, do something."

"Let her go," Sean replied.

"I am no Guardian, Nero," Aoife said. "I'm just a girl."

You have the ring of power. You defeated my brethren.

"Your brethren tried to eat us," Aoife said. "We don't wish to harm you. We only wanted shelter for the night. This was once our home."

This place once belonged to a king and a queen of unrivaled beauty.

Aoife knew he must be referring to the rulers before her father took over. "Once, long ago. Did you know them?"

There was a pause before Nero answered. *Aye, I did. But they are no longer here. It has been many years since we were free to roam the skies.*

"Why now?"

His red eyes blinked. *I do not know. Once we were free…then we were not. And now we are once again. Something strange happened to the realm. Like a shift or a rip in time.*

"Yes, you're right."

"It's right about what?" Fiona asked. "What are you saying to it, Aoife?"

Nero puffed a heated breath out of his nostrils toward Fiona.

"He doesn't like when you call him it, Mother."

"You're…speaking…to him?" she asked.

"Yes." Aoife gave a slow nod. She couldn't stop from putting a hand on the beast's snout. His scales were smooth and cool. "Do you know the wizard king who ruled from this tower?"

I know of no wizard king. Mayhap he came after our time.

"The shift separated us from the wizard king. He is my father. Can you help us find him?"

I sense a great deal of magic but not from this place. From a different place. From the west.

"Can you take us there?"

Aye, I can.

"All of us?" she asked.

He gave a nod of his giant head. *Aye, all three of you.*

Aoife's face broke into a broad grin as she turned back to Sean and Fiona. "We just got a ride."

Chapter 23

"You're crazy if you think I'm riding on that thing."

"It's perfectly safe, Mother."

Aoife followed Sean down the curved stone staircase as they headed toward the front of the ruined towers. She agreed to meet Nero there outside. Her heart pounded a wild beat as she thought about climbing on the back of the great black dragon. Just like a dragon rider out of one of her favorite books.

"You can't possibly know that," Fiona scoffed. "By the gods, Aoife, it's a *dragon* not an airplane."

"I know. Isn't it exciting?"

Fiona grabbed her arm and pulled her to a stop. "No, it's not exciting. Dragons are nothing to be trifled with. Sean, tell her."

"Far be it from me to talk Aoife out of anything she sets her mind on." He gave her a grin as the firelight from the torch flickered over his features.

Fiona huffed. "You are no help. We don't need a dragon. We have this." She held up the vial.

Aoife ignored it. "Mother, I know you're scared—"

"I am not." She gave a snort of derision.

"It's okay to be scared," Aoife continued without missing a beat. "But I think Nero knows where Niall is. I think he can lead us to my father."

She stilled as she looked at her daughter. Aoife could read a hint of hope and wariness in her eyes. "He can't possibly know where Niall is."

"He said he sensed a great deal of magic in the west."

"That doesn't mean anything." Fiona shook her head, still unconvinced. "I'd rather take my chances with the potion."

"But Nero—"

"No," Fiona said, her voice firm.

Aoife knew that tone of voice. It was the same one her mother used when she had lost patience with her when she wasn't on her best behavior. She straightened and gave a stiff nod.

"Very well."

She continued down the stairs. Several seconds later, she heard Sean and Fiona resume their steps behind her as she descended.

"I don't like this."

Aoife didn't miss the consternation in her mother's voice.

"We'll be fine, Fiona," Sean said, trying to soothe her.

"I hope so."

Outside, night blanketed the realm. Aoife came to a halt when she saw the size of Nero. He was huge. Bigger than she thought which was silly because only his snout fit through the window in Deaglan's workroom.

"Nero."

He bowed his head low and then crouched to the ground in a move that reminded her, strangely, of a cat.

Guardian.

"My name is Aoife."

I know what you are called. You are still Guardian. You have the ring of power.

She blew a lock of hair out of her eyes. "As you say."

Climb on. You first. Then man human.

Aoife turned to Fiona. "Are you coming with us?"

She shook her head.

"I wish you'd reconsider," Aoife said.

"I will find Niall in my own way," she said.

She fears me, Nero said in her head.

Aoife knew it was true but she didn't want to broach the subject aloud. It pained her to leave her mother behind.

"What if we never see each other again?"

Fiona's expression softened as she reached for her and placed a hand on her cheek. "We will. I promise. We will always find each other no matter what."

She gave her one last smile as she stepped away. Aoife hoisted up on the back of the dragon as though she had been doing it all her life. Sean quickly followed.

"If you're certain about this, Mother." Aoife gazed down at her, her heart in her throat and a sudden fear pulsing through her. She worried her bottom lip, hoping she would see her mother again.

"I am. Be safe. I will find you both."

She gave them a little wave as Nero took to the skies.

Fiona clutched the vial in her hand, her face upturned to the night sky as they lifted off and Nero's giant wings flapped and carried her daughter and Sean away.

There was no way in hell she was getting on the back of that beast. She didn't trust it—him. She didn't know why Aoife did. It was clear she wasn't going to talk her daughter out of going.

As they flew away, the other dragons fell in formation behind Nero. Fiona watched them until they were nothing more than a spec and then gone.

She took a deep breath as she looked down at the potion in her hand. It didn't have the same consistency as the Tears of the Dryad she'd carried with her for so many years. She suspected it would not work the same. She wasn't sure it would get her to Niall, but she had to try. Desperation to find him clawed through her. She uncorked the vial and took a deep breath. Hope swelled through her. It had to get her back to Niall. It just *had* to.

As she tipped the vial toward the ground, an image of her husband formed in her mind. She wanted nothing more than to see him again. But before the drop could slide from the bottle, a blinding flash appeared near her. She clutched the vial in her fist and took a stumbling step backward.

She could hardly believe her eyes when Deaglan appeared. Nor could she believe it when Cian and Queen Siobhan arrived standing behind him. Seeing the man who had destroyed so much of her life sent a blinding red rage through her. She lunged for him, the potion forgotten, intending to claw the hateful man's eyes out.

Before she could get to him, Deaglan wrapped his arms around her waist and pulled her to him.

"Let me go, Deaglan!"

"Nay, dearie." She elbowed him in the gut. He grunted but held fast. "Stop, Fiona. Stop. He won't hurt you. Will you, Cian?"

Sudden tears clotted her throat. "He already has."

Cian moved toward her. "Fiona, I—"

"Don't you dare come near me, you filthy animal. I *will* kill you."

Siobhan took offense to that. Anger creased her face. She stepped between her son and Fiona. "Mind your tongue, girl."

"And you." Fiona turned her ire on the queen. "You are nothing but a pitiful excuse for a mother. You turned a blind eye to everything he did when we were betrothed. You did *nothing*."

Red pulsed into the queen's cheeks as her eyes narrowed to slits. "How dare you. I can end you."

Fiona formed a ball of fire in her free hand. "Try."

"Ladies, please." Deaglan intervened trying to diffuse the situation. He blew out a puff of cold air and snuffed out the fire in her hand. "We will get nowhere with you two trying to kill each other."

"Fiona." Cian spread his hands in surrender. "I never thought I'd see you again."

"Never, eh? You destroyed my life. Because of you, I left behind my home and a man I loved. I swore I would kill you if I ever saw you again." She clenched her hands into tight fists. "I tried once. I will try again. And I will succeed."

The queen took offense to her threats. "You will stay away from him."

"She's right. I deserve to die. I deserve to be punished for what I did to you. And I was. For years. I was cursed by the man you loved to roam through a strange realm. Banished. Only recently was I able to return," Cian said. "What I did to you was horrible. I know it was wrong forcing you to…forcing you. I'm sorry I hurt you."

"Cian—" Siobhan said.

He held up a hand to silence her. "Let me finish. I know there is no way I can make it up to you or take back what I did. I know Niall truly loves you and you him. You deserve that happiness. Now and forever."

She stared at him as she tried to comprehend his words. He was…sorry? He wanted her…to be happy? He knew she was in love with Niall?

"Can you forgive me, Fiona?"

She chewed her lower lip as she went limp against Deaglan. His arm loosened around her but remained where it was in case she decided to go after the prince again.

"I…I don't know."

Because she really didn't. He had taken a piece of her. Something she would never get back. She pushed away Deaglan's arm but still gave the two visitors her best dagger glare.

"Mayhap in time," he said.

She ignored him as she turned to Deaglan. "Where is Niall?"

"I don't know. I'm not sure what happened when we were all

separated. Were there dragons here?"

"Aye. Aoife and Sean took off on one toward the west. They think they'll find Niall there. I planned to use this." She held up the vial.

Deaglan squinted at it. "Where in the realm did you get that?"

"Your workroom. It looked like the Tears—"

"It's not." He wiggled his fingers at her. She placed the cork in his hand. He shoved it back into the top of the bottle and then pocketed the vial. "Dangerous magic, that."

Surprise flickered through her. "What it is?"

"Where did you find it in my workroom?" he asked.

"On your shelf. It was only the pink crystals, but I found a vial labeled 'tears' and I thought that would form the Tears of the Dryad."

"Well, it's not the Tears. This liquid is cloudy."

"This is all riveting, but can we get back to why we're here," Siobhan said.

Fiona cut her an angry glance, annoyed the woman and prince were still there. "What are *they* doing here anyway?"

"Where Deaglan goes, we go," Siobhan insisted.

"I'll not have your vile son near me."

"Fiona…" Deaglan said on a sigh. "There is something you don't know."

She folded her arms over her chest. "What?"

"Cian is not Fae," Siobhan said.

Fiona blinked surprise as she looked over the man standing silent at the queen's side. She had been so blinded by her red rage she failed to notice the Cian she once knew looked different. He looked…human. His ears were no longer pointed.

"Gods. You're human." She glanced at Deaglan. "How?"

"A glamour spell," he said, and shifted from one foot to the other. He looked away, refusing to meet her gaze.

"He's been through an ordeal," Siobhan said. "He's not the same man you remember."

"Don't. I can defend myself. I don't need you to champion me."

"He'll have to prove it to me before I'll believe it," Fiona said. "And if he's human, then he cannot be your son." She folded her arms. "So who is?"

Deaglan cleared his throat. "We need to find the others."

"Not with them." Fiona pointed to the queen and Cian.

"As I said, we go where Deaglan goes," the queen said.

"Why is that so important?" Fiona demanded.

"As you pointed out," Siobhan began, "Cian was switched for a Fae child. *My* Fae child. Deaglan knows who he is and agreed to take me to him."

Fiona's brows rose to her hairline as her gaze flew to Deaglan for confirmation. He didn't deny it nor did his face seem to indicate the queen lied. A tight knot of dread formed in the pit of her stomach. Icy pinpricks danced up her spine.

"Oh, gods. She's telling the truth, isn't she?"

The old wizard gave her a grim nod.

"Who is it?" Fiona demanded.

"I had hoped we would never have to discuss this, Fiona, but it appears it is unavoidable."

"Who?" The word warbled as it caught in her throat.

"The man...the Changeling..." He paused, swallowed hard, "...is Liam."

She faltered as her knees gave out from under her and she crumbled to the ground, landing with a scuffle and a thud. A terrible sense of dread and incredulity washed over her in a heat of emotion, purging her of the cold pinpricks she felt only a moment ago.

Liam. It could not be true. Could it?

Liam stole the Time Sphere. He robbed her of her one true love. He destroyed the realm and left the Towers in ruin. He had taken everything from her.

And he would pay.

"Liam. So now I have a name for my true born son." Siobhan did not hide the satisfaction in her voice. "Why did you not tell me this before, Deaglan?"

"How long have you known?" Fiona looked up at the wizard. "Did you know who he was when I was in the human realm?"

"Nay, dearie. I swear it to be true. I never knew the Fae's human name. Not until recent developments."

Blood drained from her head in a rush. She pinched the bridge of her nose between thumb and forefinger, rubbing in hard as a sudden headache pulsed through her. If Liam was truly Fae, then that, of course, meant Sunnie was not a Halfling after all. Sunnie was full-blooded Fae.

How stupid of her not to notice before. She had been so focused on her own vengeance and hate she had never looked as closely at Sunnie as she had Aoife. She had assumed Sunnie would never have the same magic as Aoife. But she was wrong. So, so wrong.

"I have to find him. Where is he?"

"*We* have to find him. I want my son back," Siobhan said.

Deaglan met Fiona's gaze. Something about his look told her there was more he wanted to share with her. With a wave of his hand, everything around them—including the queen and prince—froze, cocooning the two of them in a bubble of magic.

"There's something you must know, dearie. Something I must tell you about the girl called Sunnie."

Hot pinpricks of fear prickled the back of her throat. She didn't like the sound of this. "What about her?"

"She's here in this realm."

Fiona pressed a hand against her suddenly roiling abdomen. "Oh, gods. She found the portal."

"And there's more. She also found the Staff of Eimhear."

She stiffened. She'd read that in the prophecy Sean found in Deaglan's workroom. She was convinced it was about Aoife. "What is that?"

"A powerful magic object once wielded by a dark sorceress named Eimhear. The staff was enchanted with her essence...her...being..." He paused, his words faltering.

Fiona gripped his arm. How much more could she take? "What happened to Sunnie?"

She could tell by the look on his face the news wasn't good. Something dreadful happened to Sunnie and he didn't want to tell her. Dread pierced through her on a wave of sickness. "What happened to Sunnie?"

"The dark sorceress possessed her."

Fiona released her grip on him as a cold sense of calm came over her. Her world tipped on its axis and then immediately righted itself. This was a mere setback. She would find a way to bring her daughter back. She was a powerful Fae. Her husband a powerful wizard.

"Then we'll save her from the dark sorceress. You or Niall will use your wizard magic and get her out of my daughter. And if that doesn't work, then I will save her myself." She could hear the hysteria lacing her words.

But Deaglan shook his head before she even finished. "It's not that easy, dearie. Taking the darkness out of Sunnie will likely kill her."

Her knees threatened to buckle again. "That can't be possible. I refuse to believe that."

"I'm afraid it's true, dearie."

She shook her head "No. There was a prophecy." She squeezed her eyes shut trying to remember the words, envisioning them on the parchment. "Something about a wizard of both Fae and Wizard blood ruling from a silver throne. That person will be the one to destroy the dark sorceress. Isn't that right, Deaglan."

His face had drained of color. Fiona sucked in a sharp breath and charged him, wrapping her hand around his arm and digging her fingers into his frail skin and bones. "Who is the prophecy about? My daughters?"

"Fiona...I...if I had known it would come to this, I would have never written it. But the magic in the prophecy cannot be undone. It's been foretold. It's unfortunate the girls are both affected by it."

"Unfortunate?" She nearly shrieked the word as hysteria threatened to bubble up inside her. "My youngest daughter is possessed by a dark sorceress while my eldest has to find a way to defeat her and thereby kill her? No. I refuse to believe it. I will find a way to save her and keep Aoife from having to fight her own sister."

"Fiona—"

"Let me out of here. I have to find Niall. He'll help me since you won't."

"You can't sift," he pointed out. "I can. We'll find him together, dearie."

She pressed her lips together in a thin line as her jaw tightened to a painful ache. She didn't want to tell him what she knew of his location but she knew it was the fastest and best way to get to Niall—if he truly was there. "The dragon said there was a great amount of power in the west," Fiona said.

Deaglan looked to the west and closed his eyes. He took a deep inhale, held it and then expelled it. His eyes opened.

"Aye, the dragon is correct. That's where we'll go." He reached a hand down to help Fiona to her feet.

"Do you think that's where he is?" She dared not hope.

He gave her a squinting smile. "Shall we find out, dearie?"

Before she could answer, he broke the magic around them and sifted them away from the ruined towers.

Chapter 24

No matter what they tried, Caleb, Brigid nor Niall could get past the iron prison. All their powers were suppressed. Niall was still shackled to the wall. Caleb had resumed his pacing, pausing only every now and then to peer out through the bars with contempt. Behind him, Brigid sat on the filthy floor with her knees drawn to her chest, dozing.

They'd been abandoned by the evil sorceress. He'd lost track of time since they'd been down there. Days could have been passed. Or weeks. He didn't know.

"It's no use. We're trapped here." Brigid yawned and leaned her head against the wall. "You may as will stop pacing, Caleb."

"I won't give up. Neither should you," he said.

He didn't want to admit he'd given up hope when it was clear they weren't getting out alive.

"Someone's coming," Niall said.

Silence descended on the dungeon. Caleb halted and held his breath as he craned his neck to see the entrance. He didn't know how Niall knew but he saw the shadow flicker along the stone wall as someone descended the steps. Light illuminated Liam's face.

"It's Liam." He whispered so only Niall and Brigid could hear.

She got to her feet and joined him at the cell bars, shivering. He wrapped an arm around her shoulders. Liam paused opposite them. Their eyes met and they stared at each other in a silent pissing match.

"What are you doing here?" Caleb demanded.

Liam moved to stand in front of Niall's cell. Keys jingled in the lock and then the groan of the hinges as he swung open the door. Though he couldn't see, he could hear more jangling of keys and then Liam emerged from the cell, arm around Niall's waist as he helped him out.

"I'm breaking you out."

He released Niall, who leaned against the stone wall while Liam went to work on their cell door.

"Why?" Caleb asked, suspicion lacing his words.

Liam paused, met his gaze. "Because it's the right thing to do."

"What about Eimhear?" he asked. "Sunnie is still alive in there. I know it."

Liam shook his head. "Let her go. I did. Sunnie is no longer in there."

But Caleb wasn't so sure he could ever give up on Sunnie.

"I have horses waiting for you on the south side of the castle. There should be enough provisions for each of you for a week's ride," Liam said.

"Where are we supposed to go? Our world is gone," Caleb said.

Liam turned back to Niall. "You need a healer. We should get you to one."

"My wounds will heal," Niall said.

"But—" Liam began.

"I will be fine," Niall insisted.

After a pause, Liam gave a nod of understanding. "All right, then, let's get you to the horses." Liam helped Niall from the wall. "We have to hurry."

They made it out of the dungeon. Liam found a secret passageway through the castle that led them through the dusty, dirty corridors right to the exit on the south side of the castle. As he promised, three horses tied to the edge of the tree line waited for them.

Morning sun streamed through the canopy of leaves. The air turned even colder than when they were last outside. Caleb could hear Brigid's teeth chattering.

"What about the Time Sphere?" Niall said.

"What about it?" Liam asked.

"I want it back."

Liam shook his head. "She's got it. There's no way she's giving it up."

"I'm not leaving here without it."

Liam huffed out a breath of impatience. "Take the horses and go. Forget about the Time Sphere."

But Niall wasn't going to give up that easily. He turned to Caleb. "Both of you get out of here. Find Fiona or my father. They can help you."

"What about you?" Caleb asked.

"I'm going back for the Time Sphere."

"You are *mad* if you think she'll ever give it up," Liam said.

"Besides, she has a protection spell around it."

Brigid spoke up. "I can break it."

"Absolutely not," Caleb said. "I promised Bryant I would protect you. Letting you go into the castle with the dark sorceress is not protecting you. I'm getting you out of here."

She shoved away from him. "Caleb, I'm not a child or a weakling. I can break the spell. I know it."

"You *don't* know that. You—"

"Caleb," she said, her voice thin. "I can do this. Let me do this, please."

"Why?" he demanded.

She cut a glance to Niall who regarded her with a curious gaze. "If anyone can repair what Eimhear did to the realm, it's the wizard king. I believe that. I want to help give him that chance."

"If you're certain," Niall said. "I'll not have you put yourself in harm's way on my account."

"I'm certain," she said with a nod.

"It will not be so easy to get the Time Sphere away from Eimhear," Liam said. "She guards it closely."

"That's why you're going to help us," Niall said.

Liam shook his head before Niall even finished. "I can't. I won't. She'll kill me."

"You honestly believe that?" Caleb asked. "You think she would hurt her own father?"

He pinned Caleb with his icy gaze. "I told you. Nothing remains of Sunnie. If there was, I'd know. She's gone. Dead. And I helped kill her."

"I refuse to believe the girl is dead."

He still held out hope deep down Sunnie was still in there. That somehow she had found a way to fight back against Eimhear. Everything that happened to her had been his fault and he had been nothing but a coward to allow it to happen. Just as he'd allowed Bryant to control him. If he could get Sunnie back, it would help lessen some of his guilt.

"We'll deal with Eimhear or Sunnie or whatever she calls herself when we get back the Time Sphere," Niall said.

"You're that determined?" Liam asked.

"I am."

He took a deep breath and gave a slow nod. "Then how can I help you?"

They heard the *whump, whump* of the leathery wings before Niall could answer. All of them looked skyward but it was really no use since the castle was surrounded by woods. They could hear it— whatever it was—but they couldn't see it.

"What is that?" Brigid's voice shook as she huddled closer to Caleb.

Liam's face drained of color. "I think I know." He waved them to follow.

The horses forgotten, they headed from the south side of the castle around to the front where there was a clearing in the trees and the sky was visible. As they made their way there, the sound grew louder and louder until suddenly the giant black dragon landed with a bone-rattling thud. He was followed by two more dragons, all crushing trees under their massive bodies.

Liam and Niall stared up at them in awe. Brigid shrieked and hid her face against Caleb's side, cowering next to him. Caleb thought dragons were nothing more than a myth. All eyes were on the two who climbed down from the back of the black dragon— Aoife and Sean.

Aoife jumped down from Nero, her heart in her throat. She thought she spotted her father from the air as they made their descent. She hadn't been wrong. She broke into a run and flung herself into his arms. He hugged her hard.

"I'm so glad you're all right." Her voice was muffled against him.

He pulled back, holding her at arm's length. She spotted his raw wrists.

"What happened to your wrists?" she asked before he could reply.

Liam stepped forward. "He was a prisoner in the dungeon but I released him."

Aoife glared at him. Her jaw set, her eyes narrowed to slits. This was the man who had raised her and yet she didn't know him at all. He had distanced himself from her, treated her as though she were nothing. He had showered all his love and attention on Sunnie from the moment she was born. He'd cast aside Aoife. She would never forgive him.

"Your prisoner, no doubt."

"No. Not mine." He held his hands up. "I swear it to you."

"Why should I believe you?" she demanded.

"Aoife—"

"No, Father. He betrayed me and my mother. He did this." She waved her hand to indicate the realm. "He destroyed the towers. He separated us."

"I played a part in it, I admit," Liam said. "But I had no idea it would lead us to this. I thought…" He stopped, shook his head. "It doesn't matter what I thought. Aoife, you have to believe me."

"No." The word cut like a knife and he winced.

"I was your father once—"

"You were never my father. You were nothing but the man who was married to my mother. From the day my sister was born, you favored her. You never loved me the way you loved her. My real father is here with me now." She nodded toward Niall. "And even though I haven't known him very long, he has treated me with more love and respect than you ever did."

Niall slid an arm around her shoulders and gave her a quick squeeze of a hug.

Guilt lined Liam's face. "You're right. I did favor her. You are also right I never treated you as well as I should have. You were Fiona's first born. Her favorite. You had a special bond with her I couldn't understand. I cannot change the past, Aoife. I can only help change the present."

"Because you destroyed it," she accused.

"It wasn't me. It was Eimhear," he said.

At the mention of the name Eimhear, Aoife and Sean exchanged a glance. The prophecy had mentioned the Staff of Eimhear, that whoever destroyed the sorceress would be the Guardian of the Staff of Eimhear. She could read the question in Sean's eyes even before he asked it.

Sean stepped forward. "Who's Eimhear?"

"The dark sorceress who cast the spell that destroyed the realm. She used the Time Sphere. She's powerful. More powerful than Niall or Fiona," he said.

Niall turned to Aoife. "Where is Fiona? Is she…?" He paused, swallowed hard. It was clear he thought something dreadful had happened to her.

Aoife took a deep breath. She had hoped her mother would

come with them but her stubbornness prevailed. "She's fine. She stayed behind because she wanted to use a portal potion to get to you. Has she made it?"

He shook his head. "Not yet."

"I knew we shouldn't have left her," she told Sean, then to Niall said, "She was too afraid to ride on the back of Nero."

"Nero?" His brows rose.

"That's his name." She thumbed to the black dragon. "He can speak to me."

Niall's eyes widened even more. "You can...communicate with him?"

She nodded.

"Impressive. There have only been a few who have been able to communicate with dragons." Pride showed in his face.

But Aoife didn't want to change the subject. "But, Mother—"

"Your mother is resourceful," Niall said. "She'll find her way to us. In the meantime, I'm getting my Time Sphere back. Brigid is a *sidhe*. She's going to break the protection spell on it. Are you ready?"

The *sidhe* nodded.

Niall headed for the entrance of the castle. Liam fell in step beside him, huffing to keep up with his brisk pace. Brigid glanced up at Caleb and everything in her expression told him she intended to go with them.

"Do you think you're just going to walk in there?" Liam demanded.

"Aye, I do."

Before either of them reached the double doors, though, they came open. Aoife couldn't stifle the gasp that rose when she saw her sister standing in the doorway holding a silver staff topped by the glowing orb. But she no longer looked like the sister she remembered. Sunnie had golden blonde hair and blue eyes. This woman's hair was stark white and her eyes were haunting silver. She was dressed in an ivory gown trimmed in gold, not the couture Aoife last remembered her wearing. Yet despite those differences, she *was* her sister.

"Sunnie, my God," Aoife whispered as she stepped outside.

Her silvery gaze touched on each and every one of them, finally resting on Aoife. A half smile tugged at the corners of her mouth.

"Well, well. What have we here? It seems my prisoners have

managed to break out of their iron cell." Her cold silvery gaze landed on Liam. "Would you know anything about that?"

"Eimhear, I—"

"Silence."

She pointed her staff at him. A bolt of white magic burst from the orb and punched him in the chest. He flew backward, landing on the ground and skidding several feet before coming to a halt at the base of a tree.

"As for you." She pointed her staff on Niall. "You will die, wizard king."

Aoife stepped in front of him. "You'll have to kill me to get to him."

"Aoife, no," he said.

Sunnie/Eimhear chuckled as she took slow steps to close the gap between them. "Aren't you a brave little thing? You are nothing like what the girl remembers."

"You are not my sister. Where is Sunnie?"

Annoyance flickered over her face. "That girl is dead. I killed her."

As soon as the words were out of her mouth, Eimhear faltered. She doubled over and put a hand to her head with a grunt.

"She's not dead," Caleb said. "She can't be."

Caleb stepped forward, moving to one side of Aoife. Sean joined her on the other, making a human wall between the sorceress and Niall. Aoife caught a glimpse of Brigid as she skirted around the group and inched her way to the open door. Brigid gave her a knowing glance before she slipped inside.

Aoife knew what the *sidhe* was doing. With Sunnie/Eimhear distracted, she intended to break the protection spell on the Time Sphere and get it back.

"The girl *is* dead," Eimhear snapped. Her cheeks had turned bright scarlet as she looked at Caleb. "Stop saying she isn't!"

Again, Eimhear faltered. This time she stumbled backward toward the open door.

"Sunnie is still in there, isn't she?" Aoife asked.

Deaglan rounded the corner from the backside of the white castle followed by Fiona and two other people Aoife didn't know. Relief at seeing her mother and grandfather swept through her. Fiona saw Sunnie before anyone. First recognition then horror crossed her face as she looked at the girl-turned-sorceress.

"Sunnie!"

Fiona made a step toward her but Aoife put a hand up to stop her, giving her a terse shake of her head. The last thing she needed was Sunnie barricading herself back inside the castle. Fiona halted mid-step.

"Stay back." Eimhear/Sunnie pointed the staff at all of them in one sweeping motion. "*That* girl is long gone. I killed her essence when I took over this body."

Even as she said it, she doubled over with a groan of pain clutching her middle. Her face turned bright red, the veins on her neck standing out. A scream of frustration ripped from her lungs as she clutched her stomach and shouted, "No!"

Aoife took a tentative step toward the girl who looked like her sister but wasn't. Hope pierced through her and she knew her sister was still in there somewhere. Eimhear hadn't killed her. Not yet.

"Sunnie, I'm here. It's Aoife. Your sister. Our mother is here, too." She waved toward Fiona. "I know you're in there somewhere. We're going to find a way to save you."

Eimhear lifted her head and met Aoife's gaze. They changed from silver to a stormy blue. In that moment, she was certain she saw her sister's eyes look back at her and not Eimhear's. But the moment of clarity was gone in an instant.

"You'll never be able to save her."

Eimhear sifted away in the blink of an eye. The door slammed closed. Aoife charged toward it only to bounce off the invisible ward that suddenly surrounded the castle. She hit it so hard she landed on her backside on the cold ground. Sean was at her side a second later helping her to her feet.

"Are you all right?"

She brushed the dirt from her pants. "I'm fine. She warded it."

"Brigid can break the spell." Caleb glanced around for the girl. "Where is she?"

Aoife swallowed the sudden lump in her throat. "She's inside."

"What? How?" Caleb demanded.

"She snuck in when we had Eimhear distracted. She must be going after the Time Sphere," Aoife said.

"She's not safe in there." Caleb stood at the edge of the ward and reached a hand to it. It zapped him. He jerked his hand back. "Eimhear will kill her to keep her from breaking the protection spell on the Time Sphere."

Sean turned on Liam who had managed to hobble back to the group. "How do we get inside?"

He shrugged. "You can't. No one can break those wards but her." He cut a glance at Caleb. "Or Brigid."

"Well, we'll just have to think of another way," Aoife said.

"Mayhap we can be of assistance," Niall offered.

Fiona noticed him then and rushed to him, falling into his arms. She hugged him hard. "Thank the gods you're all right."

"I'm all right." He brushed hair back from her face and then glanced at his father. "What are *they* doing here?"

"I should kill you here and now, *brother.*" Cian fisted his hands as he shot dagger eyes at Niall.

The wizard king started to respond but Fiona cut him off.

"But you won't. Or everything you told me about being a changed man and asking for forgiveness was nothing but a lie."

Indignation flashed over his face and his cheeks colored red as he looked away. "Apologies, my lady. You are correct."

His response seemed to appease her. "Can you get through the wards?" she asked Deaglan.

He ran a hand over his chin, his skin bristling against the gray stubble. "With our combined magical strength... 'tis a possibility." He glanced around at the group, his gaze landing on everyone and then resting finally on Aoife. "You, Aoife, are both wizard and Fae. Your magic is the strongest of all of us."

"I don't know how to break through the wards." Aoife spread her hands as if in surrender.

"We'll do it together." Fiona turned toward the closed door. "Now. Let's get my daughter back."

When Sunnie saw Caleb and the others through Eimhear's eyes, she launched a massive internal attack on the sorceress. She banged against her skull to try to make her presence known. Hearing Caleb say she wasn't dead gave her some hope that she succeeded if even a little.

It was Aoife, though, that knew her essence was still alive inside her own body. Her sister had come for her. Her sister would help her. Her mother had come, too. Her mother saw her, knew something horrible had happened to her and yet still wanted to save her from her fate. With both of them there, Sunnie had renewed hope she could banish this evil once and for all.

Eimhear sifted back inside the castle and used her magic to ward it against all those outside.

"You stupid little fool!" Eimhear shouted. Sunnie knew she was talking to her. "You will never defeat me. You will never push me out of this body."

See if I won't, Sunnie shot back.

Eimhear charged into the great hall with the silver throne and the Time Sphere. She waved a hand over it, making it come to life.

"Show me the intruders."

Images of Fiona, Aoife and her father along with the others played across the sphere. If Sunnie could weep for joy at the sight of her family, she would have.

They've come for me, Eimhear. They will do whatever it takes to save me. And you will die.

"Shut up. No one will ever destroy me. That wizard old man tried once and did not succeed."

A sound in the room caught Eimhear's attention. Brigid scurried toward the door. The sorceress used her power to close it before she could get out. When the *sidhe* reached the door, she tried in vain to yank it open.

"What have we here." Eimhear advanced on her one slow step at a time. "It appears my luck has changed. How fortunate."

Brigid pressed her back against the solid door. Eimhear cupped her chin. "Now I have a bargaining chip."

The girl jerked her chin away. "You'll never win this fight. Not against them."

"Their power is no match for mine." She gave a sniff of derision.

"It far exceeds yours," she said. "There are three wizards and a powerful Fae out there. With their combined strength, they can—"

"Silence." She hiccupped a laugh. "I've grown more powerful and will defeat them all."

The sorceress closed her eyes and chanted in a language Sunnie didn't know. A black mist filled the Time Sphere replacing the images of her family. Even the orb in her staff clouded with the same mist. The chant complete, she opened her eyes.

"Now they will face the wrath of hell."

The ground rumbled, the walls shook. But they appeared to be safe from whatever hell she unleashed. Sunnie wished she was attuned to Eimhear's thoughts to know what was happening. She knew her family was in danger. She had to find some way to break out of her internal prison and take control of her body again. But how? She didn't know how to work magic. She didn't know anything.

Embrace the magic. Reach for it and awaken it. Eimhear told her that when the transition began. Now Sunnie calmed and silenced her fears. She thought about how it felt to awaken the magic inside her, how she took control over it, how Eimhear stole it from her.

She was taking it back, damn it. Even if she had to kill herself and Eimhear to do it.

When the black mist cleared in the sphere, Sunnie could see her family again. They scattered as the ground opened around them. Giant cracks in the earth threatened them. And that black mist belched from the fissures.

Eimhear cackled. "Now you will witness all their deaths. Once they're gone, I will complete the takeover of this body at long last."

She ran her hands over her breasts and down to her hips. Sunnie cringed at the touch. She knew Eimhear was talking to her just as she knew she couldn't allow the dark sorceress to destroy what was left of her. She'd do whatever it took to make sure that didn't happen…even if she had to die trying.

Chapter 25

Below their feet, the ground rumbled. Aoife cut a glance at Sean who looked around wildly trying to pinpoint the source. Caleb stood stock still as though he knew the source of the quake, his glare firm on the closed door of the castle. Like he was trying to use some sort of mind magic to open it. Siobhan grabbed onto Cian to steady her feet while Liam inched his way toward the horses.

Coward.

The loud crack sounded again followed by a great shudder in the ground that made it impossible to stay on her feet. She collided with Sean who grabbed on to her to steady her. The ground split in two, a wide chasm opening between them and the castle.

"What's happening?" Fiona asked.

Deaglan gripped his staff, his knuckles leaching of color. He moved to stand next to Fiona and Niall. "I don't like the looks of this."

Black mist shot upward from the yawing chasm. It formed into a wraithlike hooded creature with two white eyes peering out from its darkness. It hovered over the group for a breath before turning its attention on Aoife and then diving for her.

She sucked in a sharp breath, fear paralyzing her. Sean shouted something she couldn't understand or really hear. The next thing she knew, she lost her footing and collided with the ground. Her elbow crashed first into the ground, sending a shockwave of pain through her. She realized Sean shoved her out of the way to take her place. The wraith slammed into him, covering him and making a disgusting slurp/screech sound. He flopped underneath it like a fish out of water. Fiona shrieked. Aoife cradled her injured arm against her body as she huddled on the ground, paralyzed with her own fear.

"Get it off him!" her mother shouted. "Deaglan! Niall! Do *something.*"

Deaglan used his staff to pump white magic into the thing. He managed to drive the wraith away but it was only a brief deterrent as it turned, looking for another victim. Its white pinpoint eyes landed on Aoife. It was as though it could see right into her soul. Her heart fluttered a quick beat as she looked into the eyes of the thing.

"Aoife, stop looking at it!"

She could hear her father's commanding voice somewhere near her but she could not obey. She could only stare at the thing that suddenly snarled and dove toward her.

"Aoife!"

A punch of white magic hit her in the chest. It broke her gaze long enough for her to shake her head to clear it. The wraith turned its attention on Niall then. He and Fiona teamed up to fight it while meanwhile more black mist poured from the chasm, creating a second creature. Aoife crawled her way to Sean, the cold ground biting into her. She checked for a pulse. He was alive but unconscious.

The second creature headed straight for her. She scrabbled back on an awkward one-armed crab-crawl to get away from it. In her peripheral vision, she caught sight of the stone in her ring glowing. Dropping flat on the ground, she rolled to her side, fisted her hand and pointed it at the thing much like she did at the dragon in the towers.

It shrieked, caved in on itself and disappeared.

She turned her ring on the one attacking Niall and Fiona. It, too, disappeared.

Cold sweat bathed her face as she tried to catch her breath. She looked at her parents, who stood clutching one another with surprised looks on their faces.

"Aoife, you did it," Fiona said.

"What was it?" she panted.

"A Soul Taker," Niall said.

She didn't need an explanation. She glanced at Sean. "Will he be all right?"

Before anyone could answer, more black mist belched from the earth creating more and more wraith creatures and every single one of them headed directly for Aoife. The realization hit her.

"They want me." She scrambled to her feet and shouted, "They want me. Mother, find a way into the castle."

During the whole ordeal, the wraiths had ignored Caleb while he tried in vain to break the wards around the castle using his own weak magic. Liam had made his way to the horses, but they'd been scared off by the wraiths. He instead cowered behind one of the trees watching from afar. Aoife made a mad dash around the side of the castle trying to outrun the damn wraiths.

Suddenly, Cian was at her side matching her pace with his long legs. He gave her a mighty shove to the side making her stumble. She tried hard to keep control of her footing but was unsuccessful as she tumbled to the ground. She landed hard for the second time, jarring every bone in her body. She flipped over in time to see Cian standing still, arms outstretched.

"I can't let you be the bait, Aoife," he said, his gaze locked on hers. He threw his head back and looked up at the wraiths hovering in the sky. "Come for me, you bastards."

Questions raced through her mind. Why would he do that for her? He didn't know her. She was no one to him.

"Cian, no!" Siobhan cried out.

But it was too late. The wraiths attacked him, covering him from head to toe in their black mist with that sickly slurping/screeching sound. The horror of it all stunned her to immobility but when she finally got her senses working, she forced her hand into a fist and used the magic of the ring.

It blasted into the wraiths but did nothing to stop their attack on Cian.

Nor did it stop more wraiths from spilling out of the chasm and heading for her. This time too many for Aoife to outrun. She huffed an annoyed breath as she got to her feet and started another sprint.

The great Nero landed directly in front of her, his back talons digging into the ground. His sudden appearance made her skid to a halt but not before she crashed into one of his hind legs. He didn't even seem to notice as he reared back and spewed his dragon fire all over the remaining wraiths. They turned to ash, the gray powder intermingled with small snowflakes drifting to the ground.

They wraiths attacking Cian turned their attention on Nero and charged. But they were no match for dragon fire. He destroyed them in one puff.

"Cian!"

Siobhan ran to his side and dropped to her knees. His skin was an ashen color, his cheeks and eye sockets sunken, his lips a shocking blue. The queen pressed fingers against his throat and then pulled it back, clutching her hand against her chest.

"His skin is ice."

Deaglan walked to her and put a hand on her shoulder. "He's dead, Your Majesty. They took his soul. I'm so sorry."

Guilt swept through Aoife as she looked on. He'd sacrificed himself to save her. Why? She didn't understand. Behind her, the warmth from Nero radiated over her.

"He did it to save me," she said. "Why? Why would he do that for me?"

"Redemption," Fiona said. "He did it for his own redemption."

In that instant, Aoife understood. He was the man who had raped her mother years ago, forcing her to escape to the human realm. He was the man that beat her, nearly hanged her. But somewhere along the way he had changed.

"He was my son," Siobhan said, her voice hollow. "He may not have been my true born son, but he was still my son nonetheless. And now the kingdom of Anatolia has lost its prince."

"I doubt the kingdom of Anatolia still exists, dearie," Deaglan pointed out.

Niall's jaw flexed with his annoyance as he moved to stand next to the queen. "I am your true born son. Yours and Deaglan's. Cian was my half-brother. No amount of redemption will wipe away his cruelty."

Siobhan's head snapped up as she looked at Niall, eyes narrowed and her face a dark glower. Slowly she rose to her full height and faced him. "You are not without sin, *wizard king*." She turned her ire on Deaglan. "Where is my true born son? You promised to take me to him."

Niall gripped his father's arm hard. "What is she talking about?"

Fiona stepped in between them, pushing father and son apart. "Now is not the time for this."

"My mother is right. Now isn't the time," Aoife said.

"Your true born son, dearie, is a coward and took off when things started to get dangerous." It seemed Deaglan took great pleasure telling Siobhan.

She stiffened. "Where is he? Where did he go?"

Deaglan waved to one of the remaining horses. "You are welcome to search for him. His name is Liam."

Siobhan gave him one last scorching look before she picked up her skirts and made a dash for the horse.

Sean groaned. Aoife rushed to his side and helped him to a sitting position. He was pale but appeared to be unharmed.

"What happened?" He raked a hand through his hair, shook his head and tried to clear it.

"The Soul Taker tried to kill you," she said.

He glanced down at her hand. "You used the ring of power? Or did I imagine that."

"I used it." She nodded. "It worked."

Nero dipped his giant head and gave Sean a gentle nudge. *Will man human survive?*

"Nero wants to know if you'll survive," she said with a smile.

Sean reached up and patted his snout. "I'm weak but I think I'll be all right."

She helped him to his feet. "We have to get inside that castle and save Sunnie. Are you going to help me or not?" She directed her question to Deaglan, Niall and Fiona. "Because with or without your help, I'm going after her."

"I never stopped trying," Caleb announced. "But my magic isn't powerful enough."

Aoife, Sean and the others joined him, standing in front of the castle. "Then let's help you."

She took two steps forward, standing away from the group. All she could do was go on instinct and instinct told her she had to reach deep for her magic. She closed her eyes, found the silvery thread and grasped it. She lifted her arms, palms outward toward the wards in front of her and around the castle. The magic warmed her, pulsing through her to her fingertips.

"That's my girl." Fiona's voice was near.

When her eyes fluttered open, her mother stood next to her doing the same thing.

"You learned quickly, my daughter."

"I learned from you, Mother."

Niall and Deaglan moved forward. Deaglan used his wizard staff to punch the ward with his white magic. Niall used his own wizard magic to attack. Sean and Caleb followed, though their magic was definitely the weaker of all of them.

As they stood there, each magic user pushing their own brand of magic into the wards, the invisible barrier lit in a pale blue. Cracks formed and it reminded Aoife all too much of when her mother broke the protection spell around the Time Sphere in the

Ivory Wood. That seemed eons ago, now.

The cracks grew, splintering like a spider web outward until at last a blinding flash of light exploded all around them, sending them all backward from the castle walls. The wards were broken. They had their way inside.

Sunnie peered out through Eimhear's eyes. She watched through the Time Sphere what was happening. As soon as Aoife, Fiona and the others had the wards down, Caleb charged inside without waiting for anyone. Hope soared. He was coming for her.

A scream of frustration ripped through her when the wards were broken. Brigid smirked, despite her hands and feet being shackled in iron.

"They're coming for you, Eimhear," she said. "Your life will soon be over."

"Not if I can help it." She threw a blast of magic to the closed throne room doors.

"More wards? That will not keep them out," Brigid scoffed.

Eimhear advanced on her. "Cheeky girl, aren't you? You are no match for me or anyone. You'll die before anyone comes to rescue you." She lowered her staff, the orb pulsing a bright blue light. "Or at least, that's what they'll think."

She shot light from the orb into the little *sidhe*. Sunnie had to stop her. She launched an internal attack by pounding what was left of her essence against Eimhear's skull over and over and over again. It was enough to stop her from killing Brigid. Eimhear shrieked, dropped her staff and clutched her head between her hands, squeezing.

"Stop it! Stop, you wench."

I'll never stop. Not while I have strength left to destroy you.

Sunnie could feel herself getting stronger. Some of the magic drained away from Eimhear and back to her giving her that strength. If only she knew what to do with it. But she hadn't a clue. All she knew was she had to get it away from Eimhear and back to her. It was the only way to keep the sorceress from snuffing her out.

She peeked out of Eimhear's eyes as the sorceress rocked from side to side while Sunnie continued her onslaught. Brigid awkwardly crawled from the foot of the silver throne toward the staff with the orb. Sunnie had to keep the sorceress busy while the *sidhe* got her hands on that staff. She suspected it was the only thing keeping Eimhear's magic intact and drained from Sunnie.

The silvery thread of magic floated upward to her. She grabbed on, holding it, refusing to let it go.

Someone slammed into the doors outside the throne room. They'd come for her!

The pounding got Eimhear's attention. She saw Brigid crawling toward the staff and lunged for it the same time the *sidhe* wrapped her hand around it. With her wrists shackled, she couldn't hang on to it. Eimhear snatched it up.

"You thought to take this away from me, did you? You'll pay for that." She turned the staff on Brigid again.

As soon as Eimhear had the staff in her hand, Sunnie felt the magic dwindle away from her with a violent *whoosh*. She couldn't hang on to it even if she wanted. That confirmed her suspicion the staff was the source of Eimhear's magic. She launched another attack against her skull, pulsing and pounding and doing everything she could to save Brigid.

The girl writhed on the floor, crying out in pain as the magic from the orb pounded into her with a brutal force. She was killing her and there wasn't anything Sunnie could do to stop her. As long as Eimhear held that staff, Sunnie didn't stand a chance. Eimhear didn't falter no matter how much Sunnie banged against her skull.

At the door, the wards flashed and cracked and sizzled. Even though she couldn't see it, Sunnie could hear it.

They're coming and you can't stop them.

Eimhear saw the wards had fractured and broken around the doors to the throne room. It sounded like a battering ram hitting the door over and over. She could hear shouts outside until finally, at last, the door shattered into splinters the size of toothpicks and Caleb and her family poured inside.

He lowered his head like a linebacker and charged Eimhear. Sunnie braced for impact. He slammed his weight into her, knocking her off her feet. The staff fell from her hand and clattered on the marble floor, the orb going dark.

"Get Brigid," he ordered.

For the first time since she had control of her own body, Sunnie could see into Caleb's eyes. Determination etched along his face as he tried to control the dark sorceress squirming to get away from underneath him. She had a flashback to the day beside the creek when he'd tackled her much in the same way to keep her from picking up the staff. Then he held her down and looked at her with something other than determination in his eyes. Then it had been something that made her pulse race. Something that told her he did it for more than keeping her away the staff.

Caleb! I'm here. I'm still here!

"I'm going to kill your little princess," Eimhear sneered. "I'm going to snuff out her life and expel what's left of her essence forever. And then I'll be fully reborn."

Caleb wrapped his big hand around both her wrists and dragged her to her feet, nearly yanking her arms out of her socket.

Hey, careful! I still have to live in this body.

But he couldn't hear Sunnie. He could only hear Eimhear.

He backhanded her hard across the mouth. The sting radiated through her and even Sunnie winced.

"Don't hurt her," her mother said, her tone sharp.

Still grasping Eimhear by the wrists, Caleb spun toward the *sidhe*. She lay motionless on the floor, her head lolled to one side and her legs at an awkward angle. She looked like a discarded rag doll. Deaglan stood over her, his fingers on her neck checking her pulse.

"Is she...?" Caleb began.

Deaglan merely shook his head, a grim look on his face.

Eimhear had killed her.

Though she didn't know the girl, a pang of sorrow went through Sunnie. Caleb had known her. Grief then rage flickered over his face as he turned on her. He gripped her by the upper arms, his fingers biting into her flesh.

"You killed her." He shook her with each word. "She did *nothing* to you and *you killed her.*"

"She had to die. She tried to steal the Time Sphere and return it to you. I couldn't let her live."

With Eimhear occupied and the staff on the ground, that silvery thread of magic resurfaced. Sunnie grasped it and regained control of her mental faculties. She was herself again! She could see through her own eyes. She shoved the dark sorceress back, back, back until she was nothing but a shadow.

Aoife reached for the staff.

"Aoife, thank god! The staff is the source of Eimhear's power." The words rushed out of Sunnie so quickly, she ran them all together.

Aoife's brows knit together as she looked at her, holding the staff in one hand. "Sunnie?"

"Yes, yes! It's me. I'm back."

Caleb's hands on her arms relaxed. "Is it really you?"

She turned to him, clutching his tunic in both her fists. Her eyes collided with his. A strange tingling sensation prickled through her. The same one she felt when she was with him on the embankment by the creek back in the human realm. She searched his gaze as he searched hers. He inhaled, she inhaled. They connected to one another in a way they had never connected before. It was as though she could see into the depths of his soul and knew everything he'd done had been to get back to her, to save her from Eimhear. Because he knew what sort of sorceress she was. He knew she had the power to destroy Sunnie and would if she wasn't stopped. That one look said so much.

"Yes, it's me, Cal," she whispered.

You'll pay for this, Eimhear murmured in her darkness. *I'll torture every last one of them. I'll make them burn. I'll make you watch. I'll save this pathetic excuse for a Fae man for last because you seem to favor him the most. And when I'm done killing them, I'll snuff you out, little princess.*

Sunnie gasped. Her body went rigid as her head fell back, making her cry out. Caleb wrapped his arms around her waist, holding her close.

"I don't...have...much time. She's...strong," Sunnie said.

"Eimhear is trying to control her again," Deaglan said.

"How do we save her? How do we get her out of my daughter?" Fiona said.

A beat of silence and finally Deaglan said, his voice grim, "You can't. It will kill them both."

"We have to try," Aoife said. "*A wizard of both Fae and Wizard blood will come into power and rule from a silver throne. This half-Fae, half-wizard shall be Protector of the Realm, Ruler of the Kingdom, Guardian of the Staff of Eimhear and all the precious treasures of the Fae. And should the spirit of the sorceress be released, only the Guardian, Protector and Ruler can destroy her. So it is written. So it shall be.*" She looked at Deaglan. "There's more to the prophecy, isn't there, Deaglan?"

There is no prophecy, Eimhear said.

"Prophecy," Sunnie repeated, trying to understand. Why was Aoife talking about a prophecy?

That silvery thread of magic began to slip from her. She grasped it, held on and tried hard to keep it from falling away.

"There's more," the old wizard admitted with a grim nod.

"It was the smudged wording on the parchment, wasn't it?" Sean said.

"What is the rest of the prophecy, Deaglan?" Fiona demanded.

When the dark sorceress Eimhear was put into the staff for all eternity, her soul was tied to the staff. Only a Fae with raw, untapped magic can release her, giving Eimhear all the power she needs to exist once again.

Eimhear said the words in Sunnie's head and she understood so much then. It *was* a prophecy. Sunnie had enabled it to come true. Tears leaked from her eyes. Deaglan was right. Eimhear was part of her now and forever. She would never be able to defeat her like she had hoped.

The silvery thread of magic fell out of her grasp.

"Aye, there's more. *A wizard of both Fae and Wizard blood will come into power and rule from a silver throne. This half-Fae, half-wizard shall be Protector of the Realm, Ruler of the Kingdom, Guardian of the Staff of Eimhear and all the precious treasures of the Fae.*

"*When the dark sorceress Eimhear was put into the staff for all eternity, her soul was tied to the staff. Only a Fae with raw, untapped magic can release her, giving Eimhear all the power she needs to exist once again.*

"*And should the spirit of the sorceress be released, only the Guardian, Protector and Ruler can destroy her. So it is written. So it shall be.*"

"By the gods, Deaglan. You sealed her fate!" Fiona rounded on the wizard in her fury. "You killed my daughter without ever laying a hand on her. You bastard."

Her hands turned to claws as she lunged for Deaglan. Niall intercepted her, wrapping arms around her waist and pulling her to him.

"Let me go, Niall." Her voice wobbled, tears streaking her face.

"Killing him isn't going to change anything." To Deaglan, he said, "The half-Fae, half-wizard is Aoife, isn't it?"

"It is."

"Then I have to try and save my sister." Aoife turned to Sunnie. "Do you hear me, Sunnie? I'm going to save you."

Chapter 26

Aoife had no clue how she was going to get the dark sorceress out of Sunnie's body. Sean moved to stand next to her and she handed off the staff. She lifted her hands, palms out, fingers curved inward.

"What are you going to do, Aoife?" he asked, his voice low so only she could hear.

"I have no idea." She cut him a glance, smiled. "Yet."

She said it with more confidence than she felt. Aoife released a stream of magic. It hit Sunnie in the middle of her back. She arched, her head thrown back. Her eyes went from blue to that haunting silver and suddenly it was as though she had the strength of ten men. She gave Caleb a brutal shove away from her and spun so quickly her movements were like a blur breaking the magical connection with Aoife.

Aoife stumbled back and away losing her footing. Eimhear attacked Sean, ripping the staff from his grasp and regaining control of it. She spun away from them all and headed straight for the silver throne. Aoife regained her balance as the group of magic users charged the dark sorceress.

She waved the staff with the now-glowing orb at all of them. Caleb started toward her but she pointed the staff at him. A shot of black magic smacked him in the chest. He crumbled to the ground.

"I remember you now," she said. "You were that ungrateful whelp I tried to help all those years ago."

He lifted his head, stared her down. Sweat trickled down his face. "Is that what you think? You helped me?"

"I gave you a gift. A wonderful gift of the darkest, blackest magic. You couldn't help but use it, could you?"

Aoife's head swiveled toward Caleb. Next to her, Sean stiffened.

"Too bad you will die, Caleb." Eimhear slammed the end of her staff against the ground.

A strange reverberating gong sounded and the ground began a slow crack from the end of her staff toward Caleb. The fissure increased tenfold and suddenly he was in danger of falling inside the crevice.

Sean took off at a dead run. Aoife cried out to stop him but he ignored her. He smacked into Caleb and knocked him off his feet and out of the way of the expanding fracture in the marble floor. And then Aoife watched in horror as Sean lost his footing and tumbled inside the splintered earth. He caught himself on the edge, his nail beds white as he held on for life.

She shrieked. He grabbed the edge and held on by his fingertips as Eimhear laughed a maniacal laugh.

Aoife ran to Sean, fell to her knees. She wrapped her hands around his wrists and tried to pull him up but he was too heavy. He looked up at her, met her gaze.

"Let me go. Save your sister."

"Sean, no." Her voice hitched and tears blurred her eyes. "I can't lose you."

The room lit up with blue and white light. Aoife refused to let go of Sean's wrists but glanced up long enough to see Deaglan and Eimhear locked in a magical battle—he with his wizard staff, she with her silver staff. Niall and Fiona added their magic to the fray, pushing Sunnie/Eimhear back.

"Move over and let me get him."

It was Caleb's voice in her ear as he nudged her aside. He reached for Sean as Aoife had but he had the strength to pull him up and out.

"We're even," Caleb said to Sean who nodded agreement.

Relief sputtered through Aoife as she hugged Sean, hard. There were so many things she wanted to say to him, so many things bubbling up inside her.

"Fiona, Niall, stop. This is for me and Aoife to do," Deaglan said.

It would have to wait. Sean gave her the go-ahead nod. "Go. Save her."

Aoife joined Deaglan. As Fiona and Niall stopped their magic, she added hers. They hit the dark sorceress in the chest. Eimhear shrieked with her frustration as she tried to power them back but she was no match for their strength. Aoife caught sight of Caleb sneaking around the side of the throne. It took her several seconds to comprehend he intended to rip the staff away from Eimhear.

She understood what he meant to do and concentrated all her efforts on Eimhear and keeping her immobile while Caleb grabbed the staff. Deaglan pulled his staff back and snuffed out his magic almost as though he flipped off a light switch.

"What are you doing?" she shouted to him.

"It's all you now, Aoife," he said. "You have to be the one to do it."

Eimhear pointed the staff toward Aoife. The magic hissed through her, burning her from the inside out. She shrieked with the pain. It felt like every hair on her body caught fire, every nerve-ending fried. She was sure she would burst into flame.

Caleb took that moment to lunge and grab the magical weapon in Eimhear's hand in one fluid motion. His hand wrapped around it, searing his skin as though the thing was as hot as a poker. He cried out as he gave a mighty yank and freed it from Eimhear's grip. He stumbled and fell, landing on his back and smacking his skull on the floor with a sickening crack. The staff *thunked* on the marble floor, shattering the orb into a thousand tiny shards of glass and snuffing out the magic. Aoife sent one more powerful punch of magic into Eimhear.

Her head lolled back, her mouth open in a silent scream. A dark oily substance belched from the depths of her sister and formed into something similar to the wraithlike creatures that had attacked them outside the walls of the castle. Sunnie collapsed on the ground, her body lifeless and her legs bent in an awkward position.

The wraith had silver eyes and resembled something that was left of her sister but wasn't. Aoife's arms turned to rubber as her magic spent and she dropped them to her side. Sweat dripped down the side of her face and her back. Deaglan was there, though, using his own staff of power to pump his white magic into the creature.

She made a horrible screeching sound before turning into nothing more than dust. Remnants of Eimhear's soul fluttered to the floor.

"Sunnie!"

Fiona ran to her daughter's side, gently pulling her into her lap and cradling her against her chest. She rocked her back and forth and brushed locks of her white blonde hair back from her face.

"Sunnie, can you hear me?"

"Is she…alive?" Aoife asked.

They all huddled around her. Fiona touched the side of her neck. Her breath hitched. "I don't…I can't feel a pulse." She looked up at Deaglan with imploring eyes. "Can't you do something?"

"I'm afraid I can't, dearie." He glanced at Caleb who crawled his way to Fiona's side. Blood caked the back of his hair. "But someone here can. Put her on the ground."

"Who? Who can help her?" Fiona said but refused to comply.

"He means me," Caleb croaked.

"You? How?" Fiona demanded, still refusing to comply.

"He has some of Eimhear's dark magic. He can resurrect the dead," Deaglan said.

"There are dangers—" Caleb began.

"I don't care. Do it," Fiona demanded. She gently lowered Sunnie to the floor and moved away. "Save her. Bring her back to life."

"There are dangers to bringing back the dead," he repeated. He winced and held a hand to the back of his head. His fingers came away dotted with blood. "She may be altered. There's nothing I can do about that. Are you willing to risk it?"

Her mother bit her bottom lip and glanced at Aoife, question in her eyes.

"You make the call, Mother."

She inhaled a deep breath, her eyes shuttering closed. She finally nodded.

"Very well."

Caleb's mouth thinned into a straight line giving him a grim look. It was clear he didn't want to do whatever magic he had to do to bring Sunnie back to life. She moved closer to Sean, taking his hand.

"He's right, you know," Sean said, so only Aoife could hear. "To bring Sunnie back requires him to use black magic."

"What does that mean?"

"It means…Sunnie could be no better off than when she was possessed by Eimhear."

A sick feeling crept through Aoife as she watched Caleb kneel beside her sister. Eyes closed, he placed one hand on her shoulder, the other on her hip. He began to chant something under his breath.

"A resurrection spell," Sean whispered and Aoife shuddered.

Caleb waved his hands over Sunnie's body, still chanting. He dropped his hands, opened his eyes and quieted. Sunnie lay still.

Her lifeless body not showing any signs of coming back to life. His shoulders drooped in defeat.

"I tried."

"No." Fiona shook her head. "She can't be gone. She can't be. Try again."

"Fiona—" Niall said.

"She can't be dead." She collapsed into Niall's arms and buried her face in his chest. He held her close.

"I did all I could. I'm sorry it wasn't enough." As he spoke, he refused to make eye contact with any of them. He got to his feet and turned away, his head down as he trudged toward the doors of the throne room. A deathly silence descended on them around the morbid scene—both Brigid and Sunnie dead at the foot of the throne.

Sunnie wasn't sure what had happened. One minute, Eimhear was inside her, telling her how she was going to destroy her family, her life and take over her body. The next, she was in excruciating pain and alone. Utterly alone.

For the first time in a while, there was silence in her head. The only thoughts she heard were her own as she walked through the darkness, heading toward a bright white light at the end of a long tunnel. She was determined to make it to it, to enter that light. She was certain she would no longer feel pain or anything once she entered that light.

And then she was ripped away from the light, from the tunnel. And suddenly she was coughing and crying. Her eyes cracked open. She was back in the throne room, looking out of her own eyes, listening to her own thoughts and no one else's. She rolled to her side and curled into the fetal position, whimpering with her pain.

Then strong arms slipped around her, pulling her close. The scent she smelled was decidedly male and she knew it was Caleb.

"Caleb…?"

"Shh. Don't try to talk." He ran his hand over her hair, pushing it back from her face so she could see.

"Thank the gods!" Fiona said. "Let me see her. Is she all right?"

"Mother?"

"I'm here." Fiona was next to Caleb, peering down at her with tear-filled eyes. "I'm here, baby girl. And so is Aoife."

"Dad?" The last she remembered, Liam had been afraid of her. No. Not her. He'd been afraid of Eimhear. She couldn't remember what happened to him.

"He's not here," Fiona said.

"Where is he?"

"I…I don't know. We'll find him, Sunnie. If that's what you want," Fiona said.

She closed her eyes against the sudden blinding headache. It was too bright, too loud, too everything in the room. She needed dark and cold and silence.

"Caleb, take me out of here."

He hoisted her into his arms and stumbled to his feet. "Where?"

"Away. I need quiet." She whispered it as she turned her face into his chest.

"She needs rest while she recovers."

His tone left no room for negotiation. No one objected. He carried her away, out of the throne room and up a winding stone staircase. He lowered her to a soft feather mattress. It was the last thing she recalled before she mercifully blacked out.

Caleb pulled the coverlet up from the bottom of the bed and covered Sunnie. He stepped back from the bed and watched her sleep. The slow rise and fall of her chest. The way her long dark lashes rested against her cheeks. The way her face was at peace.

Her hair was still the silvery white color but her eyes had returned to their baby blue when she'd managed to look up at him. He thought for sure the resurrection spell hadn't worked. In fact, it should *not* have worked but mayhap Sunnie was stronger than she looked. He couldn't help but wonder if there was something left of Eimhear inside her. If, when she became fully conscious, she would remember what had happened to her and if she could tell him anything about the woman who had once cared for him.

He pulled a chair over to the bed and sat, keeping his watchful gaze on her. There was a light knock at the door.

"Come," he said quietly.

The door pushed open and Sean entered, closing the door

behind him. He stood with his back against the door and the two stared at each other a long uneasy moment.

"You knew Eimhear," he said at last.

Caleb gave one jerky nod. "I did."

"You never told me."

"What's to tell?" He shrugged. "That was a lifetime ago. I was a kid."

"Tell me about it," he said.

"Why?"

A pause as Sean clenched his jaw, the muscles ticking there. "We're still friends, aren't we?"

"Are we?" Caleb countered.

"I think we are."

Caleb focused his gaze on Sunnie's sleeping form. He took a deep breath, expelled it. "I lived in a village in Kydonia. It was destroyed by Eimhear. My parents were killed. My mother, may the gods rest her soul, hid me in a wardrobe hoping I would survive, I did. But Eimhear found me. She'd always wanted a child and couldn't have one."

"She picked you?"

He nodded. "She taught me her magic. And…" He paused again thinking of that day so long ago.

This won't hurt a bit, love.

Sean waited in silence as he gathered his thoughts and remembered that horrible day when the sorceress put a little bit of her darkness inside him. She'd seared the magic into him and though she said it wouldn't hurt, it had. Oh, it had.

"Let's just say a piece of her still lives on in me," he said.

"She altered your magic?" Sean asked.

He nodded. "It's how I can use the dark magic. It's how I brought Liam back to life. And Sunnie."

"Where is Liam?"

"No idea." He shrugged again. And he didn't care. Liam wasn't a threat. He was weak. When Caleb brought him back from the dead it had permanently altered his essence and his magic. "Last I saw him was outside the castle heading for the horses like the coward he is."

"We'll have to find him."

Caleb shook his head. "Not we. You can if you're so determined but I'm staying right here." He pointed to the floor beside Sunnie's bed as though that would make it clear to Sean. "I'm not leaving her again."

Sean glanced at Sunnie's sleeping form. "What happened to her?"

"The magic in the staff. That's what. It grabbed onto her and wouldn't let go. It was by the creek back in the human realm. I tried to stop her and thought I had but I made a mistake of leaving the staff in the attic with the trunk. Bryant used a portal to get it back into Faery. Somehow Sunnie managed to get her hands on it again and Eimhear struck, overtaking her."

"She'll live?"

"So far," Caleb said. "Only time will tell."

Silence again and then Sean said, "Fiona wanted me to tell you thank you for saving her."

"Tell Fiona she's welcome."

Sean reached for the door and pulled it open.

"Sean, do me a favor, will you?" His friend paused, looked at him over his shoulder. "Bury Brigid."

Sean nodded and closed the door behind him, leaving Caleb in the chamber with the only sound of Sunnie's deep breathing.

Chapter 27

Sunnie came awake slowly, as though she were coming out of a delightful dream. But it hadn't been a dream. It had been a nightmare. A waking nightmare. For a long while, she lay in silence with her eyes closed and listened to the sounds of the room. A creaky floorboard as though someone tiptoed around the room. Water splashing. The whoosh of draperies opening and the flood of light against her closed lids.

Sunlight. How long had it been since she'd felt the warmth of dawn?

Then silence. The door to her chamber softly closing with a snick. She was alone again. Alone with her thoughts and the wild magic swirling inside her. Light and dark. It fought against each other, each one wanting dominance over the other. It was a war within herself. A war she didn't know how to stop.

Her stomach twisted in a knot, making her sick and want to retch. She swallowed hard to calm the inner voices. But they would not be calmed.

We named you Sunnie because when you were born your hair was the color of spun gold. It sparkled in the morning sunshine as though it were a halo.

Her father, Liam, had told her the story numerous times while patting the top of her head, making her feel special and loved.

Give me a child, Cadryn. It's what I want most of all. What I need most of all. A child from the union of you and me.

Sunnie sucked in a sharp breath through her nose as her eyes flew open and she sat up, clutching the bedcovers to her chest. Her heart palpitated against her chest. The last memory had not been hers. It had been Eimhear's.

You are cruel, Eimhear. Can you not see what you've done?

If I'm cruel, it's your fault. You deny me my heart's desire. I will find a way to get what I want without you.

The horror of it all flashed through Sunnie's mind so clear it was as though she watched a movie. She pressed a hand against her roiling stomach, trying to make it all go away. It wouldn't.

Eimhear destroyed a small village for the fun of it. Only a

wardrobe was left standing in the midst of the rubble of a house and inside it, a boy. He couldn't be more than seven or eight.

Well, well. What have we here? Where are your parents, little one?

Dead. The child whispered the word, his voice quivering.

Then you will come with me and I shall care for you. What is your name, little one?

Ca-Caleb.

Come, Caleb. I will teach you everything I know.

This time Sunnie gasped and shoved the covers away. She tried to get out of the bed, but her legs tangled in the covers and she stumbled, falling to the floor with a loud thump. She cried out when she landed.

Booted footsteps and then her door flew open. Caleb stood in the doorway. The look on his face said he was ready to do battle. He relaxed when he saw she was alone and then moved to help her up.

As soon as she saw him, everything inside her calmed. Her heart slowed to a normal pace. Something about having him close gave her peace.

"You all right?" he asked.

She clutched him as he lifted her from the floor and sat her on the bed. "Yes, thanks. I...I fell out of the bed."

"Is that all?" He grinned, the smile reaching all the way to his eyes. "You're not hurt?"

She shook her head.

"Good." He perched on the edge of the bed next to her. "How are you feeling?"

"Better. I think. Still tired. Like I'm trying to get used to walking around in my own skin again. If that makes sense."

He brushed her hair back from her shoulder. "It does, I suppose. You've been through quite an ordeal."

She bit her lip as she thought of everything that had happened. "Where is my father, Caleb?"

His face paled and he looked away, focusing on his hands resting on his thighs. "No one knows. He and Siobhan disappeared before we fought against Eimhear."

Grief welled inside her. He'd left her. How could he? How could he leave her without even telling her goodbye?

She knew why. When she had been possessed by Eimhear, the dark sorceress had not treated him well. She'd intended to kill him as soon as she could. Liam must have thought she, Sunnie, was dead and there was no saving her. It cut her deep to know he'd left without even trying to save her, without hope, thinking she was already dead. How would she ever find him again?

"I'm sorry, Sunnie." True regret tinged his voice.

She pushed it to the back of her mind. She would deal with it another time. Now was not that time. Now she wanted to tell Caleb what she knew about him, that she understood him. Remnants of Eimhear were inside her still and she would carry that darkness with her the rest of her days. She dragged her lower lip through her teeth.

"What is it?" he asked.

"There's something I want to tell you." She turned toward him on the edge of the bed and reached for his hands, clutching them in hers. "I know about Eimhear and what she did to you when you were a boy."

His face turned into a mask of hidden emotions. The light faded a bit in his eyes, making them unreadable.

"She taught you dark magic, didn't she?"

He gave a short curt nod and tried to pull his hands from hers. She held fast.

"She told you, did she?"

"No," Sunnie said. "She's…her memories are still inside me. I can see them. Hear them as if I were there. Some of her darkness is still inside me, too. Like you."

He lifted his gaze, met hers. "Like me."

She nodded. "You saved my life with her dark magic, didn't you?"

He nodded again and swallowed hard, his throat working.

"I think…I think I understand you, Caleb. How you feel with that dark magic swirling inside. It's hard to control and contain. I feel it even now. Sometimes it makes me sick to my stomach. Like I've eaten something bad and I want to throw up. Only when—" She paused, shook her head. "No, never mind."

"Only when what?" He squeezed her hands. "Tell me."

She took a deep breath. "Only when you're near do I feel at peace."

They stared at each other in silence. He reached up, placed a hand against her cheek and brushed his fingers through her hair. The gesture made her heart flutter. This time in the good way.

"Thank you for saving my life, Caleb. Why did you do it?"

"I've watched you grow up. Like Sean watched Aoife. I suppose part of me felt protective of you. When I knew Eimhear was inside you, I had to find a way to free you from her grasp. I only wish it hadn't taken so long." He rested his hand on her cheek. She leaned into it. "I know how much your life in the human realm means to you. I can return you, if you wish."

Return her to the human realm? After everything that's happened to her? Could she really pick up where she left off? Go back to filming movies and scratching her way to the top of the Hollywood A List to become that move star she always wanted to be? It seemed so strange now to think of she wasn't sure it was something she actually wanted anymore. She wasn't the same person she was when she arrived in Brookdale looking for answers about the death of her father or searching for her missing mother. All that had changed now. She had changed.

"I have to confess, though, with the time rifts, I'm not sure the human realm will be the same as when you left."

"What does that mean?"

"Time passes differently here than in the human realm. Days here. Years there."

Sunnie appreciated his candid honesty. If years had passed then her career was over. She had likely been forgotten by Hollywood and was nothing but a ghost. She looked at him and her heart tripped. She had a sense of belonging, something she hadn't had in all her years. She thought acting would give her that, but it hadn't. She had still felt out of place at times. Probably why she made the mistakes she made and the tabloids loved her. She knew what her decision had to be.

"If I stay, will you help me learn to control my magic?"

"I can but…why me? Your mother is much better suited. Even Aoife has more experience than me."

"She doesn't understand me. Neither of them do. You and I shared a similar experience with Eimhear. I think you understand my inner struggle with the dark and the light and you can help me control it."

He cupped her face, pressed his forehead against hers. "I would be honored."

"Good. I have a confession."

"Is it a terrible confession?" he teased.

Her pulse fluttered. "Perhaps. You may not want to hear it. When I was a little girl I had a terrible crush on you."

A grin pulled at the corner of his mouth. "Had?"

"Have." She smiled.

"You never told me."

"I don't know how." She paused, choosing her words. "That day by the creek when you tackled me. Remember that?"

"I could never forget." His voice turned husky as it rumbled through his chest.

"Why didn't you kiss me then?"

A spark of desire flickered through his hazel eyes. "I was remiss. Maybe I should kiss you now?"

"Maybe you shouldn't have to ask."

Their lips met in a tender kiss. His tongue pushed tentatively into her mouth, touching the tip of hers. It sent a spark of desire right through her from head to toe and she knew then she'd made the right decision.

Caleb was right. He had been a part of her life for a very long time. Back then she had been too self-absorbed to see it. Only now was it clear to her. She understood who and what she was. She wasn't a movie star. She would never be a movie star. She belonged with Caleb in Faery and nowhere else. For the first time in her life, Sunnie was content.

Aoife stood outside the castle walls, her face upturned to the brilliant blue sky as she watched the sleek graceful form of Nero glide across it. Far in the distance, she could see other dragons winging their way from one point to the next.

Sun warmed her cheeks and nose. After Eimhear was destroyed, winter disappeared almost as quickly as it had come. The snow was gone. Trees turned green. Flowers bloomed. And the white castle shone with a magnificent light in the daylight.

She loved watching Nero fly. He seemed so carefree. His gentle landing didn't even disturb nearby flower petals. He snuffled around her hands, reminding her of a giant dog—that could breathe fire and had scales—looking for the often-offered treat. Aoife discovered, quite by accident, dragons loved wild strawberries.

She giggled and patted his nose. "I don't have a treat today."

Pity, Nero said. *Do you wish to fly?*

In the days since Sunnie's convalescence, Aoife had taken to riding Nero through the brisk mornings. It took her breath away. She had never felt so alive or free.

"I'm afraid not today. Sunnie has finally healed and is ready to join us for the first time."

She lives. Good.

"She does. Perhaps tomorrow?"

Tomorrow then.

He gave her a friendly nudge and then took off, shooting straight up. She stood and watched him disappear in the distance, joining the other dragons.

"Is he your pet now?" Sean asked.

She turned to see him coming across the yard, a smile on his handsome face. She laughed. "I suppose he is. Funny, huh?"

He watched Nero and company flying across the heavens. "Not really. He seems to adore you. We're in Faery, after all. It seems perfectly natural you'd have a dragon for a pet." He wrapped an arm around her shoulders and turned serious. "Niall said he wants to see you. Alone."

Her brows rose to her hairline. "Alone? Even without my mother?"

He nodded. "He asked me to fetch you."

"Lead the way then."

They walked hand in hand back inside the castle. As they approached the throne room where the Time Sphere and the silver throne resided, they could hear Deaglan and Niall talking. She slowed and came to a halt outside the doors.

"Aoife, we should—"

She held up her hand to silence him and leaned toward the door cracked an inch to listen.

"Aye, it's true Siobhan was your mother. When you were a boy and grew too powerful to control, I went to her. I took you away because she didn't know how to control you," Deaglan said.

"She was relieved, in truth, because she worried for her other boy's safety."

"But that 'other boy' as you say was not my half-brother," Niall said.

"Nay. He was…" Deaglan paused, cleared his throat. "There is no proper way to say this other than to say it. Siobhan left me to marry the prince of Anatolia. She didn't tell me she was pregnant with you until she was gone. I was angry. Hurt. She took my son. You. I wanted revenge. So, I took her son."

There was a long silence. Boots scraping the floor and then Niall said, "Are you telling me you switched Cian with another babe?"

"A human," Deaglan said. "Cian was human."

"Then where is the true born prince of Anatolia? Do you know?" Impatience laced his tone. "You do know. Who is it?"

"Liam."

"Gods," Niall said on a breath. "Does Fiona know?"

"She does."

Niall paced, his boots scuffing the marble floor. "And now he's missing along with the queen. We have to find them."

"I don't think they'll be any trouble for us, laddie," Deaglan said. "The queen has lost her kingdom and Liam…well, he doesn't exactly know who and what he is."

"But he *is* Fae and he *does* have magic?" Niall asked.

"Aye."

"Then he poses a danger to himself."

Aoife had heard enough. She rapped on the door.

Niall called for her to enter then to his father, "This discussion isn't over yet." He dismissed the old wizard and then turned to her, smiling as though nothing was amiss. "Ah, my lovely daughter. Thank you for bringing her, Sean."

Sean gave a nod. "I'll leave you two alone, Your Majesty." He closed the door with a snap behind him with a snap.

Niall took Aoife by the shoulders, still smiling that goofy uncharacteristic grin.

"What? Why do you look at me like that?"

"There's something I want you to help me do," he said.

"What's that?"

He released her, waved toward the Time Sphere. "Destroy it."

She blinked surprise. "Why?"

"Fiona thinks we can heal the realm with it but I know as does my father, further tampering with time will do more harm than good. Time is something that should never be meddled with. Things can never go back the way they were. Our world is now what it is. Anatolia, Kydonia and Illyria are gone."

Her heart sank. She supposed somewhere deep inside she still held hope there was a way to go back, to return to her new home in the towers. "You know for certain?"

He gave a nod. "I looked into the Time Sphere. Everything we knew is no more. The Towers of Illyria. Lambridge Castle. Ridgeclere Castle. All gone. Swept away by Eimhear's time spell. Destroyed forever."

He walked to the Time Sphere, placed his palms on it. It came to life, showing her the ruins in the Time Sphere, rubble of what once was a regal castle, and wreckage of another place by a body of water. Her heart stuttered in her chest. She had not expected this. Though, admittedly, she wasn't sure what she expected once Sunnie had been saved from the dark sorceress. Part of her thought they would return to the Towers of Illyria and rebuild. Or her father would use the Time Sphere to repair the realm and return it back to the way it was before Liam stole it. Now, knowing that was not possible left a void inside her.

"Destroying it is the only way to keep it out of the hands of others. Even us. Even me," he said.

"What about the one in the Ivory Wood?"

"Already destroyed. It must have happened with all the time rifts."

He waved his hand over the sphere. An image of the other sphere in the Ivory Wood in a thousand tiny pieces flickered through the orb. He turned back to her, held out his hand. She took it and stepped next to him. He placed her palm on the sphere.

"Will you do it?" he asked.

"Why haven't you asked my mother?" she wanted to know.

He smiled. "There are many things I love about Fiona. Her stubbornness is not one of them. She is determined to set things right with the Time Sphere. She spent much of her time trying to convince me. 'Tis why I had to put her under a sleeping spell."

Aoife sucked in a gasp of surprise.

"It didn't hurt her," he was quick to say. "I will be able to wake her with a kiss. I couldn't have her trying to stop me and I know it's the right thing to do."

Though she knew it was the right thing to do, she didn't want to do it, either. It held such great power, such great magic. It seemed a shame to destroy it. But Niall was right in that her mother would do whatever it took to get her way no matter what.

She'd already seen that herself.

Finally, she nodded.

"What do you want me to do?"

"Channel your power into it."

He closed his eyes and focused. His hands glowed with a white light. She followed his lead, doing the same. As she focused, she felt the magic pulse from her into the Time Sphere. It didn't take long for the thing to crack and splinter and finally shatter. Niall pulled her hand back with a wild jerk. They stumbled away from it as glass tinkled to the marble floor and nothing was left but the marble stand it once sat upon.

The Time Sphere was no more.

Chapter 28

That afternoon when Niall went to wake Fiona, Aoife made her way to her sister's chamber. Even though she knew Sunnie had been awake for several days, she had yet to make an appearance. Caleb had grown fiercely protective of her. He was determined she should have her rest while she recuperated.

She knocked on the door. A moment later, Caleb opened it.

"Aoife," he said with a nod of greeting.

"Hi, Cal. I came to see my sister."

"She's resting—"

"Oh, for heaven's sake, Caleb. Let her in and stop being so over protective."

Aoife grinned when he scowled and stepped aside. But as she entered the chamber and they looked at each other for the first time, Aoife halted. She was suddenly unsure what to say or how to act. An awkward silence filled the void. Caleb cleared his throat.

"I'll let you two have some privacy." He left, closing the door behind him.

No doubt standing guard outside.

Sunnie was dressed in a pale pink gown with long flowing sleeves edged in lace. Her still stark white hair was pulled back from her face on the sides and twisted into a tiny bun at the back of her head. Her eyes were still the same clear blue. She looked the same but a little older.

"How are you feeling?" Aoife finally asked.

She shrugged. "Better, I suppose. At least I don't have someone else chattering in my head."

"You could hear her in there?"

"Yes."

"What was it like?" she asked.

Her eyes took on a faraway look. Aoife realized that probably wasn't the best question to ask. She waved it away. "Never mind. You don't have to tell me."

"It was like…having a dark presence you couldn't control inside you. She took over everything about me and tried to snuff out my very existence. She took the magic I had never used and twisted for her own gain." Sunnie perched on the side of the large bed, that same look on her face as she remembered.

"Sunnie, if this is too painful you don't have to talk about it."

"I haven't told anyone. Not even Mother." She met her gaze, clarity coming back in her eyes. "She hasn't asked. I think she's afraid there is still something of Eimhear inside me. And she's right, you know. There is." Sunnie tapped her chest. "It's here. There is a darkness there that I know will never be gone."

Aoife didn't know what to say as she stared at her sister. The perfect one. The popular girl. The one Liam loved best. Sunnie had expensive taste and loved designer clothes and yet here she stood wearing a borrowed gown looking lost, alone and a little afraid.

"I don't know why I'm telling you. I guess a part of me thinks you'll understand."

She nodded, still mute waiting for her to tell her more.

"Caleb tried to stop me from picking up that staff. I wish to God I had listened to him. I barely believed him when he told me who I really was." She snorted a laugh. "I was so wrapped up in my own life I couldn't see it for myself. I couldn't see what you and my mother are. I didn't believe in fairies. Magic didn't exist. It was nothing but a bunch of amusing bedtime stories. Turns out it was all true."

Aoife nodded again. "Yes, it was. All of it."

"When Eimhear first took over my body, I couldn't control anything. She shoved me back to the dark recesses of my mind and took control of that untapped magic I didn't even know was there. She told me vile things. Said she was going to kill me. She threatened my father. That's when I knew I had to do something."

She sat next to her on the bed and put an arm around her shoulders. "I'm so sorry."

"At least you believed I was still alive. Daddy gave up on me."

"He didn't. He couldn't have."

"I know the truth, Aoife, and I'm okay with that. I'll never see him again and maybe that's for the best." She twisted a piece of lace around her forefinger. "At least I still have you and Mother and Caleb."

"You do and we're here for you. Whatever you need."

"I told you once I never hated you. That I wanted to be like you." She lifted her head, met her gaze. "That's still true. I still want to be like you."

"You do?" Emotion clogged Aoife's throat.

"Well, duh, of course I do. You're my big sister. Will you teach me what you know?"

Aoife was touched. So much so they hugged for the first time since they were little girls. It felt good and right.

"I'm afraid I don't know much but yes, I'll teach you everything I know."

"Good. Thank you." Sunnie pulled back.

"So, you and Caleb are…?"

She shrugged. "I don't know what we are," she admitted. "I know I like him a lot. He seems to like me. We understand each other."

"I'd say he likes you more than you realize," Aoife said.

"You and Sean?"

"We intend to marry."

Her face lit up. "I'm glad. I know you've always loved him."

"Was I that obvious?"

"Duh. Everyone knew. Even Sean."

It shouldn't have come as a surprise to Aoife but it did.

"Do me a favor?"

"Anything."

"Don't tell Mom what I told you, okay?"

Aoife couldn't help but giggle. The last secret they shared they had both been under the age of ten and Sunnie had spilled red Kool-Aid on Fiona's favorite rug. "You got it."

It had been two days since Aoife and her father destroyed the Time Sphere. Fiona hadn't quite forgiven them yet but she was coming around.

Sunnie finally left her sick room but Caleb refused to let her go anywhere without him. Sunnie didn't seem to mind. Aoife started calling him Velcro Man. He was not amused.

There were survivors from the Towers of Illyria after the rift in time. They had somehow heard of the wizard king living in the white castle made of marble and made their way there. More turned up every day and the castle started to feel more and more like the towers. Fiona was overjoyed when her longtime friend,

Winnie, turned up with a ragtag group of men, women and children. They were half-starved, dirty, tired and looked as though they had been traveling for days nonstop.

"By the gods, Winnie! I never thought to see you again." Fiona enveloped her old friend in a fierce hug. Her faced beamed. "I'm so happy to see you. How did you know where to find us?"

"A few of us were living in the wreckage of a small village when a man stumbled into town, half staved. He said his horse had gone lame and he had to put it down several miles back," she said. "He told us some crazy story about a black dragon and a dark sorceress hell bent on killing the wizard king. We thought he was mad. None of us believed him until that black dragon flew over the village."

"That had to be Liam," Niall said.

"He never said his name," Winnie said.

More and more came. The castle walls were full. When there was no more room inside the walls, makeshift tents popped up outside. There were wandering minstrels and bards, beer-makers and cooks, cobblers and smiths. A makeshift village sprang from the ashes of Illyria. Niall, Deaglan and Fiona started making plans to clear some of the forest and start building an actual village to house them all. It seemed every trade was represented as they showed up one after another looking to the wizard king for leadership and guidance.

He was baffled by it all. They all were.

Aoife and Sean stood on the balcony outside their chamber watching as the first trees felled and carpenters began the long arduous task of building.

"It's not every day you see the birth of a new kingdom. They're coming from everywhere," Sean remarked, watching a group of young children running through the encampment. "I half expect Bryant to show up any minute."

"You think the agency is gone?" she asked.

"Has to be. There's no reason for it to exist anymore, is there?" He turned to her, took her hands in his. "The only place I want to be is here with you, princess."

She laughed. "A princess of what kingdom? I don't think one exists anymore."

"Of course, it does. Look." He waved toward the crowd. "We have a cook now and your mother has a lady-in-waiting. I'd say we are our own kingdom."

"And what do we call it, then?"

He shrugged. "Does it matter?"

"I suppose someday it might. If we continue to grow." She sighed. "Do you think Liam had something to do with all this?"

"Seems rather strange if he did. Why would he?"

"Winnie's story wasn't the only one about a strange man talking about a dragon. I can't help but think he sent them to us, Sean."

"Perhaps he thought they would be safe with us since your father is the wizard king."

She nodded. "Perhaps."

A knock interrupted them.

"Come," Sean called.

Her father entered dressed in a cobalt tunic, black pants and black knee-high boots polished to a high shine.

"I hope I'm not interrupting," he said as Aoife hugged him.

"Not at all," she said.

"I was hoping to have a word with you, Aoife."

Sean excused himself, leaving the two of them alone. The last time he wanted to see her, they destroyed the Time Sphere together. She wondered what he was up to this time, especially dressed as though he were prepared to hold court.

"There is something I've been thinking about these last few days, Aoife. Something I want to discuss with you."

He moved to the balcony to watch the goings-on down below. She followed and stood next to him, like she had with Sean.

"Sounds serious."

"It is. But I want to know if you'll do it before an announcement is made."

Her brows drew together in question. "Do what, Father?"

"This ordeal has made me see things differently, Aoife. My father wasn't exactly the nicest man."

"I know about Liam and Cian," she said. "That he switched them."

He didn't seem surprised by that. "He regrets it now but I understand how he felt when Siobhan left him. I felt that way when Fiona left me all those years ago. I would have done anything to get her back." He turned back to the crowd, his hands on the railing, fingers tightening. "I nearly destroyed Anatolia. I wanted blood. I wanted war. I thought it would make the pain go away. It didn't. I cursed Cian, stranding him in another realm. That curse was broken with all the time rifts."

"But you're not that man anymore," she said, placing a hand on his shoulder.

"No, I'm not. I was lucky. Fiona came back to me." He turned to her and took her by the shoulders. "It's why I want to abdicate the throne to you, Aoife. I'm tired of ruling and being a ruler. I want to spend more time with my wife before it's too late. Before there is no more time to spend together."

She stared at him in mute horror. He wanted to *give* her the throne? A shockwave went through her, making her shudder and her teeth chatter. She didn't know what to say, what to think.

"Before you say anything, just think about it."

"But…why me?"

"You are my only daughter, Aoife. A princess and heir to the throne. It's yours by birthright." He pulled her to him, hugged her.

Her arms hung limply at her side as a numbness prickled her skin.

"I don't know anything about ruling a kingdom," she muttered.

"I'll still be here to help you. I'll help you pick your royal council and soon you won't even need me." He held her at arm's length. "Promise you'll think about it?"

She bit her lip, nodded. "I promise."

He left her alone. As she turned back to the crowd below, she watched the people laughing, building, happy, sharing. A young girl paused playing with her friends to look up at her, a broad smile on her face. She waved her arm so big it made Aoife grin. Then she picked up her skirt and sprinted back to her friends, ignorant of the inner turmoil boiling through her.

When Sean returned moments later, she told him everything. He stared at her in stunned silence.

"What are you going to do?"

"I don't know." Her stomach knotted. She paced the length of the chamber. "What do you think I should do?"

"I think you should do what's right for you and I'll support you no matter what."

"That's not helpful."

"I can't make the decision for you." He spread his hands in surrender. "Only you know what's best for you."

"But it's not just about me. It's about them." She pointed to the open balcony door as music and laughter wafted on the breeze. "I don't know how to lead them. I don't know how to protect them. I don't know anything about being a queen."

"You'll learn." He kissed her forehead. "Trust your instincts, Aoife. Your gut never lies."

It took her three days to decide. She made up her mind after she talked to her sister. The old Sunnie would have been jealous and pouted. Instead, she hugged her and told her she thought Aoife would make an amazing queen.

Niall was overjoyed when she told him she would do it. Fiona not so much but slowly warming up to the idea, especially when she realized it would mean more time with her beloved.

And so, the day came when all were dressed in their finery. News of the coronation of the new queen spread like wildfire. The peasants crowded outside the castle walls waiting. Only a few were permitted inside the throne room to bear witness to the crowning of a new queen.

Aoife was dressed in an amethyst gown made of the softest silk. She could hear a slight swish as she walked and she loved it. This day reminded her much of the one when she arrived in Illyria and was presented to the kingdom by her father. But this day was much different.

Deaglan stood at the front of the room to the left of the silver throne as she made her way, walking slow sure steps. All eyes were on her and only her. Every nerve in her body was on edge. There was no turning back.

Two servants placed the thick garnet cloak around her shoulders—a royal cloak made especially for her. He motioned with his hand and she kneeled.

"Is Your Majesty willing to take the oath?"

"I am willing."

"Will you solemnly promise and swear to govern the people of this new kingdom with a just and fair hand?" he said.

"I solemnly promise so to do," she replied.

"Will you to your power cause law and justice, in mercy, to be executed in all your judgments?"

"I will."

"Will you to the utmost of your power maintain the Laws of

Faery?"

"Aye, I will. I promise to do this."

He waved her to stand and gave her a nod. She had one more line. They'd rehearsed it for hours upon hours and drilled it into her head.

"The things which I have here before promised, I will perform and keep to the last day I rule."

Another servant stepped forward, holding a garnet cushion with a simple gold crown upon it. Deaglan plucked it off the cushion and placed it on Aoife's head. He then handed her the royal scepter which was once the silver staff owned by Eimhear. Aoife insisted on keeping it as a reminder of all they lost.

Aoife's mouth had gone bone dry as she looked at the silver throne. Everyone waited for her to take those final steps. She glanced at Sean who gave her an encouraging nod. Aoife walked to the throne and slowly sat on the silver chair.

"Long may she reign," Deaglan said and the crowd repeated it.

A wizard of both Fae and Wizard blood will come into power and rule from a silver throne.

As she took her silver throne as queen for the first time, Aoife realized she had at long last fulfilled the prophecy.

From the Author

Dear Reader –

Entering the world of Fae has been so much fun for me. It speaks to me in a way no other worldbuilding does. I suppose that's why I continue to return to Faery book after book. I have a special place in my heart for Celtic things. If you've read my *Realm of Honor* series, you might see a familiar character. I had fun giving him a cameo in this book.

The events of *On the Hunt for the Wizard King* in Part One run concurrently with the events of *In the Tower of the Wizard King*. Why did I choose to write it this way? It was something the story dictated to me when I began this second book. Sometimes, books tell you how to write them and characters have very specific ideas of who they are. For a non-writer, that probably sounds pretty weird but my writer friends will understand this particular neuroses.

I wanted to tell Sunnie's point of view as well as Caleb's without forgetting about the other characters who made this series special. Aoife, Fiona, Niall and Deaglan all have a part to play as well. Will there be a book three? I've considered it. These longer works take a lot of time to write and plot so it definitely has to be the right story for the remaining characters. Everyone deserves their own happily ever after, don't you think? I welcome your feedback. Email me at michelle@michellemiles.net.

In the meantime, I hope you enjoy this second installment in the *Age of Wizards*. Thank you for purchasing and reading.

All my best,
Michelle

Acknowledgements

Special thanks, as always, to the fans who read my work. I write because I love words, creating stories and making people happy. I hope you find the joy in my words as I do.

Lots of thanks go to my beta readers and good friends Karilyn Bentley and Kat Baldwin and especially to Janice Lindstrom who read this book twice. Without them, this book would not be possible. They helped me refine and hone the story and I'm so grateful for their help and support.

To my fellow princesses, Vicki Batman and Sylvia McDaniel, for being only an email away.

And of course to my husband for his unfailing support and belief in me even when I don't. Oh, and for putting *In the Tower of the Wizard King* on his desk at work and making people stop and read the blurb and realize I don't write "just romance." I love him for that.

Praise for the Dragon Protectors

Desiring the Dragon Lord, Book 1

"Michelle Miles kicks off her new Dragon Protectors series with a bang..." —4 stars, Amazon Reviewer

"I read this book in just a couple of days. I couldn't put it down!" —5 stars, Amazon Reviewer

"...a wonderful book full of strong minded characters." —5 stars, Amazon Reviewer

Seducing the Dragon Knight, Book 2

"From the start this book has danger and a bit of mystery." —4 stars, Amazon Reviewer

"I love this author and this genre. A must read." —5 stars, Booksprout Reviewer

"I was half in love with Rafe when we met him in Desiring the Dragon Lord, but oh get me a fan and a cool drink, because his hot factor increased 100-fold in the second installment." —4 stars, Amazon Reviewer

Tempting Her Dragon Bodyguard, Book 3

"I loved reading this book and hope there are more to come." —5 stars, Amazon Reviewer

"Book three in the Dragon Protectors series a well written story that kept me turning pages. I had to know what was going to happen." —5 stars, Amazon Reviewer

"...a captivating storyline..." —4 stars, Amazon Reviewer

Also by Michelle Miles

Dream Walker
Call of the Dark

Age of Wizards
In the Tower of the Wizard King
On the Hunt for the Wizard King

A Ransom & Fortune Adventure
Highland Fling, Vol 1
Dead of Winter, Vol 2
The Citadel, Vol 3
Lord of the Underworld, Vol 4

Dragon Protectors
Desiring the Dragon Lord
Seducing the Dragon Knight
Tempting Her Dragon Bodyguard

Guardians of Atlantis
Tempting Eden
Seducing Eve
Ravishing Helene
Guardians of Atlantis Box Set

Realm of Honor
One Knight Only
Only for a Knight
A Knight to Remember
A Knight Like No Other
Shadows of the Knight

Coffee House Chronicles
Talk Dirty to Me
Nice Girls Do
Have Yourself a Merry Little Latte
Take Me I'm Yours
Sex, Lust & Martinis

Forever Yours
A Little Taste of Heaven

Shorts and Anthologies
A Dance Among the Faeries, Short Story
Eorwulf, Short Story
The Soul of Sharah, Short Story
Sinfully Sweet, Short Story
Flights of Fantasy: A Collection of Short Stories

Available in Audiobook
In the Tower of the Wizard King
On the Hunt for the Wizard King
One Knight Only
Only for a Knight
A Knight to Remember

Watch for more at www.michellemiles.net

Did you love *On the Hunt for the Wizard King*?

Try Michelle Miles' *Call of the Dark*, the first book in Dream Walker urban fantasy series available in ebook and paperback. On sale now at your favorite retailer.

Praise for Call of the Dark

"I loved this book! It's a great start to a new adventure series. It reminds me of a mashup of urban fantasy and the Indiana Jones movies with angels and demons thrown in." —5 stars, Amazon Reviewer

"I literally inhaled the book in just an afternoon! I can't wait for the next installment!!!" —5 stars, Goodreads Reviewer

"...action packed with a heroine to cheer for...I will be eagerly awaiting the next book." —5 stars, Goodreads Reviewer

"One nail-biting rollercoaster!" —5 stars, Amazon Reviewer

"Powerful...an adventure of a lifetime...I can't wait to see what happens next."—5 stars, Bookbub Reviewer

"Loved it!" —5 stars, Goodreads Reviewer

"Great characters and amazing storylines. A must read."—5 stars, Amazon Reviewer

Read more at www.michellemiles.net

About the Author

Michelle Miles believes in fairy tales, true love and magic. She writes heart-stopping urban fantasy, epic fantasy and paranormal romance with an action/adventure twist that will leave you breathless. She is the author of numerous series that includes everything from angels and demons to fairies, dragons and elves. She is married with one son and a black cat named Sir Dexter.

A native Texan, in her spare time she loves reading, listening to music, watching movies, cross-stitching, drinking wine and taking pictures of her cat. She can be found online at Facebook, Twitter, Instagram, Pinterest and Goodreads.

Your Adventure Awaits.

www.ingramcontent.com/pod-product-compliance
Lightning Source LLC
Chambersburg PA
CBHW071202100726
47908CB00002B/480